HUNTER, HUNTED

The skinwalker jolted forward and slashed Colt across the chest with its razor-like claws, shredding both his shirt and his skin. Colt gasped and shouted. He dropped to his knees as unseen fire exploded across his chest, burning and aching. He grunted, aiming his revolver at the fiend. The skinwalker sneered and cackled in delight.

The revolver kicked back as Colt fired. The skinwalker darted like a shadow and the bullet exploded in the sandstone just behind the creature, spraying it with rock shrapnel. It shrieked, the sound reverberating off the rocks and multiplying until it echoed in Colt's skull. In a blur the skinwalker moved from one rock to another, changing position so fast Colt could hardly track it, let alone take aim and shoot the damn thing.

"Watch out!" Lilly shouted.

Colt heard her an instant before he was knocked sideways by the creature. The shifter extended its wicked claws at Colt's throat with the aim of ripping it out. He held back the claws, his left arm bulging and burning with the effort, while he pulled the revolver up as close as he could between himself and the creature.

"You missed," it hissed, spittle spraying Colt's face.

The Hunter

BOOK ONE OF THE LEGEND CHRONICLES

THERESA MEYERS

ZEBRA BOOKS
KENSINGTON PUBLISHING CORP.
http://www.kensingtonbooks.com

ZEBRA BOOKS are published by

Kensington Publishing Corp.
119 West 40th Street
New York, NY 10018

All Kensington titles, imprints, and distributed lines are available at special quantity discounts for bulk purchases for sales promotion, premiums, fund-raising, educational, or institutional use.

Special book excerpts or customized printings can also be created to fit specific needs. For details, write or phone the office of the Kensington Special Sales Manager: Attn.: Special Sales Department. Kensington Publishing Corp., 119 West 40th Street, New York, NY 10018. Phone: 1-800-221-2647.

Zebra and the Z logo Reg. U.S. Pat. & TM Off.

ISBN-13: 978-1-4201-2124-7
ISBN-10: 1-4201-2124-3

First Printing: November 2011
10 9 8 7 6 5 4 3 2 1

Printed in the United States of America

This book is dedicated to my Arizona family.

*To my favorite cowboy, Quinn,
and my favorite horseback rider, Chloe,*

You two make my world.

To Marlon for always being there. Always.

To Marc for being a huge part of our lives.

*To the writers of the Valley of the Sun Chapter of RWA
and the Desert Rose Chapter of RWA,
who were my first writing home, and in particular
to Christine Eaton Jones. Thank you*

*And for Jerry, because you
look seriously hot in cowboy boots.*

In the Beginning

"Aren't you Cy Jackson's boy?"

Colt looked up at the stranger through the ragged edge of his thick, dark hair. The afternoon sun that had all but baked him alive now slung low in the sky, making it difficult for him to see more than a backlit outline of the man through the dusty haze.

"Yeah." Left behind by his pa and two older brothers to chop wood while they went hunting, Colt had spent his energy for the day. His faded red shirt, gritty and damp with sweat, stuck to his lean body. He straightened, keeping a firm hold on the smooth hardwood handle of his axe just in case he needed it. He might be only fourteen, but he knew how to protect himself and what was theirs. The hair on the back of his neck rose in warning. Strangers didn't just "drop in." The homestead was thirty miles out of town and not on the road to anywhere.

It took only a second, just a mere blink, for the stranger to launch off his horse and clamp his cold, pale hands around Colt's throat. He'd never seen anything move so fast in all his life. Hard fingers lifted Colt off the ground so that his feet swung awkwardly from his long limbs. The pressure caused sparks to pop in Colt's vision. Choking and gagging, he dropped the axe from his nerveless fingers as he clawed at the icy hands squeezing off his air.

"I'd like to kill you, just to prove a point to Cyrus, but Rathe said to bring you back alive." The stranger's breath stank so bad of sulfur it made Colt's nose burn and his eyes well. "'Course, he didn't say I couldn't have a little fun first." The unnaturally icy pale blue eyes glaring at him turned violent crimson, the vertical pupils widening with anticipation. Colt's heart stopped beating for a second.

Everything seemed to blur as his eyes bulged with pressure. The next instant, the stranger shoved Colt beneath the water of the horse trough that had been ten feet away. Glimmers of sunlight streamed in from above as the water seeped into his nose and he fought to hold his breath.

Colt dug his fingernails into the hands holding him down, kicking and squirming, anything to get a sip of air into his burning lungs. The stranger pulled Colt from the water at the last moment, before blackness clouded his vision completely.

"Where's the Book?" His voice was hot against Colt's ear.

Colt coughed and choked, the water rasping his throat. "Tell me."

All Colt could do was shake his head and gasp. He didn't know what the stranger meant.

The water closed over him again. Colt wanted to scream, but he didn't dare. There hadn't been time to take a deep breath. He fought hard against the iron hold keeping him beneath the water. Panic turned to outright terror as he realized he was going to drown.

Suddenly, above the shifting surface of the water, the stranger bucked forward, his head arching back, his mouth a rictus of pain. He lifted Colt from the water and flung him to the ground with a crunching thud, then whipped around, the axe stuck firmly in his back.

Pain ripped fire through Colt as he gasped for air and scrabbled backward, his gaze darting to Winchester, now behind the stranger. His older brother leveled the barrel of his shotgun at the stranger's head. Winn was smaller than the stranger, a young man on the cusp of twenty. But the look in Winn's cool blue eyes said he'd seen plenty.

"Go to Hell," Winn said, his voice tight and gravelly.

The stranger's mouth widened into a reddish slash in his pale face as he twisted his arm back and around, ripping the axe from his back with a wet sucking sound. His gaze flicked briefly to the glistening blackness oozing off the blade. "Already been there." The axe flew in a wide arc directly at Winn the same instant the gun exploded.

Colt screamed as Winn fell to the ground.

The stranger evaporated into nothing but a dark swirl of smoke.

Colt scrambled to his brother, ignoring the burning ache in his ribs and the rivulets of water still streaming down his face. Sod and dust burned his eyes and stung his nose as he slipped and stumbled across the ground to reach Winn. "Winn! Dammit, Winn, you still alive?"

The axe blade quivered in Winn's upper thigh, bright red blood gushing everywhere. Lord, that must hurt like hell. It had clearly struck bone. Winn's breathing was shallow, his face greasy with sweat and pain. "Don't just sit there. Tie it off."

Colt ripped off his wet shirt and tied off the limb as tight as he could to stem the flow of blood. He didn't dare try to remove the axe. He wasn't big enough to haul Winn to the cabin by himself. He swore under his breath and shivered, his skin tight with cold and fear. Winn's left eye cracked open.

"Don't swear." The words came out a bare puff of

breath. Any other time the rebuke would've stung. Now Colt was grateful because it meant his brother was still alive. He glanced up, scanning the horizon for a sign of his pa and other brother Remington.

He looked down at Winn, who was now almost as pale as the stranger had been, beads of sweat making his face shine, his lips tinting blue. "They're coming. Just stay with me."

He glanced nervously at the axe head and gulped against the bile rising in his throat. There was so much blood he was sure Winn was bleeding to death. "This is bad, real bad."

"Pa will know what to do. Just keep talkin' to me. I don't want to pass out."

"What the hell was that, Winn?" Colt hated the tremor of fear still in his voice.

"Vampire. Demon. Something unnatural."

Curiosity bit him hard and wouldn't let go. For years he'd wondered what was so all-confounded important that he'd be left alone days at a time. But when his father and brothers returned, they'd never tell him where they disappeared to or exactly what they'd done. "Is that what you and Pa have been hunting?"

"And others like it."

The thumping of running feet caused Colt to look at the tree line. Pa and Remington raced on foot toward their homestead. Pa got there first, easily outrunning Remy. He eyed Colt for a second, not bothering to ask for an explanation. He grabbed Winn's hand and gave it a hard squeeze. "This is gonna hurt, boy."

Winn's jaw jumped as he gritted his teeth. "Do it. Fast."

"Get your brother a leather strap to bite on." Colt knew he was talking to Remy, as his middle brother sprinted into the cabin to fetch the strap.

Inside Colt's stomach was an oily mess of anger and guilt. Somehow he shoulda known what that thing was. He shoulda been able to fight it off. But he hadn't. And now Winn was hurt bad. Likely as not, he'd lose his leg. Possibly even die.

"What can I do?"

Pa leveled a steely blue gaze at him. "Stay out of the way." The words were gruff, but laced with concern.

And that was the way it always was. Ever since Ma had died when Colt was seven, Pa and the two older boys had banded together and Colt had been left behind. He'd done everything he could to prove he was as worthy as his two older brothers to be included, but Pa had always turned away when he'd asked what they were hunting.

Remy came back, then crouched beside Winn to shove the strap between his tightly clenched teeth as Pa pulled the axe from Winn's thigh. Winn's scream pushed past the strap as he reflexively forgot to bite down in anguish. *Holy crap.* His piercing scream went through Colt like an electric charge he'd once gotten from one of his pa's weapons hidden under the bed, stinging and sharp. It sliced through his skull and echoed in his head, making his insides curl in around themselves away from the gut-wrenching guttural sound.

Blood gushed out of the wound, saturating Winn's pant leg in scarlet. Winn started panting through what was surely agony as Pa carried him into their cabin. Colt didn't bother to follow. He knew he'd only be in the way. The single room wasn't hardly big enough for four of them.

Hours later he heard the stiff scrape of Pa's boots in the soil behind him. Pa's hand, broad and thick, settled on his shoulder, giving him an awkward pat. The metallic scent of blood, Winn's blood, tainted the air. "He'll live. It's not your fault, Colt. Winn knew what he was dealing with. You didn't. And that's my fault, boy."

Colt turned, gazing up at his father, whose dark blue eyes were now bloodshot and shining with unshed tears.

His ma used to say they were so like Winn's it was kinda eerie. "I was trying to spare one of you boys from the life. I figured it should be you, being as you were your mama's favorite and the youngest. But I guess those bastards won't let me."

Colt fisted his hands against the damp cotton of his pants, his face heated. So many times he'd asked and been put off. He didn't dare believe the little leap of excitement in his gut or the light-headed feeling in his head. "Pa, you're not makin' a lick of sense."

His father shook his shaggy head, the dark hair thick and unkempt as all his boys'. His hand grazed over the three days of stubble along his square jaw. "Colt, it's time for you to learn exactly what you are."

Chapter 1

Arizona Territory
1883

He'd finally managed to wash the dark, sticky, tar-like blood off his hands. There'd been no hope for his clothes.

He'd had to burn them.

A man couldn't be too careful. For the likes of Colt Jackson, a Hunter born and bred, danger lurked everywhere, even in a place as innocuous as a worn-out bar that reeked of old tobacco smoke laced with the eye-watering fumes of rotgut whiskey. But neither of those blotted out the telltale stink of sulfur. Something supernatural lurked close by. He'd bet his gun hand on it.

Everything in the little mining town turned ice hub in Arizona Territory seemed coated with a ghostly layer of grit, even the chipped crystal chandeliers overhead. He felt the grit in his lungs and in his nostrils. It stank of putrid eggs and worse, probably from the smokestacks billowing white outside against an endless cerulean sky. He picked up his smeared, nearly empty glass of ice water, leaving behind a dark ring in the pale dust on the scarred, liquor-sticky table.

Hell, the only reason he'd stopped in Wickenburg in the first place was for the ice. Ever since the mines deep in the desert had flooded out and ingenious businessmen replaced the old rock crushers with steam-powered freeze machines, ice had become one of the most profitable commodities next to copper, gold, and silver in this special little sizzling corner of Hell on earth. He glared at his glass. The ice water had cost him almost as much as a good whiskey.

The lithe blond saloon girl he'd been eyeing since he walked in strolled toward him across the warped wooden floorboards worn smooth from the sand of so many boots. Her hips swayed to the sound of the out-of-tune piano plunking away near the stairs that led up to the rented rooms on the second floor. The cheap glass beading on her dark blue off-the-shoulder dance-hall dress flashed in the illumination of the gaslights overhead, creating sparkles to dance along the curves of her pale cleavage.

"Would you like some company, sugar?" Her smile didn't reach her heavily kohled eyes. She was anywhere between sixteen and thirty. How many men had she had? Worse, did he really care? He wanted the comfort of some-one who smelled sweet and womanly. Someone in whose arms he could forget, if only for a few hours, who and what he was.

Colt smiled wide. Enough women had told him his smile was dead gorgeous that he'd learned when to use it to his advantage. He'd dressed with more care than usual tonight, in clean black trousers, a starched white shirt, and a black brocade vest threaded with a pattern of silver and blue he'd been told matched the blue in his eyes. Seemed the effort had been worth it. "Yes, ma'am."

She cuddled up beside him, throwing a long, smooth

leg, bare to the thigh, over his. "So what brings you to Wickenburg, cowboy?"

He slid a hand over her smooth thigh. "Hunting."

She let out a husky laugh, full red lips tilting up in a come-hither pout. "Most men here are lookin' to strike it rich in ice. But I knew you was different the moment I saw you. In fact, I've seen your face before. What's your name?"

Colt tensed. He worked fairly hard at keeping a low profile, but every now and then a completely unwarranted wanted poster tended to circulate with his likeness. "Colt Jackson."

"Relax, handsome," she said, rubbing her hand over his chest, delving beneath the edge of his vest. He felt the heat of her hand through his shirt as her soft fingers stroked right over his heart. "We get outlaws in here all the time."

Yeah, but Colt seriously doubted they were anything like him. Her constant kneading touch began to drain the tension out of his shoulders, but only a little. His gun hand had started itching the moment he'd stepped into the bar, and his instincts had never steered him wrong before. Something in this little town wasn't right.

"So, are you famous? Are you dangerous?" she asked, her fingers threading through his shock of nearly black hair as she wriggled on his lap. Her perfume was way too strong, and verging on unpleasant. Her skin under all that makeup looked dirty. Her blond hair felt stiff and brittle beneath his fingers and he dropped his hand to her waist, feeling whalebone and crisp satin, not silky skin.

"Not exactly," Colt muttered, finding her less appealing by the moment. "Really more like a modern Robin Hood."

Glossy ruby lips pouted. "It's so much more fun when you're dangerous." He realized that it didn't matter how much he wanted or needed a woman right now, a tumble wasn't going to give him what he truly wanted and could never have—a home, a place where he belonged. No matter how delectable she looked, she wouldn't satisfy the deeper craving.

These days nothing could. There wasn't a way to feed the hunger that gnawed deep down, belly-deep. It bit into his bones and wouldn't let go. Hunting was a like a drug. Once a man knew supernaturals existed, he saw the Darkin everywhere. Once a Hunter knew that those creatures were the cause behind deaths no one else could explain, duty lay heavy on his shoulders.

Once a Hunter started hunting, he couldn't just stop.

Evil didn't take a holiday. Hunting wasn't a profession, it was a way of life.

For an instant he wished he could be like his older brothers, Winchester and Remington, upstanding citizens who didn't run from place to place even if they too were named after his pa's favorite guns. While the Jackson brothers looked a lot alike on the outside, with their pa's jet hair and wide shoulders and their ma's blue eyes and winning smile, they were different as could be on the inside.

Winn was a solid, steady, ordinary man. Remy straddled the line, looking respectable but hunting on the side. But being like Winn and Remy wasn't Colt's destiny. No, Colt had every intention of living up to the family legend his pa Cyrus "Black Jack" Jackson had started as one of the most notorious outlaws of the western territories, rather than living it down like his brothers. That was the life of a Hunter. Tracking down supernatural monsters one at a time and killing them to make the world a safer place.

Winn and Remy might have shirked their responsibilities to the Legion of Hunters, but he never would. Because once Pa had trained him, he'd revealed something to Colt he hadn't to Winn or Remy.

There would come a time when the far-flung pieces of

the Book of Legend would have to be brought together or humanity would perish. This grimy ice hub was just one more stop in his three-year search to uncover the hiding place of his pa's portion of the Book to prepare for the showdown with the Darkin, if and when it happened.

"So tell me somthin', mister. If you're a gunslinger, where's your gun?" She snaked a hand down to wrap around the inside of his thigh, rubbing suggestively at his groin and wriggling her bottom into his lap. That got his attention. It'd been a long time since he'd rested long enough to find a woman. If he'd been a less focused man, all the blood would have drained out of his brain right then and there regardless of how she'd looked.

With practiced ease she slipped one leg over the far side so she straddled him. The damp heat of her seeped right through his britches. He let out a ragged breath and she pressed forward, her soft breasts pushing against his chest as she skimmed the tip of her soft, slick tongue along his neck.

Then he heard it. Right next to his ear. The distinct sudden *flick* of a vampire's fangs being extended. He caught a sudden whiff of sulfur so strong it burned.

Colt reared up from the chair, but the vampire clung to him, her smooth legs firmly gripping his middle with the strength of a metal handcuff. Knowing he had only seconds to act, he shoved an arm between them, pushing her away from the blood pumping hard and fast in his neck.

Her face was warped beyond recognition, the brows protruded and bent, the eyes red, feral and hungry, her fangs twin white daggers bracketed by stretched ruby red lips. "Now, Hunter, you will die."

He looked her straight in those red eyes and didn't flinch. "Ladies first."

With his free hand he pulled the sting shooter from the

holster at his hip. A high-pitched keening sound split the air an instant before he shot her point-blank in the stomach.

Zzzot.

The arc of bright blue electricity catapulted her to the floor with a thick thud. She writhed and bucked on the floor like a beached fish, smoke curling in a black wisp from between her red lips.

The piano abruptly stopped. Half a dozen screams echoed in the bar as people came up from their crouch on the floor and stared at the barmaid, then at Colt with accusing eyes. Her face had already returned to its human shape. Her fangs retracted as she lay on the floor in a spreading, glistening black pool that leaked from two charred and smoking holes seared straight through her.

Shit. He hadn't intended for it to kill her, merely stun her senseless. That would teach him to use one of Marley Turlock's inventions before it was fully cooked. Marley was a brilliant inventor, but sometimes his ambitions outpaced his execution.

Colt knew better than to wait until the townspeople could get their hands on him and string him up on the nearest tree. So he did what any sensible Hunter would do. He ran like hell.

Five days later he still hadn't stopped running, but he knew he'd have to stop soon. His eyes were gritty from too much time awake in the saddle, and his clockwork horse, Tempus, was making funny grinding sounds. He wondered if perhaps he'd gotten a small stone or some other object accidentally lodged in the intricate workings of gears and springs that filled the copper belly of the beast, or just pushed his machine too hard across the dusty terrain without stopping to properly oil it. Marley would know.

Tempus clicked and whirred beneath him, the brass hooves kicking up small puffs of dust with every step through the main street. People glanced curiously at him and moved on their way along the wooden walkways.

To the untrained eye, Tempus looked like a black-and-white paint. The cowhide covering not only protected Colt from the copper getting too hot to touch if he rode in the sun too long, but also protecting the clockwork inside from rain and dirt. Only the horse's brass hooves, solid shining silver eyes, and mechanical noises gave it away. Being as Marley lived in town, the locals were probably used to seeing his contraptions of one kind or another.

Colt pulled the reins, steering the horse up the narrow, winding, dusty road that led up a steep hill to Marley's house. From a distance the house perched on the bluff over-looking the valley resembled a praying mantis more than a proper house. Various cranes and gadgets stuck out like multiple legs and antennae from the main building, and they often moved at odd intervals.

Tempus came to a rocking stop in Marley's front yard as Colt flipped off the GGD switch by twisting the horse's ear into a backward-facing position. Marley had dubbed it that when he'd shouted "Giddyup, God Dammit" at his seventh version of the horse, and it had actually moved. Colt wrapped the reins around the hitching post. Just for show. Tempus wouldn't go anywhere until pressure was applied to the plate in his back beneath the saddle, compressing the springs that allowed the GGD switch to be engaged. It was what Marley called a double safe precaution against horse thieves.

Not that a thief could get close to Marley's place. He had artificial eyes stuck here and there that were wired to an enormous lens in his laboratory. He could see who was coming or going at all hours of the day or night. Colt decided he'd hate to see which of Marley's deterrents an un-suspecting thief might run into. He'd had a close encounter once with one of Marley's spine-shooting mechanical cacti, and it had been enough for him.

Colt raised his fist to pound on the door, but it opened before he could knock. A man half a foot shorter than Colt peered at him from behind a pair of intricate multi-lensed brass goggles that extended six inches from his face and magnified his brown eyes to enormous proportions.

It was hard to tell exactly how old Marley was. The smooth youth of his face and dark brows competed with a cap of wild snow-white hair on his head. Marley attributed the premature color change to a lightning bolt that had struck him during an experiment. Colt wasn't sure, but he'd bet it was the side effect of yet another harebrained experiment gone awry. Marley's inventions, while undeniably brilliant, tended to hit big or miss horribly.

"I say, it's about time you made it back," Marley said, his words as clipped and undeniably British as his manner. He wiped his hands on his stained leather apron, then pushed past Colt and headed directly for Tempus, clucking and fussing over the machine like an old mother hen.

Colt grunted, glancing over his shoulder. "Good to see you too."

Marley was too busy checking Tempus over to reply. He was already bent over double, flipping up hatches and inspecting gears and springs, poking and prodding the beast's inner mechanics as he muttered to himself.

"I'll just make myself at home," Colt said under his breath.

Marley glanced up, his eyes magnified to the size of small saucers behind his goggle thingies, making gold flecks and the ring of darker brown around his irises stand out. "Don't touch anything."

Colt nodded. He wouldn't have dared. Last time he'd tried to move something, he'd gotten a nasty electrical shock from it. Nearly every surface of Marley's place was covered with a jumble of odd bits of brass and wire, heaps of gears and springs, and stacks of sketches. He'd find a chair and sit, maybe forage for something to drink while he waited for his friend to finish his inspection of Tempus. The only chair available turned out to be the one Marley sat in at his workbench.

He settled into the seat, thankful that it was softer than his saddle. He glanced in the direction of the kitchen and thought better of trying to navigate the trails of teetering junk piled up along the way. Instead he tipped his hat down over his eyes and relaxed for the first time in days.

Marley sauntered in about ten minutes later looking far too pleased with himself. "That horse is a marvel of mechanical engineering, if I do say so myself. I've been working on a new version that would remove the leather covering and allow the copper to act like a chemically powered boiler for steam. Make the beast move faster and more smoothly . . ." He trailed off, as he frequently did when he was distracted. Which was always.

Colt pushed his Stetson back. "Are you sure that's a good idea? I don't know how stable sitting on a steam boiler is going to be, especially if I'm getting shot at," he pointed out, his voice dry.

Marley's dark eyebrows bent down in a deep V, disappearing behind the edge of his goggles. He worried his lip with his finger. "True. You do tend to draw a lot of fire. Perhaps that method of locomotion would better serve the horseless carriage I'm working on."

A horseless carriage? Last time, Marley had been working on an improved steam flyer. "In the meantime, you might want to see what you can do about this." Colt pulled the sting shooter out of its holster and tossed it to Marley.

Marley caught it, then pushed the button. A high keening

sound split the air a second before a vivid blue wiggling arc of electricity shot out, launching a marble bust of President Lincoln off a nearby table and scattering a stack of papers. They instantly burst into flame. "Nothing's the matter with it. The Tesla coil is active. Seems to be working properly to me," he said as he stomped out the flames.

Colt tipped up the edge of his Stetson a little farther with his finger. "It blew two holes clean through the last person I used it on and nearly got me lynched."

Marley peered at the sting shooter more closely. "I see. Perhaps it requires an adjustment. It's still in prototype stage for the Tesla Rangers." He set it amid the flotsam and jetsam on his desk. "In the meantime, I've got something else for you."

Colt stood up and held out a hand. "After you, Professor." He followed Marley to what would have been the kitchen in any normal home. It was a damn good thing Marley wasn't married. Colt seriously doubted any woman could stomach the kind of chaos that Marley lived in. It smelled faintly of ammonia, and the counters overflowed with copper pots and various brown and green glass bottles, all marked with little white labels written in nearly indecipherable handwriting.

Marley pulled off his goggle thingies, handing them off to Colt. "Hold my spectro-photometric oglifiers. I don't want them too near the oven. Might change the chemistry in the lenses." Marley pulled on an oven mitt and opened the door to his large six-burner cast-iron stove and pulled out a cast-iron mold with little holes in it at regular intervals. He tipped the mold upside down over a tray, and out came a pile of bullets that looked like little, narrow, shiny cookies. "New silver bullets. Filled them with an improved mixture of powdered bone, lead, salt, and gunpowder. Should kill just about anything, natural or supernatural."

Colt grinned and clapped Marley on the shoulder. "I always said you were a good cook."

From the depths of Marley's laboratory came the clanging of a bell. "Incoming message." Marley handed the tray of bullets to Colt, then skittered into the other room, the bell still clanging. He dug through a heap on a sideboard table until he'd unburied a teletypingwriter, then flipped a switch that shut off the bell as the machine began typing out a message from Morse code. Marley waited until the typebars had stopped clacking, then rotated a few knobs and pulled the paper from the machine. He took the brass and leather goggles from Colt and snapped them back into place, flipping an extended lens over his eye as he scanned the note.

"It's from Remington. He's gone to retrieve China McGee from jail."

The bullets rattled on the tray. Colt set the tray down and ripped the paper out of Marley's hand, reading it for himself. "Damn fool," he muttered. "She's a shape-shifter. I'm lucky she got caught and not me when that bank blew to hell in the fight. What's he think he's doing?"

"Maybe he thought you two were together."

Colt grunted as he crumpled the page into a ball. "She might be easy on the eyes, but I'd be as likely to shack up with a mountain lion as that little blond hellcat. She's a good thief, but you can't trust a shifter."

"Then why didn't you just shoot her?"

"There wasn't time," he hedged. The fact was he'd been too damn busy trying to locate the deposit box of a deceased Hunter named Diego. It was rumored to hold a clue to a map revealing the location of one of the pieces of the Book. He hadn't been paying attention to how short China had cut the fuse. The damn explosives to get out of the jail had blown too soon. He suspected it was a double-crossing gone wrong.

In the end he'd climbed from the rubble before the authorities arrived and had to leave both China and the deposit box behind and move on to his next lead in finding his pa's part of the Book. He'd had no doubt she could fend for herself, and frankly she was Darkin, so he wasn't all that concerned in the first place. One less Darkin in the world wouldn't be such a bad thing. "Do you think you can get him a message?"

Marley shook his head. "His receiver isn't working. He can send messages, but I have to telegraph him in return. I'm going to fix it next time I travel in his direction."

"If you telegraph him, tell him to watch his back. That China McGee is bad news and if he needs a thief, he should look elsewhere."

"Certainly." Marley scooped up the bullets off the tilting tray and grabbed Colt's hand, facing it palm upward. "Don't forget these. I do hope they make the proper impression."

Colt grinned. "If you mean by impression a hole eight inches deep, then I'm betting they'll be just fine." He began putting them in the individual loops holding the ammunition on his gun belt. "Thanks, Marley."

Marley shoved his spectro-whozee-whatsit goggles back onto his forehead. "Don't mention it. I do my best for the cause. Where are you off to next?"

"I'm going to see a man about a mine."

"Still looking for the lost pieces of the Book of Legend, are you?"

"Last year I took down a dozen supernaturals prowling around. Last month alone it was five. This month ten. It's gettin' worse." For the last three years he'd been talking to every Hunter he could find, scouring every scrap of written information he could lay his hands on, to piece together the location of the different remnants of the Book of Legend.

The Legion had become so fractured over the centuries that none of the branches—not the Hunters in Europe, nor the ones in Asia, nor those in the Southern Hemisphere—knew the true locations of all three pieces. But his latest discovery of his mother's diary led him to believe the clue in Diego's box wouldn't lead him to Pa's part of the Book, which was his main focus.

Better to risk his neck on a sure thing than a rumor in a deposit box in the clutches of that shifter. "I don't know how big the crack has gotten in that gate to Hell, but things are slidin' through faster and faster. If we don't get that Book put back together, there's no tellin' how long humanity's got."

Marley threaded his fingers up through both sides of the cotton-like fuzz on his scalp. "I say, I didn't realize it was as bad as all that. Perhaps you ought to take this as well." He opened a drawer in his desk and pulled out a corked brown bottle with no label.

"Whiskey?"

"Holy water. You may find you need it."

Colt chuckled. "You may be right. It might be pretty hard to come by in Bodie." The saloons and houses of ill repute in Bodie outnumbered the churches by forty to one.

"Bodie?"

"According to what I found in Ma's diary, that's where the mine is."

"But isn't Winchester in Bodie?"

"Last I heard."

Marley nibbled thoughtfully on his bottom lip. "You're in more trouble than I thought." He fished around in the drawer again, pulling out another bottle with a different-colored cork.

"More holy water?"

"No. Whiskey. You'll need the water for fighting the demons and the whiskey for fighting your brother."

Colt kissed the second bottle and tipped his hat at Marley. "You're a good man, Marley. Don't let no one tell you different."

"Just do me a favor, old chap, and don't do anything foolish."

Colt chuckled. "You know me, Marley."

Marley raised one dark, bushy brow. "Precisely."

Chapter 2

The familiar stench of burnt flesh and decay woke Lilly from her deep sleep.

In the middle of her sparsely furnished boarding room, where the faded wallpaper peeled in strips from the wall, stood an enormous man. If the inhuman size of him didn't scare any sane being senseless, the pure maliciousness that rolled off him would. It tainted the very air with a palpable darkness far heavier than the night. But her fear was born not because she didn't know him, but rather because she did. Far too well.

Part vampire, part fallen archangel, and all demon lord, Rathe was Hell personified and put on Earth. His skin, dead-flesh pale, glowed eerily in the filtered moonlight coming through the thin cotton curtains over her window. He was dressed like a dapper Englishman, with a great black overcape, freshly pressed black pin-striped suit with matching vest, crisp white high-collar shirt, and blood-red silk tie. Ice blue eyes split by a vertical pupil froze Lilly to the core. Ironic, really, considering it was Rathe. She sincerely doubted Hell had frozen over. He was rather partial to keeping things hot in his dominion. But then, in the right conditions ice could burn too.

She brushed the fall of dark red hair out of her face and fought down the urge to cover herself from his hungry, predatory gaze.

"Lillith Marie Arliss, I have a job for you."

She just bet. He only used all of a person or demon's name when he wanted to bind them into service.

"Whose soul are you hungry for now, Rathe?"

Rathe laughed. The grating vile sound irritated her skin like the nagging itch of a mosquito bite multiplied by a thousand. "Someone special. A Hunter."

Lilly sat up a little straighter, flipping her long hair over her shoulder, ignoring the persistent itch. Hunters were bad news. Especially for demons. They could permanently send a demon to Hell. No furloughs to the surface world could make for one cranky demon.

"Sounds dangerous. What's my incentive?"

"Your incentive is I let you exist another day. Untouched."

When Rathe said untouched, what he really meant was untortured. There wasn't a forgiving morsel in his body.

"What exactly did you want me to do with him?"

"Seduce him, find what his father left him, take his soul, then kill him, of course."

Lilly shrugged. "Easy enough."

Rathe reached out a long pale hand, his fingernails pointed and sharp like talons, and brushed a finger along the outer edge of her cheek, then down along her neck and along her sternum, flicking the nipple that was barely covered by the edge of the black silk negligee she wore. Her skin shriveled in response. "His particular weakness is women. That's why I picked you. Who better to bring down that Hunter than an incredible succubus?"

Lilly turned away. A shiver of disgust started from where he'd touched her and wormed its way down deep into her belly. As much as she despised Rathe, he wasn't one to be argued with. As an immortal demon, she had no choice but to obey his summons or suffer however long he chose to make her suffer. After all, it wasn't like she'd ever die from his torture.

"What's his name?"

"Colt Ambrose Jackson."

For a second every sound in the room was amplified a hundredfold as her heart stopped beating. Then Lilly couldn't hear anything as the rushing sound of her own pulse pounding fast and furious filled her ears.

"*The* Colt Jackson? As in one of the three brothers of the Chosen?"

Rathe's gaze bored into her as if the question were complete idiocy.

"I'll take that as a yes." Rumors of the Chosen ran rampant among the children of the night, like a scary bedtime story told to scare little demons straight. In the Darkin world, now her world, everyone believed the Jackson brothers could be the Chosen. Three brothers who were merciless, determined Hunters unlike any that had been seen in generations.

She could see now why Rathe had chosen her and not just any succubus. For the last twenty-five years she'd been studying the legend, looking for any loophole that might get her out of her ill-conceived bargain with Rathe so she could return to her sister, maybe live a normal human life. Lilly was sure there wasn't anyone but one of the Chosen who could possibly undo what Rathe had done in capturing her soul. In her efforts to learn all she could about them, she had become somewhat of an expert on the Chosen, and on Colt in particular.

"Where can I find him?"

"Bodie."

Lilly laughed, the sound light and musical, like chimes in the wind. "That's easier than I thought." Perhaps Rathe did have a sense of humor. Going after a Hunter who liked women, and who was already in Bodie, was like offering a drunk a bottle of whiskey—the chance of refusal was nil. And she already knew enough about Colt to know precisely what to offer him to gain his cooperation.

Rathe's mouth broke into a wider reddish slash in his pale white face. Revealing two rows of pointed teeth with slightly longer canines, it was as close as he'd ever get to a smile. "You have three weeks. Good hunting, Lillith Marie Arliss." He vanished in a cloud of dark particles. At least she was alone in her room once more.

Lilly sighed. She pushed back her thin curtains and glanced out at the moon. In three weeks it would be new with an eclipse—the darkest a night could get, and a powerful time for endings and beginnings. She let the curtain drop, then flung off the covers and got dressed. There was no point in going back to sleep. Rathe might have found a sense of humor, but he'd still be impatient.

She blew on the wick of the candle in a brass holder by her bedside and it flamed to life, casting the room in flickering light and dispelling the sulfur stench Rathe had left behind. Nothing else bore evidence of Rathe's visit, not even the worn wooden floorboards covered by a braided rag rug where he'd stood, or the washstand with its chipped white porcelain pitcher and bowl. Capturing a Hunter's soul was no easy matter. If he were a normal man, she could materialize in his dreams and steal away with his soul after she'd killed him with the biggest orgasm of his life. A Hunter would never give her the opportunity. No, she'd have to make him believe he wanted her, needed her, as much as any mortal woman before he'd let himself go with her completely enough to snare his soul. And that would require gaining his trust.

The way to a man's mind was first through his eyes, then through his britches. But the way to his trust, to taking his soul if he was an experienced Hunter who knew demons, that was through his family. And in the case of Colt Jackson, specifically his older brothers.

She waved her hand, materializing three small books on the faded thin quilt on her bed. All of the books were bound in black leather that had grown shiny through wear, and each was intricately tooled with the gilded name of a Jackson brother. When she'd studied the legends about the Chosen, the three brothers prophesied to bring about the opening of the Gates of Nyx and control all Darkin, she'd never dreamed she'd ever meet one, let alone have to seduce him.

Instinctively she reached for the book with the name COLT emblazoned in gold across the black cover, caressing the familiar leather. She'd already read this book more than a hundred times from cover to cover. She knew more about him than anyone, if it was possible. Truth be told, while she had never met any of the brothers in person, she'd developed a kind of fascination with them, in particular Colt. It wasn't hero-worship, exactly, more like looking for the best chance to escape Rathe's grip on her soul. The Chosen looked like her best bet.

Lilly bade the book to disappear with a snap of her fingers. If Colt was indeed after his father's third of the Book of Legend, she knew him well enough to know there was no need for her to search for him. He'd be calling for a demon soon enough.

Chapter 3

Colt scanned the array of wooden buildings in the booming mining town of Bodie looking for the local jail. It sat in the shallow bowl of the valley among the sagebrush, a small, peaked building with a lean-to addition sagging off to the right side of it like a child off the hip of a worn-out frontier wife.

The last place Colt ever thought he'd go willingly when he was in trouble was to the local jail. But that's where his oldest brother Winn was, being that he was sheriff.

Colt trod up the sagging wooden steps in front of the door. The black iron knob was cold in his hand as he opened it cautiously, just a crack. *Click.* A gun cocked on the other side of the door, right about level with his left temple and just below the brim of his brown Stetson. His whole body tensed, waiting to see if he was going to dodge a bullet. What if Winn was out to lunch and there was some bored deputy on the other side just itching for something to shoot?

The doorknob yanked out of his hand. A large man with a head full of slicked-back black hair, a slightly crooked nose, and pair of dark blue eyes, far darker than Colt's own, stared back at him over the barrel of a revolver.

"Damn, Winn, you went and growed a mustache." Heavy and thick, the thing was as dark as Winn's hair, twisted into sharp waxed points at either end and leaving only a bit of his bottom lip exposed. It made his brother look far older and fiercer than Colt remembered.

Winn grunted. "I've had it for two years." He glanced over Colt's shoulder in both directions, then uncocked the gun and slipped it into a worn hip holster. He turned his back on Colt.

"Shut the door," he said in a low voice over his shoulder. He sat down in the chair behind the battered wooden desk that served as the sheriff's office. Behind him was a wall littered with curling, yellowed wanted posters and an iron nail holding up a leather back holster filled with a Winchester rifle. The smell of wood smoke from the small pot-bellied stove burning in the corner under a huge copper boiler cut the smell of unwashed male and the sickly faint odor of vomit coming from the cells that lined the far wall, making it bearable. "What brings you to Bodie?"

Colt took the only other chair in the place and swung the wooden ladderback around to straddle it, resting his arms across the slender back. "Well, it sure ain't the churches in town." Colt snickered. Bodie's well-deserved reputation as one of the roughest towns in the state of California meant Winn was fairly busy. "Do I need a reason to visit my brother?"

"Hell yes. You'd never come otherwise."

"Not very charitable of you."

"Not feeling in a very giving mood."

"See? You need more churches in this town, would help give folks more to think about bein' charitable. Hell, you about shot me without even seeing who was coming through the door."

Winn glanced out the window, a longing look flitting across his face. Maybe bein' respectable wasn't all he thought it was cracked up to be. Maybe that tingle in Colt's palm wasn't just about a supernatural after his ass this time. Maybe it was because Winn was ready to go back to hunting.

He turned his piercing dark blue eyes back on Colt. For a second Winn looked so like their pa that it made a little shiver shake Colt's insides way down deep. Colt wished he'd taken a slug of the whiskey Marley had given him.

Winn grumbled something underneath his breath about little brothers as he rolled his thick shoulders. "Look, I got a murder a day to contend with, sometimes more. I don't need the trouble you trail in your wake, Colt."

The truth stung. Being around normal people just wasn't something a Hunter could do. Inevitably they'd get sucked into the troubles that followed like a dark cloud of dust. "Spoken like a true big brother."

"Spoken like the town sheriff."

Colt's gaze flicked to the cells. Of the four, three were empty. Behind the black iron bars of the last cell, spread out on the robe bed and olive green wool blanket, the squatter lay facedown, his back raising and lowering in deep rhythmic breaths.

Winn followed his gaze and waved a hand in dismissal. "Don't worry about Billy. He sleeps it off in there every other night. He'll be out until daybreak. It's safe to talk."

Colt feigned a sigh. He hadn't been planning on a reunion either, but he still needed Winn's help. "I got marshals on my tail for killin' a saloon girl out in Arizona Territory."

Winn slumped back into his chair and rubbed his hands over his jaw, a small vertical crease forming between his brows. "Ah, hell. Why'd you go and do a fool thing like that for?"

Colt's shoulders stiffened at the rebuff. "She was about to sink her fangs into my neck."

Winn grunted with understanding and sat forward, bracing his elbows on his wide, scarred desk. "Still hunting, then, are you?"

Colt stared his brother down. "If you're lookin' for me to apologize, it ain't gonna happen, Winn. It's in our blood, far back as we know. And there ain't nothin' gonna change that. It's what we've been trained to do."

"No, it's what Pa trained *you* to do." Winn pointed a thick index finger at him, the crease between his brows deepening further, the ghosts of the past flickering in his eyes. "I'm not interested. I've chosen a different life." Winn had never gotten over that demon attacking Colt when Colt had been fourteen. Winn had dispatched the demon, nearly gotten killed in the process, and never done another day of hunting since, something Colt couldn't fathom.

"You ever wonder how many murders in this town might be caused by something supernatural prowling around Bodie?"

Winn huffed and stared out the window, refusing to meet Colt's gaze. "I try to stay the hell out of anything unnatural. It's hard enough to get a conviction from the crooked judge in this district without introducing a lot of hocus-pocus into the trial."

"But you know it's a possibility."

Winn glared at him. "Doesn't mean I want to wallow around in it like a pig in mud."

"Still trying to be shiny clean, the perfect gentleman, ain't you? Well, I got news for you, brother." Colt leaned forward, tipping his cowboy hat slightly off his forehead. "Marshals are the least of my worries. Hell is coming to Bodie, if it ain't followed me here already."

Winn's eyes narrowed, his bottom lip flattening into a taut line beneath the level of his dark mustache. "What'd you do?"

"Seems that saloon girl weren't no ordinary vampire.

'Course I didn't realize it until later. She was Rathe's girl. His baby girl, to be precise."

"Sweet Jesus on a shingle," Winn breathed. He rubbed his palms back and forth through his slicked-back hair, making it stand up in awkward black spikes and tufts. "He's gonna want your head for his collection."

"And he's going to do some damage getting it."

Rathe was evil incarnate. There was no need to compare him to Lucifer. The archdemon Rathe was more like Lucifer's ugly badman big brother—the one you didn't mess with. No Hunter with half a brain beneath his hat would be stupid enough to go against Rathe alone and believe he could survive.

Usually there wasn't enough left of his victims to bother with. But Rathe liked trophies. In particular he had a penchant for keeping the severed heads of his most important victims and shrinking them down into macabre watch fobs he gilded and kept strung on a fancy gold watch chain. Winn rubbed his hands over his face and sat forward in his chair, pinning his penetrating blue gaze on Colt. "Tell me you're not still searching after Pa's damn part of the Book."

Colt just stared hard at his eldest brother. There was no use in repeating the words that had passed one too many times between him and Winn. His older brother couldn't see any point in risking his life for the Legion. But Colt knew different. Pa had confided in him, and his old man's journal was part of something bigger and more important—the Book of Legend—the guide that could help him and Hunters like him ultimately defeat the darkness creeping in upon the world.

At least he hoped like hell it was. He'd believed it for so long now, he couldn't be absolutely sure it wasn't just his eager imagination, spoon-fed Hunter legend and lore from the time he could toddle, but hadn't really known what it all meant until the day Winn had saved him.

"Supernatural beings aren't just goin' to disappear because you and Remy stick your heads in the sand. They're goin' to keep coming, bigger and badder, and if the uptick in what I've seen lately is any indication, all Hell's gonna break loose soon. 'Sides, I think I know where the Book is—for *sure* this time."

Winn groaned, rolling his eyes. "Dammit, Colt, you say that every time."

"Yeah, but this time is different."

Winn leaned his head back over the top edge of his chair, closing his eyes. "How?"

"I want you to tell me the truth."

His brother cracked open an eye. "What the hell are you talking about, boy?"

"I know you know where Pa's portion of the Book of Legend is, *and* what I have to do to get it."

Winn was staring hard at him now, blue eyes blazing, lightning in a dark, stormy sky. "How'd you figure it out?"

"I've followed every clue I had, and it all leads to you, big brother. I think Pa's Book is hidden in the mountains around Bodie and you've been protecting it. It's in the Dark Rim Mine, ain't it?" Colt pressed.

Winn stood up from his chair, making the wood creak with protest as it skidded back hard on the wooden floorboards. He scowled. "Even if it was, you'd need a demon to open it for you. Pa made sure nothing human could open it and nothing supernatural would want to. And don't you even think about bringing a demon to my town." Winn pointed an accusing finger in Colt's direction.

"So now that I'm hunting here, instead of somewhere else, it's a problem?"

Winn's fingers on his opposite hand snaked down his side, fingering the holster of his pistol. "Hell yes. A big problem. I don't need to be dealing with any demon possessions. It's bad enough here with the drunk miners going after one another and shootin' each other for the slightest offense."

"Then they'd probably be too soused to notice it anyhow. 'Sides, I'll keep it right by my side, and if it steps a toe out of line, I'll send it straight to Hell." Of course, that's where all supernaturals ought to be. There wasn't one he'd met yet who'd convinced him that there was anything worthwhile or decent about them. They were monsters. The whole lot of them. And once he was done with the demon, he'd send it back to Hell just on principle alone.

"Why don't you come along?"

Winn snorted, and sat back down. "Look. I'm not going on any fool errand for some dusty old pages the old man thought held the secrets of the universe. I've got the afternoon steam stage coming in at one. We've already had it held up four times in a month. The Black Gulch Mine's entire payroll is on that stage." He unconsciously rubbed his left thigh, which still bore the rope-like scar of the axe blade. "I've got real responsibilities here."

And real fears, Colt thought, but he kept his teeth clamped shut and the words to himself. Winn had never been the same after the attack. Colt tugged his hat down tight around his forehead and stood up, swinging the chair back around to prop it against the wall where he'd found it. "Suit yourself."

He glanced back at his brother and saw his face had gone all sternlike.

"Just be careful. You know you can't trust a demon." Winn's words were simple enough, but Colt could hear his brother's real concern underneath. They'd lost every male member of their family to hunting through the ages. It wasn't a legacy he liked to ponder on too much.

Colt shrugged. "Who said anything about trusting one? I just need to find one and use it to open where Pa's part of the Book is hidden."

"It'll want your soul," Winn warned.

Colt grinned. "That's just too damn bad. I don't feel in a very givin' mood."

Winn grinned in return, the smile so similar Colt swore he could have been looking in the mirror—all except for the fat mustache with the pointed tips and the shorter haircut. A log in the small woodstove under the boiler crackled and popped, sending a shower of sparks up the flue. His brother's gaze flicked to Colt's hip. "You packing silver?"

Colt gave a single curt nod, surprised at the unspoken permission Winn was giving him to go hunting in Bodie. He turned the knob on the door, ready to leave. "Always do."

"Good." Winn took a deep breath, his broad chest expanding, and let it out real slowly, his blue eyes steady. "Colt, if you need help, holler."

Colt nodded, knowing he could count on Winn if things went to hell, then walked out the door to find a demon.

Chapter 4

"Hope to hell this works."

While Colt had gotten rid of a lot of demons, mostly by hitting them dead center in the forehead with one of Marley's demon killer bullets or with various other means combined with sheer dumb luck, he sure as shit had never summoned one. He looked at the instructions he'd dug out of a moldy old book he'd borrowed from Marley.

The high desert seemed immense in the darkness, with only the stars, a thick half moon, and his small campfire for light. Down in the floor of the valley Bodie crackled with life, but out here among the sagebrush and spindly creosote the desolation closed in, scented with wood smoke.

Colt lit four candles, one at each point of the compass, holding the fifth lit candle in his hand as he sketched a pentagram in the powder-fine dirt at his feet and enclosed it in a circle.

Marley had told him summoning a demon was about the stupidest thing he'd ever heard of, but had helped him find a reference to it nonetheless.

Colt eyed the lines in the dirt. The book had said it would hold a demon, and that the demon couldn't get out of the circle until it was released by the summoner or until sunrise, whichever happened first. Sure didn't look like much protection to him, but what the hell. Hunting came with risks.

He drew in a deep breath, letting the Latin words hum and vibrate through his chest and across his lips as he spoke them slowly and deliberately, lending his own sense of urgency to them.

A shimmer in the air, rather like the warping of a mirage in the desert heat, rippled just above the circle, followed by a curl of black smoke that grew denser until it began to form a physical shape.

At first he mistook it for a trick of the firelight. His breathing hitched as the shape solidified into a feminine form with generous uptilted breasts and gracefully sloped pale shoulders. He glanced up and found himself face-to-face with a demon far more beautiful than any had a right to be. Damn.

She looked like she'd just risen out of bed, her deep red hair a silken, fiery cloud that tumbled loose and wavy down her back. Her pale skin flushed a rosy pink, which set off her unnaturally deep green eyes. They sparkled with pleasure and delight, as if she were truly pleased to see him, and tangled his gut into a fierce mix of wariness and attraction.

Dressed in nothing more than a short black silk nightgown that dangled by miniscule strips of black satin ribbon over her bare shoulders, she—it, he reminded himself—was showing more skin than he'd ever seen of a woman outside of the sheets. Her long, bare legs were so creamy smooth he bet silk would be jealous. A seductive, knowing curve shaped her full lips into a come-hither smile that could bring any man to his knees.

"Aren't you just a tall drink of water?" As if the sight of her weren't enough, the low, husky quality of her voice danced across his skin, making him hot and hard at the same time. "What's your pleasure, cowboy? I assume you summoned me for a reason."

Colt struggled to collect enough moisture in his mouth to get his tongue to work properly. "I want you to open a door for me." His voice cracked and he cleared his throat to cover it.

Her eyes grew half-shuttered, the emerald color still unnaturally bright through the fan of her thick, sable lashes. "A man as strong as you could open any door for himself, I'm sure." She stepped forward and met with an invisible barrier, then glanced down at the lines he'd drawn in the dirt. "The circle only lasts until daybreak. Then what?" Her long, tapered fingers skimmed along the barrier, depressing the pads of her fingertips, as if it were glass.

The momentary break in her gaze on him snapped some sense into Colt. He wasn't going to take the chance that Marley was wrong about that circle holding a demon. He leveled his revolver at her. The metallic click of it cocking sounded louder than it should have in the air between them, but then Colt wasn't packing just any ordinary revolver. It was a Hunter model designed special for his pa by Samuel Colt himself, and the very gun he'd been named after.

The demon eyed the gun, caution flickering across her features. "You're a Hunter, aren't you?"

"Yes, ma'am."

The corner of her mouth rose higher in delight. "A polite one."

"Yes, m—" Colt caught himself. She was already wrapping her charm or spell or whatever the hell it was around him again. He glanced away, deliberately trying to keep her from getting a hold on his common sense.

"You just want me to open a door? That's an odd request, coming from a Hunter." She crisscrossed her arms around her narrow waist, which made her breasts press together, drawing his attention to the dark shadow between them.

"Why do you *really* need me?" Her voice drizzled like warm honey over him, smooth and sweet, and oh so tempting. Damn. Perhaps he should have covered his ears too.

"Only a demon can open the door," he replied. He refused to make eye contact with her now or look at how the firelight danced across her pale skin. He focused instead on the flicker of the candle flames that marked the edges of the circle.

"Ah. So you want me to unlock this door for you?"

"Yes."

"And what will I get out of it?"

Colt moved on instinct, flicking his gaze upward, cocking and pointing the barrel of his gun at the center of her forehead in the same instant. "How about I don't blow your sweet ass back to Hell right here, right now?"

Her eyes turned hard, assessing, taking in the measure of him like he was a raw chunk of gold and estimating what he'd be worth. "Tsk, tsk. No need to be rude. After all, *you* are the one who summoned *me*. And as a Hunter, surely you know no demon works for free. There's always a price."

Colt hesitated. "What do you want?"

The demon paused, dropping her lashes just a fraction and looking at him in a way that oozed sexual appeal. "A kiss."

"That's it?"

"A kiss for opening the door," she amended, her full lips opening just a fraction, drawing his attention and filling his mind with curiosity about what it would be like to kiss her—not just slow or quick, but soft and deep.

He ran his finger along the edge of his stubbled jaw, trying to ignore the snap of energy that fizzled and sparked in the air between them. Every normal male reaction in him said hell yes, but his brain was pulling back on the reins with a determination he couldn't ignore.

"Surely a kiss isn't too much to ask." Her voice was fine

and smooth, and seared a path right to his belly just like aged whiskey.

"That's what worries me. Every other demon I've ever met has asked for my soul."

Her sensual mouth curved into a subtle smile, just a bare uptilt of the lips that made his heart pound hard first in his chest, then down lower in his groin. "Well, perhaps I'm different from any other demon you've met."

Colt eyed her up and down. She sure as hell had that right. His mouth suddenly seemed desert dry.

She shifted, turning and putting her back against the solid invisible barrier of the circle. The barrier pressed against the curve of her ass, making the silk there look like it might have been painted on her skin. He swallowed hard.

"Surely you've kissed a girl before?"

"'Course I have."

She glanced over her shoulder with a long, lingering look. "Then what's stopping you?"

"You're not a girl. You're a demon, and if I kiss you I'm sealing a pact between us."

The soft pink tip of her tongue slicked a slow, glistening trail over her top lip. "That's right. You kiss me. I open your door."

"What about my soul?"

She shrugged. "It's not part of *this* accord."

"But you want it."

Hunger flared in her eyes. "Of course I want *you*."

Colt leaned forward, then abruptly stopped and shook himself. What the hell was he thinking? She was a demon, and there was no way a demon was going to just blithely go on its way without his soul. But for that brief space of a second, she hadn't seemed like an unnatural thing at all. She'd seemed like the most enticing woman he'd ever met.

He stepped back a pace from the circle and tried to think on something that didn't have to do with how she looked. Not that the distance was going to do him any good. The smooth, warm wood of his revolver usually soothed his nerves when he was on edge, but not tonight. He began to pace.

"What kind of demon are you?"

"Does it matter? Or were you looking for something particular?"

Colt turned, pacing back the other way. "Nah. Guess it don't matter much."

"You're stalling, Hunter. Why is that? Do we have an accord? My help for your kiss?"

Colt's brain spun trying to think of all the possible ways this could go wrong, and there were plenty. But he'd battled far worse all on his own than one lone demon who looked like sex personified. He stopped pacing and stared hard at the demon. "Why would you help me?"

"Maybe I like you."

"You don't even know me."

"Maybe I'd like to."

Colt stepped closer to the invisible barrier formed by the circle that held her his prisoner, pulled by some magnetic attraction he couldn't resist. Up close her skin was even smoother, almost the texture of rose petals, and damn, but she smelled just as good.

"I thought demons all smelled like sulfur."

Her husky laugh made him want to lean in and sample her lush mouth. "Only certain demons."

"And you're different."

"I'm a lover, not a fighter, if that's what you're asking."

"So how do you steal souls?"

"Oh, I never steal them." She batted her eyelashes at him in absolute innocence. "Men give them to me willingly."

"Why would they do that?" Even as the words left his mouth, gut deep he knew why. She was the damn near sexiest thing he'd ever been this close to.

Her lips formed a beguiling Mona Lisa smile and her

words came out a sultry whisper of promise. "Because I can do things for them. I can offer them pleasures no mere mortal woman can."

He bet. "Good enough to kill 'em, huh? You must be one hell of a succubus."

She shrugged her delicate, creamy shoulders. One of the slender ribbon straps slipped, sending the edge of her gown tipping precariously low. Both hands itched to touch her. *Ah, hell.*

He swallowed hard. "Your charms are wasted on me, demon." Colt was hoping God didn't plan on striking him dead right then and there for that whopper of a lie. "I only need you for one thing."

"I have a name, you know."

Colt's tongue tied into a knot. "Name?" he choked.

"I was a mortal girl before I became what I am now. My name hasn't changed just because I've become immortal."

He stared hard at her. Ever since the day that demon had come for him as a boy, he'd never thought of them as anything other than creatures of the damned who had no soul. But this was different. She was different.

She gave a dramatic sigh, leaning her head back against the barrier of the circle. "It's Lilly Arliss."

It took a moment for him to control his thoughts enough to find words to answer her. "But that's so normal."

She gifted him with a feminine smile that fisted through his chest and took away his ability to breathe. He thought he might have even seen a glimmer of admiration in those eyes. "You have no idea how much that means to someone like me."

"Some*thing*."

"I beg your pardon?"

"Some*thing* like you."

The pleasant curve of her mouth disappeared instantly,

the intoxicating sensation she was causing evaporating like fog, leaving a chill behind. "Now you are wasting my time, Hunter."

"I've got a name too. Colt Jackson."

She crossed her arms, her eyes hard and glittering like cut emeralds. "And why should that matter to me when I am no more than a means to an end for you?"

There wasn't a damn reason why it should, but at the same time Colt desperately wanted it to matter to her. Perhaps more than any other woman he'd ever met.

"Even now you're probably thinking of a way to send me back to Hell as soon as you've finished with me." She huffed. "You've no more honor than any other being, human or supernatural. At least my offer was genuine."

That stung. Colt's shoulders tensed. He had honor, dammit. Probably more than most men. His life as a Hunter had been built upon caring for those who didn't know what nasty uglies there really were out in the world. But considering how ruthless his reputation might be on the other side, he thought she might have a reason to see his actions in an unflattering light.

"What if I let you go when you're done with helping me?" The minute the words left his lips, he wondered why he'd even offered. What was he thinking? Letting a demon go free? What the hell had compelled him?

But then Lilly looked at him. Her deep green eyes pierced him, making him feel stripped bare to his very bones. And he knew exactly why he'd made the offer.

"Would you really do that?"

"As long as I get to keep my soul after you've helped me, then, yep, I'll release you when we're done."

"Would you be willing to help me instead?"

That took him aback. Why would any demon need his help? They were mutual enemies, good vs. evil.

"Depends."

She tipped her head slightly to the side. "What if it involved getting back at an even more powerful demon than me?"

Hell yeah. That, he was all for. "I might consider it. Who's the demon?"

"Rathe. Know him?"

Colt didn't trust himself to speak. Yeah. He and Rathe were going to lock horns pretty soon, one way or another. Better to have an ally in demon form than go up against the Lord High archdemon alone. "I'll help you."

"Then kiss me."

Colt had held back as long as he could. He leaned in toward the barrier and was surprised to find it melted around him, warming his skin like a ray of sunshine as he passed through it into the circle he'd cast. Inside the circle her allure was even more powerful. Colt's head swam and his palms grew damp. It was as if someone or something had reached into his head and pulled out his most intimate fantasies, making them real.

Miss Arliss waited for him, her oval face tipped up at him, her eyes shining with expectation. His skin tightened. Damn, was it stifling hot inside this circle? He suddenly remembered this same sensation the first time he'd approached one of the neighbor girls before the stranger had come and changed the course of his life. She'd been a sweet thing. An innocent, creamy-sweet girl who looked like she was spun out of sugar and dreams. But Miss Arliss was far more suited to his grown interests. She wasn't innocent, but neither was she jaded and used up. She was the perfect blend of enticement and allure bathed in moonlight.

He couldn't resist the temptation to touch her and see for himself if her skin was as soft as it looked. He grazed his fingers across her cheek, his thumb brushing the edge of her jaw. Her skin was smoother than heated silk.

He moved in closer, her mouth a breath away from his. The warm feminine scent of her hit him full force as he inhaled. The fragrance of her desire made his own need escalate. Colt's reserve snapped. He crushed his mouth down on hers and found it soft, warm, and willing. His desire to feel her, skin to bare skin, to sink into the warmth she offered, raged inside him.

The kiss was far more than he anticipated, drawing out not just a full range of hunger and desire, but drilling even deeper into his soul, pulling out of him the desire to tuck her against him, protect her. An image flashed in his mind of him kissing her on a wide front porch as she wrapped her arms around him, welcoming him home.

But that was impossible. A total fantasy. As long as he was a Hunter he'd never have a proper home. He'd never have a wife or any kind of family of his own, because he wouldn't risk them.

He looked down into the shimmering depths of her eyes, fighting off the urge to lose himself there. Through the sensual haze filling his mind, his training pushed forward, bringing him back to sanity. Reminding him that part of a succubus's power was the ability to make a man's deepest fantasies seem so real he could hold them.

She was a demon. A powerful one, and he couldn't afford to forget it, no matter how desirable she seemed. He pulled back, breathing hard, a hostile mix of yearning and wariness swirling in his gut. "I'm warning you." He was disgusted to hear how thick and lust-filled his voice sounded. "I don't care how good you are. If you cross me, I'll send you back to Hell in a heartbeat."

Chapter 5

The dark velvet of the night closed in around the shifting yellow circle of firelight. "Threatening your partner is hardly the way to start a productive relationship," Lilly said.

She stared deep into those determined blue eyes and tamped down the urge to rip him to shreds right then and there. While it might be satisfactory for a moment, in the long run it would ruin her chance to get the damn piece of the Book of Legend Rathe had demanded. She'd pictured meeting Colt Jackson so many times in her mind, and none of those images had matched what was happening between them now. The smell of him, virile male mixed with desert sun and leather, still swirled in the limited air supply of the circle he'd cast.

"Just want to make sure you know whose side I'm on."

"Oh, I never doubted that, *Hunter*." She forced her breathing to even out by sheer will. There wasn't much she could do about her racing heartbeat or the stream of totally unwelcome sensual thoughts cascading through her brain. *She* was the damn succubus. He was supposed to desire her, definitely not the other way around.

It made her angry that his kiss had elicited such shock-ingly strong feelings and unwanted emotions, making her breasts ache and skin crave his touch. It made her angry that he'd threatened her the second their kiss had ended. It made her angry that she'd shared something personal with him that she'd shared with none of her other victims.

And why on earth had she felt compelled to share her name with him, or the fact that she'd been human once before? Had it been because she'd already felt she'd known him? Ha. That was laughable. Being in the flesh against him was totally different than reading about his exploits in the pages of a book. He was bigger and bolder, and far more charming than she'd thought he'd be.

"So that's it?" he asked, eyeing her with suspicion.

"And look, you're still alive." Her tone was mocking, but she couldn't hide the bitter edge of anger there. In all her twenty-five years as a demon, never once had she been affected by the men she seduced. She'd rarely even looked at their faces. All she'd pictured was the look on her father's face when he'd met his match in Rathe as she took their proffered souls.

"Having second thoughts about our bargain?" Colt drawled as he looked deeply into her eyes.

Lilly steeled her spine and deliberately softened her face so he wouldn't guess at her inner turmoil. How was she to have known he'd have this kind of effect on her? "Are you? Just how many bargains have you struck with demons?"

"None. But there's always a first time for everything, isn't there?"

The words lashed at her like a bullwhip, the sting of them making her wince. A first and a last time. The truth was she'd been introduced to Hell long before Rathe came along. From the minute she could toddle, her father had exploited her keen mind and unusual looks. She'd been part of nearly every con he played and, thanks to her efforts, they'd managed a dishonest living.

"True. But it doesn't mean it always turns out the way you expect," she said, tipping her chin up a notch.

She'd grown tired of the charade her mortal life had become, the constant running and the lies. She'd wanted a normal life for her and her sister, maybe even a husband and a family of her own. But the minute she'd suggested that to her father, any ounce of kindness had vanished. He'd threatened her. If she left, he'd turn her younger sister Amelia into a means for profit any way he could. And while Amelia was a delicate beauty in her own right, she didn't possess half of Lilly's fire, determination, and cunning. She'd never be able to pull off the cons her father favored, which meant her future was bleak.

Lilly couldn't let that happen. She'd kept up the cons until she could find a way out for both herself and her sister. It had tainted her soul and shredded every ounce of decency within her, but she'd done it, by God. And she'd hated her father more by the minute. But it had taught her something valuable—there was always a way out, *if* you were able to accept the cost.

The Hunter's glacier blue gaze bored into her. "If you want me to stick to our bargain, you'd better not double back on your word, demon."

She stiffened. "I never forget a promise."

Lilly had promised herself that her little sister Amelia would never know the touch of a man until she invited it herself. There'd been only one way Lilly could think to stop her father's plans. She'd summoned Rathe, and in exchange for the fiend killing her father and sending him to Hell where the bastard belonged, something she couldn't do herself, the demon had taken her soul.

It seemed a small price to pay to protect her sister. And until now it had been relatively easy. No emotion. No true impulse. Just doing what she'd always had to do and harvesting their nearly worthless souls in the process for Rathe.

But Colt Ambrose Jackson had just done the unexpected. He'd made her *want* to kiss him. He'd made her *desire* him. Damn him.

Lilly grabbed hold of the spark of anger bristling beneath her breastbone and nourished it. This Hunter was dangerous to something far more valuable than her soul. There was no time for fleeting fantasy or idealized versions of Legend lore. Colt was a Hunter. She was a demon. The two would never mix, so why did she suddenly yearn for it to happen?

He held her at arm's distance, his hands hot against her bare skin, both of them still inside the close quarters of the protective circle in the vast darkness of the night. He didn't look like a dangerous demon slayer. His sinful good looks, set off by a strong jaw, jet dark hair that curled along his collar, and tempting mouth, were more akin to a gambler— full of promise, but too good to be true.

His broad shoulders took up most of the room inside the circle, crowding her against the invisible barrier. The smell of his skin, a mix of potent male and the wild outdoors, made her dizzy with longing, and while she couldn't retreat physically in the confines of the circle, Lilly did her utmost to withdraw emotionally. She refused to give her lust for this mortal the weight to affect who and what she was.

She glared at his hand on her shoulder. "Touching me wasn't part of our bargain."

He quickly moved his hand and she backed as far away from him as she could. "Release the circle so we can go open this door of yours. Where is it?"

He pulled at the rim of his Stetson, settling it more firmly on his head. "Dark Rim Mine."

Lilly stiffened. The Dark Rim Mine had earned its name. It ran parallel to the rim of one of the gates of Hell.

Not that the mortals knew that, but it was a favorite hunting ground for the Darkin, the children of the night. Either Colt was an incredibly skilled Hunter or he was an absolute fool.

Standing face-to-face with him, her lips still tingling from the kiss he'd given her, Lilly bet he was the former rather than the latter.

"You have a problem with that?" Colt leaned in close to her again, closing the gap she'd created until there was a mere breath of space between his broad chest and her silk-clad breasts. They tightened and ached, peaking forward, waiting for the graze of his touch. The low and gravelly quality of his voice, a man ultimately aware of a woman, picked out goose bumps over her exposed arms and legs.

Lilly bit her lip, worrying it between her teeth. "Problem with the Darkin? No." *Problem being with you? Hell yes.*

With his face half in shifting shadow from the firelight, his eyes looked a darker midnight blue. He assessed her every movement with his penetrating gaze, making her aware of just how close they were to one another. Her heart beat faster, picking up speed like a locomotive. She needed to concentrate on gaining his trust and forget about all the odd sensations he was setting off in her.

"You do realize what's down there, don't you, Hunter?"

His gaze flicked downward for an instant to the juncture of her thighs outlined in the black silk. Down deep inside her everything pulsed and tightened. When he looked back up, his sexy mouth tipped up in the corner in a wicked grin. "I think I have a pretty good idea." He ran a finger along her jaw, a touch that set off sparks all along her skin. "And the name's Colt. You might as well get used to sayin' it, sweetheart."

He was right, of course. They'd bypassed any whisper of proper social introduction and gone straight to being on quite intimate terms. Using proper names at this point was moot. Her heart did a double bump deep in her chest. Had he just called her sweetheart? Worse, with only a whisper of space between them, had he felt her reaction to the word? He was far more dangerous than she'd ever imagined. He was going to get her sent to Hell with no reprieve, to be tormented by Rathe for eternity.

Lilly marshaled whatever resistance she could gather, steeling herself against the seductive sensations he played across her easier than a bar man at a saloon piano.

"There's only a thin barrier between the worlds down there. Any one of the Darkin could attack you. We're not talking just demons. There's vampires down there that'll suck you dry to the bone. Creatures made of rock and fire that could crush then crisp you in the blink of an eye, that your bullets won't even touch. Shape-shifters that'll get inside your skin and paralyze you, using your body like a suit so you can only see the mayhem you're creating, but you'll be unable to stop it as they flay your loved ones alive with your hands and eat the meat in front of your eyes. Are you sure you're prepared for that?"

Challenge glinted in his eyes. A raw, primal power radiated off him, which made her question her powers of seduction when matched up against his. His grin lifted just a touch more, as if he'd just read her intimate thoughts. "Nothin' I can't handle. Trust me."

Lilly turned away, unable to look into his face any longer. *Trust. Not likely.* She'd never trust another soul as long as she existed, and certainly not a Hunter out to send her back to a tormented eternity. And yet, if he could help her escape Rathe, she had to take the chance.

"Are you going to let us out of this circle, or are we going to stand here talking all night about what's waiting for us?" Rathe had given her three weeks. There was no time to waste. She had to gain his confidence, yet she found herself reluctant to get too close to him. He stirred unwelcome sensations in her, sensations that would land her in a heap of trouble. The tip of his nose brushed along her cheek and beneath her ear—a skimming touch that shot straight to her toes and made a warm sensation unfurl deep inside her.

"You sure don't smell like sulfur."

"Yes, you already mentioned that," she bit out, irritation lacing her tone.

Colt suppressed the urge to grin. *Good. Let the little demon get a taste of her own medicine.* It had only taken him a few minutes to realize the only way to fight fire was with fire. If she wanted to turn on the charm, then so could he, in spades. Hell, he might even be able to consider it a secret weapon in this case. After all, her lips clung to his when they'd kissed. No matter how prickly she seemed, she was attracted to him.

He stepped back from the radiant silken heat of her curves, his foot crossing the edge of the circle. The invisible barrier slid around him like the warm caress of a sunbeam. Outside the circle, the chill silence of the night was punctuated by calls of coyotes on the hunt and scented with the dirty machine-oil smell of creosote bushes mixed with wood smoke. All that remained of the fire were the blackened husks of the logs and their red glowing hearts.

Well, he wanted a demon. Now he had one, and she was willing to open the door without taking his soul in payment. That had to count as a point in his favor, didn't it?

Through the shimmer of the circle's barrier she looked damn enticing. Things could have been worse. Way worse. He could have ended up with some ugly sonofabitch with horns, a damned forked tongue, and matching tail. Then again, maybe that would have been a hell of a lot safer than a succubus that looked like every man's fantasy sheathed in black silk.

The demon cocked the curve of her hip to one side and crossed her bare arms over her chest, which made her breasts press together in a way that made him hard and damn uncomfortable. "We have an accord. You can't keep me in here forever if you want me to open that door for you."

Colt said a silent prayer that the demon he was about to unleash on the world would go the hell back to where she'd come from willingly so he didn't have to shoot her when they were done.

"Here goes nothin'," he muttered as he glanced at the directions in the book that lay open in the dirt and worked the circle backward, blowing out the candles as he went in the opposite order he'd lit them to open the circle he'd cast. Unfortunately, that brought him pretty damn close to the sweet curve of her derrière pressed against the barrier. He tried his level best to ignore the view as he completed his trek around the circle's perimeter.

The shimmering barrier dissipated into nothingness, and Colt put his hand on the smooth wood butt of his revolver. No use taking chances. Not with a demon anyhow. He stepped back and eyed her. "You might want to put on somethin' decent before we head into Bodie. No use in calling attention to ourselves."

The demon—he refused to think of her as Miss Arliss, because that just led to all kinds of fantasies he couldn't afford to indulge—snapped her dainty fingers and the short black silk sheath vanished, replaced by a high-collared wide-striped emerald green gown, gathered up in the front to knee-length swag, which exposed fishnet stockings. If he'd been a less observant man, he would have fixated entirely on those legs and not even noticed the large bustle and train, or the smart white kid gloves, but being a Hunter meant he was always observant of the details. Her fiery tresses were coiled into some elaborate knot at the base of her slender neck. Atop her head sat a feminine version of a black top hat with a wide green ribbon around it and a variety of green and black feathers clustered at the back. The color of her gown enhanced her exquisite pale skin and made the color of her eyes even more enchanting.

"Better?"

Colt cleared his throat. What would have been better was if he'd never seen what lay beneath that gown and had it seared into his brain, but he wasn't about to suggest she change back. "Ain't that a little fancy for tramping through an abandoned mine?"

She picked up the long, bustled train of her gown and swung it around as she turned. "Mmmm. Perhaps you're right."

She snapped her fingers. The fancy green gown and matching hat vanished, replaced by a serviceable stretch of pale blue sprigged calico with a rim of white lace that traced the edge of a square-cut bodice framing an enticing display of female assets. A small blue and white cameo threaded through a wide black velvet ribbon at her throat showed the faint throb of her heartbeat. Colt wanted to put his mouth there. The front of the skirt gathered up about her knees, and she still had those damn stockings on, the line at the back tracing every curve all the way up. He swallowed hard against the lump in his throat.

"Surely you have no objections to this."

Oh, he had objections. By the barrel-full, but that wasn't going to get him through the hidden door in the Dark Rim Mine, so they were best forgotten. "We're wasting time."

"Then let's not dilly-dally. Do you wish to walk, or shall I meet you there?"

As tempting as it was to have her use her powers and get to the mine faster, Colt resisted. There was no telling where she would go if he let her out of his sight. No. It was better to keep a firm hand on the demon while they were partnered up. "Neither. We'll ride."

The demon shrugged. "Suit yourself, Hunter."

"Colt."

She rolled her unnaturally bright green eyes. "Fine, Mr. Jackson."

He doused the fire with the remaining dregs of the coffee he'd made to keep himself alert. It let off a fragrant coffee-scented steam as it hissed and popped against the coals. The minute the light of the fire disappeared, the desert darkness closed in. Colt tightened his grip on his gun as he kicked dirt over the smoldering remains of the fire. The lingering scent of wood smoke persisted. Overhead the stars sparkled like gold dust cast over a swath of black velvet.

Colt reached out, clasping the demon's hand in his own. The touch sent an arc of awareness shimmying up his arm. Colt knew enough to tell that it wasn't some dark demon power, but plain old lust bolting through his system. Her hand felt small, delicate, and distinctly feminine in his much larger one.

"Watch your step."

"For a skilled Hunter, I'm surprised you don't know that demons have excellent night vision."

He glanced over his shoulder, not trusting her as far as he could fling her. "Who says I'm holding your hand to help you out? Maybe I just want to make sure I know exactly where you are."

"Don't trust me, do you?"

"No, ma'am."

"Good, because for the record, *Colt*," she said his name like an epithet for something far more loathsome, "I don't trust you either."

"Perfect."

Her footsteps came to a sudden halt, yanking on his arm with a surprising strength.

"You're not making me ride *that* thing, are you?" He glanced back. Her pert little nose was all scrunched up like something stank to high heaven.

"That was the plan."

She stared hard at the silver eyes of his horse. "But he's . . ."

"Mechanical. Yeah. He is. Means he's more reliable."

"More like he doesn't have a mind of his own."

Colt had never considered that a downside. Tempus did what he was supposed to when he was supposed to without any attitude, rearing, or crow hops. He didn't need food or water, just a few squirts of machine oil and a good winding now and then. After his brothers and Marley, Tempus was one of the few things he could rely on in his life.

"I don't go anywhere without my horse."

"That must make things interesting when you take a woman to bed."

"Not what I meant."

She shrugged. "I wasn't arguing, merely observing your statement had other implications."

"You always talk so much?"

"I don't see why that should matter."

He shoved his foot into the stirrup and mounted. "Ready?" She gave a slight squeal of protest as he leaned over, using his forearm to brace hers as he pulled her up behind him. He flipped the GGD switch forward and Tempus rumbled and clicked as the gears and springs began their work.

The demon hugged him tight around the middle, her sweet breath coming in short little puffs over his shoulder near his ear and her heart beating fast against his back.

Colt suppressed a grumble. He should have listened to Marley. Given enough time, Marley might have been able to invent something that could open the door just as well as a demon. But time was the only luxury he didn't have. The crack in the Gates of Nyx was gettin' bigger by the day. He could feel it in his bones.

"How long do we have to ride this thing?"

He chuckled. "What's wrong, demon? Afraid?"

Her cheek brushed against his back as she shook her head. "Of your horse? No. Don't like it—it's souless—but it doesn't scare me."

"Then why do I detect a little fear in your voice?"

She lifted up a little and leaned into him, putting her lips close enough to his ear that he could feel the heated brush of them as she spoke. "If you had any idea of what's truly waiting for us in that mine, you'd be scared too."

Chapter 6

The dark monolith of the mountain, rising in jagged peaks above them, appeared ominous in the cool, pale wash of moonlight. Lilly shuddered against Colt's back, the circle of her arms tightening around his waist.

"Sure this is the place?" The warm puff of each word she breathed into his ear was counterpoint to the chill biting into his exposed skin. Hell no. He wasn't sure at all. He'd been told the entrance could be found here, but that didn't mean it'd be easy.

Milky moonlight illuminated the roughly milled wooden boards crisscrossed over the stygian darkness of the entrance. Distinctly uninviting, it shouted KEEP OUT.

"Can't you feel the evil in there?" she persisted, as if that were going to change his plans one whit.

"That's just a draft of cold air from the shafts down below." His reply sounded calm enough, but jitters worked away on the inside of him as the darkness seethed in front of him. What was that sayin'? Abandon all hope ye who enter . . . *Stop that*. There was no use thinking that way. He hadn't even got off his damn horse yet. What was he going to do? Scream like a girl? Run because his belly squirmed and his nerves stretched tight told him to? Hell no.

Lilly shifted behind him, her small soft breasts rubbing against him in an unconsciously seductive slide that caused his groin to swell. "That's what you think," she muttered.

No, that's what he had to make himself believe. Didn't matter how it felt. There was no choice. A cold slip of air slithered unnaturally around Colt's legs and his hands tightened reflexively on Tempus's reins. It wasn't just icy mine air, and he knew it. The palm of his gun hand was itching and the rotten egg odor was noticeably stronger the closer they came to the opening. Something dark and unnatural waited down in the depths of Dark Rim. Okay, likely there were a lot of somethings just waiting.

Unfortunately, they were between him and his pa's portion of the Book. "Don't matter anyhow. Winn confirmed that this is the place."

"What exactly are you looking for that you'd risk coming up against the Darkin in their own backyard?"

Colt hesitated. He wished he could tell her. But he didn't dare. He didn't trust the demon enough to confide in her. Not yet. Maybe not ever. "You'll find out when we get there."

He twisted, lifting her slightly so she could hitch her leg over Tempus's hard metal rump and slide down to the ground. He flipped the GGD switch backward and dismounted. The rhythmic metallic clicks and whirring of Tempus's inner workings came to an abrupt halt, leaving the night in stifling silence.

"Well I don't like it."

"Neither do I." Colt glanced at her. The moonlight picked out the overlarge whites of her eyes, the telltale greenish glow at the center, like a wolf or mountain lion, marking her as a demon. She'd woven her arms together over her chest, her body rigid, closing in upon itself. She was scared. Damn scared. And she was a demon.

Ah, hell. This was going to be bad. The palm of his

left hand began to burn from the powerful itching there. "Let's go."

Colt grabbed his saddlebags off Tempus, dumping them at his feet, then turned to pry at the boards, grunting as the splinters dug into the calloused skin of his hands.

Directly behind him came the soft feminine clearing of a throat. Colt glanced back at her. Lilly's legs encased in a fine mesh of fishnet stocking were visible up to just above the knee.

"Allow me. I might as well be of some use."

In that getup? He stifled a chuckle. Might as well let the little lady try. He backed up one step, removing himself from the temptation to look further at her.

She leveled her chin in determination. "You might want to stand back."

He took another two steps back just to humor her. Her eyes narrowed as she focused and held out her small hand, palm facing the door, then created a fist in midair. With a crackling pop of splintering wood, the boards collapsed as if grasped at the center by some giant invisible hand. She pulled her fist back, the nails groaning as the boards peeled away from the wooden beams. The boards dropped into a pile of kindling beside the entrance amid a cloud of dust.

Colt blinked back the swirl of particles in the air. "Impressive." Her responding smile made his heart skip a beat. Damn but she was gorgeous.

She broke eye contact with him, staring at the dark, gaping entrance to the mine. "Are we in the right place?"

He pointed to the two-foot-thick beam that formed the lintel holding up the weight of the mountain over the entrance. Gouged into it were the roughly lettered words Dark Rim. "Yes, ma'am. Welcome to the edge of Hell."

Colt picked up his saddlebags and dug out a long brass tube Marley called a self-contained coil illuminator. A lens was secured in one end and it rattled a lot when shaken, but

Marley had assured him that shaking it would produce enough stored energy to produce a fire-safe torch. Something about copper coils and magnets that Colt didn't completely understand.

He'd never tried it before. New inventions from Marley always were a gamble. Colt knew he had a fifty-fifty chance of either getting a great source of light, or of having his eyebrows singed off. But bringing an oil lamp in his saddle pack hadn't been practical and using a pitch-soaked torch would give them light enough for an hour, maybe two.

He held the tube out as far away from him as he dared and shook it hard. The rattling was loud enough that it stirred a few bats out of the mine shaft and they streaked off into the dark night sky. He flipped the switch and a soft blue glow grew in an ever-widening circle at his feet. He swung the saddlebags over his shoulder and moved forward. They left Tempus outside the entrance and ventured into the dark recesses of the mine.

The rocky dust beneath their feet became damp about fifty feet inside. Colt flashed the illuminator on the walls and saw only a small, dark trickle of moisture seeping like tears from the rocks.

Deep down his gut twisted. He hoped the reason these mines had been abandoned had nothing to do with flooding. From the map he'd sketched based on Winn's poor description, the hiding place of his pa's piece of the Book of Legend was down deeper in the shafts. If the shafts were flooded, there'd be no hope for getting it. He had a distinct dislike for water. Since he'd been fourteen he didn't get any deeper than his waist in it, and that was only in a washtub.

"You don't look so well, Mr. Jackson."

Leave it to the demon to state the obvious. "I'm not the kind that likes to be confined."

"Don't tell me you're afraid of the dark." There was humor in her voice.

He gave her a cocky grin. "Not of the dark, darlin', just don't like our odds down here. The sooner we get what we're looking for and get out, the better."

"And what are we looking for?"

"A door."

"To what?"

"A door. That's all you need to know." They had come to a series of three shafts branching off from the main tunnel.

"Which way do we go?"

He pulled the coil illuminator closer, using it to cast a pool of bluish light on the crudely drawn map in his hand as he balanced his saddle packs over his shoulder. "If I understood my brother, it should be down the shaft to the left."

She shivered.

"Cold?"

"Something's coming."

Even though the sulfur scent in the air hadn't grown any stronger, Colt's gun hand began to itch worse the farther they traveled down the left tunnel. A hushed, rasping sound, like the whisper of a hundred voices, began to grow the deeper they moved into the earth. Colt pulled the demon closer. "Whatever it is, I don't like the sound of it. Stick close to me." He pulled his gun from his hip holster.

She nodded, and glanced behind them. Her eyes widened and Colt spun around to see what had caused her reaction. In the light of the illuminator the walls of the passage itself seemed to be shivering, moving as if the rock were a blanket and something crawled along beneath it.

Then it transmogrified, the rock pulling away from the walls of the tunnel-like living, breathing things, built like men, but so broad and so tall they hunched in the tunnel. Their flat, featureless faces only looked like faces because of the twin glowing red eyes and gaping dark maw. Small puffs of dust, almost like spurts of steam, issued from the creatures' joints as they lumbered toward him and Miss Arliss.

"What in the hell are those?"

"Scoria soldiers. Guardians to the Darkin. Don't just stand there, shoot them!"

The gritty, grinding sound of rock against rock as they moved caused the hairs on Colt's arms to prickle. "Hold this." He tossed the coil illuminator to the demon and held the gun out in front of him, trying to take aim. But at what? All he could see were mounds of massive rock limbs and glowing red eyes headed straight for them.

Each step the rock monsters made created more dust and grit in the air, obscuring their vision and making it harder to breathe. Colt coughed and shoved the demon behind him, then fired off one of Marley's special rounds right between a pair of glowing, ember-like eyes. Then another. Chips of rock flew in all directions from the hole blasted clean through the rock. A fragment grazed his cheek. Colt lifted his hand to the stinging spot and found his fingers red with his blood. The Scoria soldiers just kept coming, oblivious to the gouges in their rock forms.

"Damn supernaturals. Bullets aren't going to do it," Colt muttered. He pulled her with him as he ducked behind an outcropping of rock forming the edge of a smaller side tunnel.

"Got any dynamite?"

"Yeah, sure, in my back pocket," he smarted off. "Hell no. How was I supposed to anticipate these things?"

"I told you—"

As if he needed the reminder. "Move!" He shoved her ahead of him down the smaller passage. The rock monster closest to them roared and swung down hard with a massive boulder of a fist, causing the rock ledge above them to shatter and rain fragments down on them.

"But they'll only follow us."

"Not if I can help it." Colt wished like hell he still had the sting shooter of Marley's. He'd be glad to blow a few bigger holes in those rock monsters, maybe shatter them completely apart. Instead he did the next best thing. He pulled a tin of lucifers and the bottle of whiskey Marley had given him out of his saddle pack. Marley had been right about needing the whiskey, but wrong about the application. He didn't need it for Winn. Colt pulled the cork out with his teeth as he handed the packs off to the demon.

She glared at him. "Do you really think now's an appropriate time for a drink?"

"None better." Colt kicked back a slug of the whiskey, already regretting what he was about to do next. He pulled the tail of his light blue cotton shirt out of his denim pants and ripped off the bottom edge. He stuffed the strip of fabric into the open bottle, then lit it off with a lucifer he struck against the rocks. The fire hissed to life, brilliant in the darkness. He kissed the bottle good-bye, knowing it was a damn waste of fine whiskey, and chucked it back against one of the support beams.

He yanked the demon close and put his back to the opening of the passage. The sound of shattering glass was followed by an explosion that knocked both him and Lilly forward. Colt twisted, trying to spare her the worst of the slam to the dirt and rock-strewn floor of the cavern, but purposely ended up on top of her to protect her from the flying debris. A river of flame licked along the rock and exposed wooden beams. The beams creaked, followed by a loud crack that echoed off the walls like a gunshot. An avalanche of rock rained down on the dismantled monsters, sending a plume of dust over the top of Lilly and Colt.

Beneath him she wriggled, her soft and distinctly feminine curves pressed distractingly against him. "What did you do?" she sputtered, her tone indignant.

"I just blew our little rock friends back to the Stone Age." Colt was proud of his display of ingenuity.

Miss Arliss wriggled harder and Colt leveraged himself off of her before she could tell how all that movement had got his attention. Her green eyes glinted with inhuman color in the low light of the coil illuminator. "What you did was collapsed our only exit."

Colt glanced back at the tumbled wall of rock behind them. *Damn. She was right.* He peered down into the blackness ahead of them, took the coil illuminator from her and shook it hard, hoping like hell it would still work. It threw a beam of blue light in the dusty darkness, but the illumination didn't extend more than a few feet.

The dust swirled and eddied back toward them when it should have been billowing away from the explosion, not toward it. "There's got to be another shaft that connects to this one." He pointed at the shifting dust clouds. "There's still air flowing this way."

He offered the demon his hand to help her from the ground. She stared at it for an instant, then took it reluctantly. "So what's behind the door we're looking for?"

He gave her a sly grin. "Good try." He took off his hat and dusted it, then patted himself down coughing at the dust that billowed up from his clothes.

Lilly huffed. While she could understand that he didn't trust her any more than she trusted him, it galled her all the same. It was difficult at best to find something when you knew what you were looking for, but damned near impossible when you didn't. Until they found that door she wasn't going to get any closer to escaping Rathe.

"You know, I have different senses you don't. If I knew what we were looking for, I might be actually able to help you find it faster."

"You mean you'd find it faster with or without me."

"That's not what—"

Colt whirled, grasping her in a firm but gentle, no-nonsense grip on her upper arms. The coil illuminator still in his hand threw light up toward the ceiling, giving an eerie uplit cast to his rugged features, and exposing the dark stubble growing thicker on his jaw and chin. He pulled her close enough to him that her breasts brushed his chest. "Coy doesn't become you. I know you're smarter than that just by looking at you."

Her skin and hair were coated with a fine powdering of dust leaving them feeling gritty. Beneath the hems of her skirt, her bruised knees throbbed. They'd gotten scraped and her fishnet stockings torn on the rough floor of the cavern when the blast had propelled her forward. As succubi went, she was sure she looked like hell.

Lilly tried to pull back from his magnetic touch. It was causing small sparks to fire just under her skin in a most distracting manner. Despite her own misgivings, she wanted him to kiss her again. Not because of some pact, but out of pure desire.

She wet her lips, tasting the dust that lingered on them. "We have a pact. I'm going to help you find whatever it is you are looking for by opening this door you're seeking."

"True. But that doesn't mean you'll forget the pact you've made with your master either, does it?"

"*You* summoned *me*, remember?"

The thumb of his right hand brushed over her upper arm in a slow back-and-forth skimming movement that tightened her skin in an all over body shiver.

"Just look for the door and you'll find out what's behind it the same time I do. Deal?"

Exactly how annoyed would he be when he discovered that she already knew. And how quickly would he renege on his promise to let her go free or, more importantly, help her disappear once he knew she wanted the piece of the Book of Legend as much as he did?

"Fine. I'll stop asking."

"Good."

Colt dropped his hands from her, making her feel noticeably cooler. He pulled the map out of his pocket where he'd stuffed it and shook it out.

"Looks like there's another branch in the shaft up ahead."

Lilly peered over his shoulder at the page. "How much farther?" His long, blunt-tipped finger ran along a crooked line following it across the page.

"Another mile, maybe mile and a half. The map isn't exactly to scale. Winn said when the temperature got warmer, we'd be getting close."

Not surprising. If the crudely drawn compass points in the corner were anywhere close to true, they were headed south, closer to the rim of the Darkin realm, rather than away from it. No wonder the Scoria had been waiting for them. They might as well have danced right across the welcome mat to Hell itself.

"I suppose you'll want these back now," she said, holding the saddle packs out to him. Colt slung them over his shoulder, turned on his heel without a word of thanks and started walking.

At the next turn, the trail descended steeply, and a runnel of water made the rock slippery. The demon grabbed hold of his arm, heedlessly bumping her hand against the gun in his low-slung hip holster.

His gaze snapped to hers, his skin tightening. That had been awful close to her rubbing the precise part of him that was most interested in the demon. "Careful there, darlin'. You might set it off."

The sound of rushing water grew louder, filling the chamber. Colt's chest tightened reflexively, a giant invisible fist squeezing all the air out of his lungs.

"Sounds like a river or waterfall." Her tone was a mixture of curiosity laced with boredom.

Yeah, he heard it. And he prayed it was neither. "Winn didn't mention any waterfall or river. In fact, he didn't mention any kind of water at all."

She pressed in against him, her breasts warm and soft against his back. A pleasant buzzing started at the base of his skull growing louder and filling his ears, drowning out the sound of the moving water that terrified him, making him think about how he'd like to sample just one more kiss from Miss Arliss before he sent her back to wherever she'd come from. He inhaled the cinnamon rose fragrance of her. So different. So much better than sulfur.

"Perhaps we took a wrong turn."

His vision snapped back into focus. The sound of the water grew louder as they continued walking down the slope.

They rounded the bend to find the tunnel through the rock led to a natural underground cavern more than fifty feet tall. The light from the coil illuminator was too weak to reach to the vault of the cavern, but it did well in picking out the giant stalagmites jutting up from the floor like a ridge of teeth and stalactites that dripped down in giant stone canines from the ceiling. At the far end of the cavern a wall of water cascaded from thirty feet above, flooding their path.

"Looks like we're going to have to go through the waterfall to keep going." Her tone was so blithe it pissed him off.

Beads of sweat popped out on his skin. Just the sound of the running water had him in a lather. The thought of having to drench himself for who knew how long under thousands of gallons of water pelting down on him, obliterating his air, left his stomach queasier than a greenhorn after an all-night party on white lightning.

He gripped the map in his hands, making the paper snap taut. "We're going to have to find another way around."

Chapter 7

Miss Arliss swiveled, looking around the cavern. "Unless you know a clever trick to walking through the rock, I suggest you plan on walking through the water."

He deliberately ignored her. "Maybe you were right. Maybe we took a wrong turn." He turned to go in the opposite direction of the waterfall, back up the slippery, steep path.

He damn well knew they had to go through that waterfall, and he'd rather be whipped on his bare back than do it. Colt stopped dead still as her hands feathered in a light, skimming touch up along his arm. "You don't have to do this alone. I'm right here with you." The silken, sultry quality to her voice made his mind fill with thoughts of tangled sheets and sweet female warmth. More than that, it lulled him into wondering what it would be like to be with Miss Arliss if she were human.

She led him by the hand into the mist coming off the waterfall. It roared as it fell, far more feral than any supernatural beast he'd ever encountered. Every sensation he'd experienced underneath the surface of that water trough when he was fourteen came back with a vengeance. The burning in his lungs, the clammy, cold sluicing over his skin, reaching in and numbing him to the core. It wasn't something he could control, dammit. His breathing became shallower, faster as his heart rate sped up and his lungs started to shrink in his chest. Her grip on his hand tightened.

He pulled back. "You don't understand."

The demon didn't hesitate. She stood up on tiptoe, her soft curves pressing against his chest, and wrapped her arms over his shoulders and around his neck. Her lips were dewy soft and warm as she kissed him. A shock, like something from a sting shooter but far more pleasant, arced through him, energizing every cell, making him feel invincible.

He liked women. A lot. He liked how they smelled, how they tasted, and how they felt. Her sensual assault was like giving a drinking man a bottle; he simply couldn't resist.

Colt threw his arms around her waist, pulling all her warmth closer until it filled his senses. Damp heat steamed off them. The tip of her tongue slid along the seam of his mouth, slick and warm, and he couldn't resist the temptation to taste her. She was sweet and spicy, cinnamon and honey. She ground her hips against him. Colt couldn't think straight. Hell, he couldn't think at all past the thrumming pulse of sensual heat she was wrapping around him.

In the next instant water poured down, drenching them both, streaming over his hat. He broke their mind-numbing kiss with a startled intake of breath and found they were on the other side of the waterfall.

They had passed straight through.

Colt blinked in astonishment.

"See, that wasn't so bad."

He gazed down into her eyes. Droplets of water sparkled in her long, dark eyelashes. "You did that on purpose." His voice was rough with longing and need. For an instant he was insane enough with desire to want to plunge back under the water just so she'd keep kissing him.

Her lips, slightly swollen and rosy from their kiss, tilted into a sweet, sexy-as-hell smile. "You're welcome."

Now Colt was rattled for another reason altogether. In the space of a heartbeat she'd taken over his ability to think with the touch of her body and the heat of her kiss. Hell, she'd overridden a fear that went straight to his gut. Not to say that he hadn't enjoyed it, but if she could do that, then exactly how much power did she possess and how deep in trouble was he?

The air on this side of the waterfall was noticeably warmer. Wisps of steam curled in white mist off her clothing as well as his. For a second Colt was grateful for the reassurance that it wasn't just his overactive libido causing the heat he sensed.

He tried to right himself by gently, but firmly, unlacing her delicate fingers curled into the hair at the nape of his neck.

"Don't worry so much, Colt. I'm not going to let anything happen to you on this venture. You're safe with me," she said.

He very much doubted that. He was anything but safe with her. A beautiful woman was a weakness for him, but a woman who could make him forget himself, forget his deepest fears, his darkest memories, that was a force to be reckoned with.

Resorting to a glib smirk, he tried to cover his discomfort and put some distance between them. "Maybe I did that on purpose just to get you to kiss me again."

The succubus gave him a knowing smile in return that said *maybe I wanted you to.* His stomach dropped to his shoes. Damn. She was testing him, and there was only so much a mortal man, Hunter or otherwise, could bear.

She reached up and pulled the pins from her hair, letting the dark, wet, red tresses curl down along her back. She ran her fingers through it, separating the curls with her fingers, where they dried instantly into spirals of flame-colored silk.

Damn, it was hot in here. Colt swallowed down a thick lump hard. His fingers were itching to follow the same path as hers, but he forced his hands to stay at his sides and instead rubbed the butt of the revolver in the holster at his hip.

"So where do we go from here?" The sweet lilt to her voice started to suck him in all over again. His brain spun with visions of having her naked beneath him. Of waking up with her, slumberous and soft, tucked in beside him each morning.

Stop it. Get hold of yourself, Colt berated himself. Letting her kiss him like that had been a mistake. There was no denying that having her kiss him in the heat of the moment had been damn near the hottest thing that had ever happened to him with all his clothes on, but it was still a mistake. And if he didn't watch himself, next time it could likely be a soul-stealing mistake. He'd forget himself. Forget who he was and why he shouldn't want her. Next thing you know he'd be thinking about nights by a warm fire and a cozy bed. Home-cooked meals and how it'd feel to be welcomed into her arms each night. Things a Hunter had no business thinking about. He had to be careful from here on out if he wanted to find Pa's piece of the Book and forgo a one-way train ticket straight to Hell.

"There should be a second large chamber up past this stretch of the shaft." He stalked past her, deliberately not looking back to even see if she followed. He could tell by the soft, lingering feminine scent that overpowered the dank, damp, swampy smell of wet earth and the stench of sulfur in the mine that she was still right on his heels.

"So this door. What's it supposed to look like?"

Winn hadn't known. He'd never seen it, merely repeated word for word what Pa had told him. Leave it to Pa to leave out the waterfall, unless that had come later. Who knew? Things underground could have changed in the last twenty years. But one thing would never change. They were closer to Hell than he'd ever been before, which made him damned uncomfortable.

"Not sure. All I was told was that we'd know it when we saw it."

The coil illuminator didn't like being wet. *Clack. Clack. Clack.* It refused to work, so Colt shook it harder. *Clack ClackClackClack.*

"Let me." She held out her hand, and in it materialized an oil lamp. She lifted the glass on the lamp and blew on the wick, making it light.

Colt had realized her kisses were hot, he just hadn't realized she could actually create flame with them! "Well, aren't you handy?"

She gave him a sly grin. "On occasion." She started walking and he took a moment to admire the sway of her hips beneath the damp calico still clinging to her. She paused, glancing back over her shoulder at him. "Are you coming?"

"Not yet, but give me time," Colt muttered under his breath. How he could find a demon so damn captivating, when he'd spent years destroying anything from the Darkin realm, was beyond him. What was it about this one demon that had him tied into knots like some green boy fresh off the farm?

He should be planning how he was going to send her back to Hell, not admiring the way her creamy skin glowed in the lamp's light. They might be united for the moment in their search, but he hadn't a single doubt in his mind that Miss Arliss would turn on him the moment she'd gotten what she really wanted.

Water dripped off the cavern ceiling, plunking in the damp rocks at their feet as Colt tried to analyze the situation, discover where his weakness lay. True, she was an incredible combination of unusual beauty and sensual appeal, but certainly it had to be more than that. He wasn't that easily led astray, was he?

'Course, he'd never been up against a succubus before. Vampires, certainly. Shape-shifters, demons, chupacabras, even a fire wraith, and now Scoria soldiers, but never a succubus. It was a bit unnerving to realize that perhaps he did have a weakness. Well, if it was a weakness, best to find out how to challenge it and reinforce his defenses. He had a duty to humanity that outstripped any of his own personal interests.

He caught up to her side in a few fast, long-legged strides. The damp, swamp-like smell of the mine shaft was replaced by Lilly's distinctive floral-and-spice scent that tugged at his gut. Colt did his level best to ignore it. Maybe if he just inhaled deep enough he'd get used to it and wouldn't be able to smell it any longer. He inhaled as deeply as he could. The scent dug deeper into his soul, causing an eddy of need to wash through him. Damn. That wasn't working.

Maybe he just needed to talk to her, find out she was no different than that scheming shape-shifter China McGee. But before he could speak, she turned those unnaturally bright green eyes on him. They bored straight through him, stealing the breath right out of his lungs, making the words on the tip of his tongue fade into nothingness.

"Have you killed every child of the night you've met?"

Her question shocked a little sense into him. He tore his gaze away from hers and stared straight ahead into the dark tunnel ahead. "Almost every one."

"So, one escaped the great Colt Jackson?"

He shrugged, thinking of how he'd narrowly wriggled

out of the rubble at the bank, leaving China behind for the authorities. Better they put a shape-shifter in jail than him for trying to steal Diego's safety-deposit box. "I wouldn't exactly call it an escape, and neither would China McGee."

"A woman?" Her brow arched.

"I wouldn't call China McGee exactly a woman. She's a shape-shifter."

"So you've had a relationship with a supernatural?"

"I wouldn't call what China and I shared exactly a relationship."

"Well, obviously you are intimate enough to call each other by your first names, and she was helping you."

"More like helping me by helping herself." Diego had been a Hunter in the same generation as Colt's pa. His safety-deposit box supposedly held a clue to the location of a map, which would lead to another piece of the Book hidden south of the border. China had brought the information to him in exchange for payment. He'd told her he would pay her when he got hold of Diego's safety-deposit box. Not that it was his problem now. He had his pa's part of the Book to track down. Remington could get the box from China, decipher the clue, and find a way to get hold of that map, and it would probably be a whole lot smoother and more legal than blowing a hole in the back of the bank.

"And you left her behind?"

Colt locked his unflinching gaze on hers. "Absolutely." He held no illusions about China. Anything she did was for her own benefit. And while attraction had flared between them, it had always been tempered by wariness and distrust. He'd yet to meet a Darkin he could trust. They'd screw you every single time. His chest ached as he thought of how often his family had suffered at the hands of Darkin, and Colt grew irritated with himself at how his common sense seemed to dissipate around Miss Arliss's considerable charms.

He had to be better than good as a Hunter. If he was going to bear the name Jackson within the Legion of Hunters, he had to be just as good, just as sharp, as both Winn and Remy. Being the youngest wasn't any kind of excuse for being softheaded around a female Darkin, no matter how tempting she seemed.

He'd already given his brothers a reason to taunt him when he'd been booted by China. He sure as hell wasn't about to listen to them tell him Pa had wasted his training on him because of another Darkin who seemed too good to be true. The shaft narrowed, forcing him to walk close enough to brush shoulders with her. She slowed her steps, causing him to slow too.

She turned into him, setting the oil lamp down beside them and placing her dainty hand over his heart. The heat of her touch seeped through his shirt, making him break out into a sweat. "Am I mistaken in thinking there's a heart in that broad chest of yours?"

"Yes, ma'am," he said, his voice solid, despite the increased pace of his heart beneath her hand. "I'm a Hunter through and through." His groin throbbed with a beat that matched his pulse. Hell, he didn't need a heart to want a woman, did he? But this wasn't a woman. This was a succubus, he sternly reminded his libido. *Duty. Honor. His family name among Hunters*, he recited in his head.

She stepped in closer to him, the flare of her hip grazing his erection. She made a sound deep down in her throat, almost like a purr. "Hunter you may be, but you're human too. So was I, once upon a time. I wish I still were."

Everything around him seemed to fade out as her sweet face filled his vision. Her bright eyes turned sultry as she slowly blinked, looking up at him through her lashes. Her breath smelled sweet, like a cinnamon roll. Colt got lost in the moment. Damn, he just wanted a taste. Just one more taste. The tips of her curls tickled the side of his neck as he leaned in to kiss her.

A low, feral growl issued from behind him and brought reality back into sharp focus. Sulfur suffused the air. The hairs on his head all tightened, making his scalp prickle and itch almost as hard as his gun hand. He gazed into the darkness over his shoulder, unable to pick out anything except a glowing pair of red eyes, chest height, tucked in tight against the rock, but approaching them slowly, black against darker black.

As the dark beast entered the edge of the yellow oil lamp light, Colt could make out the massive shoulders and ridge of raised black hair along the hellhound's back. More importantly, he could see the grizzly bear–sized mouth full of bared, glistening dagger-like teeth just beneath the scarlet eyes, which flickered with the glow of red-hot coals in a campfire.

The thing was the size of a buffalo, black as night and as angry as a pissed-off mama bear. Its sides bellowed in and out, its breath a stinking wind that reeked of sulfur. It stalked them slowly and deliberately, laying down one massive paw in front of the other, dark curving nails clacking against the rock floor.

Normally hellhounds came after you when they were guarding something, an entrance to Hell, something of supernatural significance, or hunting down a soul bound for damnation. He'd never fought off a hellhound before, but based on the description he was pretty damn certain the creature eyeing him like a prime cut of steak was one. He knew of only one Hunter who had fought a hellhound and managed to survive. That was if you called missing both legs and having half a face that hung in limp chunks survival.

Without hesitating he whipped out his revolver and pulled the trigger. *Click.*

Nothing happened. The Colt revolver had misfired.

Shit. His stomach shriveled into a tight, uncomfortable knot as his brain spun searching for options to defend them against the beast. "Dammit. Must be wet. Any suggestions for dealing with a hellhound?"

"No."

He threw her an incredulous look. "You're the Darkin here. I thought they'd at least give you some idea how to deal with your own kind."

Her brows knitted and mouth hardened. "Normally we don't have to. They only sic the hellhounds on people they want brought back dead or alive, but preferably dead. You could try to bargain with it."

"Bargain with it! Are you insane?"

She shrugged. "Good dog. Nice dog." She materialized a thick-cut raw hunk of steak and shook it.

The hellhound shifted its glowing red eyes in Miss Arliss's direction, but flattened its ears tighter against its buffalo-sized skull. She tossed the steak into the darkness behind the hellhound. It snapped as the steak sailed past, but didn't go after it. Instead it growled low and deep. The vibration of it reached right through Colt's gut and rattled his spine. "Not interested in steak."

"Really? Hadn't noticed," she said dryly.

"No reason to settle for an appetizer when you've got a full course and dessert sitting in front of you, I suppose."

"At least there's only one of them." Lilly scooted back, but kept her hand latched firmly on Colt's forearm and her eyes keenly focused on the hellhound stalking them.

She really had only two options. A: she could help the Hunter send the hellhound back to the depths from which it spawned, or B: she could let it take him. The problem was, if she let it take him, she'd still have to find the door he was searching for herself and she'd be no closer to getting rid of her ties to Rathe and getting back to being human. Therefore, there was really only one option—beat back the hound. This was going to hurt.

"Watch out for its teeth."

"You don't have to tell me that." His tone was condescending and irritated.

"No. It's the venom. They aren't just razor sharp. They've got a fast-moving acid that paralyzes the victim, but allows them to continue to feel all the pain."

"Nice to know. Suppose that'll leave you to clean up the mess when it's done chewing on me."

She glanced at him, daring to take her gaze off the hound for only a second. "It works on Darkin and mortal alike, lethal to both. So if you want my help, you're in this fight too."

Colt eyed her suspiciously, but she knew he was smart enough not to argue with her. "So how do you plan on getting out of this?"

"Any way I can."

"So pretty much kill it or die trying."

"Pretty much." Lilly steeled herself for the fight and materialized a whip from thin air. Bright red flames licked down the length of the black leather lash.

Colt's eyes gleamed in the flickering firelight. "Do I get one of those?"

She obliged, and with a shimmering of the air Colt held a twin to her whip. He tested the grip in his hands as he stared down the hellhound.

"Ever use one of these before?" She pulled back and let the whip snap. The gunshot-like crack echoed off the rock walls. The hellhound stepped back one pace and snarled.

Colt's avid expression made her hope dwindle. "Nope. Guns are more my thing." All eagerness and no experience meant he was likely to end up maimed or dead.

"It's all in the wrist. Keep your elbow and wrist loose. Flick it at the last moment. Follow my lea—"

Colt pulled the whip back and let it snap. The end flew back, pulling a strip of shirt and skin off his shoulder. The rest of the pale blue cotton around the wound caught on fire, and he hastily patted it out as he cursed.

"Damn touchy, aren't they?"

Lilly barely had time to mutter under her breath before the hellhound lunged, snapping at Colt. She pulled the whip around her, keeping her movement fluid and supple until at the last instant she flicked her wrist and let the flaming end fly. The whip curved through the air. *Crack.* It snapped across the beast's three-foot-wide nose, stripping off a ribbon of black flesh. The hound howled and snarled, swiveling toward her, red eyes glaring.

A second later two more pairs of red glowing eyes appeared in the darkness behind it.

"Oh, this just keeps getting better and better," Colt muttered. "Three of them?"

They closed ranks, the two hounds in the back right on haunches of the irascible lead dog, filling the breadth of the cavern, their mingled growls rumbling the cavern enough to send down a shower of rock dust from overhead.

"The more, the scarier," she replied. Damn. Damn. Damn. If this was Rathe's sick idea of a joke, it sure wasn't making her laugh. Three hellhounds? Wasn't that a bit of dramatic overkill, even for a demon lord? Lilly muttered a few choice curses underneath her breath.

"I'll take the one on the right. You get the one on the left." Colt shifted his stance, preparing to strike.

"What about the one in the middle?"

"Greedy, are we?"

"No. Just didn't want you to forget we had extra helpings for dessert."

Colt gave her a wicked grin. "Just the way I like it."

Men. Always hungry for more. Lilly focused on the hellhound in front of her. She let the whip fly. The fiery lash made an orange arc in the air, striking the hound's cheek and nearly taking out one of its glowing red eyes. The beast roared. *Crack.* She heard Colt's whiplash echo in the air. Together they held the three hellhounds at bay.

"Try circling to see if we can get behind them." Colt's cool tone belied his focus. Together they lashed and drew back, a deadly duel with the three hellhounds as they adjusted their position so that the hounds were now in the direction of the waterfall, and the untried tunnel and unexplored second cavern at their backs.

The hellhound snapped at her. She jumped, avoiding the poisonous fangs. She pulled back the whip and let it fly again. But as it sailed backward, it struck an unintended target.

Colt cursed loudly. She glanced back to see his gun hand tucked beneath the pit of his other arm and his gun lying in the dust. He was glaring at her as hard as the hellhounds surrounding them were. "You might warn me before you strike."

The hellhound he'd been fighting bit the whip, grabbing it like a toy, shaking Colt violently.

"Let go of the whip!" she yelled at him. He did and dropped fifteen feet to the dirt.

Momentarily preoccupied, she failed to notice that hellhound number three had joined up with the lead hound in the center and they were nearly nose to nose, mouth to mouth, with her in the center, a bone to be fought over.

"Oh no, you don't." Lilly pulled back the whip, hoping to lash them both, but the hellhound closest knew that whip and moved a split second before the lash connected with it. It snapped at the whip, catching it between its enormous teeth and ripping it out of her hand like a plaything. It shook the whip, striking the second hound and nearly striking her in the process with the swinging handle, then tossed the offending item across the cavern. It roared in irritation, then raised one massive paw in the air, moving to squash her flat.

She hit the dirt and rock floor of the cavern with a thud that shoved the air out of her lungs like a punch to the gut. There wasn't time to think on it. A giant paw was coming down toward her. Fast. She rolled to the side, narrowly missing becoming ooze between the hellhound's toes.

She shoved the curtain of hair out of her face and spotted Colt's revolver in the dust and scrabbled for it. "Colt!"

He'd risen from the cavern floor and swiveled in her direction. She tossed the revolver in the air. For an infinite moment it seemed to hang suspended in slow motion just like her stomach, weightless and fluttering with uncertainty. The hellhound closest to her snapped at it, but missed. Colt caught the revolver and with long-honed reflexes cocked it and fired in one lightning-fast motion. The dead center of the hellhound's head exploded with a fist-sized hole, splattering the wall just above her head with black ooze and chunks of hellhound gray matter.

"Duck!" He fired off two more shots in rapid succession, landing one in the center of the hellhound's hip and taking down the third hound with a shot to the throat. The howl of pain from the giant beast rattled the rock walls. The beasts then erupted into a blaze of fire one after the other. She had to raise her arm to stave off the broiling heat. The mine shaft acted like a funnel. Fire shifted, moving with lightning quickness toward them, obliterating everything in its path.

There was no time to think. He caught her by the arm as he ran past her down the dark tunnel, and she pumped her arms and legs hard and fast to keep up with him.

The gnashing of giant teeth, agonized howls, and the crackle of the fire started to fade as the darkness consumed them. The stench of burned fur and flesh lingered thickly in the air, a noxious cloud making them gasp and wheeze. They both were out of breath and doubled over by the time they stopped. *Clack. Clack. Clack.* A feeble blue light emitted from the coil illuminator.

Colt stared at Miss Arliss with amazement, his chest still heaving. Her face was unnaturally pale and the demon glow of her eyes obvious in the bluish light. "You just helped me send those hounds back to Hell."

Still breathing hard, she shoved back an unruly tendril of dark red hair that had come loose in the scuffle. "Well, I couldn't let them take you to Hell when we were this close, now could I? Besides, I've never really liked hellhounds. They stink." Her elegant nose scrunched up.

"But it was your own kind." His tone echoed his suspicion.

"Darkin—yes, but not like me." She folded her hands together, as if unsure of what to do with them. "I don't want to be a Darkin any longer. I've never wanted to be one, but I had no choice."

His brow bent. This was the first he'd ever heard of a supernatural who didn't want to be one. Pa had never mentioned it was even possible. Perhaps it was a trick. "What do you mean? Don't most demons become demons by choice?"

"More like by bargains badly made. We all think there's a way out, until you find out there isn't."

"So what did you bargain for?"

"I saved my little sister from becoming a whore to support us."

Colt launched into a coughing fit and pounded his chest with his fist. Hell's bells. He certainly hadn't seen that coming. "Can't say as I've ever heard a lady be so blunt before."

She gave a shrug of her dainty shoulders, but her eyes still held shadows of the past. "I haven't had the luxury of being a miss with delicate sensibilities. Not when I was mortal, and certainly not now."

If she weren't a succubus she would've been damned near the perfect woman. Soft sensuality and feminine curves over a core of iron-hard determination and stamina—a woman who wouldn't wilt every time a supernatural came near—a woman who could cope with the Hunter life.

His mother had been such a woman. But her steadfast loyalty and unyielding resolve hadn't stopped the demon's bullet that killed her. He'd been so young all he'd remembered were her soft kisses brushed against his forehead at night and her warm hugs and the cinnamon-sugar cookies she'd bake for him, always letting him have one before his brothers. Pa said there wasn't another woman like her on Earth, and he believed it. But then Miss Arliss wasn't a woman, she was something more. Colt had to admire her grit even though he was determined not to let her powers sway his better judgment any further.

"Let me look at that wound of yours." Only now did Colt realize that his shoulder burned. He glanced down. The singed edges of his shirt were charred around the long, dark slice in his skin that was raw and blistered and bleeding sluggishly. He glanced up at her. "It's fine."

She arched one brow. "I didn't think Hunters were supposed to lie."

"Who says I'm lying?"

The look she gave him said he ought to 'fess up. It did burn worse than he wanted to admit. "If it makes you feel better, you can look at it."

She stepped closer to him, that unique female scent of

her drifting up and crowding out the unpleasant stench of burnt hellhound. Her long, tapered fingers pulled back the edges of his tattered, burned shirt with infinite tenderness. The tip of her pink tongue touched the center of her upper lip and Colt had the ridiculous notion that kissing her would make the pain go away completely.

"I may have something to soothe that, but I'm afraid it's going to leave a mark."

"Yes, ma'am. I think it is."

She opened her palm, and a small blue glass jar appeared in it.

"What's that?"

"Healing salve. It'll take away the burning, but I'm afraid this is going to take a while to heal."

"Sometimes injuries from supernaturals never heal." Colt was thinking specifically of Winn and how the demon had crushed the will to hunt right out of him. It had left Winn with a scar on his thigh, but had messed him up worse on the inside. Colt had a sickening feeling that if he let himself get too attached to Lilly, it might happen to him too.

"So how'd you become a Hunter?" She opened the metal latch on the glass jar and dipped her fingers into the glistening white salve.

The question seemed so normal that he'd almost answered without thinking. He hesitated a moment. He had no business talking with her like this, and yet she'd fought back-to-back with him against the hellhounds. He owed her something. A little information about his past seemed harmless enough. "I was born into it. My family is part of the Legion. Has been since way back when." The trail she left as she touched him was cool and relaxing, soaking into him like water into the parched desert sands. Something he'd needed desperately but hadn't known he had until it was given to him.

"You're famous in our world, you know."

From the light throb, just below the black velvet ribbon around her throat, Colt could tell the touch affected her too. She glanced up at him, her green eyes bright and wide, shining with something more than just admiration.

"Hardly a hero, I'm sure."

"But you're part of the Chosen."

"Isn't that like the bringer of destruction to your Darkin world?"

She latched the top back on the jar, then waved her hand over it, making it disappear into thin air. "No. The Chosen are the bringers of balance. We need you as much as you need us. What would light be without darkness?"

Colt had spent enough time out in the desert to know exactly how that felt. The sunshine could seem unrelenting in its intensity. There were times where the darkness came as a blessed relief after a long day. "Monotonous," he answered. His mind opened to the possibility that perhaps he needed her to be with him for longer than just finding the Book. Maybe there was more he could learn from this delectable demon.

Unable to resist any longer, he pulled her closer. His shoulder stung, but Colt didn't give a damn. He just wanted to hold her for a moment before all hell broke loose again. "So what are you going to do once we find that door?"

She looked up at him, her eyes luminous, her chest pressed close to his so that he could feel her heartbeat against his ribs, just as real, just as rapid as his own. "That's a silly question, Colt." This time when she said his name there wasn't any animosity in her tone, and her fingers slid along his jaw, testing the texture of his lips and making him ache with a longing that wasn't physical alone. "When we find that door, I'm going to open it for you."

Chapter 8

In every con there came a point where you had to take a risk. That point had just arrived.

Despite her promise to open the door for Colt, Lilly still hadn't figured out precisely what she was going to do once he got his hands on the pages from the Book of Legend. Rathe had demanded it. Furthermore, he wanted Colt dead. Just how far was she willing to go? Certainly she could seduce Colt into giving her the Book, but was she willing to turn Colt over to the archdemon and lose her one chance at becoming mortal again because she feared Rathe?

"Where are we?" Colt cast the light from the coil illuminator, exposing the uneven rocky ceiling of the shaft, which had begun to widen and slope upward. The temperature had markedly increased, causing Lilly to worry some at the trickle of moisture between her breasts and the possibility that her state might be evidenced on the calico of her dress. The fetid, damp smell of stagnant water combined with the earthy scent of wet rock to saturate the air in the humid heat.

"My best guess is we're nearing the second cavern."

He shook the coil illuminator a few times, but it refused

to produce any brighter light. "Could you snap us another oil lamp?"

"I can do one better." Lilly balled up her hand, blowing on it until her palm grew warm and the flutter of small wings beat against the cage of her fingers. She opened her fist slowly and released the red fireflies into the air.

Their dancing lights scattered far and wide, soaring out through the tunnel opening and into the chamber. Lilly followed, with Colt quickly falling into step beside her. The fireflies seemed to multiply until there were thousands of them. Their individual light bounced in small dots of color off the rocks as they bobbed and bounced in the air, but combined they lit the space with a warm reddish glow.

"Haven't seen fireflies like that before."

She tilted her lips up in a coy smile. "Unless you go to Hell sometime, you never will."

"They're kinda pretty." The way he said it made it obvious he wasn't just talking about fireflies from Hell. He locked gazes with her, his pupils dilated a fraction, the dark nearly swallowing the deeper blue.

Lilly forced herself to remember that he was a Hunter first and a man second. "Not everything from Hell is horrible. Sometimes they just reside there out of circumstance."

An eerie green glow filled the shaft in front of them, and Lilly pinched her nose at the increasing stagnant stench. She inched closer to Colt, unsure of what awaited them. The map in Colt's hand seemed to come to an end with X marking the spot.

The floor of the shaft sloped upward enough that they couldn't see over the rise, but based on the smell alone Lilly had an idea they were close to still water. Colt was going to balk. They'd never get the Book, not if it required him to swim. She slowed down, forcing Colt to lag in his steps.

"What's wrong?"

She sighed. "Just how far are you willing to go for what you're looking for? I know you are willing to kill for it, but are you willing to die for it?"

He eyed her warily. "If I have to."

"What about swim?"

"Excuse me?"

"Swim. Are you willing to swim for it?"

Colt stiffened. "Why?"

They crested the top of the rise. The trail ended below them at the shores of a wide, acid green lake, which glowed with an unearthly phosphorescence that lit up the stalactites overhead in ripples of green light.

"Because you might wish you had died instead," she said flatly.

They walked down to the shoreline of black sand, which ran in both directions until it disappeared in the darkness. It was impossible to see how big the lake was.

The light of the fireflies bounced and reflected off the water as ghostly female forms, transparent and as oddly green as the water, drifted with sightless eyes and placid smiles just beneath the surface.

"What in tarnation? More water? Are you sure we aren't already in Hell? Maybe we crossed the border back there," he ground out, irritation lacing his tone.

The succubus shrugged. "Everyone has their own personal version of Hell. Just figures that a Hunter wouldn't be afraid of flames and brimstone."

He blatantly ignored her comment. "And what are those things?" He pointed to the placid figures in the water.

"Naiads, water sprites. The minute you touch that water, they'll try to lure you in deeper. Don't give me that superior I'm-a-Hunter-and-I'd-never-succumb look. Trust me, you won't be able to resist."

He turned his gaze back to the water, transfixed. "We'll have to find a way around."

"It could be a thousand miles," Lilly pointed out. "Straight across will be quicker."

He turned his head slowly to look at her again. "Across? What for?"

"That." She pointed, and his eyes reluctantly followed her finger.

On the far shore, a small rock ledge jutted out of the cavern wall, extending just over the surface of the water. Above it was a black shiny door made of what looked like volcanic glass set into a rough wall of gray granite.

"Damn." He shook his head, scrubbing his face with his hands. "You sure there ain't another way?"

Now was her chance if she wanted to ensnare him. His guard was as down as it was ever going to be. She could take his will, bend it to her wishes, but then, then she'd never know if his response was genuinely to her or just to her succubus powers. Here was the risk, staring her straight in the face. Daring her to take the chance.

What's it going to be? If she glamoured him, it would be easy as pie to hand him and the piece of the Book over to Rathe. If she glamoured him, he'd become just another of Rathe's thralls and never be strong enough to help her fight the demon lord and become human once more. Choices. Choices.

Lilly took a deep, steadying breath and decided against glamouring him. He seemed to be a man capable of reason, and willing to keep his word. Those were few and far between, nigh extinct, in her experience, but she liked to believe a few still existed. It was one of the few things that kept her faith in humanity alive and well. "Well, it looks like if you want to get to that door, we're going to have to find out how potent those naiads really are."

* * *

Overhead the fireflies began to wink out one by one, until only the greenish glow of the water remained. Colt swallowed hard, pushing his toe up to the edge of the water but not getting it wet. He could do this. He had to do this. *It's just water. It ain't gonna kill you.* His gaze connected with hers.

"Do you want me to go first?" she asked. There seemed no guile in it, but Colt couldn't be sure. Maybe she wanted to get to the door first. Maybe she was hoping that the naiads would simply drag him down and drown him as he tried to follow her.

He frowned. "No, I'll go first. Just take care of my hat and my saddlebags. I don't want them getting wet again." He peeled off his Stetson and tossed it at her, then shrugged his saddlebags off his shoulder, letting them drop to the black sand.

Miss Arliss caught his hat and arched her brow. "What about your boots?"

Colt grumbled and peeled them off one at a time, dropping them into the black sand as well. "Happy?"

"You could keep going—if you didn't want to get your clothes wet," she replied archly, setting his hat down next to his boots and the saddlebags.

Colt rubbed his hand through his hair. "Don't give me any fool ideas, woman. I've got enough to deal with." He took three quick rapid breaths in and out, getting up his gumption to go into the lake, then stepped one foot in the strange water. The surface immediately broke into ripples of movement. *Hell's bells. This isn't regular water.* His whole form turned rigid at the contact as the naiads' voices, light and musical, filled the cavern, echoing in harmony off the rocks.

"What do we have to do to make them stop singing?" he

called back to Miss Arliss without taking his eyes off the strange water. Translucent, pale green feminine hands and fingers undulated along the surface.

"Get what you're after," she answered. "There's nothing else."

Colt swore under his breath as the long, tapered green fingers of several dozen hands shimmied up his foot, grasping and stroking at his calves, then his knees and thighs. It would have been erotic except that the pounding in his chest wasn't the excited kind; it was born out of pure gut-wrenching terror.

Nothin' hurts worse than losing. When Hunters lose, people die, he told himself, repeating the mantra his father had drilled into him again and again. He entered the water up to his knees with a jerky stride, pushing himself to ignore the warning bells clanging like an accompaniment to the naiads' song. His knees suddenly seemed spongy and almost unable to hold his weight.

The skin on his face turned damp with sweat, and his heart swelled, filling his chest and his throat, making it damn uncomfortable to breathe. He could literally feel the naiads pulling on the stiff denim of his pants, pulling him deeper into the water. He hesitated, hand on his gun belt. But there was nothing to shoot at. Nothing to torch to a crisp. They were liquid, for God's sake.

"I'm right behind you. Keep going," Miss Arliss said, but he could barely hear her over the loud, insistent song of the naiads that was even now drowning out his own thoughts.

He forced his field of vision down to only one thing: the smooth sheet of obsidian ahead. Nothing else was there. Nothing else mattered. He willed himself to move one foot, then the other deeper into the swirling liquid, even as his logical mind rebelled as the glowing water pushed up farther, chilling him to the core.

The singing of the naiads became louder, a cacophony, drowning out the sound of even his own heartbeat in his ears. *Perhaps dropping into the water, letting it wash over me isn't such a bad idea.*

Colt shook his head and blinked hard. No, that wasn't his thought, it was the song of those damn water nymphs.

The bottom of the lake felt soft and insubstantial beneath his feet, like a thick layer of mud that gave way, but then sucked and pulled before it would release him. Colt was damned if he'd go under and concentrated on keeping his footing. No turning back now.

The cold hit his knees. His thighs. His groin. His waist—hell's bells. He was doing it! Elation inflated his chest. A hundred feet and he'd be on the ledge.

The water lapped around his chest. Naiads pulled free of the surface of the water, their translucent faces eerie and beautiful. One grasped him with her liquid arms around his neck, pressing her mouth to his in a kiss.

The glowing waters slid around his lips, cool and intimidating. Colt tore away, his arm swinging through the naiad, turning her into a spray of droplets as his foot slipped in the silty bottom of the lake. The singing continued to swell. More naiads collected around him, pressing their bodies against his, their lips to his cheeks.

He suddenly lost contact with the bottom of the lake. Panic, white hot, raced through him. He thrashed, desperate to touch down, his arms colliding into the naiads gathered around him. He raised his hand to cover his ears, but a smooth, solid hand stopped him.

"Stand up." It was the succubus's voice in his ear, clear, strong, and decisive. Her grip on his wrist was sure. "You're through the deepest part. The water is only up to your shoulders if you just stand up."

Colt forced himself to ignore the slick, suffocating sensation of the water on his skin and pushed his feet downward. To his surprise they connected with something solid. Despite his spongy knees, he stood. The liquid retreated slightly, but not enough to rid him of the horrible sick swirling in his gut telling him he was going to drown.

His vision blurred as his lungs refused to function. An insistent pushing at his back told him Miss Arliss was still there with him. As long as she was touching him, the naiads' hold on him was like a light current in the green water tugging at him, but not able to pull him under. But Colt had no illusions. If Miss Arliss weren't there, he'd have been under the water long before he reached that door. So far the demon had proven herself far more of an ally than a handful of other Hunters he'd known. And that was saying something.

"Can you make it?"

Colt took his gaze off the black shiny door ahead just long enough to catch a glimpse of Miss Arliss. The ends of her flame-colored hair floated in the water, spreading out around her like fire on water.

His tongue was dry and almost too thick to speak. "I'm fine. You don't need to baby me."

She shook her head. "I know. We all have weaknesses. Water just happens to be yours."

"Still ain't right," he grumbled. Inside Colt hated that weak part of him. Sure, normal people, even demons perhaps, had weaknesses, but not a Hunter. And so far, between the water and his attraction to Miss Arliss, he seemed to have two whoppers. But they were almost to the door. Once he got his hands on his pa's portion of the Book, he'd be able to look at it and find out what he was supposed to do next.

The naiads turned feverish in their attempts to hold him and the succubus in the water. They undulated against him, their hands stroking every inch of him, but Miss Arliss's touch was more solid, more warm and real. It didn't just touch his skin, it touched something deeper inside him, making his heart pound not with fear or anxiety but with fierce determination.

They reached the outcropping of granite that formed the ledge before the door. Colt dug his fingers into the rock and pulled himself out of the water, laying his cheek against the solid rough surface and sucking deep, gasping breaths of air into his burning lungs as if he'd been under the water the whole time and the rock was his lifeline.

He reached down, offering Miss Arliss a hand to pull her onto the ledge beside him. Her small hand locked around his forearm as he heaved. There was a slap of wet cotton hitting rock as she lay on her back shoulder to shoulder with him, both of them breathing fast and heavy as if they'd run the distance rather than waded through it. Every muscle in his body burned.

"We made it." Her words were simple, but the experience had been anything but.

Colt turned his head to gaze at her. Her cheeks were brilliant pink from exertion. "You make it sound like it was easy."

Miss Arliss bent her arm, resting it on her forehead, her hair pooling in wet coils about her head. Colt reached over, removing one of the strands that stuck to her smooth cheek. "I don't think I would have made it without you."

Colt meant every syllable. He knew he wouldn't have made it this far without her help, despite his training. No Hunter could have taken on those hellhounds alone. He couldn't have challenged the strange lake full of naiads alone, and for that he owed her something.

She worried her full bottom lip between her even, white teeth. Desire stirred down deep. He knew what those soft wet lips felt like, how inviting and sweet they could be. He gritted his teeth and refrained from kissing her, but he was damned tempted.

A sadness filled her eyes he couldn't quite figure out. Was she sad their partnership was almost at an end? The truth was, he had a hard time reading her. Up until now he hadn't spent much time or effort to understand women. Enjoy them, certainly, but he knew he'd never be able to stay any one place long enough to make understanding a woman worth his time. Now it put him at a distinct disadvantage, which made his gun hand itch. He wanted to understand this unusual creature and make her understand that her efforts meant something to him.

"I guess what I'm trying to say is thank you."

She shook her head slowly, the sadness seeping into her voice. "Don't thank me yet."

Colt struggled on the narrow ledge to stand without bumping her into the lake, then helped Miss Arliss to her feet. She gazed up at him as they stood chest to chest and toe to toe. "Colt, I hope whatever is behind this door doesn't change things between us," she said into his shirt, her breath warm through the fabric against his wet, chilled skin.

Colt knew better than to touch her. It would make him want things he couldn't have—spending time with her, finding out what made her smile, being sappy and sentimental—things a Hunter didn't have the luxury of doing with a woman, even if he wanted to.

Once they opened this door and he got his hands on those pages, everything for them would change. He'd get the Book and convince his brothers of the need to unite it. He'd find a way to free Miss Arliss from Rathe's grasp. And she'd be human again, and he'd be . . . moving on. Even if he didn't have to overcome his reservations about her once being a demon, there was nothing he could do about who and what he was—a Hunter with a mission.

Colt spread his hands along the damp calico that wrapped her small rib cage, his fingers tracing over each dip and curve. Damn, for a demon she was delicate, but then she was tough as nails too. The soft feminine scent of her curled about him as her skin heated. He crooked a finger under her chin, forcing her to meet his gaze. "I made you a promise. I don't do that lightly."

Her hands fluttered at his chest. "I know. It's just that no one's ever escaped Rathe before." The heavy sigh she exhaled pierced right through him, squeezing his heart. "I've wanted to get away for so long now I'd almost given up hope. No one in the Darkin realm was positive the Chosen would survive Rathe."

Colt gave her a confident smile born not out of false hubris, but painful hard-earned experience. "Rathe's already tried to kill me once. He sent one of your kind out to bring me and my brothers in when we were just kids. Damn demon nearly drowned me, and just about cost my brother Winn his life."

"That's why you don't like the water."

Colt didn't trust himself to say any more. Admitting his deepest fears to her had been monumental enough for him. He just gave one curt nod.

She stood there, staring up at him with wide eyes, shining green and jewel-like, brimming with trust. "If there's anyone who could get me away from Rathe, it'd be you. I just know it."

A little bit of pride fired up in Colt's belly, the warmth of it wiping out the last of the chill from his dip in the lake. "Well then, what are we waiting for? You've been curious enough to know what's behind this door. So, go on, open it."

Lilly peeled herself away from him. As a demon, she knew praying was useless, but some habits were just too hard to break. She sent up a silent prayer to the God who'd forgotten her that the Hunter beside her was strong enough to stand whatever Rathe would send in retaliation.

She took a deep breath, then reached for the door. The glassy surface of the rock had no handle and no hinges. It was held shut by the supernatural forces at the Darkin's command.

She held her hand against the cool flat door, reciting an incantation that should have opened anything related to the Darkin realm. The smooth sheet of obsidian didn't so much as shimmer.

Behind her, Colt grumbled. "What's wrong? Why isn't it opening?"

Lilly glanced back at him. "I—I don't know. That should have done it."

"Try it again," he said, an edge of desperation to his voice.

She obliged him, knowing it was folly. Focusing her whole power on the door, she recited the opening incantation again. Still nothing. It simply would not budge.

"I don't understand. That should have done something."

Colt stared hard, the blue of his eyes dark and stormy as he concentrated. "There's something we're missing."

Lilly felt the heat of his avid gaze the instant it shifted from the door to linger on her mouth.

"A bargain with a demon is sealed with a kiss," he said. His tone was huskier than it had been a moment before. His rough fingertips reached out, brushing a light, tingling touch over her lips.

A white-hot spark of awareness arced out and downward from the point of contact, running along her nerves and racing all the way to her toes and fingers. Lilly gasped, everything inside her tightening like a clock spring wound to the breaking point. Desire, dangerous and impulsive, swirled and eddied in the breath of space between them.

Without another word, he pulled her hard and tight up against him. Lilly didn't resist.

The first time they'd kissed there'd been surprise and suspicion. The second, he'd been so focused on his fear he'd been unable to block her and had responded more. But this time, this time when he kissed her, Lilly discovered something far more potent, more drugging in the press of his firm lips to hers. She tasted trust mixed with desire. The heady combination burned through her, heating her to the core like nothing else could.

"That was some kiss," she said, the moment she could breathe again.

A light flared to life behind his eyes, making them glitter. "That's it."

"The last kiss?"

"No. But your kiss—"

"My kiss has opened the secrets of the universe?"

"No, but it may be what we need to open the door." He put his hands lightly on her shoulders.

"A demon's kiss?"

"Why not? It's worth a try." He gently spun her around to face the obsidian portal. Lilly took a deep breath and let it out slowly, sending up a prayer Colt was right. She pressed her lips, still hot and tender from his kiss, against the cool, smooth stone.

Like smoke in the wind, the black stone vanished in a shift of particles. Lilly yelped as she fell forward into the unexpected opening. Only Colt's quick grasp around her waist kept her from falling face-first into the alcove.

The walls of the hidden room were studded with glittering crystals, making it look as if they had stepped inside an enormous geode. With the first footstep into the alcove, the crystals began to glow and sparkle, pulsating with green phosphorescent light. At the center of the little room stood a waist-high polished black marble pillar supporting a smooth wooden box.

The glossy surface of the age-darkened wood reflected the greenish light. The ornately filigreed golden hinges that resembled roaring lion heads and the clasp shaped like a triple cross glinted. All they had to do was reach out and grab it.

"Think it's a trap?"

"Could be. But if it took a demon's kiss to open the door, whoever put it here assumed it would take a Darkin to get this far. And I don't know of a single supernatural, 'sides you, who'd actually want the Book of Legend reunited."

Colt stared at the small wooden box, the greenish hue of the light reflecting in his eyes and giving his face a goulish hue and an intensity that shook her to the core. She'd do well to remember that while he'd needed her help down here in the tunnels, that would all end the moment he opened that box and got what he was after.

They'd no longer be on the same side after that. And she certainly didn't count on him keeping his word to help her escape Rathe. He was a Hunter after all.

"Do you want me to pick up the box?" she offered. Her voice shook slightly, betraying her insecurity. He was so fixated on the box that he didn't even answer her. Damn, she should have glamoured him when she'd had the chance. Without the piece of the Book, would she even have a bargaining chip to force his hand in helping her escape Rathe?

Colt flexed his fingers. Every sense was coiled tightly. Here on the edge of Hell, anything was possible. The floor could drop away, the walls could collapse inward. Worse, the water might rise, trapping them inside the alcove and drowning them. He'd stared so hard at the box, trying to see if there were any visible triggers, that his eyes had become gritty. He blinked and glanced at Miss Arliss.

Her calico dress had turned dark blue from their swim and was still dripping water around the hem. The wet cotton clung to her form, surpassing his imagination, and he had imagined plenty. Her pale skin was flushed a delicate pink, which made him wonder if the tips of her breasts would be rose or apricot. Her lush mouth was slightly open, her small hands balled eagerly in front of her, her eyes bright, like a woman aroused.

Colt tore his gaze away from her and forced himself to ignore the tight, heavy heat in his groin and his increased pulse. *She's a succubus*, he told himself, *purposely designed to sway your thoughts and take over your body. Control. You need control.* He took a deep, shuddering breath and flexed his fingers. Retrieving the Book was too important to let inappropriate thoughts and feelings interfere.

Inside that box were the pages his father had guarded with his life—the knowledge Hunters had passed on for centuries from one to another beginning with the three brothers in medieval times who had broken it apart. Each brother had trained their own portion of the Legion in each generation. Some said the Book of Legend had a power of its own, but Colt had never believed it. Of course, he hadn't believed in the prophecy of the Chosen either.

Now, given that the Gates of Nyx were opening wider, he hoped he'd been wrong. Defeating Rathe and keeping the realm of the Darkin from overtaking the world and enslaving humanity was going to take a hell of a lot more than three brothers said to be some mythical leaders. It was going to take a damn miracle. And in that box was the start of the miracle.

"Here we go," he said more to himself than to her. He reached for the box, praying it wasn't a trap. His fingers curled with reverence and surety around its thick corners.

Gently he lifted it from the shiny black pedestal. The age-darkened wood was warm to the touch and worn satin smooth, as if it'd been handled by thousands of hands.

He straightened, then blew out a breath he hadn't even realized he'd been holding. They were still alive.

He gave Miss Arliss a cocky grin as he moved his fingers to pry open the lid. "That wasn't so bad."

That's when the rumbling started. Panic drained her face of color. Her eyes widened and her gaze darted about the room. It was bad, really bad, if the demon was worried.

The grinding of moving rock filled the cavern. Gritty dust fell from the ceiling, catching in the back of his throat and itching there. The crystals began to fracture and crack, their greenish phosphorescence turning crimson.

"If you were waiting for a sign that it's time to go, the messenger just arrived!" she shouted above the rumble.

Chapter 9

The once placid green water of the enormous unnatural lake was a bubbling, boiling red. Naiads grappled and strained, creating a turbulent surface, their transparent bodies as fiery scarlet as the water. Elongated hands clawed for purchase on the stone ledge inches from Colt's feet.

"Nobody invited you up here," he said as he stomped on a hand that nearly grabbed his foot. The naiad shrieked like a damn banshee.

He heard an ominous crack, watched a fissure do a crazy zigzag along the ledge. Nowhere to go. Ah, hell! Miss Arliss screamed as the ledge beneath their feet crumbled.

He hit the scalding lake feetfirst. Plunged into the hot, viscous liquid, thick and rank like whale oil, the clutching hands of the naiads pulling at his clothing, hair, skin, forcing him beneath the surface. Where was Miss Arliss? he wondered, frantically trying to evade the grasping hands and keep his head above the roiling surface. Was she there with him in this liquid hell or back on the last shards of the ledge, safe?

But it was hard to think about anything other than his burning flesh and staying alive.

Don't fight it. Relax. The water feels good.

The hell it did. A cool hand gripped his sleeve, then slid lower to his hand as he sank beneath the surface, and the contrary thoughts invading his brain dissipated like mist. A pent-up breath burned within his chest. His muscles went rigid as panic once again shot through him. Breaking the surface, shockingly one arm still locked around the box, he gasped, kicking against the viscous fluid for all he was worth. Finally—thank God! Finally, his toe scraped bottom.

Still gripping his hand, the succubus bobbed up beside him, red hair slicked back from her face. "Just keep in touch with me until we reach the shore. They might make our way difficult, but they can't take you if we're connected."

A bubble of raw fear swelled in his throat. "I've only got one free arm." Hold on to Miss Arliss, or drop the box? Neither was a viable option. There was no way he was letting go of the box, even if it meant fighting the naiads every inch of the way to the shore.

"There," she said, gripping his shoulder with her other hand before she released her tight grip on his fingers. "Now you have a free hand. Let's go." Her fingers on his shoulder dug in, becoming a death grip.

They struggled through the thick water, the rushing liquid-spirit bodies bumping against them and grasping at them like an undertow.

The shore seemed as though it were receding with every laborious step, yet Colt knew they must be making progress. He could now see his Stetson, boots, and saddle packs, small brown dots on the black sand. Colt's limbs were lead weights, pulling him down in the water, making it a challenge to keep just his nose and mouth above the surface.

"Don't you dare give up!" Miss Arliss yelled.

He didn't have the heart to remind her that he was only

human. They were never going to make it. Hell's bells, he could barely move. The liquid of the lake was the consistency of warm aspic.

He was going to die for nothing. The portion of the Book he held would be lost forever in the depths of this cursed lake. He'd failed not only his calling, but his brothers. Without these missing pages, there was no way the pieces could be reunited.

"We're almost there. Keep going," Miss Arliss urged. With her small, strong hands she pushed him through the water, unwilling to let go.

They were in the middle of the lake when Colt's vision began to turn black at the edges, his heart seeming to beat right behind his eyes. "I'm not going to make it. Take the Book," he gulped, struggling for air. "Take it to my brother at the sheriff's office in Bodie. Winn will know what to do with it."

She tugged harder. "Save your breath. Move, Mr. Jackson. Don't you dare quit on me now."

He didn't know how they made it to the shore. He just knew he pitched forward in the lake as the bottom sloped up out of the water, forcing him to crawl onto the gritty shore beside his hat. Exhausted, Miss Arliss collapsed beside him, her pale, wet cheek resting against the black sand.

"I hope it was worth it, Colt Ambrose Jackson."

He blinked and stared hard at her with stunned disbelief, his chest still heaving. "What'd you say?"

"I hope it was worth it, Colt Ambrose Jackson?"

Colt lifted his head. Confusion crowding his brain. "You know my middle name." Middle names weren't just names in the Darkin realm. They were a means of control. She could have put him under a glamour at any time since he'd released her from that circle he'd cast. She could have owned him body and soul and there wouldn't have been a damn thing he could have done about it, and yet, she hadn't.

She turned away from him, placing her back to the sand and staring up at the arch of the cavern above them. Her delicate profile was utterly feminine, and Colt couldn't drag his gaze away.

"I know a great deal more about you than that," she said softly.

"You're not at all what I expected from a demon."

She turned her head to look at him. Her unnaturally green gaze caught his briefly. And there it was again. That sensation that she could reach in and twist his very heart around her little finger. The knowing that if he let her get to him, she'd forever change his life. His breath hitched.

In an instant those same eyes turned wary and guarded. "Demons are just like mortals; every one of us is different," she added, her tone defensive.

"You don't have to look at me like that. I'm not going to dispatch you just because we found the box. I'm going to help you escape Rathe. I promised."

Tears welled along her lashes and she looked back across the bubbling red water. A tear slipped down her cheek, leaving a glistening trail against her creamy skin. He'd said he'd help her escape Rathe. Clearly she didn't believe him. She wanted to, but she couldn't for reasons he had yet to understand.

She swiped her face with the back of her hand, then sat up, dusting the black sand from her palms. "You ought to open that."

Colt's fingers flexed on the box under his hand. "I've been working more than three years now to find my pa's part of the Book of Legend." His fingers traced over the ornate gold filigree of the latch and hinges. The box wasn't nearly as old as what it held. "Funny how something so small could make such a big difference. The whole future rests on what's in this little box."

His eyes focused on hers. "You sure we should open it now? I mean, look at me." He gestured to his sagging wet pants and tattered, singed shirt. "I'm soaked in God knows what and it might drip all over the pages. And isn't opening it here kind of like sending up a flare to the Darkin, saying, 'Hey, we're over here! Come and get us.'"

"Perhaps. But it sounds like you're searching for reasons not to open it. I'm scared too, but eventually you're going to have to open that box."

The temptation to crack it open and look was immense, but the risks outweighed the benefits. Gut deep he knew what was inside. It was Pa's part of the Book. Everything he'd researched and discovered had led him to it. "It can wait until we get outside." His voice cracked as he picked up his hat and settled it back into the familiar, comfortable place on his head.

"Are you sure?"

He had to admit she did have a point. After all they'd gone through to get the box, they should at least look inside. Hell's bells. For something this monumental, it was worth the risk.

She scooted closer, her breath catching as his fingers popped open the latches on the wooden box. The strange water of the lake seemed to bead and roll off the smooth black finish of the box, leaving it perfectly dry. He held it reverently; a jolt of expectation zipped from his fingertips to his scalp, making the hair all prickly. Slowly he lifted the rectangular lid, and the scent of old wood, mellow and musty, rose with it.

What was waiting for him was nothing like what he'd expected.

Nestled deep in the box on a ripple of burgundy velvet

was a single small scroll of yellowed paper curled in upon itself.

A crushing invisible weight pressed in on Colt's chest, making it hard to breathe. The edges of his vision started first to darken, then turn red. Rage boiled up inside him. He clamped down hard with his jaw, the grinding sound of his teeth filling his ears. Not the Book. Not. The. Damned. Book. "Damn filthy liar," he growled.

Lilly leaned in closer, crowding into him, glancing first into the box and then expectantly at him. "Where are the pages? Where's the Book of Legend?" Panic laced her voice.

For a second his brain stuttered. She'd known all along about what he'd been searching for, but she'd never hinted at it? He was so angry he couldn't take time to absorb this new bit of information.

"They're not here! Nothing's here but this!" He snatched the scrap of paper and crumpled it in his hand, then threw the wooden box he'd been willing to die for down into the black sand at his feet. He stood, stalking away from the box and away from the demon who'd brought him here.

"Maybe there's a hidden compartment. Something."

Colt glanced back. She'd picked the damn box out of the sand and was turning it over and skimming her fingers along it, searching. Her determination was as fierce as his.

"Leave it. It's worthless." His tone was harsher than he intended, but he couldn't control it. He wanted to tear the rocks of the cavern down with his bare hands. He wanted to punch something, preferably Winn. But Winn wasn't around.

"But what about the Book?"

Yep, what about the Book. The Book he didn't have a blasted chance in hell of finding. His lip curled into a sneer. She'd known about the Book and never let on. If she could do that, what else was she capable of hiding from him? Ironic, really. This close to Hell and he hadn't been able to find what he'd been searching for. Now he was back to square one, partnered up with a supernatural he'd vowed to send to Hell, yet as much as he doubted her, he trusted her in equal measure. Trusted her and admired her courage and strength. Hell, was even beginning to like her. Too much. It had to have taken a lot for her to give her soul to save her little sister. It had taken even more for her not to glamour him when her need was equal to his own. If she could be that stalwart and loyal, so could he. And that's the precise moment where he stopped thinking of her as Miss Arliss or a succubus, and instead as Lilly. His to protect and help, just as he'd promised.

Colt shifted his gaze to his fist. The crumpled paper was growing damp in his palm. He released his hold, letting the paper unfold slightly.

He sighed and pressed it open with his fingers. The writing was small, some swirling gibberish thing-a-ma-do. "What the hell is this?"

The weight of her small hand on his shoulder was so light he barely felt it, but it was the heat and scent of her that caught his attention as she peered around his arm. "Looks like it's in some kind of code."

"That yellow-bellied horse's ass."

"Surely you aren't talking about your father." She sounded a bit sarcastic, as if she had one she thought of in precisely that way.

"No. My brother. He sent me down here knowing it was a wild-goose chase. He's afraid of joining the Book of Legend together."

"Are you certain?"

"There's only one way to find out. We're going to jail."

Chapter 10

Both of them knew getting out of the Dark Rim Mine wasn't an easy proposition. Lilly peered back at the tunnel entrance they'd come through, which yawned like a dark open maw high above the frothing red underground lake. "Which way now? We can't go back out that way. It's blocked past the waterfall."

Colt knew she was strong, but how strong? "Don't suppose you could use your powers to take us out of here."

Lilly gave him a look that clearly said no. "That would take a more powerful demon than me. I can materialize to a place I've been to before and I can materialize small objects without a problem. But two of us? Impossible."

Colt cast a narrow-eyed glance, scanning the rock walls. "Mines always have more than one entrance. They'd need ventilation shafts. We'll find one of those and make our way out." His frown ironed out a bit. "There."

He pointed to a small, dark opening in the rock at the far end of the black stretch of shoreline. It was tall enough to accommodate them only if they crawled through it. Not by any means his first choice. He didn't like tight spaces that left him no room to maneuver. Hunters stayed alive because they thought through how things could go wrong and prepared for them. But there was no preparing for what had happened so far, especially with his changing feelings for Lilly, and he wasn't fool enough to believe it was going to get any easier any time soon.

Lilly's shoulder brushed his. Despite what they'd already been through, she still looked fresh-smelling, sweet, and womanly to him. She had a sense of humor and a dogged determination and was brave enough to stand with him shoulder to shoulder even against tough odds. If he weren't a Hunter, she could have been damn near perfect.

"Fighting our way out of the Darkin realm is far more difficult than fighting our way in, but I think I can guide us out." Lilly's voice seemed to shrivel. The haunted look in her eye told him she'd seen far more of the Darkin's ruthless side than he had, even as a Hunter.

Putting his life in Lilly's hands didn't seem nearly as horrible as it had before. There'd already been several times that day alone she could've let his ass be dragged off to Hell in the bat of an eyelash, but she hadn't. Considering how difficult it had been to find the worthless box in the first place, he didn't relish the idea of fighting God only knew what to get out of the mines. He still didn't have the pages, which meant he had more work to do once they got out. He shot her a smile, touching his fingers to her cheek. "You haven't failed me yet, sweetheart."

"You know as well as I do that nothing down here is what it appears to be." Lilly sighed, stretching her hands toward the top of the cavern, which rippled with reflected red light from the water. She fixed her gaze on the small, dark opening and started toward it.

Colt fell into step beside her. "Can't be worse than anything we faced so far," he offered, but his words were far bolder than he felt. The truth was he had no idea what they were up against. Finding the box empty except for the small scrap of paper hadn't helped. For the first time in a long time, Colt allowed doubt to creep into the fringes of his certainty.

Would he ever find the pages? And if he did, would he find them in time?

Lilly dropped to her knees, giving him a delectable view of her small, curvy backside as she crawled into the low opening in the rough rock face.

"Stop looking at my behind!"

Colt bit back a smile as he followed her. "Since it's only twelve inches from my face, hard to miss. Besides, it's a very pretty behind, Miss Lilly."

She made a rude noise. "What am I to do with you?"

"I can think of several things," he said dryly, removing his hat and unshouldering his pack. "Unfortunately, none of them here or now. Can you see anything up ahead?"

"No. Can you give me the coil illuminator?" Her voice echoed inside the passage.

He pulled it from his pack and placed it in her outstretched hand. A blue glow lit up the narrow space.

Colt gritted his teeth. In a tunnel too narrow to turn or stretch in, all they could do was crawl forward. The glow of the coil illuminator she held limned Lilly's body, its illumination not penetrating behind her. That put him in the uncomfortable position of staring at the very enticing feminine curves of her bottom shifting beneath a clinging swath of blue calico as she crawled just a few inches in front of him. If the view weren't enough to frustrate a man, being shoved in the space roughly the size of a barrel, unable to do a damn thing about his growing attraction to her, was worse. His hands and knees were scraped raw and starting to bleed, and his shaft was aching in response to watching her move.

"Stop a minute."

Lilly stopped dead in her tracks and whispered, "What is it?"

Colt gripped the hem of her skirt and ripped it awkwardly in the tightly confined space. "Here." He handed her the first strip as he went back for another. "Wrap this around your hands to protect them. This rough surface is going to shred your skin." It probably had already cut up her tender palms, he was sure. But she hadn't uttered a word of complaint.

"Thanks. Tear some for yourself while you're back there turning my dress to rags."

No point protesting that he was too manly to do so. His hands were already burning like fire. He ripped a couple more strips and wrapped his hands. "Okay. Keep going."

The cushion helped, and they both moved a little faster.

"How far does this thing go?" Colt muttered as he pushed his hat and pack just ahead of him as he moved. The tunnel narrowed, getting even more suffocating, making them crawl along on their bellies an inch at a time.

"Can't be much farther," Lilly retorted. The tunnel became a mere seam between the rocks, squeezing them as they pushed through. Panic started to pound fast and furious in his chest, thundering in his ears, as Colt realized he was stuck, unable to move forward and unable to scoot backward.

Sweat beaded his brow and upper lip, and he said, as evenly as his manic heartbeat allowed, "Stop. I can't move, I'm stuck fast." This would be a lousy way to die. No glory being buried inside the Dark Rim, his gun still in its holster, his hat in his hand.

Colt forced himself to blow all the air out of his lungs, twisted his head to the side, and pushed forward hard. The rocks scraped his ears and cheeks as he moved. A soft hand grabbed firmly around his wrist and pulled, stretching the tendons in his arm and shoulder. Damn. She was stronger than he realized. But then a lot of things about this woman weren't at all what he'd expected. She was soft, but tough.

Beautiful, but deadly. And Darkin, but not. She was caught in between, same as him. Both of them part of the supernatural that lay in between humanity and the world of the Darkin.

Colt jettisoned forward out of the mouth of the tunnel onto hard, uneven ground. He groaned, rolling over. Rocks dug uncomfortably into his back, and his skin felt dirty and abraded, as though he'd been tied behind a stagecoach and dragged to Bodie and back. "Damn. I'm glad I'm out, but remind me never to do that again."

Clack. Clack. Clack. The bluish light of the coil illuminator seemed brilliant in the inky darkness. Colt blinked, holding a hand before his eyes as they adjusted to the light Lilly held.

"You might not be so glad once you see where we are." The black ribbon about Lilly's throat moved as she swallowed hard. Death and decay lent a sickly odor to the air. She pointed a shaking finger in the direction of the cavern that opened up in front of them.

Colt looked around. "What the . . ." The floor and walls looked white and fuzzy. He sat up with a start as he realized that the floor of the cavern was covered in pale bones. Thousands of them. The rocks beneath him weren't rocks at all, but bits of skeletal remains.

He leapt to his feet, his skin too thin and uncomfortable as it suddenly shrank tight to his body. "Whatever calls this cave home is hungry." He pushed a coyote skull away with the toe of his boot, then reached out to touch the haphazardly woven sparkling white cloth-like substance covering the walls.

"Don't touch it," Lilly hissed, her voice low and insistent. "Can't you see it's a web?"

Colt yanked back his hand. Upon closer inspection, the white filaments of the thickly woven web were glistening with clear pearls of liquid. The stuff was probably sticky as hell. As Lilly moved the light about the cavern, grisly husks—animal and human—appeared from the gloom, their flesh decayed and dried like mummies. An upward glance showed more desiccated bodies suspended from the ceiling, shrouded in webbing.

"Well, there's one good thing about this." Colt placed his hat firmly on his head, then shrugged into his pack.

Lilly turned and glared at him. "How can it possibly be good? We've got either an army of spiders waiting to pounce on us or one enormous spider that's hunting somewhere else."

"No. We've got to be close to the surface."

"What makes you think that?"

He jerked his thumb at the floor. "There's no way it could have found this much food wandering into the mine aimlessly. It has to hunt on the surface and bring its prey here, where it feels relatively safe from other predators."

Lilly gazed around them and gestured to the remains dangling from the ceiling. "Based on the size of its prey, it's probably large enough to cover a lot of ground," she pointed out. "We could still be a good distance from the surface."

Colt tugged his Stetson down lower on his forehead. "Either way, we need to move."

They struggled across the uneven piles of bones, slick, shifting, and smooth beneath their feet, toward the large opening of the cavern. Twice Colt grasped Lilly's arm to keep her from falling among the macabre debris.

"Thank yo—"

Colt held up a hand and silenced her, then pointed to the funnel-like opening of the webbed cavern. The sound of skittering rocks and an unfamiliar rasping *click, click, click* was echoing in the tunnel beyond.

Colt's gun hand itched like holy hell. "That don't sound good."

They inched out farther into the mine shaft, careful not to catch themselves in the sticky web lining the walls and draped in diaphanous sweeps from the ceiling.

A glint of something shining in the darkness caught Lilly's eye and she swiveled in its direction, holding out the coil illuminator so they could see it better.

Eight soup bowl–sized eyes came into view over a pair of pointed mandibles, each as long and thick as Colt's arm and tipped with a deadly black shining fang. Their razor-sharp edges rasped as they clicked with the monster-size spider's movement. A distinctive red hourglass four feet long marked the undercarriage of its enormous globular black body. The spider suspended itself from the ceiling with long, thin legs as its eyes avariciously took in what must look like two meaty snacks.

Lilly gasped. Her body went rigid beside him, all color draining, turning her skin ashen as sun-bleached wood. Colt tugged on her sleeve. "Lilly." He said her name low and harsh. "Move!"

She didn't budge. Didn't even blink. Damn, the spider seemed to have mesmerized her; either that or she was utterly terrified. His heart sped up, his senses growing sharper in the presence of danger. The spider crept forward. Its bristled, hairy forelegs stretched out toward them, then lunged.

There wasn't time for words. He unceremoniously yanked Lilly off her feet as he wrapped a thick arm around her waist and pulled her out of range of the spider's piercing fangs.

He shoved her down the hallway, placing himself between her and the enormous arachnid, then spun back to face the monster. "I ain't heard any dinner bell yet."

With practice-honed reflexes he pulled his revolver from its holster, using one hand to fire and the other to recock the gun as fast as he could, firing off three quick shots.

From the corner of his eye he could see Lilly jerk with the ricocheting sound of each shot.

The spider bucked backward and screeched, two of its eyes blown apart. Dark liquid splattered the rock wall and dripped from the gauzy web in long, stringy black strands. One leg had been shot clean through and twitched on the ground. Great. Only seven to go.

It lunged forward again, angry, snapping fangs and giant mandibles at him. A scream tore from Lilly's throat as she huddled on the floor of the tunnel. He pulled six more bullets from his ammunition belt and shoved them in the revolver chambers as fast as he could. Marley's special bullets weren't going to stop this monster. It was too damn big. Time to improvise.

Instead of shooting at the advancing creature, he fired the six rounds at the wooden support beam over its head, sending out a shower of splintered wood, debris, and bones. The beam weakened with an audible crack and the rock it had held in place came crashing down on the spider. It screeched, writhing and still alive, but pinned down.

Lilly coughed against the dust. Colt hauled her up from the floor with his free hand. "You hurt?"

Colt knew that glassy-eyed look. Shock. Fear. She swung her head slightly from side to side, still too shaken to speak properly. "Good. That ain't going to hold it long. Can you run?"

Lilly nodded mutely, but it was all the reassurance he needed. He took her hand firmly in his and pulled her along after him.

Clack. Clack. Clack. Clack. He shook the coil illuminator hard and fast, sending a blade of blue light slicing through the darkness ahead of him. Lilly pressed her hand to her side, her breath sawing hard in and out as she struggled to keep up with him. Slowly the screeches and thrashing of the creature faded and the walls of the tunnel became barren rock once more. They took several turns down smaller shafts that veered off the main tunnel.

"I have to stop," she wheezed. Lilly sagged against the wall, her legs looking wobbly and unstable.

"The sooner we get to the surface, the better," Colt muttered. From the tightness in his forehead, he could tell the worried crease between his brows was growing deeper.

She swallowed hard, making the ribbon around her throat bob with the motion. "We're lost, aren't we?"

The hopeless, lost tone of her voice caught him off guard. He turned his piercing gaze on her. "What happened back there? For a moment I could've sworn you'd turn to stone."

"Rats and spiders. I hate them both. We didn't stay very often in hospitable places. So my childhood was filled with them skittering over me in the dead of night, but nothing this big, this terrifying."

Colt rubbed a reassuring, steady hand over her shoulder. She was still shivering. "We'll find a way out. All we have to do is pay attention and leave a trail so we know if we've doubled back." How they were going to leave a trail he had no idea. He was fresh out of bread crumbs, and leaving a trail of Marley's bullets would only be worth it if he left them *in* something. He eyed her skirt speculatively. "Do you think you could spare some more calico?"

Lilly plucked at her torn skirts. "Since I'll never wear this rag again, I don't see why not." She handed him the coil illuminator, her brows bending in concentration as she searched for the seam of her dress in the fading light. Lilly ripped off a two-inch strip from all along the ragged bottom edge of her skirt, which now reached just above her knees, and handed it to him.

He tore a small bit off the fabric and stuffed one end of it in a crack in the rock at eye level. "That should do it."

Lilly shook her head. "If you think a few scraps of fabric

are going to get us out of the Dark Rim, you're deluding yourself."

Again the hopelessness he heard hidden there made him wonder what exactly she was thinking. Had it all been more than she'd bargained for? Was she going to leave him here in the depths of the mine and hope he'd never come out again? Maybe that had been Rathe's plan all along. "I suppose you could always just materialize yourself out of here. One of us might as well get out of this in one piece." Colt squeezed his hand tight, hating that the caustic edge to his tone revealed his inner doubts.

Lilly leveled her gaze at him. "Why are you always looking for me to shoot you in the back? I haven't left your side thus far. I'm with you until we find the Book."

Damn. Double Damn. At some point he had to stop being so suspicious of her and start taking her actions as proof of her loyalties. His jaw worked, chewing over his next words. He caught her gaze, wanting her to know that his words were genuine. "You didn't deserve that. How about we call it a truce?" He held out his dirty, masculine hand to her. "You protect my back, I'll protect yours. Deal?"

She gazed at his offered hand, then placed her smaller one in his. Her touch set off a bolt of awareness in him. Her skin was pale against his tanned hide, her fingers long, slim, and feminine. She looked like a fragile thing and yet she had inner depths of strength, and a hard past that had formed her into the kind of woman he didn't think actually existed—one that could steal his heart if he let her. She lowered her lashes, a faint smile tugging at her bottom lip. "You know I only seal a deal with a kiss."

His heartbeat kicked up the pace again, but this time from desire rather than a fear-fueled rush. Using his grip around her hand, he pulled her forward into his chest. They stood toe-to-toe, the heat of her seeping through his clothing. A spicy hint of cinnamon and sweet perfume of roses rose from her, tempting him. The press of her thighs against his brought to mind far more pleasant images of what they could have been doing in the darkness. "Have it your way."

She tipped up her face and gave him a heart-melting smile that curved up at the edges just enough to make her thoroughly kissable. "Not often."

Colt couldn't resist. He brushed his mouth against the soft smoothness of her lips before pressing harder, molding her mouth to his, tasting the sweetness of her as he traced the seam of her lips with the tip of his tongue. Lilly responded in kind, opening for him. The soft silken slide of her as she explored him made him hot and hard all over.

Lilly didn't just arouse him, she brought out something more in him, not just trust, certainly, but a desire to protect her, to help her find her way back to being human and maybe even find her sister. She took his mind away from its constant drive to search for the Book. She made him wonder what it might be like to have never been a Hunter at all, to have a normal life, like his oldest brother.

He abruptly pulled away from her drugging kiss. "Pleasant as that is, it's not likely to get us out of here. We best get going again."

Lilly, her cheeks flushed a pretty pink, nodded. Colt didn't let go of her hand, and she didn't pull it out of his grip.

They walked on through the branching tunnels but didn't come back across the small scraps of blue-sprigged calico Colt was stuffing at regular intervals in crevices and cracks in the rock walls.

Lilly stopped short, pulling on his arm. He glanced back at her. "What is it?"

"Do you hear that?"

He listened more intently. Then he heard it. The faint clanking sound of tools against rock. They followed it. As the sounds grew louder, the shaft ahead began to glow with faint ruby light.

The rhythmic clanking became augmented by the hiss of steam turbines and the grind of crushing rock as the shaft ended on the edge of a rock pit inside a large cavern in the earth. Through the columns of steam Colt could see the gray, faded forms of men along the rock walls, all at work, just as they had been in life.

Hundreds of miners worked the rock that had been formed into concentric layers up the insides of the cavern with the steam-powered rock crushers working away below. Water, probably siphoned off from the waterfall they'd passed through earlier, sluiced in through iron water ducts, pouring into the boilers and filling the wash boxes where the crushed rock was rinsed to pan out the gold.

"Ghosts," Lilly murmured, her mouth so close that it tickled his ear.

"Think I figured that out for myself, thanks. They're probably the men that got trapped and died in the cave-in that closed the mine." The bad thing about ghosts was when it came to a fight, if they landed a punch it was solid as any live fist, but if you tried to hit back, you were swinging at nothing but air. They could inflict a lot of damage if you got too close. And the odds from where he sat weren't good if they were noticed. "Why in the hell are they still mining?" Colt muttered. "Ghosts don't need gold."

"They aren't mining it for themselves."

Colt turned to gaze at Lilly, his eyes asking why.

"It's for Rathe and the other archdemons. They're obsessed with the stuff."

The news that archdemons craved gold wasn't as shocking as the revelation that there was more than just Rathe skulking about as a demon lord in the Darkin realm.

"You mean to tell me there are more powerful demons like Rathe?"

Lilly nodded. "One for every archangel."

Colt swore under his breath. The stakes of keeping the Gates of Nyx closed were far higher than he'd ever imagined.

"If we can skirt around the edge of the pit, we might be able to make it through over there, without them noticing us," Lilly said as she pointed to a dark shaft opening across the cavern.

At this point Colt was game for just about any plan that got them the hell out of the Dark Rim in one piece. "Fine, we'll try it your way."

They wove along the edge of the pit, hiding behind rock outcroppings and mining cars. Lilly's footsteps made a clinking sound as she stumbled over a pile of rusted iron chain.

Colt put his index finger to her lips, warning her to be quiet.

Lilly silently mouthed back the word "sorry."

Carefully, and as quietly as possible, Colt gathered up a good length of the chain, wrapping around his fist. There was no telling when it might come in useful with this many ghosts around. Iron and salt were about the only thing useful in dispersing them temporarily, and Marley's bullets wouldn't spray the salt when fired like a hand-packed shotgun round would.

"Just stay quiet and stick with me," he said.

They were within twenty feet of their exit when a long wolf whistle of appreciation pierced the air. Suddenly, everything grew very quiet. Hell's bells.

Colt's gaze darted to find every ghost miner starting in their direction. Damn. He should have known. Lilly was a succubus. There was no way something that shouted pure sex wasn't going to catch the attention of a bunch of miners who'd been working away for God knew how long without feminine company. And that had been before they'd died.

"Going unnoticed was a good idea. But I don't think it worked," he ground out.

From the crowd of miners came two ghosts, one thin and angular and the other stout and wide with a pickaxe resting on his thick shoulder. They stepped deliberately toward him and Lilly, blocking the way out.

"Let us pass," Colt said. He rested the heel of his hand on the butt of his holstered revolver and let the chain around his left hand slip a few links so it rattled ominously.

"You can pass," the ghost answered, then licked his thick, fleshy gray lips as his pale hungry eyes shifted to Lilly.

"But not the lady," the thinner ghost said. His gap-toothed grin grew wider as his long hands flexed.

"You're ghosts! She's not any good to you."

The fatter one's eyes narrowed greedily. "Just 'cause we're dead don't mean we forgot how it works." The tell-tale bulge in his britches set a firestorm off inside Colt.

They weren't going to touch Lilly. Period. "Last chance. Move it or I'll do it for you," he growled.

The fat ghost came barreling down on him, his pickaxe held high. Colt moved on instinct. He swung the length of iron chain out like a whip, lashing straight through the miner, dissipating him into grayish mist. The axe fell with a clatter to the ground. The thin one beelined it straight for Lilly.

She held out her hands, her delicate brows pinched with concentration, and he bounced back as if he'd hit an invisible wall. The ghostly miners amassed, hundreds of them now shoulder to shoulder, pressing in on him and Lilly.

"Duck!" Colt let a few more links slip and sent the chain

spinning in a dizzying circle over his head, like a metal lasso. Every ghost that connected with the chain vanished into a puff of grayish dust. Keeping the momentum going, he reached down and grabbed her and they started inching forward toward their exit, back to back. His shoulder was burning from the weight and effort of keeping the chain moving.

"Watch out!" Lilly yelled. Colt's arm jerked back hard, nearly pulling his arm from the socket as the chain wrapped around the very real shovel hoisted by a ghost behind him. Colt whipped around, the chain slipping from his damp grip, but he kept the shovel from cleaving Lilly's skull.

Lilly blasted back four ghosts. Her skin glittered with beads of perspiration and she was breathing hard. The fight was beginning to wear her down. They were outnumbered by hundreds to one.

Colt racked his brain. "You said you can materialize objects."

"Yes," Lilly said, then grunted as she sent the ghosts coming at her bowling end over end.

"I need a bag of salt. Now."

Lilly held out both hands and closed her eyes. A ten-pound burlap bag of salt appeared at Colt's feet. He dug his fingers into the fabric and ripped the bag open. "Stand behind me," he ordered, knowing the salt would burn her as a demon, just as it would dispel the ghosts.

He threw the salt in a wide arc, the ghosts screaming as they vaporized. The silence afterward was only punctuated by the hiss of steam from the turbines below and their harsh, rapid breathing.

"We've got to get out of here now. Salt will only get rid of them for a little while. They'll be back, and we don't have time to find and then burn and salt their remains."

"I can't walk over the salt," Lilly murmured, looking at the white sparkling crystals scattered all over the floor.

Colt didn't argue. He scooped Lilly up into his arms and marched right over the salt, getting them out of the cavern as quickly as he could before the angry ghosts returned.

Chapter 11

It took them four hours of muddling around in the dark with a coil illuminator that faded in and out and required extra shaking, but they escaped the Dark Rim Mine without incident and rode Tempus back to Bodie.

Colt held fast to Lilly's hand as he kicked open the door to the Bodie jail. Raw anger throbbed behind his eyes. After all they'd been through, Winn was nothing but a damn coward hiding behind a badge and a desk. For all Colt knew he'd probably destroyed or hidden his pa's pages elsewhere. Well, now was the time for him to 'fess up.

The deep furrows over Winn's face smoothed out and his eyes clouded over with confusion as he took in their ragged condition. "What happened?"

"We found the damn door. We got in. We got the wooden box open. There was nothin' in it! Nothin' but this scrap of paper." Colt threw the yellowed bit of paper on his desk. "And we nearly got killed for our troubles."

Winn grasped it, unfolding the aged brittle parchment with care. His eyes narrowed as he twisted the paper first one direction, then the other, obviously trying to make sense of it, same as Colt had. "It's in code."

"No shit, Winn. What'd you do with Pa's part of the Book?"

Winn's gaze lifted from the page, boring deep into Colt. "I didn't do a damn thing with that Book. Pa just said to keep watch over the thing. I haven't seen it since he hid it down deep in that mine when we were kids."

Unspoken hostility eddied in the air between the Jackson brothers, making it crackle. "You're tellin' me somebody else got to it first?"

Winn's gaze shifted, landing squarely on Lilly. "Not someone, some*thing*."

Colt shifted his stance, stepping slightly in front of her. He'd be damned if he'd let Winn harm her now, especially since there was no reason to blame her. "She's been with me the whole time."

"This the demon you summoned to help you out?"

Colt gave one quick nod.

Winn huffed out a disgruntled sigh, his eyes coolly assessing Lilly from head to toe in a way that made Colt hot under the collar. He was mad as a wet hornet at Winn, but this was something that stung differently and burned hotter. Just the thought of anyone harming a pretty, burnished hair on her head made him seethe.

"You sure know how to pick 'em, I give you that," Winn muttered.

"Point is, she don't know any more about this code or the missing location of the Book than we do."

Winn picked up the scrap again, turning the page sideways, then upside down. "It's written in a circular fashion. Starts at the center like a spiral and coils outward."

"Like a spring." Lilly's voice snapped both men to look at her. "It's like a lock, and you're holding the key to the spring in the lock."

"Huh," Winn said, the one word conveying a host of

unspoken I-don't-give-a-damn-what-you-think messages loud and clear.

"So what do you think it says?" Colt pressed, the impatience giving his voice a raw edge.

"Have no clue. You're gonna have to have Marley pick this one apart."

"He's not a code-breaker."

"He's not, but Balmora is."

Colt released his hold on Lilly and pushed his Stetson up at the brim with his index finger. "Balmora?" He'd never heard Marley mention that name before.

"Some fancy-pants contraption he's been building for the British government." That explained it. Marley rarely talked about an experiment still in the development stages, especially when he was working on it for a paying client.

Colt leaned in, planting both fists firm on the scarred expanse of Winn's desk. "Come with us. If they've found Pa's Book and moved it, there's no telling how fast this is gonna unravel."

Winn shook his head, spreading his hands wide on the surface of his desk. "Can't. Got an important foreign dignitary showing up this evening."

Colt shoved away from the desk. "Can't be bothered with the supernatural when you've got such important matters to tend to, eh?"

"Don't start with me, boy. I was hunting before you were walking."

"Which is exactly why we need you to come along."

"He's right. Rathe is planning something," Lilly said.

Winn glared at her. "And I'm supposed to trust you?"

Colt stiffened, his skin heating. He'd had the exact same feeling toward Lilly at first, but she'd more than proven herself trustworthy down in those caverns. "We've got a deal. She's going to help me get the Book."

Winn's glare shifted to his little brother. "Dammit. Didn't I tell you not to give your soul for that Book?"

"I didn't. She wants our help."

Winn rolled his eyes and gave his head a small shake. "They all say that, brother."

"She wants to get away from Rathe. She wants to return to being human again."

Winn glanced at Lilly, skepticism etched in every worn line of his face. "Is that true?"

Lilly stepped around Colt. While the brothers looked awfully similar, there were distinct differences. They shared the same thick, nearly black hair and stunning blue eyes, but where Colt's were the dark, fathomless blue of the ocean, his brother's were a shade lighter. The effect was chilling.

She swallowed down hard on the lump in her throat. "No one has ever tried it before, but the way I see it, if anyone could find a way to break Rathe's hold on my soul, it would be the Chosen."

Colt grunted and scraped his scuffed brown boot over the gritty wooden floor. "Told you before, Lilly. We're not the Chosen."

Her momentary shock at him using her given name was overcome by her indignation. She balled up her fists. "You don't *think* you are. Big difference. Doesn't mean you're not."

"Either way, don't matter," Winn said, clasping his hands over the back of his head. "You two need to get to Marley on the double. I'll see what I can do about tapping into a lead on the second part of the Book for you, but I'm not going on any fool's errand to fetch it back."

"You know we're going to need more than just Pa's part of the Book, don't you?"

Winn snorted. "Now she's really got you addled, boy. They were never meant to be brought together. That's why the Legion separated them in the first place. It's too damn dangerous."

Colt shook his head slowly. "That's where you're wrong. If what I think is happening is true, then we need to get those other pieces. Pa told me this might happen." That got Winn's attention.

"We don't even know where the two other thirds of the Book are located."

"A lead is all we need."

Winn stared at him long and hard. Colt knew the moment Winn realized there was no changing the course that had already been set. He might not want to hunt, but he could help find the missing pieces of the Book of Legend.

"If I find anything, I'll send word through Marley," Winn said simply.

Colt didn't need more than that. Winn might not be going with them to discover the secrets in the code, but he was still willing to back him up, even if it meant going along in a scheme to bring the pieces of the Book back together.

Chapter 12

Overhead the noon sun gleamed a brilliant white in a cloudless field of blue. The air above the rocks and parched earth shimmered in the heat, making the cactus in Marley's front forty acres appear to wriggle.

As they approached Marley's door, Colt stiffened. In a short time he'd grown so accustomed to Lilly's presence he hadn't considered what Marley's reaction might be to her in his home. Lilly had been in step behind him right up to the front door. He glanced at her over his shoulder. "You'd better wait here."

"Why?"

"Marley Turlock is many things, but tolerant of supernaturals is not one of them."

Lilly crossed her arms and speared him with an incredulous look. The lace framing her neckline was wilted and dirty from their trip to the mine, and her hemline ragged and torn, but that didn't dampen her appeal one whit. Her skin was still flawless cream, her curls shiny, as if the dirt and grime had never touched her. She was still just as enticing, still every inch a succubus. "Surely he can make an exception."

"Trust me. I know Marley. This'll all go a lot faster if I don't get him all riled up."

She blew at an errant red curl that had dipped down over her forehead, making her lips pucker for an instant. Lust hit him in a fevered rush. Colt wanted to do much more than merely kiss her. Her red curls, a cascade of silken fire, begged for his touch. A waft of sweet roses, delicate yet at the same time seductive tickled his nose, enticing him to nuzzle along her neck. She was seduction, plain and simple, and Marley would shoot her on sight.

"Fine. But don't expect me to wait all afternoon," she muttered.

"You've got a better place to go?"

Lilly squinted up at the unbearable midday sun beating relentlessly down on them. Her skin seemed to glitter in the sunlight, but Colt knew from his own state it was perspiration. "No, but it's hot as hell out here."

"You would know."

"So just how long should this take?"

Colt shrugged. "I don't even know what this Balmora thing is, so it'll take as long as it takes. Just sit down on the other side of that wall in the shade and I'll be back out as soon as possible."

She didn't look happy, but she did as she was told. Colt waited until she was around the corner and out of sight before he rapped on Marley's door.

No one answered. He tried again. This time he heard shuffling, a thump, and a muffled curse from inside. Marley opened the door, still rubbing his shin, his goggles firmly snapped into place over his face, making him look like a white cotton-tufted bug with large brown eyes.

"Colt!" He broke into a delighted smile and gestured Colt inside. "Come in. Come in, old chap. Good to see you. I was a bit worried if you'd return the last time I saw you. Obviously you survived the run-in with Winchester."

"Yeah. Not the touching family moment one hoped for, but at least we didn't exchange lead," Colt said as he stepped inside the shaded, cool interior of Marley's home.

Marley shut the door behind them. "And the item you were seeking?" He blinked expectantly, rubbing his hands together with anticipation.

Colt scowled. "That's why I'm here. Winn says you got some special decoder machine you've been designing for the Queen."

Marley's eyes glittered. "Yes. Balmora. She's even better than Tempus, if I do say so myself. The gear ratios necessary for a true analytical engine required extensive redevelopment of the—"

Colt put his hand up, stopping Marley's inevitable long-winded lecture on things he didn't comprehend, nor had any wish to. As long as it worked, that was all that mattered. He pulled the small scrap of paper from his leather vest pocket and held it out. "Can Balmora decode this?"

Marley took the scrap of paper and peered with hugely magnified eyes at it. "Far trickier than anything I've tested her with so far."

"Her?"

Marley grinned widely, making his eyes seem even larger, if that were indeed possible. "If you're going to build something, why not do it with style?"

"Her?" Colt repeated. "Marley, you been working alone too long."

Marley pulled his goggles to the top of his head and waved his hand as if to displace Colt's suggestion as he turned and started navigating the teetering piles of stuff piled up around his home. Dust mites danced in a beam of sunlight coming in through the gap between a pair of heavily tasseled, forest green brocade curtains. An entire wall of all different sorts of clocks all shifted to noon and began to chime. The resulting tumult was so loud and discordant that Colt covered his ears.

"Has nothing to do with it, old chap. Follow me," Marley called out over the cacophony of chiming clocks.

"Sure it don't," Colt said under his breath. He followed Marley through the narrow hallway past stacks of books and canning jars full of gears and springs toward a back room he'd never been to before.

The door itself was black wrought iron, complete with a spinning combination lock on the front, like a bank vault. Marley muttered a series of numbers and directions to himself as he turned the tumblers. *Thunk. Thip. Thunk, thunk.* The bolts in the door shifted, allowing Marley to heft the heavy door open. He used both hands and had to put his weight into it. Colt knew he wouldn't accept his help, and leaned a shoulder against a nearby wall as the heavy door opened in one-inch increments.

Unlike the rest of Marley's home turned giant laboratory, this room was conspicuously bare. The jumble of materials had been shoved against bookcases and glass cabinets lining the walls. In the middle of the room was a large shape hidden beneath a pristine white sheet.

"Here she is," Marley said with great pride. He whipped off the sheet. There at an elegant polished cherrywood table sat a mechanical woman.

She was quite astonishing, a miraculous work of art. Her fine, aristocratic features were sculpted out of flawlessly smooth silver skin, with wide expressive blue glass eyes and fat copper curls caught up in an elaborate cog and jewel-work clasp. Brass lace edged a very refined brass dress, and inset on her chest sat a large red heart-shaped jewel. Every inch of her had clearly been lovingly polished until it gleamed. Marley took a large brass turnkey in hand and reached behind the elaborately carved cherrywood chair she sat in.

Colt heard the clicking of the key as Marley turned it. Inside Balmora the cogs and mechanics sprang to life, awakening the automaton, and the garnet jewel heart on her metal gown began to glow.

"Good afternoon, Miss Balmora," Marley said.

Colt was astonished when she blinked, turned her head toward Marley with recognition, and smiled. "Good afternoon, sir." Her voice was light and musical, but still had a mechanical tinny edge to it.

Colt whistled long and low. "I've seen a lot of your inventions, Marley, but you have outdone yourself. Whatever they're paying you, I'd ask for double."

Marley's dark eyes danced with excitement. "Just wait until you see what she can do, old chap." He turned back to address the decoding automaton. "Miss Balmora, we have a puzzle for you. It is in code. Can you identify the code and then translate it for us? American English, please," Marley specified. He fed the paper into a slot in the table-top in front of the automaton. Gears and clockwork hummed as the paper disappeared from view.

Marley turned to Colt and grinned like a giddy school-boy. "I've been giving her increasingly complex codes to prepare her for anything the Queen's ministers might throw at her. She's developed quite nicely."

For a second Colt thought he might have heard more than just pride in Marley's voice. Perhaps even a touch of adoration.

Balmora blinked, tilting her head to one side slightly as if she were listening to something. "It is in notation and riddle form. Language: Navaho. Processing translation for you, sir."

There was the clacking sound of typing immediately followed by a paper being fed up through a slot in the table into Balmora's metallic hands. "Shall I read it, sir?"

Marley nodded. "Yes. Proceed."

"Have tried to seal the Gates. It is no use. This piece alone will not do it. It will require the complete Book. At the height of the mountains, where legends are born and reborn from the ashes, is the eye through which we must pass to sew the tapestry of our Chosen destiny."

Marley took the page from her hands. "Thank you, Miss Balmora. That'll be all."

"My pleasure, sir." She blinked, straightened herself to sit up straight, then closed her eyes as if going to sleep. The clockwork inside her kept moving and clicking, and instead of a steady glow the red jewel heart throbbed off and on, like a slow, measured heartbeat.

Marley turned toward Colt, ushering him out into the hallway. "I'll wait until she runs down before I cover her up. Did what she decode make any sense, old chap?"

"The first part is a message from Pa. The second might take some time to figure out. I'd have to see if Remy or Winn can make sense of it."

"Sense of what?" Lilly's voice drifted up from where she stood among the teetering piles of books, papers, and machinery bits that lined the narrow hallway and cluttered nearly every inch of Marley's home, worrying a bit of copper wire between her nimble fingers. Colt's heart stuttered for a beat, knowing she was in danger.

A red light began flashing on the leather utility belt Marley kept strapped about his waist beneath his lab coat. And he whirled about. "Demon! Get down!" he shouted as he shoved Colt sideways into the front parlor room behind a table stacked tall with glass beakers, tubes, and wires.

"This'll take care of her."

Colt didn't know precisely how Marley had found the sting shooter in his mess of a lab, but he had it aimed straight at Lilly. A high-pitched whizzing sound issued from the gun. *Zzzot*.

An arc of blue electricity went spinning across the room.

A crowded bookcase directly beside Lilly erupted into flames. Marley's sting shooter seemed to be more powerful than accurate, but Colt wasn't taking any chances.

"Marley! Marley, for the love of science, stop!"

Lilly had the good sense to duck as Colt grabbed hold of the sting shooter and placed himself between her and Marley as he attempted to wrestle the device out of Marley's hands, but Marley was having none of it.

"My God, what are you doing, man! There's a demon!" He squeezed the trigger, and the high-pitched whine of the shooter preceded another blue stream of electricity arcing out randomly, bouncing off a mirror in the hallway, through the open vault door, hitting Balmora in the process.

"Balmora!" Marley jumped up from their place behind the cluttered desk, rushing to his automaton, the demon clearly forgotten in the heat of the moment. Colt and Lilly were right on his heels.

Balmora's silver skin and brass accents glistened for a second as the electricity danced in delicate sparks along her body. Marley's cottony fuzz of hair stood out straight as he touched her and got zapped for his trouble. He shook his hand, sticking his finger in his mouth, and glared at Colt. "What are you waiting for? You're the damn Hunter, go hunt down that demon!"

Lilly peeped out from behind Colt's broad back.

"No." Colt stepped back between the frazzled inventor and Lilly.

"No? No! Are you bloody well out of your mind?"

"I brought her." His tone was low and lethal, giving a clear don't-cross-me message Marley couldn't ignore.

Marley's grasp went somewhat limp with surprise. "You brought a demon? Here! To my lab? What in the bloody hell is wrong with you? Whose side are you on? Get her out of here!"

But there was little point to Marley's rant. Colt turned to find Lilly had vanished.

The quick shift from the cluttered laboratory of Marley's home to the cold pristine black marble floor of Rathe's throne room momentarily stunned Lilly. Her hairs had lifted with apprehension and her stomach swished uncomfortably at Marley's, but now a cold, clammy sensation bathed her skin and her stomach shriveled to the size of a pearl shoe button. An arc of an electric spark singeing her was nothing compared to what Rathe could do if he was displeased, and there could be no doubt he'd materialized her to his throne room for a reason.

The heat in the room made the very air shimmer, and a reddish glow lit the rugged stone walls from below as if the entire floor floated on a pool of red-hot magma. Rathe, bracketed by a Scoria soldier on one side and a chimera on the other, sat ensconced on a throne of obsidian that glittered malevolently.

Despite his dapper British-tailored coat, suit, and intricately tied white cravat, Rathe wouldn't have summoned her for afternoon tea and a bit of a chat. He wasn't the type.

"Lillith Marie Arliss, you are deliberately saving that Hunter's life. Did you think I wouldn't notice?" His long, pale finger caressed the assortment of golden shrunken head fobs that shivered on the watch chain at his waist. The deep ruby stickpin in his snowy cravat glittered like a shining droplet of blood.

Lilly suppressed a shudder. Her brain spun so fast she was certain Rathe could hear it whirring. *Think, Lilly. Think. You are smarter than this demon.* "Actually, I was hoping you'd notice," she said, rising up slowly from the floor.

"And why is that? Do you wish to be tormented?" A feral gleam glittered in the ice blue of his eyes, which quickly shifted to ominous yellow, the vertical slit widening in anticipation. The chimera beside him let out a deep lion growl. Its snake tail undulated in the air toward her, flicking its forked tongue, tasting the air for her desperation.

"No," she said, snapping her fingers and changing into a tightly cinched dark green bustled gown with a very low neckline. She smoothed her fingers down the copper and gold brocade on her underbust corset, letting her hands come to rest on the flare of her hips. "It's just rather difficult to get your attention. You're awfully busy."

He arched one thin dark brow and steepled his fingers, their tips touching the reddish slash in his face that passed for a mouth. "I see. And what is it you require?"

"He is still searching for the piece of the Book of Legend. It wasn't where he thought it would be."

"And that is why you dispatched three of my hounds, my Scoria soldiers, a lake full of naiads, and Morticia?"

"Morticia?"

"My black widow spider."

She twisted one of her curls around her finger, looking at him through the lowered fan of her lashes. "You did say to do whatever it took to recover the piece of the Book and obtain his soul, didn't you?" she said, slipping the tip of her index finger into her mouth and caressing her bottom lip. Playing the coquette with Rathe was a gamble. He'd either find it amusing or annoying. Lilly's stomach shriveled further.

Rathe tapped the tips of his fingers against the waxy pale skin of his face. His sharp aquiline nose and deeply carved cheeks made him seem aristocratic, but it was the cruel slash of a mouth and his icy eyes that showed his true nature. An archdemon lord, merciless and cold. The rancid odor of decaying flesh grew stronger as he shifted forward in his seat. The snake tail of the chimera hissed at her. "You have seven seconds to state your request. What is it you require, penny-girl?"

Lilly bowed, and stayed bent, refusing to let her rage at the hated moniker betray her. Her father had called her that, both because he hated the coppery color of her hair when she was a child and because he'd said she wasn't worth more than a penny to him unless she plied the con trade with him. She'd thought she'd escaped that dreaded name when she'd sent her father to Hell, but Rathe remembered. He always remembered. And it was a festering wound that never healed, and that he'd prod when she was most vulnerable, reminding her more clearly than ever why she wanted to escape him. "I need more time, my lord. I need to fully gain his trust."

"Impossible. The Gates of Nyx must open by the next dark moon."

Lilly shifted uncomfortably. "Of course, my lord." She glanced upward, fixating on the yellow gleam of his eyes. "But what if there was a chance not to get just one piece of the Book of Legend, my lord, but the entire thing? Every. Single. Page. Every secret, every spell, every trick that Hunters have amassed over the centuries to control and eliminate Darkin, all at your disposal."

Rathe's entire demeanor changed. He leaned forward with obvious interest. The yellow in his eyes intensified to gold, his deathly pale skin stretching taut over the sharp angles of his cheeks. The Scoria soldier fixated his glowing red eyes on Lilly and the chimera sat on his haunches, shaking its great mane. "Such a thing is possible?" Rathe asked, his voice grating and sibilant.

"Colt Jackson believes he and his brothers must unite the Book to keep the Gates closed."

The slash in Rathe's face widened into what could be called a grin, if it hadn't been so terrifying and vile. It revealed pointed, vampire-like canines amid his other pointed teeth protruding from black gums. "The fools. This is indeed most interesting." He touched the fobs again, rolling them between his fingers, and Lilly thought she heard them squeak in protest. Considering they were severed shrunken heads coated in molten gold, it wouldn't surprise her if he'd somehow managed to keep them cognizant as some extra form of torture for his own sick amusement. "And you think you can convince them to give it to you?"

Lilly deliberately modulated her voice, making it as seductive and smooth as possible as she tossed her hair over her shoulder. "Not I, my lord, but *you* could. Especially if you had an item to bargain with."

"And what would that be?"

"Colt Jackson."

"I see."

"Once he's discovered his father's portion of the Book, you could use him to get the other two brothers to give you their portions." Rathe didn't believe in the prophecy of the Chosen, had openly mocked it in his court. But deep down Lilly suspected that if they were to defeat the archdemon lord, all three brothers would need to be together, facing him as one united front.

"If they discover them in time."

"Yes."

"I grow tired of this game between us, Lillith Marie Arliss. You need more than time; what do you require for this?"

She hesitated. It was one hell of a gamble she was taking. "My freedom, my lord." Lilly waited as he sat as still and silent as stone. Her pulse pounded in a heavy swoosh and whoosh in her ears, interrupted only by the grinding sound of the Scoria soldier's rock body as he twisted his massive head to observe Rathe's reaction and the growl and hiss of the chimera as he paced about Rathe's chair.

Chapter 13

"Dammit. She's gone."

Colt's chest squeezed uncomfortably. He'd become so accustomed to Lilly's presence that the lack of it left a noticeable void. When had that happened, he wondered. Colt prayed she was close by, somewhere. If Balmora's decoding was right, he still needed her. Clearly that had to be the reason for his discomfort, he told himself.

"Excellent," Marley said with some satisfaction.

"No. Not excellent," Colt said with a little venom tainting his tone. "She's the one I summoned to help me find Pa's piece of the Book. Now I'm gonna have to find out how to fetch her back." Colt darted into the room where Balmora was, grabbed up the dust cloth, and used it to start smothering the small fire the sting shooter had started in the bookcase in the parlor.

Marley slapped his hand to his forehead, nearly knocking loose his brass spectro-whatzee-whosits goggles perched on the top of his head. "You didn't actually summon one from those books I gave you, did you?"

"Why else would I have asked for them, for some light reading?" Colt said, turning from the still-smoking bookcase and chucking the singed dust cloth to Marley.

Marley caught the cloth and shrugged. "I thought it was perhaps a research endeavor, given your line of work." He shook his head, muttering to himself about Hunters and ludicrous ideas. "So you say she's working for you?"

"For the moment. Yeah. No telling what'll happen when I turn her loose after we find the piece of the Book." Again that unfamiliar twinge started up in his chest at the thought of her leaving.

"You aren't seriously contemplating letting her go, are you? Working with the enemy is preposterous," Marley continued to bluster. "She could turn on you, lead you astray. My God, man, how do you know she isn't just a spy?" He threw a concerned glance back at Balmora, who was very still, her jewel heart void of light.

"Simmer down, Marley. She's already saved my skin more than once. And she wants help escaping Rathe in exchange for finding the Book. She wants to be human again." If Lilly were human, would she still be interested in being around a Hunter like himself? No, she'd want to find her sister. He was certain of that. But what about after she found her sister? Would she seek him out again? The thought made the ache dissipate.

Marley huffed, throwing an angry glare at the space where he'd last seen Lilly. "Demons belong in Hell."

"I agree, but that ain't going to help us find the piece of the Book, now is it?" Colt gathered up the papers that had scattered and handed them to Marley.

"I suppose not," Marley grudgingly replied. He stuffed the dust cloth under one arm and took the proffered pages with the other hand.

"But she can. You understand, Marley? If Balmora's interpretation is correct, I'm going to need her help."

Marley's nod was reluctant. "I don't envy you, old chap. The clue doesn't even say where to start."

"Remy's the one who's crafty with words. If anyone can figure out Pa's riddle, it's him."

"I suppose you plan on taking *her* to sec Remington, then," Marley said with distaste as he took the papers Colt had handed him and crammed them into an already crowded drawer. He shook out the dust cloth, noting the dark brown singed ring and a few new holes in the cloth, and laid it over a desk sporting an assortment of twisted bits of glassware connected to copper pots and long silver cylinders.

Colt didn't have time to worry about Marley or his misconceptions about Lilly. He needed to find her again and make tracks for Arizona Territory. "Thanks for deciphering the note, Marley."

"Wait. Before you go, you ought to stock up on some more ammunition and take this with you." Marley held out a metallic-looking gauntlet with a keyhole in the back of the hand and leather straps and buckles along the forearm to attach it.

"What's that?"

"Vertical Mechanical Lift."

Colt turned it over in his hand, looking at the intricate gears that ran along the slim channel set into the palm of the device. "This the thing you were using when you suspended yourself off the roof to fix the telescope?"

Marley nodded, a touch of pride lifting his lips. "The very same."

Colt shrugged, then tucked the device in his pack. "Well, you're still in one piece, so I suppose it's safe enough."

Marley handed the sting shooter to Colt. "I modified it again."

Colt took the sting shooter and tipped his head toward the automaton. "Hope it didn't hurt Balmora."

Marley's eyes watered a bit. "You know where the

bullets are stored, don't you? Get what you need. If you'll excuse me, I must see to her." He turned away from Colt and toward his beloved invention.

Colt tugged his brown Stetson down tight. He headed for the kitchen and pulled several handfuls of the special silver bullets Marley had manufactured for his pa's specialized Darkin-killing Colt revolver from one of the kitchen drawers. One by one he refilled the spaces on his ammunition belt, then headed for the door.

He'd barely made it two steps past the entrance before she materialized from the shadows. Relief washed over him in a cooling rush. She'd changed into a fresh forest green satin gown with a black and copper brocade corset that dipped beneath each breast to emphasize the swell of her bosom, the flare of her hips, and the inward curve of her dainty waist.

Colt shook a finger at her. "Don't you ever do that again."

"What? A girl can't freshen up when she's been tramped through a mine, attacked by hellhounds, and threatened by some mad scientist?" she said without heat. She smelled of a flower garden in the midst of summer, heady roses and sweet honeysuckle and fresh cool green things.

"Don't disappear like that. I gave you an order to stay outside until I was done with Marley." Sure his tone was a bit harsh, but damn it all, she'd given him a scare by just vanishing like that. He'd become far more attached to her than was good for him.

Lilly crossed her arms, making her breasts swell to the point where they almost spilled out of the confines of her gown. "Yes. But see, that's a problem. I don't take orders very well."

The creamy expanse of her plumped-up breasts tempted him to lean forward for a better peek. Colt forced himself to focus on her face. "You always hightail it off to wherever you've been when things get bad?"

She glared at him. "You know that's not true. I didn't vanish out of the mine, did I?"

"That's not the point."

"Then what is?"

Colt ground his teeth and tugged his hat down tighter. He didn't need anybody's help. Didn't want it. He'd do fine on his own. But it was more than that. He didn't want to lose her, but he had no right to keep her, and the combination made him feel at a distinct disadvantage. "I need to know if you're still gonna help me find what I'm searching for."

The disappointed moue of her soft pink lips made him feel instantly like a worm, but this was the time to use his head, not his other senses, which were far too attuned to her.

"We made a pact," Lilly said simply. She folded her hands in front of her, but Colt noticed her grip was tight, causing her flesh to form white crescents around each fingertip. Either he'd upset her or she was toying with him. Neither made him feel any better.

Colt pulled his shoulders back, attempting to preserve what little barrier there remained between them. His growing attachment to her wasn't right. Didn't matter how strong it seemed. She was a demon, he reminded himself sternly, and with a demon there were unbreakable rules. And you sure as hell didn't trust one with your heart. "Yes, I gave you a kiss, you opened the door, which means that pact is over."

"But the thing you were looking for wasn't there," she countered.

He turned on his heel and glanced over his shoulder at her. "Not your problem."

Her proud features fell and Colt caught a glimpse of the

concern shimmering in her eyes. "But you promised to help me."

"You offering another pact that don't involve my soul?"

She paused for a moment, then took in a deep, reluctant breath. "Yes. I shall help you find the piece of the Book you are searching for in exchange for another kiss."

The tension in his shoulders and chest relaxed. "Sounds good. But you don't follow orders well."

"A pact is an agreement between equals. Not a superior giving orders to an underling," she said with asperity.

Colt made a noncommittal grunt. "You seem to be able to take orders from Rathe fine enough."

"I do have a mind of my own," she countered.

"That's what worries me." He paused, tugging on his hat, making sure it was firmly in place, then checked where he had holstered the sting shooter to make sure it wouldn't go off inadvertently. He cast a cautious glance at her. "I wouldn't have let Marley hurt you. You know that, right?"

Her mouth tipped up in an almost shy smile. "Perhaps. But it seems I must admit that you were right about Marley's dislike of supernatural beings."

"Where'd you go?"

She shifted uncomfortably and cast a scathing look over her shoulder at Marley's house. "Rathe wanted to check up on my progress. Believe it or not, he wants me to help you find your father's portion of the Book of Legend."

Colt shoved his hands into the front pockets of his pants to keep himself from throttling her. He'd been stupid to feel so comfortable around her. Hell, he'd almost begun to trust her without reservation and let himself fantasize what it might be like to be with her for longer than just this mission.

"Oh, I believe it. Makes it a lot easier for him if I do the work and take the risks in getting to it so he can have you steal it."

* * *

Lilly made a sour face. She was getting tired of his contrary attitude, especially when she'd been the one almost fried by his inventor friend. "I came back, didn't I? I didn't let you die any number of times we were down in the Dark Rim, did I? I battled through and went with you to your brother's jail."

He moved so quickly Lilly could have sworn he was a demon himself. He certainly looked the very devil at the moment, his blue eyes dark and stormy. "None of which means anything if you thought you could use me to help you." He trapped her against the wall, his hands bracketing her, making her distinctly uncomfortable. She was strong, but not as strong as he was. "How about you stop beating around the bush and tell me the truth?"

"Rathe wants you *and* the Book. That truth enough for you?"

He pulled back just a fraction. "You mean it, don't you?"

"He thinks he can use the Book to permanently open the Gates of Nyx."

Colt gave a harsh bark of laughter. His strong jaw was dark with stubble and flexed as he gritted his teeth. "Good luck with that. He'd need all three to do much of anything, same as us." He had the keen-eyed gaze and muscular build of a predator. Rathe might think Colt could be easily controlled, but just looking at him, Lilly knew the truth. He was stronger, more wily, and better able to deal with the demon lord than anyone she'd ever met.

"He knows that."

The intensity in Colt's gaze changed, turning more sensual, and somehow that was far more unsettling than his hostility. The determined edge to his mouth was still there, but it had softened, begging to be kissed, and the predatory light in his eyes gleamed just as brightly.

She sucked in a breath, but it didn't do any good. She still couldn't get enough air. He leaned in closer, invading her space, the mix of leather and male determination saturating the air around her. "So are you going to get him all three portions of the Book?" The smooth quality of his voice rubbed against her skin like dark silk.

Lilly swallowed hard, her heart beating hard, but not from fear. "Tell me something. If you can send a demon back to Hell permanently, can you also rescue one?"

He leveled his killer blue gaze on her. "Haven't ever tried."

"But you could, in theory."

His brows dipped down, his mouth twisting into a seductive smile. "Yeah, I suppose."

"And would you?"

She waited a heartbeat. Then two. He purposely didn't answer her, but she saw the flicker of uncertainty in his eyes. He was at war with his own feelings, instinct raging against training and no clear victor in sight. Lilly understood the battle only too well. A similar one raged within her as well. As a Darkin she should be fulfilling her duty, getting the Book and taking his soul. But this wasn't just any man. This was Colt. And every minute she spent with him only intensified her unrealistic dreams of becoming human once more and inspired fantasies of what it could be like to actually have him as all her own.

He moved in closer, putting her on intimate terms with the firm wall of his chest. Her breasts tightened, aching as they rasped against him.

"What exactly did Rathe want with you? Surely it wasn't just to give a report." His tone grew husky as his gaze lingered on her mouth.

She turned away, unable to bear the intensity of his stare

any longer and the way it wormed down into her deepest fantasies about him. He leaned in closer, the tip of his nose skimming against her cheek and down along the length of her neck and back up again, making shivers follow in its wake. His lips brushed against her temple, his warm breath filling her ear. "Tell me, Lilly," he whispered.

His lips, warm and solid, replaced the skimming touch. A full body shiver started at the edge of her jaw and shimmied all the way down to her toes.

She turned and gasped. Big mistake. His sinfully sculpted mouth captured hers, sucking her bottom lip, his clever tongue lightly brushing against hers, the slow slide teasing and seductive. Everything in Lilly responded with heat, melting from the inside out.

The scent of leather, male, and desert wind washed over her as his mouth pressed more firmly to hers, branding her with his touch. His hand slid from the wall to cup around her rib cage, pulling her firmly against him with his palm while his thumb traced along the upper edge of her corset until it found the juncture where it disappeared beneath her breast.

With slow, deliberate strokes, his thumb caressed the outer curve toward the tip of her breast, making it peak and tighten and rasp against the dark green satin of her gown. Lilly couldn't stop herself from arching into his touch. It just felt so damn good to let herself go, and he knew exactly how to make her respond. But more than that, he touched her heart at the same time. Heaven help her, she was falling in love with him.

He broke their kiss, dragging in a ragged breath. "You certainly know how to tempt a man, I'll give you that." The low, rough words vibrated through his chest, making everything in her twist up even more, begging for that one touch that could release it all.

It took everything she had to be honest with him. "I'd be

the best you've ever had, but that wouldn't satisfy you." She knew what he didn't—this was no longer just physical attraction arcing between them, but something far more rare, far more lethal.

He ground the ridge of his erection against her. "I think I'd be willing to give it a try."

Lilly groaned. "I think the price would be higher than you're willing to pay."

"You're a demon. Don't you like taking souls?" he teased.

She looked to the right, not wanting to face him or the truth. Up until now soul stealing had been gratifying. But he was different. He was an honorable man, the first to treat her with some dignity and respect in her entire life. The first to make her desire him more intensely than any man she'd ever met. The first to make her believe that escaping her damnation and having a normal life with a man who would treat her as an equal was a possibility. The first to consider what it might be like to love a man without reservation and have him return that affection.

"If I took your soul, I'd damn us both. As good as we'd be together, there's too much at stake to risk it." *Like my heart.*

Colt blew out a ragged warm breath against her neck, the sound of a man on the edge of his control. "Risk or not, that doesn't mean I'll stop thinking about what it could be like between us." He pulled back, and the instant change in temperature from his heat against her made the aching cold spear all the way through her to her heart.

She was never going to be able to be with Colt Jackson. Not while she was still a demon and he a Hunter. And certainly not as the one woman who mattered to him most.

When her thoughts had turned in that direction, she wasn't exactly certain. She only knew that in addition to reuniting with her little sister, despite her advanced age, she now yearned for something to fill the growing Colt Jackon–shaped hollow in her heart. Lilly gave a resigned sigh past lips that were still tingling from his kiss. "So now that Marley's decoded your message, where are we going?"

He pulled his hat down low and started walking to his mechanical horse. "To see my other brother in Tombstone. Marley's machine decoded it from Navaho, but it's a riddle only Remington would likely understand. He and Pa both had that way about them. We'll ride Tempus into town and catch the train there. It'll be faster."

He held out his hand to help her up, and with reluctance, Lilly stepped forward and took it, wishing it were so much more and knowing it never would be.

Chapter 14

Tombstone. Had a real cheerful ring to the name, Colt thought sourly as he and Lilly, dusty and tired, rode into town on the Ohnesorgen Stage from Benson. That was as far as the Southwestern Pacific Railroad went for Tombstone. It had been sit on the dusty stage, rent a horse, or walk, since he'd had to leave Tempus back in Bodie. Time was of the essence and the train was faster than Tempus, but he'd paid for the convenience in different ways.

First he'd had to sit, pinned against her, in the narrow wooden train seat, her soft shoulder rubbing against his arm, with an entirely far too distracting view of the shadowed valley between her plump breasts. Even on the stagecoach, his nose filled with dust and the odor of horse sweat, he could detect the alluring floral-and-spice scent that seemed to cloak her skin. Both made him hard as a board and distinctly uncomfortable, requiring that he place his hat on his lap a good portion of the time.

Despite the jostling and bump of the stagecoach, where they'd been crammed shoulder to shoulder, three per seat facing one another, Lilly seemed to fare just fine. She looked as fresh as the proverbial daisy in her green taffeta gown accented with the copper and gold brocade corset that practically put a display shelf underneath the low-cut neckline of her gown. Colt had wanted to punch the man who'd deliberately sat on the opposite side of Lilly and was even now enjoying the display. Just remembering it made him agitated. He huffed. Succubus. Attracting male attention came as naturally to her as breathing. Didn't mean it didn't rile him up any less. Just the thought of another man's gaze or hands on her made him feel the need to hit something. Hard.

Colt pulled his hat down low against the glare of the afternoon sun as they stepped out of the hot, stuffy confines of the coach and into the fresh dry air scented with sagebrush and new wood. He offered Lilly a hand down from the coach, not trusting any other man to understand the difference between a succubus's natural powers and their own actual attraction. Once she withdrew her hand from his, she propped open a parasol, a black fringed little thing, which she seemed to have materialized upon exiting the coach without attracting undue attention.

"The sooner we get there, the better," Colt muttered. "Shall we?" He offered her his arm and they took a stroll from the stage stop at the far end of the town's main thoroughfare toward his brother's offices. Colt immediately began to understand the appeal of Tombstone for his brother. It was booming. Hell, half the buildings were new since the last time he'd been here.

On one half of Allen Street were the respectable businesses. The other half harbored saloons, game halls, and bath houses that doubled as brothels, where discordant, badly played piano music and the loud boisterous noise of the gamers carried out into the street. But that was exactly how his middle brother Remington liked to play things. He straddled the line between Hunter and normal solid citizen, between big brother and little brother, between straight shooter and maverick.

Colt kept them to the respectable side of the street, if for no other reason than he didn't need to fight off a half-dozen men overcome by supernatural urges to meet a succubus they thought they could buy for a dollar. Their footsteps echoed on the wooden plank walkway beneath their feet.

About halfway down Allen Street was Remington's building. Everything about the two-story building looked predictable and utterly normal: the brown-painted boards offset with white trim, the symmetrical four-pane windows on either side of the double doors. Only the fancy cut glass in the doors gave a hint of something different. Beneath the first-floor wooden awning that covered the plank sidewalk swung a sign on a black wrought-iron hanger. The elegant black lettering, outlined in gold paint, read BARTEL & JACKSON, ATTORNEYS AT LAW.

"He's up on the second floor."

Lilly grasped his arm, stopping him, her brow pinched with concern. "I've got a funny feeling about this."

He bet. Colt grinned. "Afraid of being with two Hunters in the same room, are you?"

Lilly cocked her head to one side and wrinkled her pert little nose, her eyes narrowing. "No. He's got something supernatural up there with him. I can smell it."

Colt tensed and sniffed the air. Lilly was right. He detected a faint whiff of sulfur, but it was overlaid by the heavier smell of black tea and vanilla. His stomach dropped in a swift dip and an itching started up in his gun hand. It'd be okay, but it wouldn't be pretty. He'd only come across one supernatural being that smelled like that. China McGee. "It'll be all right. Remy's got it under control. I think I have an idea who's up there with him."

Lilly raised a silky brow, her vivid green eyes sparkling with awareness. "Another supernatural that doesn't concern you? Interesting."

"Interesting ain't the word for it," he grumbled. "Trouble is more like it."

He opened the door for her. "He must be doing better at law than I thought. These are new." The cut leaded glass sent a splash of sparkles over the walls of the wide central staircase as they headed to his middle brother's offices on the second floor. Colt ran his finger over the smooth wall. "See they repaired the plaster too."

"Some redecorating you brothers did together?"

Colt grunted. "Small misunderstanding. Few gunshots. Nothing major." Of course it had been about China, and the fact that she was here now didn't bode well. He was already agitated enough thinking about how Remy might react both to the truth hidden in the pages of Ma's diary and to Lilly. He would either be outright hostile like Winn or attracted to her like him. Either choice wasn't putting Colt in a good mood.

Lilly stood just behind him as he opened the door with BARTEL & JACKSON painted on the glass. Lined with oak filing cabinets and bookcases crammed with volume after volume of leather-bound books, his brother's office smelled of lemon and beeswax wood polish, leather, paper, and the faint, sour, chalky scent of india ink. Colt reconsidered giving Ma's diary to Remington, especially given he didn't trust the current company.

Tilted back in the secretary's chair at an oak desk in the center of the room sat a buxom blonde. Dressed in a pale brown, fringed leather jacket, a faded blue button-down chambray shirt that stretched tight across her chest, and skintight brown leather buckskin pants, she had her dirty cowboy boots propped up on the desktop.

Whoever the woman was, she clearly had no respect for other people's possessions, Lilly thought.

"Hello, Colt. It's been a while." The way she purred the words made every hair on Lilly's body stand up in agitation.

Colt grunted with a curt nod, but Lilly noted his gaze didn't linger long and instead darted to the open doorway behind the desk. Through it stepped a man almost the mirror image of Colt, all except for the deep cleft in his chin, the shorter haircut, and the well-tailored gentleman's coat over a crisp white shirt with a red paisley vest. A small black ribbon was tied at his neck and matched his fancy black pin-striped pants.

"Did I just hear you say—" His blue eyes widened along with his mouth into a giant heart-stopping smile. "Hey, little brother!" He rushed forward and swung his arms around Colt in a bear hug that knocked a huff out of Colt. "Good to see you. Especially all in one piece."

Lilly tried to stifle her grin. She had a hard time thinking of Colt as needing to be protected by anyone.

Colt pulled out of his brother's arms. "Good to see you too, Remy." His gaze shifted over to the woman at the desk. "See you've got China working with you." Lilly noticed how his shoulders stiffened and how he deliberately avoided eye contact with the woman as if she made him distinctly uncomfortable. Considering how her gaze seemed to track his every move, as if he were a rodent to be toyed with, his attitude was understandable. Lilly didn't like the sneaky little smile playing on the other woman's mouth or the way she kept glancing from one brother to the other as if waiting for fisticuffs to start.

"Yep. Got her out of the Bisbee jail, no thanks to you." Remington nudged his brother with his elbow, but his face went soft and his blue eyes out of focus as his gaze settled on Lilly, warming her to her toes. "And who is this charming young lady? Certainly you'll introduce us."

Colt glanced back over his shoulder, his brows knitting together slightly in the center and his jaw flexing as if he'd rather do anything but that. "This is Miss Lilly Arliss. Lilly, my brother Remington and Miss China McGee. Lilly's helping me find Pa's part of the Book."

Remington pushed past his brother, purposely knocking him aside with his shoulder. He bowed slightly from the waist, never taking his eyes off hers, and lightly grasped her hand in his smooth one, brushing a warm kiss over her knuckles. "A *pleasure* to meet you, Miss Arliss." He continued to hold her hand a moment longer than propriety demanded. The air crackled with challenge between the Jackson boys.

Lilly felt her cheeks warm with a blush. There was no doubt that the brothers owned charm in spades. Colt quickly wedged himself between them, breaking Remington's hold on her hand.

"I didn't haul us all over God's creation to watch you kissing hands and sweet-talking ladies. Pa didn't leave pages. He left a *riddle*. The kind of thing you're so good at. Need you to solve it so I can go find what we're looking for and not waste any more time."

Remington turned toward his brother. "You didn't find his piece of the Book?"

Colt shook his head slowly, his jaw tight. "Nothing in the damn box but a scrap of paper with a riddle written in Navaho."

"You don't speak Navaho, let alone read it. For that matter, neither do I."

"Yeah. But Balmora apparently does."

"Balmora? You mean Marley's analytical decoder machine? You saw it?"

Colt's lips twitched. Lilly lifted her fingers to her own mouth, which tingled at the thought of how warm and firm his sculpted mouth had been when he'd kissed her. "I think he's going to have a hard time letting her go to the Queen, when the time comes."

"Her?"

"I'll explain later. Right now, can you make heads or tails of what Pa meant?"

Colt fished the page Balmora had spat out from his pocket and unfolded it, handing it to his brother.

Remington scanned the page, his lips moving as he read to himself. Remington had an equally appealing mouth, she thought. But he wasn't Colt. Colt somehow seemed darker, more powerful in an elemental way, than his more refined brother. She didn't know if it was the way his dark hair curled over his collar and ragged bits of it shaded his eyes or simply the powerful build of his shoulders.

Remington brushed his fingers back through his short dark hair. "Well, the first part is pretty straightforward. We're going to need the whole damn Book of Legend to close the Gates of Nyx."

"I figured out that part myself, thanks," Colt said sarcastically. Lilly stepped lightly around the office, running her fingers over the fine leather volumes in Remington's library, as the brothers leaned over the desk deciphering the riddle.

She cast a cautious glance beneath her lashes at the other supernatural in the room. She was surprised the Jackson brothers were so openly discussing matters in front of her, but perhaps the shifter already knew more about their search than she did.

China shared the same wildness about her that Colt possessed. Perhaps it was the predatory nature in both shifter and Hunter. Her long, honey-colored hair lay in careless abandon over her shoulders and halfway down her back and she was leaning forward, her elbows on her knees, feet braced wide apart like a man's. Her keen gray eyes darted from one Jackson brother to the other in front of her, as if they were tea cakes and she was deciding which she'd like to eat first.

The skin on Lilly's face tightened with heat and anger. *I think not.* For a moment she contemplated turning on her full charms as a succubus just to prove to the shifter that she could draw Colt's attention back to her with next to no effort. China's silver gaze locked onto hers as if she'd heard Lilly's thought. Lilly sucked in a quick breath, then lifted her chin and avoided her direct stare as she continued to inspect the books.

"At the height of the mountains, where legends are born and reborn from the ashes . . . Phoenix birds are reborn out of ashes," Remington murmured. "Legends—another word for myths and superstitions. It could be the Superstition Mountains outside of Phoenix."

"What about the eye part?" Colt pressed his fisted hand to the top of the desk. His shoulders and arms were so tense Lilly could see the ripple of muscle as he moved.

"Alone it doesn't make any sense, but see where it says sew and tapestry in the rest of the line?"

"Yeah?"

"Ever heard of the Lost Dutchman Gold Mine story going around?"

Colt snorted. "Who hasn't?"

Lilly glanced back at the men and saw that China had moved. She was out of the chair and standing awfully close to Colt, her hand resting on Remington's shoulder. She seemed to sense Lilly's stare and locked gazes with her, her lips turning into a self-assured smirk as she gave her a silent message through her eyes. *Mine. Back off.*

"Well, legend has it Jacob Waltz used the rocks called the Eye of the Needle and Weaver's Needle as landmarks to the mine," Remington said.

"So you think Pa was in cahoots with Waltz?"

Remington turned away to face the windows and shrugged his broad shoulders. Even in his expensive suit, he didn't look half as handsome as Colt, and that was saying something, but if China thought she was going to get her hooks into Colt, she had another thing to consider.

"Maybe. Maybe not. Point is that if you were looking at those mountains or Phoenix, I'd think the Eye of the Needle is the place to start."

"You're leaving something out," Lilly interrupted. She deliberately strode up to Colt, placing her hand on the broad expanse of his back, and leaned between the brothers, pointing to the paper they were looking at. Nearly in unison both brothers turned their identical blue gazes to her amply displayed charms. Colt's eyes widened a bit and he swallowed hard, while Remington colored slightly. Colt cleared his throat and gave Lilly a heated look that made her stomach quiver.

Remington's intense regard didn't make Lilly's heartbeat speed up, so she focused on him as she said confidently, "You missed the last two words." She leaned her shoulder into Remington and threw a "take that" glance at China. The shifter's eyes flashed silver, then narrowed as she spun away on her boot heel.

"Chosen destiny," Colt grumbled, crossing his arms. "So what? Means we get to choose how it all turns out by our actions."

She tilted her chin up. "No. 'Chosen' is capitalized."

"Yeah, so?"

Lilly grasped hold of Colt's arm, letting her fingers skim over the hard curve of muscle there. "Do you really think your father would have done that if he didn't mean you three boys? You are the Chosen."

Colt pulled away from her touch and rubbed the back of his neck. "Ah, come on, Lilly, don't start up with that again."

Remington chuckled. "I hate to say she has a point, but perhaps she does."

"It's your destiny to reunite the Book of Legend, and all of the Darkin know it."

Colt cast a glance at Remington. "I've got something you need to see."

"More important than the clue?"

"Could be."

"Well, let's have it, then."

Colt pulled a worn leather journal from his pack and handed it to his brother.

"What's this?"

"Ma's diary. Had it with me all this time. There's clues in there, like the one I found about Diego's map. Things that Pa should have told all of us, but didn't. Soon as you can, read it."

Behind the three of them came the clearing of a throat and the tap of a boot against the wooden floorboards. "Excuse me, hate to break up this little tea party, but didn't you say you'd need to reunite the whole Book of Legend?"

They turned and looked at China. "That clue you got out of the safety-deposit box. That's to a map that leads to one of the pieces, isn't it?" She shifted her piercing pale gray eyes between Remington and Colt.

The brothers glanced at each other. Something passed between them, though neither spoke, before they turned, united, back to China. Colt shrugged. "Could be."

China threw up her hands and growled. "Great. A bunch of idiot Hunters out to save the world and it 'could' be the key to the next piece. You know, it's a wonder that we didn't both get caught in that last heist."

Remington stepped over and leaned in closer to China. "I did tell you that I tend to be the brains of the family."

China huffed, brushed the fall of her blond hair off her shoulder in irritation, and turned away from them. Both brothers gave a lingering look at the tight spread of leather over the shifter's derrière. A simmering, annoying feeling swam in Lilly's gut. A woman in pants, shifter or no, simply wasn't decent, she decided. Why hadn't she thought of that?

"Let me know when you actually want to do something about finding what you're after, instead of just cackling about it like a bunch of old hens," China threw back at them as she stared out the window.

"I think your analysis of the riddle was wonderful," Lilly said to Remington, grasping his arm and finding it not nearly as thick as Colt's beneath her fingers.

Remington turned back to her and gave her a sinful grin that made even a succubus take a second long look. "Thank you. Nice to know someone appreciates my efforts."

"Oh, I'm glad you can make sense of it," Colt said gruffly. "But that doesn't change the fact that we still don't have a single piece of the damn Book in our hands."

"True." Remington grasped and held the lapels of his long coat as if he were in court debating. "But we do have a good lead to the second piece. The clue in Diego's safety-deposit box starts just outside Tombstone."

Colt took off his Stetson and smoothed the edges of the firm felt brim between his fingers, then locked gazes with his brother. "We're running out of time, Remy. I can't go to Phoenix looking for Pa's part of the Book and go on a hunt for the piece Diego heard about at the same time."

Remington glanced over at China. "What if China and I were to go after it?" China shifted, cocking her head to listen in, but refusing to face the three of them.

"You'd do that?"

"I'd be willing to sacrifice a few weeks in the office for you if it meant saving the world," he answered, his words laced with sarcasm.

Colt gave him a brotherly slap on the shoulder. "That's mighty big of you, Rem."

"Nobody asked me if I'd be willing," China interrupted as she turned away from the window and strode slowly up to the brothers, positioning herself between the Jacksons and directly across from Lilly.

Lilly glared at her. Didn't the shifter know when to back down? "Do you have any idea of what will happen if you *don't*?"

China glared back. "The end of annoying Hunters?"

"How about the start of a new world order, featuring a sadistic archdemon lord at the helm?" Lilly volleyed back.

China stood up a little straighter and glared at Remington. "Well, why didn't you say so?"

Remington put up his hands in defense. "I just found out, like the rest of them." He jerked his head toward the window. "What the hell is that nois—?"

A mixture of screams, the whinny and galloping of spooked horses, and the thunderous crash of wood splintering came from the street outside the office. A shadow darkened the interior of the office. As one they ran to the windows.

Lilly had never seen anything like it. "What *is* that . . . thing?" she demanded of Colt.

"It's a dirigible, a class A, I'd guess from the size of it," Remington answered over the din coming up from the street. The silver fabric skin of the giant dirigible, at least two hundred feet long and fifty feet across, glittered in the afternoon light as it descended over Allen Street, scattering the citizens and animals below.

"That better be good news," Colt said as he whipped out his revolver and cocked the hammer back. "I've just about had my fill of bad news."

"You ever seen that insignia before?" Remington pointed at the red castle turret bracketed by black bat wings emblazoned on the side of the dirigible.

"Nope. You?"

Remington shoved back the edge of his long coat and pulled his gun from his hip holster. "You packing silver?"

"Marley's special bullets."

Remington nodded. "Then let's join the welcoming party, shall we?"

Lilly grasped Colt's shoulder. "I've seen that insignia before. That's vampire. European or Russian royalty."

"You tellin' me we got a vampire nobleman just deciding to drop in for a visit?" Colt grumbled.

China snickered, crossing her arms. "Since when would that be so strange for you two? You are Cy Jackson's boys, after all."

Lilly pointedly ignored her. "Based on the size of their dirigible, I'd say it's either a very small vampire nobleman with a very big inferiority complex or an entire battalion of vampires."

"Have any idea which royal house it might be?" Remington asked.

Lilly squinted in thought. "Could be Petrov, or the house of Drossenburg. Both have bat wings in their insignia."

"Nothing like a little subtlety," Colt muttered. He eyed Remington and knew his brother was thinking the same thing he was. Colt turned toward Lilly and China. "You two stay put. We're going to check this out."

"And miss all the action? No, siree," China spat back, her face hard with determination. In a flash her form began to change. It was like looking at a watercolor portrait that suddenly had water poured over it. Everything grew smudged and shapeless for a moment as the particles rearranged themselves into the form of a great golden mountain lion. The mountain lion roared, baring an impressive set of white canines, and everyone took a big step back.

Lilly was pressed against the wall, her smooth, silky skin a definite shade paler than normal. Maybe she'd never seen a shape-shifter like this before. Only a desk stood between the two of them, and the big golden beast began to pace Remington's offices, its head bent low and ears pinned flat to its enormous head.

"If she wants to go out and greet the vampires, I think you ought to accommodate her," Lilly offered, a tremor in her voice.

Colt grimaced. He'd seen China transmogrify enough times to no longer find it impressive. She was such a damn show-off. He pointed at the cougar. "Fine. Come along, but don't attack unless they provoke. Got it?"

"We need to know exactly what we're dealing with first," Remington added. The big cat growled low and deep and blinked in acknowledgment.

"We'll be right back," Colt said to Lilly, then opened the office door.

"Unless there's trouble," Remington said with a smile, "then we'll be back in about thirty minutes."

Chapter 15

Colt cursed under his breath. Vampires. He hated vampires. They were too damn unpredictable and a bit too uppity for his taste. The only thing Colt did like about vampires was that they weren't around fifty percent of the time. Through the leaded glass doors they could see the dark shadow of the dirigible on the street. A dark shadow meant the sun was at its zenith. No chance they'd be coming out, unless they were fully covered in protective clothing. So why park the thing smack dab over the center of town in broad daylight instead of waiting for dark? Clearly this wasn't an attack.

"What do you reckon they want?" Remington muttered as they clomped down the stairs, guns at the ready, the golden mountain lion trailing behind them with soft padded thumps.

"Hard to say. But make no mistake, they'll want something," Colt answered as they swung open the fancy doors to the sidewalk. "You know vampires. They *always* have an agenda."

A wash of dry heat, smelling of horse, dust, and the oily scent of creosote, tightened the skin on Colt's face. It shimmered in the air, distorting everything beyond the massive shadow of the dirigible overhead that blotted out the desert sun.

A ladder, constructed of rope and wooden rungs, hung down from the lowest deck of the airship. It swung perilously close to the building, threatening to break a window or two. Colt shaded his eyes with his hand as a dark form emerged, then started to descend the swaying ladder. He narrowed his eyes against the backlit shadow, but couldn't make out who or what it was, though from the shape and the boots it looked to be a man.

"About time you made it out," a familiar voice shouted. "I was beginning to wonder if Marley had told me wrong about you coming here." *Winchester*. A pair of tight-fitting, dark-lensed brass goggles obscured his face, and he was wearing his black oilskin duster and his favorite black Stetson.

The coiled tension in Colt's shoulders and back slipped away as easily as taking off a coat. He slid his revolver back into the holster just below his hip, the weight of it as comforting as Winn's voice. "What in tarnation are you doing on a vampire dirigible, Winn?" Colt called out.

China rubbed her furry cheek and chin up against Colt's leg and he shooed her off. She answered with a low rumble in her chest and padded away to sit closer to Remington.

Winchester made it farther down the ladder and hopped the last few feet to the ground. The dust billowed up in a cloud around him as he pulled the dark goggles down to rest around his neck. "Was made an offer I couldn't refuse."

Remington gave their older brother a narrow-eyed look, glancing upward at the dirigible. "You in trouble?"

"No. Not yet. Seems the vampire royalty in Europe thinks they could use our help in tracking down a missing third of the Book. The Contessa says they sent her here to request our assistance."

"Who *they*? Vampires? They want *our* help?" Disbelief tinted Colt's tone.

Winn shrugged. "Simple matter of survival. If Rathe wipes out humanity, their food supply disappears."

Remington grimaced and Colt saw his hands tighten reflexively on his guns. "Hardly seems like the best of reasons for us to forge an alliance with them," Remington muttered more to himself than his brothers.

People were beginning to peek out from behind their closed doors. Across the street the tinny sound of a piano started up again. As odd as the dirigible was, nothing could get the hardy souls of Tombstone ruffled for long. A gust of wind blew, kicking up dust along the mostly deserted street and making the rope ladder sway. Colt peered up at the windows to Remy's office and saw Lilly silhouetted there, looking down at the unfolding tableau on Allen Street, her arms crossed, nibbling her lip.

Of course, who were he or Remy to judge Winn? Colt cast a glance over his shoulder at China, who was now cleaning her face with a large paw. He was working with a damn demon, and Remington had paired up with a shapeshifter. Their pa would be twisting in his grave if he could see his boys working side by side with the very supernaturals he'd trained them to slay.

"Considering how little time we've got, if Marley's calculations are correct, I don't see much of an option. If we want to discover where all the pieces of the Book have been hidden, we'll have to split up," Winn answered. "You two any closer to decoding Pa's message?"

Colt caught Remington's gaze for just an instant, then turned his attention back to Winn. "Remy thinks it's got something to do with either the Weaver's Needle in the Superstition Mountains or a place called the Eye of the Needle on the outside of Phoenix close to McDowell."

Winn rolled the sharp, waxed end of his mustache between his fingers, his dark brows bending together in concentration. Colt could almost see the gears spinning as he calculated in his head. "Phoenix," he paused for an instant. "I could get you there in about an hour."

Raw-awrr. From behind them the mountain lion growled, and Winchester gave it a pointed look. "What is that? And what is it doing here?"

"You mean *who* is that," Remington corrected him.

Winchester nodded with understanding. "Shifter?"

"China McGee," Colt and Remington said in unison.

Winn's eyes widened slightly in recognition and his gaze darted to Colt. He at least had the decency not to let his jaw drop. "Not the same one who—" He waved his hand as if shooing the thought away. "Never mind. I don't want to know."

Remington tried to hide his amused smile, but Colt saw it and punched him in the arm. That was the thing about brothers. They never let you forget anything, especially if it was embarrassing, and his first run-in with China had been a whopper, leaving him buck naked and tied to a bed. That had been several months before she sought him out dangling information about Diego's safety-deposit box in front of him.

"It wasn't my fault," Colt growled. *Raw-awrr* the mountain lion growled again in retort.

"She begs to differ." Remington holstered his guns and flipped his long jacket back over them. "Despite that, she's agreed to go with me down to follow the clue Diego left about the map in Mexico."

Colt gazed up at the black wings of the sigil on the dirigible. "You sure the Contessa would be all right with extra company?"

Winn smiled, and it lifted the ends of his mustache. "We already have Tempus on board. Thought we might drop it off for you. We're flying to Europe."

"And now Phoenix is on the way to Europe?" Colt knew it was actually northwest of where they were now, but if Winn and the Contessa were willing, it'd be a hell of a lot shorter trip than taking the train and a lot more comfortable than him and Lilly riding Tempus double.

"It could be. Are you up for it?"

Colt nodded. There was no use wasting time. "Let me go and fetch Lilly down here from Remy's office and we can get going."

Winn's face darkened. "You still hanging on to that demon?"

Colt pulled back his shoulders a bit and set his jaw. Winn had a hell of a nerve throwing it at him when they all had uneasy alliances to deal with at present. "She's with me until we find Pa's part of the Book."

The look in Winn's eyes changed. There was only so far he could push as a big brother, and Colt had long ago passed the point of taking anyone's advice but his own. "Just watch yourself," he said simply.

The tension gone, Colt jibed back, "Look who's talking. You better consider wearing extra starch in your collars. You might need it, considering the company you're keeping."

Winn's mouth tipped up at the corner. "Fair enough, little brother. Go fetch your demon and let's be on our way."

Colt took the steps two at a time back up to Remington's office. It occurred to him that in a very short time, he'd stopped thinking of Lilly as a demon at all, and as, well, Lilly. Not a mortal woman, but not a supernatural being to be destroyed on sight either. Somehow she'd wormed her way into the no-man's-land between the two and straight into his heart.

If there was one thing Colt knew, it was that gray areas tended to be very dangerous, even deadly. Black-and-white always made quick reactions born out of gut instinct easier, and therefore safer. With Lilly he was treading dangerous waters in more ways than one. And he sure as hell didn't know how to swim.

He opened the door to Remington's office. Lilly's curved silhouette was outlined in the window by the light. The bronze and copper threads in the brocade of her corset sparkled and the sunlight turned her hair into a fall of molten fire down her back. Colt's breath hitched. He inhaled the scent of spicy sweet, warm female flesh and cleared his throat. Damn, she was one hell of a woman. "Ready to go?"

She turned, her eyes a bit wide, her lips curving into a tempting smile. "You weren't jesting. That really did take less than half an hour." She jerked her head in the direction of the dirigible outside the window. "I notice it's still here. Did you get rid of all the vampires, then?"

"Nope. We're hitching a ride with them."

Her mouth dropped open and she thumbed over her shoulder. "On that?"

Colt nodded and reached out to take her hand. "Yep. Let's get going."

Lilly shuffled back, clasping her hands behind the small of her back just above her bustle. "Oh, no. No. No. No. You didn't say anything about air travel."

Colt couldn't resist teasing her. "Afraid of heights?"

The tremor in her lip was all the confirmation he needed that it was no teasing matter. His chest tightened with regret. Damn. He hadn't meant to upset her. Colt walked toward her slowly, like he would a skittish mare, keeping his voice steady and soothing, his fingers a gliding touch up and down her arm. "It'll be all right, Lilly. I'm not going to let anything happen to you. You can trust me to look after you."

Her eyes sparkled with unshed tears. His stomach clenched tighter and he hoped she wasn't going to cry. He wasn't sure he could handle that. Considering how very real, and debilitating, his own fear of water was, he should have known better than to joke about this. Her fear was clearly very real to her.

"It'll only be an hour. You're a strong woman. Think of all we've already made it through. This can't possibly be as bad as three hellhounds or that spider."

She gave him a tremulous smile.

"I know you can do this." Colt wrapped her into his arms. Lilly laid her head down on his chest. Her heart was beating hard and fast, but with fear, not desire. Colt's own heart recognized the frantic pace.

He stroked her hair, doing everything he could think of to soothe her frayed emotions. "I'll be right there beside you the whole time."

Lilly lifted her head and stared into his face, her eyes glistening with unshed tears. "I'm sorry to be such a milk-water miss about it, but I just—" Her voice cracked and her throat moved as she swallowed. "When I was very small my father told me to climb to the top of a tree or I wouldn't get to eat for a week. I was terrified of heights, but I did it, knowing it would be worse if I didn't. And while the crowds gathered and discussed how to get me down, he picked their pockets. In the end, I was up there, petrified, my fingers turning numb, for four hours, not knowing if I was ever getting down. I truly believed I was going to die up there."

Colt winced. "Sounds like a character from a Charles Dickens novel."

"Unfortunately, not much better," Lilly said as she shrugged, but her shoulders sagged a bit more, curving into him, absorbing the solace he offered her. It was tempting as hell to just hold her, comfort her, and let them both believe he could and would protect her from anything, that they could freeze time and stay in each other's arms without the rude intrusion of the world, but he knew it was impossible.

She wasn't a real woman—not yet. Any ideas he had about living a life beyond his quest for the Book were purely fantasy. She was still tethered to Rathe, and Rathe still wanted his head as an ornament for his watch chain. Winn and their fast one-way airship ride to Phoenix were waiting, and their time to find Pa's part of the Book was dwindling fast.

"We really should go," he said softly into her hair.

Lilly raised her head, her gaze falling to what lay outside the windowpane. She heaved a resigned sigh. "What's the worst that could happen? It's not as if I'd die if it did indeed crash." Resolutely she slipped her hand in his and he squeezed it tight, although her comment did give him pause for thought. Just how reliable was the dirigible? He'd never actually been on one before.

They tramped down the stairs and out into the bright Arizona sunshine. Colt didn't miss the long, lingering gaze Remington gave Lilly or the deep, throaty growl that rumbled around China's pursed lips, even though now she'd transformed back into her human female form.

Winn had snapped the dark goggles back into place, the brass edges of them glinting gold in the afternoon sun. He dug deep in the pockets of his duster and fished out two pairs of similar goggles, handing one to Colt and the other to Lilly. "You'll want those once we get up in the air. The sun seems even brighter up there, and there's some dust."

Lilly and Colt dutifully pulled the goggles on, and Colt made sure his hat was down good and firm on his head.

Winchester started up the rope ladder and Colt prodded Lilly to follow.

"You can't climb up after me. You'll see up my dress."

He grinned. "Better me than half the population of Tombstone, don't you think?"

She nibbled her lip between her teeth.

"I just figured you'd feel safer with one of us before you and one of us after you. That'd be twice as many hands to catch if something happened. But you're welcome to climb up after me if you want."

Her lips twisted into a little moue of displeasure but she grabbed hold of the rope ladder. "Have it your way."

Colt chuckled. He could only dream of having his way with her. It wasn't ever going to happen. "Keep climbing and don't look down and you'll be just fine," Colt directed.

Colt leaned over and took Remington's hand, giving it a good hard shake, then pulling his brother to him. "Be careful. And don't trust the shifter," he said into Remington's ear.

Remington pulled back and nodded. "Don't do anything I wouldn't do up there."

"Well, that just leaves me open for all kinds of things, now don't it?" Colt's gaze drifted to China for an instant and he saw a longing there, mixed with enough anger that he didn't envy Remy one little bit. He'd rather take his chances with a succubus than a shape-shifter any day. He grinned. "Happy hunting, brother."

He scrabbled up the rope ladder, giving particular appreciation to the view he had of Lilly's curvy derrière. The rope ladder swung in the breeze and Lilly gave a high-pitched squeak, but she continued climbing.

Colt grasped onto her ankle to steady her and she nearly kicked him in the face for his trouble. "You'll be fine. We're almost there." The broad silver expanse of the dirigible's underbelly looked even bigger up close. Colt could see the individual ribs that formed the frame beneath the stretch of the fabric just above the broad, flat expanse of the gondola bottom only ten feet or so above his head.

Winchester disappeared over the edge of the gondola deck for a second, then leaned over to offer Lilly his hand. "Hold on and I'll help you up."

Colt's hold loosened out of shock and he slipped a little on the ropes. He made a mental note to stop gawking at the airship and hold on tighter. Winchester had never offered a helping hand to any supernatural before. Not that Colt could remember, at least. There must be something all-powerful amazing about the vampire Contessa to have changed his attitude so drastically. A mixture of worry and curiosity swirled in Colt's gut. His arms burned with the effort of climbing. He sincerely hoped the vampire hadn't glamoured his brother.

Lilly's tiny black button-up boots disappeared over the edge as Winchester helped pull her onto the deck. Colt kept climbing. He waited for a few seconds to see if Winchester was planning on helping him up as well. "Hello? Anybody still up there?"

Winchester leaned over the edge, his goggles pulled down loose around his neck. "What's taking you so long, little brother? You're holding up the circus."

Colt grumbled beneath his breath and reached the top of the ladder, then used the last bit of strength he had left in his arms to boost himself through an opening in the half wall surrounding the polished teak deck of the dirigible's gondola. For his trouble he came nose to toe with his brother's boots.

Winn looked down at him with a genuinely amused smile. "Took you long enough," he chided.

Colt pulled the goggles down to his chest. "If you wanted me up here faster, you could have helped."

"And risk making you look bad in front of these lovely ladies? Not a chance."

Colt glanced to the side and saw the tips of Lilly's scuffed and dusty little black boots right beside a pair of knee-high black boots that were polished so highly they gleamed like Oriental lacquer. His gaze traveled up an equally shiny dress of taffeta the blue-black color of raven wings with a tightly nipped waist, puffed shoulders, and a high neck to find a pair of piercing whiskey-colored eyes peering back at him. The woman's dusky beauty was both dark and alluring, but the undercurrent of danger surrounded her like a cloud of expensive perfume.

"Another Mr. Jackson, I presume?" she asked. Her Eastern European accent made "Jackson" sound more like "Yakson" to Colt.

He sprung up from the floor and dusted off his hands on his denim pants before he took her gloved hand, covered in fine black kidskin, and kissed it lightly on the back. He flashed her a smile. "The youngest, and the most handsome, at your service, your ladyship . . ."

Winn unceremoniously took the young woman's gloved hand out of Colt's. "Lady Alexandra Porter, Contessa Drossenburg," he said, his tone tinged with a ripple of irritation Colt could feel, "my *little* brother, Colt Jackson." Colt didn't miss Winn's emphasis on "little" as if it somehow referred to his anatomy and not just the age difference between them.

"So this is the Contessa." She had to be an old vampire to be out this long in the bright desert sunshine even if the whole gondola hung in the perpetual shade of the dirigible's balloon.

The woman gave the slightest inclination of her head. "It seems we are to transport you to Phoenix, along with your charming companion." Her voice was like warm rustling silk, smooth but husky and inviting at the same time.

"Yes, we're much obliged, ma'am, um, Lady Drossenburg," Colt corrected himself, unsure of exactly how to address a vampire noble.

Her full, dusky, mauve lips curved into a sensual come-hither smile. "It is my pleasure to help the Chosen," she answered, then turned away from him without missing a beat, as if she were used to being superior to those around her and his thanks a foregone conclusion. Colt bristled just a bit. Yep. No doubt about it, she was a vampire all right. Cocky, insufferable bloodsuckers.

Her head snapped around, her tawny eyes narrowing in warning as if he'd said it out loud rather than merely thought it. She looked down her long, aquiline nose at him. "Fair warning, sir, this ship is filled with vampires. And we can hear your thoughts as clearly as if you'd spoken them out loud."

Colt gulped back a sudden uncomfortable swell in his throat. "Yes, your ladyship."

She gave him a curt nod and turned back, heading for the large intricate Tiffany stained glass double doors that adjoined the deck. The motif of the red castle with black wings swung past Colt's nose as Winn opened the door to let the ladies enter the interior of the dirigible first.

"Mind your manners, boy. No sense in offending the vampires before we know if they can help us find the missing part of the Book," Winn whispered harshly into Colt's ear as he passed.

The top level of the dirigible looked surprisingly modern, like a plush hotel lobby, surrounded by windows. Huge potted palms, their long, fringed green boughs ruffled by the breeze coming in the open doors, broke up the large open space. Heavily stuffed and elegantly carved

chairs and settees were grouped like small parlors for
gentle conversation or tea. Underfoot a thick oriental car-
peting in rich burgundy and gold interspersed with the
black points of the vampire's crest muffled their steps.
There was even a roaring fire in the grate of a marble fireplace at the far end of the room.

Colt couldn't help himself. He was drawn to the huge
fireplace. Stone cherubs held the ornately scrolled columns
aloft. Upon closer inspection he saw the cherubs had fangs.
A small shiver slithered over his skin and he took a quick
step backward. A fire. In the air. It would certainly give
Marley a conniption to have missed it.

"Fascinating, isn't it?"

The familiar voice startled him. "Marley?"

The inventor grinned. "So good to know that I can oc-
casionally surprise even you Jacksons," he said with
amusement.

"What are you doing here?"

"Your brother and the Contessa offered to assist me in
delivering Balmora to Her Majesty."

Colt's gun hand itched and a slight whiff of sulfur made
him draw his revolver and cock it in one swift motion,
pointing it an inch from the center of the fake Marley's
forehead. "Who are you really?"

Marley sighed dramatically, rolling his eyes, and suddenly the image smeared and shifted, the white cottony hair
growing longer, blond and silky, the body turning taller and
curvaceous. "What gave me away?" China asked.

"First, Marley don't like supernaturals, so I seriously
doubt he'd take an offer of riding aboard a vampire's dirigible. Second, I think it's going to take half of the Queen's
army to pry Balmora out of Marley's hands. He's not going
to give her up willingly. Third," he wrinkled his nose, "I
can still smell the sulfur on you."

"So I'm a little rusty," China groused with a shrug.

"You're sloppy. There's a difference. You should know who you're impersonating better than that. And you didn't answer my question."

"I attached myself to the ladder as a mouse when they hauled it up. Remington wanted to make sure it wasn't a trap. And, for your information, at least I'm not heartless like you. I can't believe you left me behind."

Colt turned back to the fire so he didn't have to see the wounded look in her eyes and the angry set of her mouth.

"Look. If I'd had any chance of getting us both out, I would have. As it was, Remington came to get you. If anybody could talk you out of that jail cell I knew it would be him, not me."

"Regardless, you still owe me." The petulance in her voice left no doubt China intended to collect on the debt. "And by the way, I'd watch that demon if I were you. She's already got you hooked."

Her assessment rankled and Colt didn't feel like discussing it, especially not with China. "Tell you what, you protect my brother's back if you two go out searching for Diego's map and make it back, then we'll talk about what I owe you."

A low growl started deep in China's throat. For a moment he thought she was going to shift, then he sensed the female warmth standing right behind him and caught a whiff of Lilly's unique fragrance in the air. Damn. Caught between a succubus and a shifter. Not a good place to be for a Hunter. And a hell of a place to be as a man.

"We'll talk when we get back," China said between gritted teeth, then turned on her booted heel and strode off across the lobby of the airship, the fringe on her jacket swinging with the motion of her hips.

"What did *she* want?" Lilly asked, her tone as bristly as an annoyed porcupine.

"Difference of opinion about a job we did a while back. Thinks I still owe her."

"Certainly sounded like more than that."

"Can't always trust that a supernatural is going to stick to their word."

"Or a Hunter, for that matter," she said with some bitterness.

He snapped his gaze to her and stared at her hard. As much as he hated to say it, he needed to clear the air between them before anything happened that was as big a mess as the misunderstanding that had somehow happened between him and China. He needed to make her understand.

"I'm not going to let you torment my brothers."

"Excuse me?"

She had the temerity to look surprised at his comment, which made Colt feel he needed to be even more direct. "We had a pact. You agreed not to take my soul. But you didn't say nothin' about leaving my brothers alone. Two out of the three Chosen wouldn't be bad. I suppose it would satisfy Rathe. Except nothing ever does."

"What are you talking about?"

Now his skin was starting to itch with irritation. She still wasn't getting it. "I saw the way Remy looked at you. And the way you looked at him."

"Yes, normally one looks at the other person with their eyes. I believe that's rather mandatory."

Colt cursed under his breath and glared at her. "No. He *looked* at you—undressed you with his eyes."

The angry lines on her face softened with understanding, the scent that cloaked her growing more pronounced like roses in the summer sun so that it filled the air around him. "Think about it, Colt. It's part of my allure as a succubus. Some are just more immune to it than others. Your brother is mortal. If he hadn't reacted in some way, we'd have known he was a corpse, or worse yet, a vivified corpse."

"That explains him. What about you?"

The angry flash in her eyes reignited. "Me?"

"You were *looking* at him too, hell, rubbing up against him like a damn cat. China even noticed it."

Her lips pulled together into a tight little twist as she paused for an instant, sighed, and closed her eyes. When they opened she seemed far more serene. "While your jealousy is quite flattering despite it being Neanderthalic, it's misplaced. I've always been fascinated by the Chosen. You and your brothers are all part of that mythology, whether you wish to accept it or not. And speaking of the shape-shifter—"

"So you were admiring him like a museum piece? Is that what you're telling me?"

"Just how close were the two of you during your brief association?"

The fact that she had completely changed subjects and was back to hounding him about China was not lost on Colt, but put him on the defensive nonetheless. He straightened, turning back to face the fire, trying to resist the urge to reach out and touch Lilly. "Close enough to know better, and distant enough not to care."

"So it's worse than I thought."

His gaze darted to her. "What's that supposed to mean?"

"The shape-shifter fancies you."

"What?"

She waved her hands in a fluttering motion as if stirring curls of incense to disperse them. "The air was simply saturated with the smell of it. Only now she loathes you as well. Which makes her attraction to your brother even more complicated."

Colt's shoulders sagged a bit. It was true. All of it. How

was it possible she had guessed? "You got all of that out of one sniff?"

Lilly crossed her arms, making her bosom swell in dangerous proportion over the top of her gown. Colt tore his gaze away from the soft swell of creamy skin and deliberately focused on the flickering blue parts of the flames dancing in the fireplace. "Call it a gift, or a curse, depending on what side you're on."

"And what do you call it?"

"Doesn't matter, because I can tell all the same exactly what's going on." She turned and walked away from him, avoiding the windows on the opposite side of the dirigible, to sit in a chair as far from him as she could, her back ramrod straight.

Colt knew better than to follow. He just stared at her graceful silhouette outlined by bright light streaming in the windows, feeling completely out of his element surrounded by supernaturals, suspended in the air over the desert.

There were things about Lilly he just didn't understand. How could she read him so easily when she'd only been in the room with him, China, and Remington for less than a half hour? Besides seducing men to surrender their immortal souls, what other powers did she possess as both a demon and a woman? And exactly how tied to Rathe was she?

While he felt he could trust her, given she'd been completely blunt about Rathe's intentions and stayed with him thus far, he wasn't absolutely sure. He hadn't trusted anyone other than his brothers and Marley in so long that just contemplating it seemed foreign. And if that weren't all enough to confuse a man, his interest in her had turned from one of mere lust-fueled attraction to wanting to protect and help her in her quest to become human and find her sister. He actually cared, dammit.

Then a thought burned through him faster than a lightning bolt: he might actually love her.

Colt turned away, clenching and unclenching his hands, totally unsure of how to handle the situation, and went searching for Winn. When in doubt it was best for a Hunter to focus on his work.

The airship was divided into three different decks, each dedicated to a different purpose. He took the stairs and went from the upper observation and dining deck down below to the secondary deck divided into long halls leading to what he guessed were individual sleeping cabins, and ended in a cargo hold where he found Tempus secured to the floor by ropes.

Beneath that, at the base of the gondola, he found the gas jet fires that heated the air inside the balloon for lift and ran the steam turbines for the steering props. It was so loud and hot, beads of sweat trickled down into his eyes. Colt swiped them away with the sleeve of his shirt.

"A marvel, is it not?" He turned to find the Contessa. The light from the flame shooting upward over the gas jets made the row of highly polished gold buttons along the left side of her gown glow.

"Is this where the fire comes from in the fireplace on the upper deck?"

She smiled. "Very astute of you."

"But don't you find hot air more limiting than the lifting aether?"

"More limiting, perhaps, but far less flammable."

Even though the conversation was totally benign, Colt was getting uncomfortable around the vampire. He'd had one too many close encounters where his neck had been on the line, literally. "Do you happen to know where my brother is?"

"Of course. I shall show you."

As they walked, the Contessa's skirting and bustle shushed with each step. "Tell me, Mr. Jackson, why is it you detest vampires so?"

He stiffened slightly at the direct nature of her question. "I guess for the same reason all Hunters do. You feed on humans."

"But we were all human once. Does that not count for something? Surely we can find common ground, *da*?"

Like hell. Finding the Book wasn't going to change a vampire's diet. But then he and his brothers couldn't be picky about allies at the moment. "It depends."

"On what?"

"On if you're serious about keeping the Gates of Nyx closed."

The Contessa came to a stop before a dark wooden door with a round brass porthole in it. "Mr. Jackson, you must understand. The Chosen are as much our salvation as they are for your own kind. Surely you can see that we need one another. We have been guarding Europe's part of the Book for six centuries. If we didn't want to help, we wouldn't."

"I suppose that's true enough."

She stepped to the side and clasped her black-gloved hands before her. "Your brother is through that door."

Colt swung open the polished mahogany door with caution, still not trusting what might be on the other side. As the Contessa had promised, Winn sat at a table cluttered with charts and maps muttering to himself as he took notes.

"Am I interrupting?"

Winn looked up at him. "Of course you are. You always do. Sit down anyway."

His brother had stripped down to a shirt with a vest over the top and discarded his coat, collar, tie, and Stetson.

Colt ran a finger along the inside edge of his own shirt collar. "Doesn't your neck feel a little exposed?"

Winn grinned at him. "She's not that kind of vampire."

Colt snorted. "What, the kind that don't drink blood?"

His older brother shook his head. "I don't have time to explain it all to you. Look, I've got an idea where Pa might have stashed his pages. If my calculations are right, Waltz's mine should be somewhere close to this military road, practically in sight of it."

"You really think Pa stashed the pages in the Lost Dutchman's Gold Mine?"

"Why not? Waltz was a Hunter from the old country. Chances are he's got it hidden well enough nobody would find it if they didn't know the Hunter lore."

"How do you know that's not some wild-goose chase?"

"You have any better ideas based on the clue he left us?" Colt shook his head. "Good. Then listen up, little brother. This ain't going to be easy."

Chapter 16

Lilly couldn't stop bouncing her booted foot. She perched on the edge of a very comfortable settee covered in deep plush burgundy velvet, one of several cushiony chairs and sofas scattered about the large and luxurious lobby of the airship. Sitting in the middle of the settee, she was as far away from the windows surrounding the room as she could possibly be.

Saying she was not fond of heights was an understatement. Beyond the expansive windows, the cerulean blue of the sky seemed almost serene, until one contemplated the distance between the insubstantial cloth-and-metal framework of the airship and the rocky earth far, far, far below.

She closed her eyes and breathed out slowly, trying to calm her quickly beating heart. When she managed to slow it down enough to qualify as somewhat normal, she opened her eyes to find the Contessa headed toward her.

Lilly envied her poise and grace. She seemed to float on air as she crossed the thick black and burgundy Turkish carpet. Considering where they were, the thought of floating on air made a bubble of hysterical giggles tickle the back of Lilly's throat. She giggled, then coughed, covering her mouth with her hand to mask her nervousness as the Contessa took a seat on the settee beside her.

The woman fairly breathed nobility. Her straight posture, her demure grace, even the fine, smooth quality of her pale skin all made her seem larger than life to Lilly. But it was the cool, assessing, superior gaze of those tawny eyes that made Lilly understand why vampires were among the most deadly and independent of the Darkin.

"Are you enjoying air travel, Miss Arliss?"

Lilly hesitated. She'd never been comfortable around people from high society, and the Contessa seemed to be from the highest echelons. She always felt that they'd see the dirt and ragged hems from her disreputable childhood no matter how far she'd removed herself from her beginnings. She didn't want to offend the elegant lady vampire. "It's smooth. Much better than a stagecoach or even a steam train, but—"

A spark of kindred understanding twinkled in the Contessa's eyes, relaxing Lilly's tension. "But it makes you sick to your stomach, *da*?"

Lilly placed a hand to her overheated cheeks. "Does it show that badly?"

The Contessa offered her a warm, kind smile. "You just look the way I feel when I am on a sea vessel—a bit green."

It was socially not what one would normally say, but honestly, Lilly liked it. It made the Contessa seem more real to her rather than some untouchable vampire princess.

"Just the thought of how much space there is between the bottom of the airship and the earth makes me nervous." Lilly didn't tell her that thinking about it made a fresh surge of panic spark along all her nerve endings making her skin prickle and itch all over.

"I think tea is in order." The Countess held up her black-gloved hand and materialized a small, cut crystal bell between her fingers. She shook the bell, and the light tinkling sound of it brought out a uniformed crewman within moments. "Tea for Miss Arliss and myself." He nodded and whisked away before Lilly could manage a thank-you.

The nervous knot in Lilly's stomach was still growing larger. She didn't know how to make polite conversation with a Contessa and she'd certainly never taken tea with a vampire before. The closest she'd ever come to conversing with nobility had been when she'd been begging for a coin or two as a child, or when she'd surreptitiously entered a ball using a forged invitation in hopes of stealing the lady's jewels while the party went on below stairs.

"I hope you don't misunderstand me, Lady Drossenburg. Your dirigible is amazing."

The Contessa waved her hand in the air. "Do not think on it any longer. I understand this feeling. You are not meant for the air as I am not meant for the sea."

"Is Miss McGee going to be joining us?" Just thinking about China McGee made Lilly squirm uncomfortably in her seat.

"No. She left via her own means back to Tombstone."

Lilly chanced a guess. "She turned into a bird?" *Like a hawk or an eagle or some other bird of prey?* she added silently to herself.

The Contessa smiled, her teeth very white and very even. Not a fang in sight. "*Da*. She makes a very impressive raven."

Lilly suppressed the urge to comment about exactly how obvious Miss McGee had been in her attentions to Colt and how unwanted they were. It wouldn't be ladylike, and she was already feeling awkward enough.

Thankfully, their conversation was interrupted as two crewmen returned with tea. One carried an ornate golden object that looked rather like an elegant brass teapot balanced precariously atop a large brass urn emblazoned with the enameled image of the Drossenburg crest. There were two metal handles sprouting out of the sides of the urn, a twisting tap on the front, and a little coal chamber beneath it.

The second crewman carried a silver tray bearing two translucent white china cups rimmed in gold and an assortment of elegant little rounded tea cakes covered in powdered sugar, various finger sandwiches, and matched silver pots of honey and bright yellow lemon wedges. They placed both on the table and vanished.

Despite her discomfort with air travel, Lilly's stomach grumbled with interest at the tart citrus of the lemon and the slight almond fragrance drifting up from the tea cakes. The Contessa filled her cup first from the teapot at the top, a dark, thick, fragrant brew, then from the tap on the urn, which produced steaming hot water. She added both a wedge of lemon and a generous dose of honey to her tea.

The Contessa gave her a brief glance laced with gentle amusement. "It is a samovar. The tea is strong, so add the water to it as you wish." Having never seen such a tea apparatus, Lilly followed suit. She helped herself to a small sugar-coated tea cake and several small sandwiches, then used the delicate etched silver spoon to add a lemon wedge and a generous dollop of honey to her steaming tea. She took a bite, and the soft subtle flavor of powdered sugar was accented with almonds in the cookie-like tea cake.

Mouth a little too full, Lilly glanced up to catch the Contessa's tawny gaze on her face. She flushed with embarrassment when she noticed that the other woman hadn't taken any food of her own.

"You are a supernatural like me, are you not, Miss Arliss?"

Lilly nodded as she reluctantly placed the tea cake on the little plate provided, licked the trace of powdered sugar from her lips, and took a sip of the fragrant tea. The warmth spread out from her stomach to her limbs, and for the first time since she'd been in the air she relaxed slightly.

"What do you know of the Chosen, Miss Arliss?"

"Only what I've discovered by reading their archives and from Darkin lore." Even before she'd been turned to a succubus, books had been Lilly's sanctuary.

The Contessa's amber eyes lit with interest and she leaned slightly forward in her seat, her raven-colored taffeta skirts and bustle rustling slightly with the movement. "And what do you know of the oldest, in particular? Does he have any weaknesses I should know of?"

"A few."

"Would you mind if I summoned some key members of my crew to hear as well? Anything we can learn to protect them during our mission could make the difference."

Lilly was uncomfortable with sharing what wasn't even hers to share, but wasn't exactly sure how to refuse the request. For one, she was a guest on the Contessa's airship and, two, vampires weren't known for being terribly tolerant of other Darkin, whom they felt were somehow inferior, and, three, she was nobility. One simply didn't refuse them anything. "If you wish," she answered simply.

Within a moment six vampires materialized in a curl of dark particles like smoke in the room. They clustered behind the Contessa's settee. They all shared the same whiskey-colored eyes as the Contessa, but unlike her, those eyes were filled with avid male interest. Inwardly Lilly smiled and relaxed. These were common male vampires, not highborn like Lady Drossenburg.

Lilly batted her lashes slowly at them, letting a subtle, coy grin spread across her lips. They leaned forward ever so slightly, and she knew she had their undivided attention.

She suddenly felt far more in control than she had since Colt had summoned her.

Colt returned to the upper deck to find Lilly surrounded by a bevy of male vampires that looked like they were lined up at a buffet. The crewmen, all wearing identical uniforms of black, accented with highly polished golden buttons and the Drossenburg crest embroidered in red and black on a field of gold on the right chest pocket, seemed to be totally fixated on her.

He cleared his throat, and her gaze swiveled in his direction. "Are you ready to get off this thing?"

She nodded, which made the red waves of her hair bounce in a way that was far too alluring, just begging a man to slip his fingers through the fiery silk. He had no doubt from the looks of the crew that every one of them was thinking the same damn thing.

Colt eyed the vampire crewmen. He didn't want to take them all on, but he would if one so much as showed a fang. "Don't you gentlemen have duties to attend to? I'm sure the Contessa wouldn't be pleased if she were to see you all here."

A few looks passed between them, as if they all shared some little secret he wasn't privy to, which irritated the hell out of him. They bowed to Lilly, said their good-byes, and shuffled off in different directions.

"What were they doing here?"

She sighed, swirling a ringlet of her red hair around her finger into a tight twist matching the twist in his gut. "They just showed up."

"I see that, the question was why?"

"I'm a succubus."

"Yes, but they're vampires. Your charms shouldn't affect them."

Her sigh came out an irritated quick exhale. "You Hunters think you know everything. But you don't. There's still more you haven't discovered about supernaturals. Vampires still retain something of their humanity. Therefore what's left of it is just as affected by the demon powers as any mortal man."

Colt reached out and slipped a ringlet of her hair around his finger, sampling the texture. His pupils dilated slightly. "Just like there's some humanity left in certain demons?" He was still wearing his rough frontier clothing—the denim pants he favored, the rumpled cotton shirt, the long brown duster, and the well-worn brown Stetson. Something about that rugged exterior made her tighten and coil with longing.

She stood, bringing them face-to-face. The strong edge of his jaw was rough with stubble, at odds with the smooth, sculpted firmness of his mouth. Lilly's body eagerly supplied her with all the details she remembered of how he could kiss. She inhaled at the thought and was hit with the scent of long, cool nights in the desert, and leather, which clung to him.

He leaned in just a little closer, close enough to kiss her, making her heart resume its faster-than-normal pace, this time from desire rather than fear. "That's more by accident than design," she replied.

Colt released the curl and she could tell his reserve had been firmly put back in place. Her heart contracted. Every time he seemed on the verge of declaring his real feelings to her, he backed away. He glanced out the windows, where the peaks of the tallest mountains were now level with the ship's windows. He took off his hat, smoothing the brim of it between his fingers. "Winn said we should be landing outside McDowell in about ten minutes."

"I thought we were going to Phoenix."

"This is closer to the mountains."

All the better for crashing into them. Lilly chastised herself for being so negative. "Do we have to climb down the ladder?"

Colt settled his hat back on his head. "No. We're gonna unload Tempus out of the cargo hold, so they're taking the ship all the way down this time."

Lilly weakened with relief. "You have no idea how much I was dreading the climb down."

He grasped her hand and held it. This time the look in his eyes wasn't one of desire, but of protection and concern—as close as she'd ever been to love. "I think I have a pretty good idea." His gesture wrapped her in a kind of warmth she'd never experienced before. The kind of warmth that came when someone genuinely cared for you.

Heartened, Lilly threw her arms around him in a hug.

He stiffened slightly. "You aren't going to start crying, are you?"

Lilly laughed softly into the collar of his coat. Colt might not have been ready to say the words, but his actions spoke volumes. He cared about her. "No."

Colt pulled out of her arms as he straightened. "Want to go for a walk around the deck before we leave?"

Lilly shook her head. "No thanks, I'm perfectly happy to stay safe and sound in here until we stop."

He tipped his hat. "I'm going to look around a bit, then see what needs to be done to unload Tempus."

Lilly remained firmly entrenched in her burgundy velvet settee while the airship slowly descended. The hiss of hot air being released from the vents had the same impact on her as that of a snake. A shiver followed by the quick dip and roll of her stomach made her queasy.

She glanced out the windows to see Colt bent over the rail, observing the crew and taking it all in. Lilly squeezed her eyes shut and gripped the settee's arm harder, wishing she had the guts to go out and grab hold of Colt instead. A thick hard lump centered just below her throat at the top of her chest ached. If he fell . . . she couldn't bear to think of it. When had he become more to her than a means to an end? When had she fallen for this rough-and-tumble Hunter? She certainly wanted to escape Rathe, and for the longest time that had been her only goal. But being with Colt had changed that. The Chosen weren't just a myth. He was a virile flesh-and-blood man who made the world alive in brilliant color, when for so long she had felt it was nothing but endless shades of gray.

She gasped slightly as the enormous airship thumped on solid ground, bounced up slightly, then made grinding noises as it scraped along the rocky desert soil.

"You can let go of the chair now. We've landed."

Lilly pried open one eye and looked at the Contessa. "You're certain we're safe?"

The Contessa's eyes twinkled with merriment. "The younger Mr. Jackson is waiting for you."

As Lilly walked on unsteady legs with the Contessa out to the viewing deck to disembark, she could see they'd come to rest in a barren stretch of dirt and rock. In the distance she saw the town veiled in the layers of dust hanging in the hot, still air. Other than a few houses, the only other building was the old fort constructed out of the same reddish tan stone that littered the landscape. Half tumbled down, it blended in so well that it was hard to discern it from the desert.

Lilly, nearly giddy with happiness that her first airship ride was finally over, remembered to thank the Contessa for her hospitality before heading toward the narrow wooden plank walkway linking airship and earth.

Colt came around from the back of the dirigible, riding Tempus. The leather with cow-like blots of black on white made it look more like a real horse, but the click and whirr of its clockwork parts as it moved, its brass hooves and solid silver eyes gave it away as a machine. The mechanical horse came to a rocking stop and Colt slid off, jogging up the ramp to offer her his assistance.

Lilly grasped his thick forearms, grateful for his presence. "Thank you," she murmured. He gifted her with a stunning smile that made her heart thump harder. She took ginger steps, watching where she placed her feet as she walked down the narrow planking thinking that falling at this point would be not only painful, but most embarrassing. She heaved a great sigh the moment her boot touched terra firma.

He left her side and mounted the paint, bringing it over to her. Lilly looked at Tempus with chagrin.

"Surely you aren't planning on making me ride that beast right after I've already suffered through riding on an airship, are you?"

"Not unless you want to."

Lilly nearly stumbled over her own feet in surprise. "Really?" She supposed she still didn't trust anything she couldn't understand, and unfortunately that still included Colt's mechanical horse.

"We're going into McDowell first and see if we can pick up some supplies and maybe a guide who knows these mountains. Then we'll get on the horse." He grinned.

Lilly resisted the urge to grumble and tried to retain her ladylike decorum. Just when she thought she had Colt figured out, he went and changed again.

"Can you walk with me?" she asked gingerly.

Colt hesitated. "I would, but Tempus doesn't move unless the plate under his saddle is depressed by the rider's weight. It's a safety feature Marley created."

"I see."

"I can walk him beside you if you want."

Lilly considered it for a moment. She wasn't any more comfortable with the thought of the big mechanical beast stomping on her than she was of it potentially throwing her to the ground if she rode it.

"You go on ahead. I'll follow."

His brows bent down with disapproval. "I'll walk with you." Lilly materialized her favorite black fringed parasol and opened it against the broiling sun. The meager shade was better than nothing, and there was none to be had unless she planned to lie underneath a creosote or jonco thorn bush or up against the prickly trunk of a saguaro.

Only the sound of Tempus's metal hooves clicking against the occasional rock punctuated the sounds of wind-rattled sagebrush. High overhead a hawk, searching for a meal, let out a screeching cry.

The town, if it really could be called a town, was a collection of sad sun-bleached wooden shacks surrounding what remained of the old adobe fort. Stuck here and there was a twisted mesquite tree, the green leaves so small the branches almost looked feathery in the brilliant sunlight. Wood smoke from a cooking fire mingled with the smell of roasting meat, cooking beans, and dust in the air.

The few people Lilly saw were crusty frontier types. From the crude condition of their homes, their dusty denim and duck cloth clothing, and scattered tools, she guessed they were miners. Tied in the shade of one shack was a gray mule, its head hung low. Its long ears flicked away annoying flies in the heat, and like everything else in the town, it seemed tired.

In the part of the old adobe fort building that remained intact they found a small mercantile. It smelled of vinegar from the pickle barrel, and a thin layer of dust seemed to cover everything. Lilly sneezed three times in a row. She looked around while Colt picked out the supplies. Bolts of calico and canvas sat on the shelves. A straw bonnet hung from the ceiling, the ostrich feathers rather sad and droopy, alongside a saddle and a pair of boots. Harnesses hung between baskets, and a doll stared blankly at a random selection of dusty farm implements.

A dusty display of nails caught her attention. She glanced back at Colt and the storekeeper, and noting that they paid her no heed, picked up a few. You never knew when nails might come in handy. Some might call her collecting habit a vice, but a hardscrabble life of conning people for a living had bred into her the unbreakable need to be resourceful. She picked up bits and items as she came across them to bolster her sense of security. With quick fingers, she deftly tucked the nails in her reticule along with the copper wire she'd acquired at Marley's.

She glanced once more just to be certain neither of the men had noticed.

"Got any fresh meat?" Colt asked.

The old store clerk's salt-and-pepper walrus mustache huffed outward with an annoyed breath. "Fresh out. Won't get more until next month on the wagon train."

"What about tinned biscuits?"

"Nope."

"Tinned beans?"

"Those I got." The clerk pulled three dusty cans from the shelf and added it to the pile on the counter right next to the five-pound bag of salt, another of flour, some cured meat, and a few bits of hard cinnamon candy. "You wouldn't happen to know of a guide for hire, would you?" Colt asked the clerk as he paid.

The clerk just shook his head, his enormous mustache making even a lip twitch indiscernible. There was a reason his establishment seemed to be lacking business, Lilly thought, and it wasn't just because they were on the edge of practically nowhere. She knew they weren't going to get very far this way. If they were going to get any kind of assistance, she was clearly going to have to intervene.

She sauntered up slowly to the counter, her lids half-shuttered, and gave the store clerk a stunning, but demure smile. "It's too bad you don't have any maps," she said sweetly, with just a twinge of a pout. "Without a guide it's going to be next to impossible to find."

Colt forgotten, the clerk's head swiveled as he fixated on her as if she'd just stepped out of thin air and he could see nothing else. "What are you lookin' for, ma'am?"

"The Lost Dutchman's Mine."

The clerk burst out in a warm laugh. "Ma'am, if I had a map to that I'd be richer than Croesus. There ain't a miner been through here yet has found it."

She widened her eyes just a touch. "Oh, I *know* the gold isn't real, just a story in the penny dreadfuls. But I want to see where that thrilling legend started. My darling here promised that he would take me to see the famous mine, as a birthday present."

The clerk eyed Colt for a second, as if summing him up, then returned his gaze to Lilly. "Shucks. I don't know if it'd actually help any, but Ol' Pete probably knows those hills just as good as anybody. If it weren't for more than just a walkabout out there for a day or two, he might be willin' to go."

"Really?" Lilly leaned in closer, her lips tilting just so. "Do you know where I might find this Pete?"

Two minutes later, with directions in hand, they stepped out of the mercantile with their supplies. It was like stepping into a woodstove oven after being inside the cool interior of the adobe building. The branches of a mesquite tree near the entrance to the mercantile burst into noise as they passed under it with the buzz and hum of insects. The dry air was so hot it tightened her skin and made her squint.

Lilly put her hand up to her forehead, blocking out the sun, and looked for the dirigible. It glinted and flashed in the sunlight, like a lone, small, silver fish in a huge blue ocean, growing smaller and smaller as it drifted off to the east.

"I never seen the like—what'd you do to him?" Colt asked as he readjusted his hold on the supplies in his arms.

Lilly gave him a sultry smile as she unwrapped one of the lemon-fizz candies the store clerk had given her free of charge for her birthday. "Only what a succubus is designed to do. Just be glad I didn't ask him for his soul while I was at it."

"Was it true, what you said about it bein' your birthday?"

"No. My birthday isn't until September. But it was a sweet gesture of him, don't you think? Want one?" She offered the open sack of candies to him.

Colt shook his head and muttered something under his breath about women, deceit, and wiles as he packed away the supplies in his saddlebags. Tempus stood absolutely motionless, his silver eyes never blinking. Lilly put the small paper sack of candies in her reticule and shivered despite the perspiration pooling between her breasts. The automaton gave her a case of the willies, not because it was a machine, but because at times it could be so lifelike, but had no emotion, no mind, no soul. Lilly knew better than to comment on Colt's grumblings. Despite what Colt might think, he was just as dangerous to her well-founded sense of self-preservation.

Already she'd put herself in jeopardy with Rathe on Colt's behalf more than once on this journey. And Rathe was only going to be so patient for so long before he called her back to his domain for a report. Lilly worried her bottom lip between her teeth.

There was no telling just how long Rathe's patience would extend. Once they found that Book, he'd expect her to return to him with it—and Colt—in hand or there'd be hell to pay. Literally. Up until now it had been a calculated risk. Getting the Book had been more about her freedom than saving the world from Rathe. But knowing the Chosen were real, that Colt was a flesh-and-blood part of it, and that she loved him—even if she hadn't told him so—had changed things. There was a chance the Chosen could overthrow Rathe, and by helping them she could gain her freedom and a chance to be with Colt. But there was an equal chance she'd get the Book, Rathe would slay the Chosen, and then he'd torture her mercilessly for ever having helped Colt in the first place.

The problem was, Lilly was caring less and less about her own well-being and more and more about the mission of the Chosen, and Colt in particular. Was becoming human again worth risking a world to be human in? If Rathe won, torture for both Darkin and human would be the rule, not the exception. And if the Chosen closed the Gates of Nyx, would they declare war on the Darkin who were left? And what about Colt and his brothers? If they lost, what horrible fate awaited them? She had a growing belief that in the end she'd be forced to choose between serving Rathe and helping Colt. And deep down she knew her heart had already put her lot in with Colt's.

Colt finished buckling the saddle pack and pulled down the edge of his Stetson against the afternoon sun. "Ready to go meet our guide?"

Lilly offered him an encouraging smile. "The sooner we get going, the closer we'll be to bringing together the Book."

A sad look flitted across his eyes for an instant, then was gone just as quickly. Or had she just imagined it?

"You're different from other Darkin, Lilly. You've still got a heart, a sense of right and wrong and a passion to do something about it. And as much as you've suffered so far, you deserve to be free from him. I'm sorry to have to ask your help when you've already done so much, but I need you to help me find the Book. I'll do whatever I can to help you make a break with Rathe and find your sister, but I can't make any guarantees, you know that, don't you?"

His praise made a warm sparkling sensation fizz through her veins. While he hadn't said as much, perhaps, like her, Colt was thinking of her as more than just a passing fancy. She reached up, curling a bit of her hair around her fingers, and nodded. "You just set your mind on getting your pa's part of the Book right now. All that can come later."

Much later, as far as she was concerned. A sharp sensation needled in her chest. He was such an honorable man in so many ways. One of the good guys, even if he looked like an outlaw. There had to be a way she could protect the man she loved from what Rathe had planned. But she'd better come up with it soon. Time was running out.

Chapter 17

"Are you sure he'll make it up into the hills and back?" Lilly asked, her mouth just beneath Colt's ear as she rode behind him on Tempus. She hadn't wanted to get on the mechanical monstrosity, but walking all the way was out of the question, and she didn't have a clue where they were going and therefore couldn't transport herself there. The only thing that made it bearable was being this physically close to Colt.

Colt chuckled. It vibrated through his back, causing his shirt to rasp against her breasts. "Just because he looks ancient doesn't mean he ain't tough as nails, sweetheart."

Pete, the guide he'd hired, truly did look older than the rocks around them. His weathered face was a leather brown that blended in with the color of the landscape and was deeply etched with lines, just like the mountains in the area were crisscrossed with rich veins of copper, silver, and gold. Clearly he needed the work. His clothing was so thin and worn it clung to his bony frame, and his hat was frayed at the rim. The guide didn't talk much, even when she'd tried to charm him. He just sat on his gray mule far enough ahead that they could see him, but not so far as to be out of earshot.

Lilly shifted behind Colt, a strange tingling sensation fizzing in the back of her skull. "I can't put my finger on it, but there's something about the man that makes me uneasy." She sniffed the air but detected no scent of sulfur or of anything else. This actually turned out to be a blessing in her estimation, since they were actually upwind from the old man and he stank to high heaven of rotgut whiskey and a body gone unwashed since his clothes were likely new.

"Afraid I can't protect you from one harmless old man?" he said, teasing her.

Lilly twisted, peering over her shoulder. The sun was sinking in the sky, almost touching the hills on the horizon. "We aren't going to make it into the mountains before dark, are we?"

"Not at this rate. We'll stop and make camp in the next hour," Colt replied.

Up ahead of them the jagged peaks of the Superstition Mountains turned purple in the dusky light. Heat still shimmered up from the desert floor. Her skin seemed to shrink to her bones. She was a demon, far better able to handle the heat than either of the men. She could only imagine how Colt or the old guide felt. 'Course, the old man had probably done a lot of hard living out here, judging by the look of him, and was probably used to it.

Even beneath the covering of cowhide, the metal of Tempus's body still seared in the ambient heat of the air, the clockwork within turning with a rhythmic hum. Riding Tempus double was exhausting.

"How are you holding up?" Colt asked.

"All I can taste in my mouth is dust. There's not even enough moisture in there to make it mud."

Colt chuckled. "Yeah, I'm surprised Tempus is holding up so well. I'll have to wind and oil him once we make camp."

Lilly shifted again. She wished she could say the same.

Her bustle was shifting back and forth as they rode, making her distinctly uncomfortable. And her thin cotton drawers were hardly adequate padding against the constantly thumping motion of her thighs against the hard metal of the horse. She could only imagine what Colt might suggest to soothe the soreness, which made her heat with a blush from the roots of her hair to the tips of her toes.

She wriggled at the thought.

"What's wrong?" he asked.

"It's this bustle. Riding astride, two to a horse, it's a nuisance."

"I can take it off you if you like," he teased.

Lilly didn't dare answer him, considering what she'd actually been thinking of.

"Just think, somewhere in those rocky crags rests our best hope for defeating Rathe," he added. "We find it, we win."

Lilly sighed as she leaned forward to peer over his shoulder. "That's if we find it before our guide gives out."

"Oh, we'll find it, all right."

She didn't doubt it. Colt was tenacious enough to do whatever it took to find his father's portion of the Book. She sucked in a breath and held it, her breasts pressing in a most distracting manner against his back as she hesitated.

"What? Just say it, woman."

She let out her pent-up breath in a slow steady stream. "Isn't our bigger problem finding all three? I mean, you said we can't close the Gates of Nyx with your father's portion of the Book alone, can we?" She pressed her cheek to his warm, broad back. Beneath his shirt the muscles shifted in rhythm to Tempus's movements. She inhaled the scent of leather and the outdoors, which clung to him, enjoying it. He was so solid, so strong, so very human.

"Nope. But you just leave that worry to Remy and Winn," he replied, the deep timbre of his voice resonating through his back. "If we get this piece, we can at least slow it down. If we can't close it all the way, then Rathe can't open it all the way either."

Lilly hoped it was the truth. She hugged Colt fiercely about the waist.

He grunted in response. "You can stop worrying. We're almost there."

She gave a mirthless little laugh. "If only it were that easy."

He turned. She looked up and he gave her a wide, heart-stopping smile that for a moment made her believe that anything, even this, was possible. "Why shouldn't it be? I'm here, aren't I?"

She sighed. She shook her head. "Because you know as well as I do that nothing is that easy." He had bravado in spades, but they were up against more than finding all three parts of the Book. Ultimately they were up against Rathe and his legions of Darkin.

"Yeah, but it can't be any worse than being on the edge of Hell, swimming in a lake filled with killer naiads, can it?"

"Don't tempt fate," Lilly suggested, "you never know."

Close to the base of the mountains the guide stopped his swayback jenny and twisted around to wait for them, his face covered in evening shadows. He tipped back his battered hat and pointed to a pinnacle of rock that peeped over a deep V between the darkening slopes of the mountains.

"Just between those two hills there is the military trail that'll take us to the Eye of the Needle," he said, both his manner and his voice dust dry.

"We'll make camp here tonight," Colt ordered. The guide gave a single nod and swung himself off his mule with far more grace than Colt would have expected.

Behind him Lilly sighed with relief. She had to be sore from the ride. Riding double on Tempus meant she sat either in his lap in front of him or on a blanket roll behind his saddle.

He helped her down from the horse and settled her on a blanket while he and the guide went about the business of setting up camp for the night. In a half hour's time he had a respectable fire, a hot pot of coffee, and a start on a dinner of beans and biscuits. He'd oiled and wound Tempus and had laid out their bedrolls for the night. Not bad, he thought. The air was cooling off quickly, and over the mountains a waning moon silvered the landscape.

Their guide sat on the ground leaning against the side of his mule, who'd bedded down for the night, just outside the rim of firelight. The old man stared out into the night sky.

That was just fine by Colt. He was more interested in watching how the firelight played over Lilly's delicate features and created flaming highlights that danced in her hair. Her eyelids drooped, her long dark lashes fluttering against the smooth skin of her cheek as she tried hard to stay awake.

She looked delicate and vulnerable, not at all like some vicious demon determined to strip away his soul. His chest tightened. How in the hell did he think he'd free her from Rathe? Rathe would want the Book, he knew that already. But he'd probably want something more. No demon lord was going to settle for an even trade. He'd want a better deal, or no deal.

He sat down beside her, tucking her into his side so she could rest her head on his chest. It wasn't purely out of good manners, Colt admitted to himself. He liked how the warmth of her soft curves pressed into him, made him think of exactly how she'd felt pressed up against him when he cornered her at Marley's. Lord, the girl could kiss.

He'd done his damnedest to avoid something similar

since. The realization that he might actually be falling for her had been a sobering one. She was just too much temptation, and while their bargain didn't involve his soul, Colt was wise enough to know that he wasn't too far off from willingly surrendering it, or anything else she asked for.

She sighed and in her sleep wrapped her legs over his, snuggling deeper into his chest, brushing against the hard length of his shaft. He blew out a rattling breath, and the next inhale he took was scented with Lilly's distinctive perfume. Damn. "Shoulda known better than to call on a succubus," he muttered to himself as he concentrated on the firelight.

Sometime in the night he finally drifted off to sleep, Lilly's supple body still curved against his, his arm about her holding her tight.

In his dreams they were back at the cabin of his childhood, the last place he'd thought of as home before his identity had gone from being just plain Colt Jackson to being a Hunter. He toyed with the hot red silk of her hair, letting it slip between his fingers as she smiled up at him, eyes luminous with desire, her lips partially parted, waiting for a kiss.

Hunger tore through him. He kissed her hard, putting everything into the kiss. She moaned, arching into him. The soft curves of her breasts pressed against his chest as she wrapped her arms fiercely around his neck and slid her leg up and around his hip, cradling him against her damp heat.

Then the dream changed. Instead of being entwined in Lilly's arms, feeling the warm heated silk of her against him, he was on the outside looking in. Lilly's body was wrapped around his brother, Remington. Her skirts were bunched about her hips as he leaned in against her, her back to the wall of their old cabin, her long, bare leg twined about his thigh like a snake.

Colt choked and sputtered, unable to breathe. Red exploded across his vision.

He leapt to his feet, the distance across the dry prairie grass seeming to grow farther and farther no matter how hard he ran. And then, suddenly, as in all dream worlds, he was there. He gripped his brother's shoulder, spun him about, and held nothing back as he let his fist fly, landing a solid right hook to Remington's jaw.

In slow motion Remy's head snapped back. Colt hit him again and again, until Remington began to block him, beat him back, his eyes gleaming with raw fury. Colt fought harder, drawing blood. "She's mine, Rem. Mine, you hear?"

Remington laughed, but it sounded wrong, dark and vile. Evil. "Wake up, Colt. You're a fool. It's just the succubus's spell. You can't trust her. You'll never be able to trust her." Then Remington's face melted and shifted into the pale face of the demon who'd tried to drown him. The demon launched himself at Colt, slamming them both to the ground, and shook him hard.

Colt woke to find himself being shaken for real, the back of his head bumping against the ground. "Colt! Colt, wake up!" Lilly hissed in his ear.

"Whoa. Hold up there. I'm awake." He sat up on his elbows, blinking at the pale red glow of the embers of their campfire, trying to get his eyes to adjust so he could clearly see her face. "What's wrong?"

"You were having a nightmare, thrashing around and grunting like you were on fire or something. It woke me. When I looked around I didn't see Pete."

It was dark, and the light of the moon etched the landscape in a stark interplay of light and shadow. "He's probably just gone off to take care of necessities."

"With his mule?"

That got Colt's attention. He got to his feet and stoked the fire, making it leap to life once more from the glowing coals. The orange glow lit a wide arc around them, but beyond the reach of the fire's light, the desert was still velvet night caressed with silver.

She was right, of course. Their guide and his mule had left nothing behind them but prints in the dirt.

Lilly huddled close against him. "What if something got him?"

Colt patted her back gently. "Maybe he's just gone on ahead. Makes more sense to travel at night out in the desert."

Lilly shivered and changed the subject. "What kind of nightmare were you having, anyway?"

Colt stiffened. "Just old memories. Nothing for you to worry yourself over. Try to go back to sleep."

She snuggled back in beside him. Colt watched the fire die down and become nothing more than glowing coals that eerily reminded him of the eyes of those Scoria soldiers he'd encountered in the mine. There was no use in trying to sleep, because he knew he wouldn't. The dream had been too intense, too real, and his emotions were too tangled up. Since when had a girl ever come between him and his brothers? Never. That's when.

What bothered him more was that he recognized that he wasn't just jealous in his dreams. Back at Remy's offices, he'd felt a flash of something and mistaken it for annoyance, wanting Remy to stop gawking at Lilly and get to business. But here, in the silent desert night, there were no illusions to hide behind. He'd been jealous, pure and simple. And no female had ever done that to him before.

Dawn crept over the mountaintops, washing the sky in a blush of peach and pink. It had cooled off enough in the night that his breath came in whitish puffs in the air. Their camp at the base of the mountains was still in shadow, but farther out the drops of dew sparkled in the spines of the cactus, and small cactus wrens were twittering and hopping about searching for breakfast.

Beside him Lilly stirred. Damn. Half-asleep, her hair softly tousled, she looked like she'd just gotten out of bed. In other words, sexy as hell. Her silky leg shifted against him as she stretched, and his mind didn't have to go far to imagine what it would be like to wake with her in a soft bed instead of a couple of blankets on the rock-strewn desert floor. He wanted a lifetime to see that same look on her face every morning.

But that wasn't going to happen. Not now. Not until he'd found a way to get her away from Rathe so she could become human again. If that was even possible.

Lilly blinked, her eyes feeling gritty, and rubbed one eye with the back of her hand. There was no need for a mirror to tell her she probably looked absolutely awful.

"You ready to wake up and take on the world?" he teased softly. Lilly lightly smacked him in the chest with her palm.

"Do you have to be so impertinently cheerful before there's even been a proper sunrise?"

He chuckled. "Not a morning person, are you?"

"Hulloooo." The call came from above them, echoing off the rocks. Beneath her ear, Colt's heartbeat sped up as he quickly moved to get hold of his gun. Lilly shifted to look up. The old man waved to them from atop the rocky cliff face.

"What's he doing up there?" Lilly murmured.

Colt didn't wait to find out. He leveraged her off his chest and began packing up camp before she'd even had time to put her boots back on. "Maybe he just wanted to scout ahead to make sure he knew where he was taking us," he said.

"In the dark?" Lilly countered. She ran her fingers

through her snarled hair, trying to work it out into curls instead of knots.

"Unusual, I admit, but then if we really find it, are you going to fault his methods?" He rudely pulled the blanket off her and began folding it into an impossibly neat and tidy little square, which he stuffed into his saddlebags.

"I suppose you really did mean it was time to get up."

He gave her a smile. "As much as I'd like to spend all day with you curled up beside me, that's not going to help us find the Book."

Lilly had to admit he had a point. She rose and readied herself as best she could, helping with their quick breakfast of beans and bacon, and scouring out the pans with sand before they started their trek up the mountain path. She looked up the vertical and fairly smooth mountainside towering over them, then glanced at Tempus. "Will he— it—be able to climb up there?"

"No. Too steep and too slippery. He'll fall, and thousands of dollars of Marley's money will end up in a million useless pieces in the ravine, or worse, he'd fall on one of us. My brothers will mourn my passing, and you'll never become a real girl. So to answer your question, no. Tempus will stay here to wait for us; you and I will walk." Colt slipped off Tempus and helped her dismount, then rummaged in the saddlebags. "We'll take what we need with us and leave the rest," he said as he pulled out a variety of items that he stuffed into a leather shoulder pack. She recognized the coil illuminator and the sting shooter, but not the other devices. "That should do it." They left Tempus at the base of the rocks.

The sun was growing impossibly hot as they scrabbled up the loose rock in the trail, winding their way through the larger boulders interspersed with brush until they reached the barren promontory of reddish rock where the guide waited for them. A slit of blue sky could be seen in the center of the spear that slanted up sixty feet high toward the sun, giving it the needle-like appearance.

Colt swiped away the sweat streaming down his face with his sleeve. Lilly doubled over for a breath. It was a good thing she was a demon and not a human, or she never would have made it up that hill in one afternoon. No wonder the old man had come up so early; it had probably taken him all night to get up here, and it certainly would have been cooler. Underneath her corset her shirtwaist and chemise were soaked through. Finally, they caught up to the guide.

Pete's wizened, leathery face peered at them from beneath the brim of his battered hat. He ambled forward on his thin legs, far more agile than Lilly suspected.

"'Bout time you made it up here. Took ya long enough," he said, then spat a dark stream of tobacco juice into the dirt, a bit of it dribbling down and staining his white-whiskered chin.

"So where is it?" she asked, between panted breaths.

"Down in that gulch. Cain't see it from the military road we followed up here from the fort. Have to get up above and look down from the Eye of the Needle," the old man answered, his voice crackling with disuse.

Colt took off his hat and raked his fingers through his sweat-plastered hair, resting his hands atop his head. His damp shirt clung to him and a heart-stopping smile lit up his whole face. It stole Lilly's breath away. Even travel-worn and covered in grime, Colt Jackson was a splendid specimen of man. "I'll be darned, old-timer. You did it. You found the mine," he said, a distinct note of relief in his voice.

"Oh, I've known where it is for years," the guide answered, chuckling softly to himself.

Lilly watched in horrified fascination as his gap-toothed smile transformed. The skin of his face beginning to sag as if it were wax melting in the heat of the day. Suddenly the old man's fingernails extended rapidly into black, shining claws, and he reached up and tore at his own sagging skin until it came away in thick fleshy ribbons, exposing grayish scaly skin beneath and leaving a shredded suit of the old man's body behind on the rocky ground.

Lilly screamed, and it echoed off the rocks. A skinwalker. The worst kind of shape-shifter.

Pointed teeth stretched in needles from his black gums as his eyes went from rhuemy blue to dark yellow, the pupils stretching upward to become vertical slits. This time when it spoke the voice was gravelly and raw, like a longtime cigar smoker in a saloon, making all the hairs on Lilly's skin prickle and tighten with revulsion. "Now that you know where it is," the shifter paused, licking its wide jaw with a hideously elongated red tongue that snaked up across his gray cheek, "nobody will ever hear from you again."

Colt didn't have time to think. He shoved Lilly behind him with one hand and pulled and cocked a revolver with the other. Lilly's sudden change in footing didn't hold. She screamed as she slid in the scree, the loose rock over stone leaving no chance for solid purchase.

"Colt!"

He whipped around just in time to grasp her flailing hand before she went over the edge to the thirty-foot drop below, and he pulled her up behind him. She grabbed hold of the pack strapped to his back. But the momentary loss of concentration cost him.

The skinwalker jolted forward and slashed Colt across the chest with its razor-like claws, shredding both his shirt and his skin. Colt gasped and shouted. He dropped to his knees as unseen fire exploded across his chest, burning and aching. He grunted, aiming his revolver at the fiend. The skinwalker sneered and cackled in delight.

It didn't know Marley had packed these silver bullets with powdered bone and ash added to the gunpowder. The revolver kicked back as Colt fired. The skinwalker darted like a shadow and the bullet exploded in the sandstone just behind the creature, spraying it with rock shrapnel. It shrieked, the sound reverberating off the rocks and multiplying until it echoed in Colt's skull, a sound so annoying it made his eyes nearly cross. In a blur the skinwalker moved from one rock to another, changing position so fast Colt could hardly track it, let alone take aim and shoot the damn thing.

"Watch out!" Lilly shouted.

Colt heard her an instant before he was knocked sideways by the creature. The impact sent him flying in one direction and his pack in the other. The shifter extended its wicked claws at Colt's throat with the aim of ripping it out. He held back the claws, his left arm bulging and burning with the effort, while he pulled the revolver up as close as he could between himself and the creature.

"You missed," it hissed, spittle spraying Colt's face.

"Yeah, but at this range my aim is bound to improve." He fired, and this time the narrowed black slits of the pupils widened with recognition before the creature stiffened and fell in a slump off him.

He lay there for a moment just breathing. God, it was good to breathe.

Lilly crouched beside him, tears streaking the dirt on her cheeks. She cradled his cheek in her palm. "You're alive!" Her kiss was swift, full of equal parts fear, joy, and passion.

The contact made Colt's head buzz and everything in him sit up and take notice. She pulled back just as quickly as she had planted the kiss on him.

"That was the idea, wasn't it?" he teased, then launched

into a fit of coughing, which made the cuts on his chest burn even worse.

"Let me look at those." Lilly gently pulled aside the shredded strips that remained of his cotton shirt and winced. "I have to get those cleaned out before I apply any salve to it. We need to find water."

He felt like an absolute idiot for not knowing it had been a shifter, but the old man had smelled so bad, he hadn't noticed the telltale sulfur scent or had the itch in his gun hand. Colt had to admit that perhaps shifters were his weak point. Usually he was pretty adept at picking out supernaturals, but this made twice a shifter had made a fool of him.

He pushed himself up and glanced down the gulch at the dark opening, which was mostly obscured by thorny green mesquite. Where there was greenery out here in the Sonoran Desert, there was water. "If we want to clean up anything, we need to get down there. You up for going down that gulch?"

Lilly cast a glance at the deep crevasse and her throat moved as she swallowed. "Don't suppose we have a choice, do we?"

"Not if you want that water and we want to find out what that skinwalker was protecting."

Lilly lifted herself resolutely from the ground and offered him a hand up. It was a simple gesture. Normally he would have ignored it, thinking it a sign of weakness on his part, but considering the circumstances, he thought he could make an exception. He gazed into her face as he put his hand in hers.

Lilly had been there, resolutely by his side, since he'd started this expedition, and he had to admit that he'd grown accustomed to having her there. She didn't make him feel weak. In fact, quite the opposite. With a touch, she made him feel alive, and graced with her provocative smile, he thought he might just be able to tear up and throw whole mountains.

"What's that look for?" Her tone was teasing, but there was a girlish uncertainty in the recesses of her gaze he hadn't seen before.

"I'm thinkin' you're beginning to grow on me."

She smiled prettily and the uncertainty vanished. "Are you trying to charm me, Mr. Jackson?"

"Yes, ma'am."

"That shifter's poison must be working faster than I thought," she mumbled as she shook her head and glanced down over the edge she'd nearly tumbled over.

The gulch wound down, twisting and turning between the larger boulders, a ribbon of green hidden deep in the reddish brown rocks. Far down below at the base of the hill, the tan strip of the military trail snaked into the mountains. The skinwalker had been right about one thing—there would have been no way to see the entrance to the gulch from down there.

"How are we going to get down there?" Lilly murmured. "If we try to walk it, we'll just slide off and end up speared on a cactus."

Colt chuckled, then stopped. It burned too badly. He retrieved the pack that had been lost in the scuffle with the skinwalker. "Marley truly does think of everything." He fished out a length of rope and the mechanical glove fashioned from brass, leather straps, clockwork, and pistons.

"That isn't going to fire more electric bolts, is it?" Lilly asked, her voice laced with wariness.

"Marley called it a Vertical Mechanical Lift. I thought he was nuts for suggesting I take it. The thing is damn heavy, but it's made for exactly something like this."

He flipped the glove-like device over, and Lilly could see the slim channel that ran through the center of the palm lined with rows of small gears. "He said the gears act like little teeth in the rope." He flipped the contraption over and pointed to a green glass button. "This one makes the gears move upward, and this," he pointed to the red glass button, "is supposed to make the gears go in reverse."

"Have you ever tried it before?"

Colt grinned. "Nope. But I watched Marley lower himself from the edge of his roof with it, so I know it at least works, unlike some of his other more harebrained inventions."

"Like the sting shooter?" she jibed.

"Yeah, that."

He looped the length of rope around a rock protrusion, making sure to cross it over itself so it wouldn't slip, then slid the metal glove on. It was fingerless at the tips, jointed at the fingers and wrist to allow for movement, and extended to his elbow. He tightened the leather straps with buckles to adjust it to fit his forearm, wound the small key on the back of his hand, and took hold of the rope, lining it up in the channel of the metal glove. The little gears clicked and engaged, digging into the rope like the shifter's claws had dug into him.

"Come here and hold on to me and we'll go down together."

Lilly eyed the metal glove with doubt. "It might support you, but are you sure it can support both of us?"

Colt grinned at her. "Only one way to find out." He motioned for her to move closer.

Chapter 18

Lilly circled her arms around Colt's neck, placing his chin perilously close to the distraction of the rose-scented silk of her breasts. His groin tightened in response. He put his arm about her dainty waist to secure her to his side.

"You might want to wrap your legs around my waist." The words slipped out before he had a chance to really think about the additional torture that might cause him.

Her sleek brows arched at him. "And that would be—"

"To ensure you don't fall."

She gave him a sly smile. "If you insist." She wrapped her legs around him, locking her ankles together just below his waist, which had the most unfortunate result of pressing her damp, warm heat firmly against his already hard length. Colt groaned.

"Am I hurting you?"

Only in the best way possible. He shook his head. How on earth could he tell her that wounded and half hanging off a sheer rock mountain face, he wanted nothing more than to bury himself in her decadent silken heat? Despite everything they'd been through, it certainly wasn't something one said to a lady, especially when he suspected it might just be his lowered immunity to her charms as a succubus. "Chest burns," he replied tightly.

She looked slightly crestfallen. "Oh, of course. I'm sorry. Let's proceed."

"Could you press the green button?" he asked.

His voice was so strained, Lilly began to truly fear that she was too heavy for his one-handed hold on the rope despite the mechanical advantage.

She depressed the green button and the clockwork sprang into action, lowering them slowly and smoothly down the length of rope toward the gulch.

Lilly realized she was practically sitting atop Colt, their most intimate places pressed close together as he leaned back, his feet walking backward on the rock as they moved. A flash of heat stole across her skin. Surely she had no business thinking of him in such a fashion, but Lilly found she couldn't resist. With his every movement he rubbed against her, creating the most delicious friction. Her breasts tightened.

"How close are we?" she whispered in his ear.

"Not nearly close enough," he answered, a ragged edge to his voice.

Inch by inch they lowered until they reached the base of the gulch. For all the dry desert around them, the lush greenness of the gulch was like a hidden Eden. *Probably complete with snakes*, Lilly thought as she glanced around. There were so many places they could hide. She shivered.

Colt disengaged the rope from the glove, then slipped it off, pulled off his pack, and stowed the glove away. "Let's spread out and start looking for the entrance to that mine. You take the left side of the gulch, I'll take the right," he ordered.

Lilly speared him with a sharp gaze. "First, how about

we treat those cuts? Shifter poison can sometimes cause delirium."

Colt grimaced. "Fine." He turned away from her and stripped off what remained of his shirt.

Lilly's brain went muzzy. She'd only seen part of his bare torso before when she tended to his shoulder, but seeing him with no shirt at all was a truly different experience altogether. He was muscular in the way the classical Greek and Roman statues portrayed the heroes of another age, but instead of stark white, his skin was a golden bronze punctuated here and there by paler scars, his back a ripple of muscle with every movement he made. He turned toward her, revealing a dusting of crisp hair across his wide chest that arrowed down toward his waistband.

Her heart gave a funny little flutter that seemed to amplify somewhere about her stomach, and then lower. She tried to focus on the innocuous lash mark from her fire whip, which was still a red streak against his shoulder, but her gaze couldn't help but stray to the fresh wounds on his chest. The blood had dried to a thin crust about the edges but the center of each of the four slices was still open and raw.

Colt had the audacity to grin. "Like what you see, do you?"

Lilly blushed furiously. "Well, yes, everything but the cuts, naturally," she blathered like a ninny rather than a sultry succubus, but she couldn't help herself. She'd never been affected by the sight of a man's body like this before.

A trickle of water burbled down between the rocks. Cicadas buzzed and hummed loudly in the pale green boughs of the palo verde trees matching the buzz and hum happening in her veins.

"Come over here and let me clean those."

He stepped toward her, hands at his hips just above his holstered guns, and watched her as she moved. He seemed to be enjoying her distracted state. Lilly scooped the cool, clear water in her hands and washed his skin with her bare fingers. His skin tightened, the muscles flinching as she touched him. She glanced up and caught his gaze, unfocused and hazy with desire. "Am I hurting you?"

"No. I'm fine." He lied.

Just running her hands over his impressive chest made her fingers, and far more unmentionable places, tingle with awareness. "You're going to need salve on—"

He moved so quickly his kiss cut her off mid-comment. His lips were hotter than the air around them, and his clever hands slipped around her back, then dipped lower, cupping her bottom and pulling her into him as his tongue delved deeply into her mouth, starting a sensual slide against her tongue. Invisible sparks flew along her skin everywhere they touched.

Lilly's knees started to soften, refusing to hold her up. He grunted, and she realized she was pressing hard against the very cuts she'd been cleaning, hurting him and dampening the front of her gown in the process. She abruptly pulled back. "Sorry. Sorry," she said softly.

Colt pressed an index finger to her tender lips, making them ache for another kiss. "Shh. You don't have any reason to be sorry."

"But I hurt—"

He pressed harder with the finger and locked his vivid blue gaze deeply with hers. "You don't have any reason to be sorry."

Not yet. Lilly pushed him and the unwanted thought away. "We'd better get you patched up and find that cave before it gets dark." *And before I do something we'll both regret.*

He reluctantly released her and stayed stoic as she materialized her jar of healing salve and applied it to his chest.

"If this stuff works as well on these cuts as it did on the whip burn, I won't need stitches."

She smiled at him wanly. The thought of having to stitch together his flesh, more of him being hurt enough to need it, did not do good things for her stomach.

"Could you get me the fresh shirt in my pack?"

Lilly dug into the pack and found the shirt and something else far more interesting. A little black velvet drawstring pouch. Definitely not something a man such as Colt would normally have just hanging about. With quick, efficient subtlety, born from too much practice as a child, she loosened the drawstrings and peeked inside. A set of crystals she'd never seen before were nestled inside the black velvet. She snatched out the shirt and the little velvet bag with one smooth movement. Perhaps it was the survival instinct bred into her, but a little insurance never hurt when you were going into situations where the balance of power might tip out of your favor. And right now she was far too dependent on Colt.

She held up the shirt so that he had to turn to slide his arms into the sleeves, and the moment his back was turned she tucked the velvet pouch under the voluminous folds of her bustle.

"Feeling better already," he said as he buttoned his shirt. He picked up the pack, secured the buckle and strap that held it together, and heaved it over his shoulder. "Ready to find that cave now?"

"No," Lilly said, "I'm ready to find the Book."

Colt gave her a wide grin. "We'll have a better chance of finding it before dark if we split up. You take the upper half of the gulch and I'll trek farther down."

Lilly glanced up the narrow canyon. If she was going to be climbing over rocks and mucking about in a stream, she needed a change of clothing. She glanced back to make sure he was out of eyesight farther down the gulch before she materialized a pair of the buckskin pants she'd seen China wear. Lilly tucked her hand into the front pocket and her fingers met the smooth softness of the velvet of the pouch, the long thin nails, and the curvy bit of copper wire. Good, it was all still there. She'd never worn pants before, and they seemed a bit confining and hugged tightly around her hips and posterior.

Across the small creek, trunks of mesquite trees the size of Colt's waist crisscrossed the gulch, wedged against the rocks and twisted and cracked against one another in a big tangle. Lilly climbed the snag, finding it much easier in the pants, and noticed the worn pale line that etched the rocks three feet above her head, marking the last time floodwater had filled the canyon. There'd been a lot of force to push these trees from their roots.

She climbed over a few boulders, pausing to wipe her forehead on the sleeve of her shirt. It was cooler in the gulch and the water made a pleasant sound as it splashed over the rocks, but this was still the desert. The air was dry enough to make her lips tight and parched. She sidled down the opposite side of the boulders and found herself at the end of the gulch, facing a wall of almost solid dry rock. This couldn't be it. Where was the water in the stream coming from?

Lilly tramped back to the flowing water and followed it to a spot between the boulders. Two large rocks had fallen together, forming a narrow triangle big enough for her to pass through if she crouched a bit. Beyond the rocks were only bushes.

"Find anything yet . . . yet . . . yet?" Colt called out to her. His words echoed off the rocks. A stream of cooler air slipped around her legs, chilling her calves above her booted ankles. It smelled of damp earth and musty underground air. Lilly pushed past the bushes to find a large opening in the rock.

"It's here! At the end of the gulch," she shouted. Colt's

footsteps became louder as he doubled back in her direction and came scrambling over the boulders.

His eyes widened with appreciation as he glanced at her change of clothes, making a shiver of awareness zip up her spine.

"We're close now, I can feel it," Colt said, the excitement in his voice vibrating in the air like the buzz of the cicadas.

"Close, but not there yet." Lilly pushed the bushes aside and held them back. The wash of cold air sent chills racing over her skin. The cool dampness of the cave seemed both refreshing and ominous in the desert air.

Colt's brows bent down as he looked at the trickle of water coming from the mouth of the cave. "Not more water," he grumbled.

She tried for levity. "Weren't you the one who said it couldn't be any worse than the last cave we were in?"

He glanced back at her with a heated stare that said her attempt had failed. "What was I thinking?" Colt pulled off his pack and fished out the coil illuminator and gave a resigned sigh. "Shall we?"

"After you," Lilly replied.

Colt chuckled, but it had a nervous timbre to it. "You just want me to go first."

Considering she was still in pants, and he'd likely be paying attention more to her assets than the cave, Lilly nodded, placing her hand on his broad back. "Absolutely."

Chapter 19

They plunged into the darkness of the cave with only the coil illuminator for light. The stale, damp air washed over them, smelling of mildew and neglect. Colt stepped over the thin stream of water trickling through the center of the floor, taking care with his footing since the pack on his back threw off his balance slightly.

"Where to now?" From the slight tremor of her hand on his back, he could tell she was scared.

"Working on it." He tilted back his hat slightly and ran his hand across the rough surface of the rock near the entrance, doing a tactile and visual search. His fingers found it before his eyes did. Hewn into solid bedrock was the Legion's symbol, a triple cross, three increasingly larger lines stacked horizontally over a single, long, vertical line. A sense of triumph bloomed in his chest, sending sparks of renewed energy out through his veins. "Eureka!"

He quickly brushed away the dust and cobwebs, his fingers lingering on the indents of the image as he shone the illuminator on it. A hard lump lodged at the base of his throat, making it difficult to swallow. Had Pa made this mark before he taught his three sons about their heritage? True, there were other Hunters in the United States, all trained out of the same piece of the Book. But considering his pa was the one charged with guarding it, there was every chance that he'd been the one to make that mark to reveal this place to be a Hunter's design. And he'd found it, not Winn or Remy. Him. The one they didn't want to become a Hunter.

"Did you find something? Let me see," Lilly asked as she pressed closer, gazing over his shoulder. The sweet, seductive scent drifted off her warm skin. Climbing down the side of the gulch had been torture enough, and they were closer to the Book than they had ever been. Colt turned swiftly, cupping her smooth cheek in one hand and kissing her soundly, reveling in this feeling like he could take on the world and win.

She stared at him with wide eyes. "It's a sign you're supposed to kiss me?"

He chuckled, running his fingers over the mark once more and tugging his hat down firmly on his head. You couldn't exactly call a Hunter giddy, but he was damn close.

"It means we're on the right track. This is the place." He was talking faster than normal, but the energy, the drive to press forward now that he knew they were on the right track, couldn't be ignored.

"How ca—"

He held up a hand, cutting her off. "Trust me. I know. Watch your step. If Pa hid it here, there's probably a few traps. Hunters don't leave anything unguarded, especially something as important as this."

"You Hunters are an odd lot, you know that, right? Suspicious, paranoid loners."

Colt grinned at her. "Better odd than dead. I take it you haven't run into many Hunters you actually like." He skimmed his hand along the rocky walls, smoother than the walls in the Dark Rim Mine. A result of being a natural cave instead of one hacked and hewn out of the rock by man. That didn't mean he liked it any better. Both had the potential to be hazardous to a Hunter's health.

"Can you blame me?" she answered. "They tend to dispatch Darkin first and ask questions later."

The shush of their footsteps echoed in the cave, as did the steady, rhythmic plink of drops into the small creek that seem to take up the middle of the cavern floor. This wasn't just collected dampness from the cave. Somewhere there was a water source. Colt grimaced. He wasn't looking forward to finding out exactly where all that water was coming from.

He moved the bluish stream of illuminator light around, looking for any kind of trip wire among odd natural shapes in the rock. The stalactites and stalagmites that dripped down from the ceiling and speared up from the floor seemed to join together in a thick, stone, harp-like arrangement. But what he was looking for was the unnatural, unmistakable signs left by other Hunters. Something beyond just the mark at the entrance to indicate they were headed in the right direction. The musty, metallic scent of the cave was growing stronger the deeper they went.

"You and your brothers have more charm than most Hunters I've come across." Her voice echoed in the confined space, and she walked very close to his side, careful to keep her footsteps in the circle of the light.

"You sure it isn't just because we're the Chosen?"

"That only adds to your reputation," Lilly said. A brief flash of white in the light let him know she was smiling.

But Colt was only paying her half a mind. The sound of bubbling water pricked his ears and made him stop. He swung the light in the direction of the sound. About fifteen feet overhead, a smooth round opening twelve feet across was cut into the rock. Water poured down from the edge of the opening in a constant small supply, like an enormous drain, creating the creek down the center of the tunnel.

The illuminator was fading fast. In the waning light he searched for another incised mark in the rock or a Hunter's symbol that could serve as either a lead or a warning. They couldn't afford to be careless. One wrong move in this cave and neither of them might see daylight again. *Clack, clack, clack.* He shook the illuminator and the light increased some, but not nearly enough. At this rate he estimated they might have an hour of light left, if that. Then they'd be dependent on whatever light source Lilly could create, or be left in the dark.

"Do you think we're supposed to go up there?" Lilly asked, a slight tremor to her voice.

Everything within him resisted the idea. With the diameter of that opening, all kinds of water could easily flow through there. "The tunnel turns right up ahead, let's keep going and see what's there first."

They walked on, turning the corner, and found themselves in a large, dead-end room with a vaulted ceiling. It looked like the interior of a mausoleum, the rock of the cave chiseled straight and smooth. It smelled like one too. Earth, dank moisture, decay, and metal. Colt held the illuminator higher and stepped closer to the nearest wall. Lilly's steps slowed and she tugged on his sleeve, making the light jiggle and dance. "Colt—Look!"

"Hard to miss." A large bronze door at least ten feet tall and streaked with verdigris was set into the solid stone.

Colt's hands shook. This was what he'd been waiting for, working for. He had to be close to the Book now.

This was the easy part.

Except it wasn't. Of course it wasn't. What about this quest had been easy? Not a damned thing. Because there wasn't just one giant, verdigris-encrusted door facing him as he swung his light about the oddly shaped turret-like room—there were *five*.

It was a given that four out of five were traps of some sort. Beside the door frame of each was a small rectangular slot cut into a rock. It was big enough for a hand. If one didn't mind having a hand cut off, he thought. He couldn't rush this. He had to be methodical, cautious, and smart.

One at a time.

Lilly wasn't nearly as suspicious. "I bet the lever to open it is in there." She reached forward.

He grasped her slender wrist. "Don't!"

She hesitated, her fingers less than an inch from the dark opening, and sent him a frowning glance over her shoulder. "You have another suggestion for opening the door?"

Her eyes tracked the direction of his gaze and she crossed her arms, cocking her hip out to one side, her left eyebrow rising slightly. "Don't tell me you are afraid of the bugs that might be crawling about in there?"

He grunted. "Hardly. I think it's a false door, and possibly a trap."

She glanced at the door and back again at him. "It looks normal enough to me. How can you tell it's false?"

His brows pinched together, his gaze darting to the different images around the door, trying to make sense of it all. "The insignias are all wrong." He pointed to the three insignias molded in relief, one on either doorpost and one on the lintel above the door. "They're out of order. In Hunter lore the eldest brother of the medieval knights, Cadel, who took the last third of the Book, was the lion of the Legion. Its greatest defender. See that lion head? It should be on one of the side posts, not at the top."

"But if he was the eldest, and the leader, it would make sense he was at the top, wouldn't it?"

Colt shrugged. "It's possible. But if they were in birth

order he'd be on one doorpost or the other, not on the lintel over the door."

He peered closely at the other two images standing out from the metal door frame, rubbing his stubbled cheek in deep thought. "That one to the right, the raven, is the symbol for the youngest brother, Haydn. He took the middle portion of the Book to the edge of the known world."

"Then what is that one?" Lilly asked in curiosity. "It certainly doesn't look like any animal I've ever seen."

"That's because it's a palm tree." Amusement laced his tone. "That's Elwin's. He was the peacekeeper between the other two. He took the first third of the Book. As close as I've been able to find, he took it to southern Europe, but lore loses track of it after the age of the explorers."

"So how do we know which order they are supposed to be in? Birth order?"

That sounded logical enough to Colt. "Let's try oldest first." He took the illuminator and swung the light about the square walls of the room, each inset in the center with a tall bronze door. Around each door the symbols appeared in a different arrangement. "We have to choose the one with the right combination."

Lilly went with him to inspect the images surrounding each door. It was time-consuming, and he grew impatient as the light of their coil illuminator grew even dimmer. But this was too important to screw up now. He took his time to compare the images on each door. And when he was done, he went back and did it again. And then a third time.

Every ten minutes or so he gave the coil illuminator a shake. And every time, while it revived, the light was just a little less bright and stayed illuminated for a shorter time.

"Well, which one is it?" she asked, her tone slightly exasperated.

"I think it's this one." He handed Lilly the light and cautiously reached into the opening beside the door, feeling blindly for a lever. As Lilly had predicted, the whole space came alive with movement of things creeping and crawling over his skin. Finally he found a lever the size of his thumb, but the opening of the slot was too narrow for his forearm to move forward any farther, so he grasped the lever with his fingertips, and pulled. The sound of gears grinding rumbled somewhere behind the wall. He pulled his hand out and shook off the assortment of insects, then put his hand on the center of the door and pushed.

With a screech of unused metal, the door swung abruptly inward. The footing beneath him seemed to crumble. A pit too deep to see the bottom of yawned before him in the meager light of the illuminator. His arms flailed as he tried to find something, anything, to grasp and stop his fall. His fingers slid along the smooth metal of the door frame, unable to find purchase. Lilly dropped the coil illuminator and grabbed him about the waist with both arms and dug in her heels. They teetered backward and collapsed in an inelegant heap, Colt on top of Lilly, on the dry rock floor, his holstered gun bruising his hip and his hat tumbling off into the dirt.

He rolled off her. "Are you hurt?"

Lilly moaned, but sat up on her elbows, the glow from the coil illuminator uplighting her face. "I'll be fine once I get my breath back." She rubbed her ribs. "You're heavier than you look when you're on top."

A very different image flashed in Colt's mind. He shook his head and didn't dignify her comment with an answer, even though his body certainly responded to it. He snatched up his hat, dusted it off by slapping it a few times, and settled it back into place on his head. He didn't need his thoughts taking that wayward turn. He needed to be focused if he wanted to keep them alive.

"I'm taking a wild guess that birth order isn't the correct combination," Lilly said with sarcasm as she dusted herself off, picked up the illuminator, and took the hand he offered to pull her to her feet.

"We're missing something." Colt kicked a small rock on the ground, sending it skittering away to clang on one of the metal doors. He should be better than this. There was no room for error. The next door could just as easily trigger an explosion that could collapse the entire cave, killing them both. Which would leave Remy and Winn not only without a brother, but without means of closing the portal because they wouldn't have the third piece of Pa's Book.

What other combination made sense? That's when it hit Colt. He pushed back his Stetson with his index finger so it rested toward the back of his head. "I can't believe I didn't see it before. The images need to be in the same order that the pieces of the Book of Legend fit together. Only a trained Hunter would know that."

"And the demon with him," jibed Lilly.

Colt grunted. "Yeah, well, I think that's rather an exception to the rule. I can't think of a single Hunter who's paired up with a demon until now."

"Just be careful," she murmured.

Her concern was touching, in an annoying sort of way. He hadn't had much mothering, and the few times his brothers had warned him off of something it was more like adding a match to kindling, firing him up to take an even bigger risk the next time.

He located the door with the palm tree on the right, the raven up top at center, and the lion on the left. The brothers' symbols in the same order as the pieces of the Book each of them had taken when it had been separated. Colt reached for the opening, and he mentally prepared for the sensation of a million little prickles as the insects skittered over his skin.

"Wait!"

He jerked his hand back. "What? Did you see something."

She pulled straight a bit of copper wire between her fingers and shaped the end into a shepherd's crook. "Use this. No reason to get a bunch of bug innards on your hands."

Colt shrugged and took the wire, peering at it, admiring her resourcefulness. "This looks like the wire Marley uses in his coil illuminators. Might work real well." He wasn't positive, but in the dim light it seemed that Lilly's coloring heighted slightly.

"Well, try it," she urged.

Colt slipped the wire into the opening and fished about for the lever. When it stuck, he gave it a good tug. The lever shifted forward. Behind the door there was an echoing thump, followed by the *clickity-clack* of moving gears. He handed the wire back to Lilly and pushed on the door. This time the bronze door shifted easily inward as if resting on wheels and a track of some kind.

Colt waited for a moment in case he'd been mistaken a second time. When the only thing that happened was a cold draft of stagnant musty air swirling out around his legs, he crossed the threshold cautiously, Lilly close on his heels.

Inset into the riveted bronze wall was a sconce with a strange torch set into it. It looked vaguely like an old bronze torch, the handle twisted and narrower at the bottom and wider at the top, terminating in a wide rim with an inch-thick cotton wick at the center. He lifted it out of the sconce. From the sloshing sound, there seemed to be some liquid in the long metal handle. Colt touched the wick and rubbed the slick substance between his fingers, then sniffed. From the oily pungent aroma of it, Colt recognized it was kerosene. He pulled a small box of lucifers from his pack and struck one, illuminating the oil lamp. The coil illuminator was so faint, Colt turned it off completely and tucked it into his pack.

"Looks like we're in the right place. There's no way this just happened by accident."

Lilly hunkered close. Too close. The heat of her was a big contrast to the cool air of the tunnel, and her unique spicy floral scent filled his nose, blotting out the stench of kerosene smoke. The pale yellow light of the torch revealed a long, rectangular hallway crafted from thousands of bronze tiles and supported with large, arching, riveted bronze beams. The metal had aged to a greenish patina with the moisture in the tunnel over the years. The colors, coupled with the dancing torchlight, gave the impression of being underwater. Colt shivered.

"It's cold in here," Lilly said as she huddled closer, rubbing the sleeves of her short blue jacket. The color enhanced the peaches-and-cream tone of her skin and made her hair look a deeper, darker red. Colt took an appreciative peek at the curve of her derrière in the buckskin britches. They looked even better on Lilly than they had on China, and that was saying something. He berated himself for being so physically responsive to her. Clearly she had his senses scrambled. But it was more than that. He'd become accustomed to her presence, to the sound of her voice and the quality she lent to the very air she breathed. It was relaxing and intoxicating at the same time, and thinking of losing her made a strange ache start deep in his chest.

"And dangerous," Colt added. There was no way this was going to be an easy passage. Hunters had constructed the tunnel both as a protection to what was secreted away here and as a means of funneling unwanted visitors into booby traps designed to eliminate them every step of the way.

"God only knows what's up ahead. Stay behind me, and rest your hand on my shoulder. Step where I step, and let

me know if you see or hear anything suspicious. Ready?"
He was truly as concerned for her safety now as his own.

She placed her hand on his shoulder as they moved
with deliberate slowness down the hallway. All that talk
about demons seeing just fine in the dark didn't seem to
matter when she was well and truly frightened, Colt
thought. And she was sensible to be scared. He focused on
the details of the construction, trying to work out exactly
what they were facing. In the realm of Hunters, it was up
to him to protect her.

The walls were crafted from six-inch-by-six-inch metal
tiles inscribed with Hunter symbols meant to neutralize
Darkin powers and fitted so tightly as to appear nearly
seamless. On the floor were large squares of metal, about
twelve by twelve, that echoed with each step they took. He
listened carefully to the sound for any changes, which
might indicate a different surface underneath, but it was
difficult with the echo of their footsteps on the metal walls.

Colt would bet his last gold dollar the panels on the
floors and tiles in the walls were trap doors and triggers.
This whole place was nothing but a dynamic machine,
constructed from a series of complex devices operating in
convoluted ways to perform the simple task of killing
them. He'd heard other Hunters talk about them before.
It'd taken the brains of a mad scientist and the cunning of
a skilled Hunter to create something this elaborate and
Machiavellian.

"Why are Hunters always fascinated with being underground? Why not just put the Book of Legend in a safe
place under lock and key?" Lilly asked with asperity, her
voice echoing as she huddled close to Colt, her small hand
gripping his shoulder. Even though the air smelled of
disuse and dust, the light floral scent of her tugged at him.

Colt didn't know how to answer, but he did his best.
"When the original leaders of the Legion of Hunters broke

the Book of Legend apart in medieval times, they escaped through the catacombs beneath the church. They've been hiding out, a secret presence in society ever since. Maybe being underground is all Hunter ancestors ever knew."

Lilly looked at him thoughtfully. She'd always thought of Hunters in general as paramilitary types who had no compunction when it came to Darkin. For them it was kill or be killed or keep someone else from being killed. No matter how one looked at it, Hunters and Darkin were oil and water—the two simply didn't mix. So why did her stomach give a strange flipping motion whenever Colt gazed at her intently? Why did helping him find the Book seem to be becoming more important than even escaping Rathe or reuniting with Amelia?

Perhaps the Chosen had more powers over the Darkin than they were aware of; perhaps it was just her growing awareness of her feelings for Colt. He'd certainly caused her to react in ways she'd never felt before and made her yearn for impossible things—a home, hearth, and family of her own. Someone who'd treat her as his equal. Someone to love.

He reached out, touching his fingertips to each wall as he walked. She kept hold of his shoulder, unsure of what might happen next. Beneath her hand his muscles were hot, taut, and rigid. He was just as unsure as she was.

Colt came to an abrupt halt in front of her, and Lilly ran into the wall of his broad back. *Oof.* "What now?"

"Trip wire." He held the torch lower to the ground so she could see the light reflect off the thin metal filament stretched tight across the hallway. He stood and took care to step over the wire, then held out his hand to help her do the same. Lilly was grateful not to have her long skirts or a bustle hampering the maneuver. Perhaps there was something to be said for a woman wearing britches now and again after all.

"How did you even see that?" she asked, moving to stand shoulder to shoulder with him.

Colt pointed to the lion in relief formed into the metal of the wall just before the wire. "I didn't have to see it. I felt the symbol and knew it was indicating something, so I stopped and looked around. There was the trip wire."

"What do you suppose it does?"

Colt followed the wire with his gaze and pointed it out to her. "See how it moves up along the wall, and there connects to a pin, which connects the lever, and then to that large round stone in a track? If we'd tripped on the wire, then the chain reaction would have started."

"And?"

He glanced upward and held the torch higher. Huge stones, nearly the width of the hallway, were suspended above them in the tunnel. "The ball starts rolling down the track, knocking loose the pins holding those stones, and they'd have started crashing down one at a time, forcing us down the hall and blocking our exit."

"Or crushing us right where we were standing."

Colt just nodded.

"So trip, and you're likely to be flatter than a johnny-cake."

"Yep."

She shook her head with disbelief. "And you Hunters think *we're* dangerous to your kind. I'd say you're more of a threat to one another."

Colt grabbed her hand in his, his strength and reassuring manner flowing into her through their touch. Lilly had never been protected by anyone all the while she was growing up. And certainly not by Rathe. Colt's manner touched her heart.

They kept moving. "There's no way Pa could have done

all this alone. It would have taken several men to be able to create these walls, design the protection devices, and to lift and secure those stones in place. And if they've gone to all this effort to plan and build this, then it's got to be here somewhere." He turned and locked his gaze on hers, his face serious. "Whatever you do, don't touch anything."

"It's like we're walking inside a clock, isn't it, and these are all the gears and mechanisms."

"Yeah, a clock that'll kill you."

Lilly nibbled on her bottom lip and nodded. He turned back toward the unexplored end of the hallway, slowly walking forward. She focused on the greenish glow of the walls. It was nearly impossible in the flickering light of the oil lamp he held out in front to see anything well, let alone clearly, but she could see symbols etched into the surface of the metal, symbols that kept Darkin unable to use their powers to enter this place . . . or to escape.

"How do you know where we're supposed to go?"

"We'll know when we get there."

"Brilliant. That makes me ever so comfortable with the idea that we're trapped inside a dynamic killing machine."

"At least it's not Hell," he retorted.

Lilly thought of a few choice words for him. Yes, this wasn't Hell, but the constant fear, the cold dread thick and uncomfortable in her stomach didn't feel much different to her than being under Rathe's thumb. Only the solid connection of him, flesh to flesh, gave her any comfort in this place.

The unnatural silence of the metal tunnel combined with the lonely echo of only their footsteps started to gnaw at the frayed edges of her nerves. She needed something to take her mind off their present predicament. "Tell me some more about the Legion."

Colt hesitated a step, turning his head back to her for a

moment, then kept moving deeper into the machine. "Why, so you can use it against us?"

Her skin heated with annoyance. After all she'd done thus far, and he still didn't trust her. "Don't you think I know enough to have done that by now, if that was my intent? No. I need something to keep my mind off where we are and what we're doing." That and she *was* curious. All the Darkin books on the Legion and the Chosen were vague on how they'd begun.

"What do you want to know?"

His willingness to share despite his words of distrust drew her even more closely to him. "What happened after the three brothers escaped?"

"They went their separate ways, trying to get the pieces of the Book as far apart as they could."

So that's why Rathe had no idea where they were and was so eager to have the Chosen collect the pieces for him. The Hunters themselves didn't know where all three pieces were secreted. A smart strategy if a group didn't want anyone to discover their secrets. "Did they ever see each other again?" she asked to keep the conversation going.

Colt shrugged. "I don't know. The legends don't talk about that part much. They only tell us which brother founded which line of Hunters. Each line has a separate specialty in hunting. Some Hunters are more skilled at killing vampires, and others are better at hunting demons. Depends on what's prominent in the area where you live. Stay to your left for about four steps."

Lilly looked down and saw the outline of four different squares inlaid into the floor. She pressed herself against the wall, following his lead. "And what if the information you needed to know was in a different portion of the Book of Legend?" she asked.

He glanced back at her. The torch threw his face into a play of light and shadow, making it look far more sinister than she'd ever seen it. "Then you learned it by trial and error, unless you happened to come across another Hunter from a different line who could train you. We worked in isolation for centuries, but with the telegraph, the postal system, and air travel, Hunters have been able to band together more as our numbers have dwindled."

"So nobody wants to be a Hunter anymore?"

Colt's laughter had a rusted, dull edge to it. "Nobody chooses this life on purpose, sweetheart. It just sort of happens and takes over." He stopped, looking at a shaft of light cutting across the interior of the tunnel. He looked at it intently, then took off his Stetson and waved the hat quickly in the beam of light. *ZZZOT.* An arc of blue electricity several times more powerful than a sting shooter zapped a smoking black spot on the metal wall behind them. Rivulets of electricity sparked along the length of the wall, disappearing into the darkness of the tunnel. Lilly gasped.

"Duck underneath the light," he instructed as he settled his hat back on his head, crouched down, and kept moving forward.

Her heart was pounding out a loud tattoo in her throat. She swallowed hard past it and pulled herself together to follow him.

"If you're lucky enough to live long enough to have children," he continued, "you spend the rest of your life fearing they won't grow up."

His comment gave her reason to wonder, exactly what would life with Colt be like if they were to survive this machine and Rathe? Would he not want children? Would he give up hunting? No. She knew him well enough to know he'd never do that. So would she be the woman waiting at home alone for news she'd been widowed, or would she be in the battle by his side? By his side, definitely, she decided. She huffed with exertion and fear. "And here the Darkin are the ones believing they alone are hunted."

"I wish." Colt pushed back his Stetson, and for once the shadow moved enough that Lilly could see his eyes clearly. They were determined, but also held a deep sadness, a sadness she'd never heard him voice. "I'll tell you a little secret. My mother never wanted me to be a Hunter."

The news was unexpected and made her heart twinge. The softness she glimpsed in his features made her imagine what he'd looked like as a boy. A bright boy, she imagined, and it made her love him all the more. He'd had parents who truly cared for him, who hadn't seen him as a means to an end. Yet in the end he was nearly as alone and isolated as she. "Why?"

He cupped the back of his neck with his hand and rubbed it. "Ma saw what the men in our family were up against." He gave a mirthless little chuckle. "Hunters aren't known for having long life spans. Guess she was just hoping one of us would survive the life."

"Well, with this kind of thing lying about, I'm sure I can understand the shortened life span," she replied.

Colt turned to her, stepping closer, his chest nearly pressed against hers, making her heart stutter a beat, then beat harder to catch up. "You know, if it weren't for the Gates of Nyx being opened, we wouldn't have to do this. Any of this. You could have been just a woman and I could have been just a man."

"And we never would have met," she finished for him.

"But if we are the Chosen, won't it end all this anyway, I mean, if the prophecies are right?"

He moved closer still, the blue of his eyes sparkling, his breath heated on her cheek. Lilly backed up against the wall and he placed the flat of his large hand on the wall beside her shoulder. "If you are truly the Chosen," she said, her voice so soft it was nearly a whisper.

He inhaled next to her ear, pressing a kiss just below her earlobe, causing everything inside her to tighten. "If I am truly the Chosen . . ." His words rumbled husky and deep in a way that made her shiver.

"Then it's not the end," she breathed. He pulled back a fraction, placing their faces nose to nose. Caught between the unyielding cold metal of the wall and the hot, unyielding wall of his chest, all she could focus on was his face, his mouth.

"It isn't?" he whispered, brushing his lips in a feather-light touch over hers.

She gasped at the tingle, opening her mouth. "No. It's just a new beginning."

He pressed his mouth to hers in a searing kiss that shot sparks down to her toes and wrapped a tight loop around her heart, tying it to him. Everything within her responded. Colt angled closer, placing his other hand beside her shoulder on the opposite side, creating a cage she never wanted to escape.

A sudden grinding sound and vibration behind her head pricked her ears. An instant later, the wall behind Lilly slid open, causing her to stumble backward out of his arms.

She caught a fleeting look at Colt's stunned expression before the door slid shut between them, closing her inside absolute darkness.

Chapter 20

The wall shut with a loud *clang*.

"Lilly! Lilly, can you hear me?"

She pounded on the metal wall separating them. "Get me out of here!" Her voice was muffled, but audible, and from the tenor of it highly displeased. "Colt Ambrose Jackson, you get me out of here right *now*!"

"Don't touch anything. I'm working on it."

A tremor, born of panic, made his hands unsteady. He had absolutely no idea how to get her out.

He wasn't even sure exactly what had happened. One minute he was kissing her soft, willing mouth and the next the wall had opened and swallowed her whole. He ran his palm across the smooth, cold metal. Not a handle. Not an edge. Not a hinge to be found. If asked, he would have sworn an oath that the damn thing had never moved in a hundred years.

"Are you even trying anything?" she shouted, her voice thickly muffled.

What was the last thing he'd done? He'd kissed her. That couldn't have been the trigger. Colt shook his head. *Think, dammit.* He'd been so focused on the feel of her curves against him and the softness of her skin that he hadn't paid any attention to precisely where he'd placed his hands.

He peered more closely at the wall. It was covered in small tiles, no bigger than six inches square, that all looked the same. He'd leaned against her as he'd kissed her, and must have inadvertently triggered one of those tiles. Where had his hands been? Which one had he inadvertently pushed? Closing his eyes, he imagined he was still kissing her, how she'd felt, which stirred him up all over again. Holding his hands in position around an invisible succubus, Colt cracked open an eye, took a guess, and pressed one.

There was a sudden *swoosh*, *thunk* on the other side of the wall that made him jump back and the wall vibrate. "No!" She yelled. "Not that one!"

"What happened?"

"Something big and heavy just came swinging by and nearly hit me."

Colt held the torch aloft. Glinting in the flickering light was a razor-thin outward-bending crease. Clearly it had been a good-sized blade of some kind that had just about found its target. Hell's bells. No more time for mistakes.

Sweat began to itch on the back of his neck. While the temperature within the tunnel seemed constant, Colt might as well have been out in the noonday sun. He tried hard to think of exactly where she'd been positioned when he'd leaned forward. He pressed another tile and an ominous grinding noise began. Damn. Double Damn.

Suddenly he noticed that the passageway was starting to get gradually smaller and smaller as the wall behind him inched closer. If he didn't pick the right tile, right now, he'd be squashed like a bug, and Lilly would be entombed forever in this Hunter-devised maniacal killing machine.

Colt frantically skimmed his shaking fingers over the cold metal tiles. Which one? He tried to ignore the wall encroaching on his back. God. Was there any air in here, or were his terrified lungs constricted by fear for Lilly, and for himself?

Think, boy. Think!

Sweat beaded his brow and upper lip as he rubbed his damp hands together. He closed his eyes again, letting his fingers and his Hunter instincts take over. There. His fingertips encountered a tile that was slightly warmer in temperature. He pressed the heel of his hand against it with a silent prayer.

The wall slid open.

Lilly catapulted out of the opening and into his arms, nearly bowling him over and knocking his hat and the lit torch to the ground. "Finally! You have no idea—"

But the moving wall behind him hadn't stopped pressing forward, skidding his hat and the torch along on the floor. He grabbed Lilly about the waist, lifted her up against him, and attempted to drag her back into the opening she'd just escaped. The torchlight guttered out.

"What are you doing?"

"Trying to keep us from getting killed!"

Lilly whipped around and slapped a tile. The moving wall bearing down on them ground to a halt, then slowly started to retreat.

Colt's breath was sawing in and out. He felt around for the torch and relit it, then stared at her in astonishment. "How'd you know which one to push?"

She raised a brow. "I could still see the imprint of your hand on it."

"In the pitch dark?" Colt shifted his gaze and stared hard at the wall. All the damn tiles still looked identical to him. "That must be some pretty amazing eyesight you've got."

Lilly shrugged, glancing quickly up and down at him. "I'm incapable of seeing through walls or clothing, but Darkin vision is better than human vision at spotting human heat in the dark."

"What else can you see?"

Her brow arched upward. "That there's more between you and China McGee than you've been telling me."

Colt grunted, pulling away from her and scooping his Stetson up from the floor. He dusted it off and settled it back on his head. "True, but hardly likely to get us out of this machine."

Lilly's eyes narrowed. He turned away from her and started walking, leaving her to follow in the flickering shadows.

"I would have thought by now I'd more than proved myself to you," she bit out.

"Oh, you have, but just because you've proven trustworthy doesn't mean I trust easily," he replied without heat.

"Because of her, or because it's me?"

Colt locked his intense gaze on hers. She sucked in a startled breath in response. "Neither," he said plainly.

"You said your mama didn't want you to become a Hunter. Then why did you, Colt?"

A flash of the demon's face, pale and sinister, swam into his view, the yellow eyes indelibly marked on his memory. "Because a demon didn't give a damn if I was a Hunter or not, only that I was Cy Jackson's son. He would have killed me and the rest of my family that day if Winn and Pa hadn't known what to do."

"And China?" she pressed.

"China just showed me I was still green as a Hunter."

"And it still rankles."

A corner of his mouth lifted at the thought of how she'd conned him, leaving him to wake without his weapons or his clothes, let alone his gambling winnings. It'd been a hell of a strip card game involving some strong Kentucky Red Eye and a big head on his part, thinking he could outwit the sexy-as-hell shifter and have some fun while he was at it.

"Yeah. I've tried to never forget myself around another

supernatural again." *Until you*, he added silently. He thought she winced at the comment, but she said nothing.

They fell into a companionable silence as they walked down the tunnel, following the twists and turns. Her shoulder brushed against his, causing a growing friction that was making him restless inside. Every once in a while he'd pause, checking the walls for some indication they were headed in the right direction, but he did his level best to ignore the increasing heat she was stirring up inside him.

Not only was this the wrong time and place, she was the wrong woman. She wasn't even human, and he damn well had better start remembering that, even though his johnson didn't seem to agree. Sometimes there were lines you didn't cross. Rules that had to be followed. Having an intimate relationship with a Darkin, let along falling for one, was one big hell of a bad decision for a Hunter. Darkin were business, not pleasure, and certainly not someone to love. Usually. But then again, Lilly wasn't your usual Darkin.

The steady rhythm of her breathing was somehow comforting and maddening at the same time. He'd been hunting alone for longer than he wanted to admit. And the sweet, intoxicating fragrance that flowed around her was so damn feminine and inviting that he found himself taking deep breaths just to indulge in it, then getting angry at himself for doing so.

He had to remind himself that was what a succubus did. Enticed a man to madness, convinced a man to throw caution to the wind. Made him believe he was the only man for her and that she was all that mattered. But no matter how it rankled, Colt had to admit what he was beginning to feel for Lilly wasn't just plain old lust—it was something far more dangerous for a Hunter—an attraction that made him want to tuck her in tight against him and never let her go. He loved her, dammit.

Lilly's boots scraped against the floor as she stumbled.

He grasped her elbow. "Are you—" Colt stopped and cocked his head. *Oh, shit.* The grinding and click of gears could be heard behind the metal sheeting of the wall. Her breathing sped up as she lifted her braced hand from the depressed pressure plate in the wall. Whatever she'd done, it hadn't been good. He tensed.

"Colt . . ."

He swung around, and the torchlight bounced unevenly with the movement as he searched for a sign of what was coming. "What?"

"Something is happening . . ."

"I know, dammit!" *Clunk, clunk, scree.* At about shoulder level, long thin hatches slid open. "Get down!" Colt tackled her about the middle, knocking her to the floor. Two massive scythe blades, hooked and sharp like the ones carried in drawings of the Grim Reaper, snapped out of the walls. They swung so fast, raking in unison along the hallway where their necks had been, that the air whistled with their movement. *Whoosh.*

Scree. Clang. The long hatches slid closed, making the walls look innocuous once more—a long, tiled hall of greenish bronze, punctuated with riveted ribs. The torch still burned as it lay beside them.

They lay face-to-face on the floor, Colt cradled between her buckskin-clad thighs. Colt rose up on his arms, afraid of crushing her, yet keenly aware of how soft and warm she felt beneath him. Her breath was coming in short, shallow pants, born out of panic. In the light of the torch he could see her cream complexion flushed bright pink and her eyes clouded with dark fear. Her curls spread out a tumble of dark red silk over the floor. She'd never looked more alluring.

Talk about bad timing.

But then wasn't his entire partnership—for want of a better word—with Lilly fraught with ill timing?

Inwardly Colt cursed himself. "Some tunnel, huh?"

"Are you sure your father even wanted you to find this thing?"

"He did, but apparently whoever built this contraption wanted to make damn sure the Hunter who found it was worthy." He rolled away from her, careful to check the walls and listen for any sounds before he stood upright again. He liked having a good head on his shoulders and wanted to keep it that way. More importantly, he wanted to make sure Lilly kept her pretty head on her pretty shoulders.

He offered her a hand and she got unsteadily to her feet. She brushed herself off and pushed her loose hair back over her shoulder. "How long do you think we've been down here?"

Colt pulled the watch out of his pocket and looked at it in the light of the torch. "Six hours too long." He glanced up at her. From the sag of her shoulders and the faint smudge of darkness beneath her eyes, he could tell she was tired. Hell's bells, they'd already spent the better part of the day trekking up the mountain, down the gulch, and now into the mountain itself, where this machine was encased like a constantly beating heart.

"What if we don't find your third of the Book, Colt?" she said quietly as they started walking once more. "And I hate to point out the obvious, but what if we never get out of here?"

Colt refused to think of that as an option. He would find it, or die trying. Without all three pieces of the Book of Legend, there'd be no closing the Gates of Nyx completely. Without all three pieces, Rathe would take over the world and the human race could collectively kiss its ass good-bye. "We ain't got time to worry about it, because we are going to find it," he answered. "And we will get out of here."

The long hall branched left, a conspicuous pile of huge brass cogs and gears stacked like remnants of some repair was in the corner. Colt considered picking one up, just to see if he could use it as a wedge in the next damn trap door that opened, then thought better of it. Messing up the stack could very well be another trap.

She caught his gaze and smiled at him wanly, but it didn't reach her eyes. He'd seen that defeated look before. Winn's eyes had looked no different on the day the demon had hurt him so badly he'd nearly died. A small part of him crumpled inside, wanting to wipe that look away and make her smile instead.

The corridor terminated in a round room, arched into a verdigris-streaked brass dome at the top. Lilly looked around, and her shoulders slumped. "A dead end?"

"Don't say that." Colt turned and gently cupped her cheek in his palm. Her skin was smooth, warm and fragrant like the petals of a rose in the sun. He traced his thumb back and forth over her cheek, indulging in the feel of it. "We aren't dead yet. We're going to get out of this with the Book, Lilly, and we're going to get you away from Rathe . . . I promise on my soul."

"Don't make promises you can't keep," she murmured softly, her voice blunted with pain. "Look around. We're lost. Hopelessly and totally lost." Her lashes turned darker as moisture gathered in her eyes, threatening to spill over into full-blown tears. Colt didn't think he could handle that. He pulled her into his arms and ignored the ache from the wounds still healing on his chest, letting her cling to him. He rubbed his hand slowly over her back and placed a kiss on the top of her head, inhaling the fragrance of her, letting it fill him up.

She hiccupped, her body trembling. A cold wash of dread slid down his spine as hot dampness started to saturate his shirt right over his heart. Aw, hell. That did it. "How about this, I promise that'll we'll stop shortly and rest for the day."

She nodded against his chest and gave a slight sniffle. "Why?" Her voice was so small, so soft that he nearly missed it.

"Why what?"

"Why are you willing to help me?"

He stroked her hair. "I promised," he said simply. He didn't need more of a reason than that. A Hunter's promise was ironclad. His honor, his ability to trust his brothers in the Legion, depended on it.

Lilly gazed up into his face, her green eyes luminous and fringed with dark spiky lashes. "How big a fool do I look to you, Colt Jackson?"

Her words hit him like physical blows, triggering his defense. "You don't believe a Hunter can have honor when it comes to a supernatural?"

She nibbled her lip. "If what you want to call it is honor, then you're the first Hunter I've met with it."

For a moment he couldn't look at her. There was simply too much push and pull, confusion and mixed emotion. Duty. Honor. Loyalty. Love. Aw, hell. He'd reached the tipping point with her where he couldn't lie to himself any further. There was more of him invested in Lilly than just his libido; she'd somehow slowly claimed his heart.

He peered at the walls looking for some sign of what they should do next. There, at the center of the floor, was a small lion's head. He stepped on it. A huge crunching thud echoed under the floor. Clicking noises preceded a sudden jerk beneath their feet as the entire room, floor and all, began to spin on its axis.

As the room rotated slowly, it cut off their access to the hallway, leaving them trapped, but gut deep Colt knew it was this or declare a stalemate and just sit there. They had to take the next step if they wanted out. They had to take the risk. He took a deep breath, then let it out real slow. "If you wouldn't call it honor, what would you call it?"

* * *

Lilly turned her gaze away from his broad shoulders and chiseled stubborn features as she contemplated how to answer him. She didn't want him to see the unnatural feelings that were colliding inside her. The hero-worship she could understand. He was the Chosen, a legend in her world. But the small dull ache building in the pit of her stomach when she thought of what her life would be like if he freed her from Rathe and then walked away into the sunset, well, that was more difficult to comprehend.

"I don't know. Attraction, maybe. Friendship?" she offered.

On one hand she wanted him to be attracted to her, and not just because Rathe had made it her mission to romance the Book away from him. On the other she feared what an emotional entanglement with him might mean. She'd learned the hard way very young not to trust a single soul—her father had seen to that. Putting all her chances of escaping Rathe into Colt's hands was a huge risk. For so long she'd contemplated what she might do if she wasn't Darkin anymore, how she'd find Amelia and start life over. Putting her trust, her heart, in a Hunter's hands was a risk she'd been sure she wouldn't be willing to take. Until now . . .

Colt's touch was soft, but his eyes weren't as he brushed an errant curl away from her temple. "I can tell you whatever is happening between us is far beyond friendship." Her whole world felt like it was spinning, and while logically she knew the floor beneath her feet and the room she stood in rotated, she couldn't help but think some of this instability was in her unusual responses to Colt, because this kind of spinning made her head and chest feel light.

Never having made many friends when she'd been mortal, Lilly was ill equipped to make a comparison. "How do you know?"

He pressed two fingers to her sternum right above her breasts, and the touch went all the way down to her heart. "You feel it in here, way down deep. Friendship don't do that."

Her breasts tightened and ached, waiting for his touch to glide just a bit farther to one side or the other along the inside swell of her breast. But he didn't, and the ache increased.

"Neither does honor," she countered. She'd had enough of waiting for him to admit the growing attraction between them. She grazed the back of her hand lightly against his hardened length.

His lips twitched. Desire flared in his eyes.

She lowered her lashes. "What are you thinking about right now?" she asked, her voice barely a whisper.

"How good you looked in britches." He cupped his other hand around the smooth roundness of her bottom, pulling her in tight against him. Lilly gave a little gasp at the sudden counterpoint of soft against hard. Colt might be good at playing stoic, but he couldn't hide the evidence of his desire. "I've been thinking about it since I watched you walk around in them things. They're like a kidskin glove, hugging your curves. Give a man plenty to fantasize about. I think they might be even more tempting than that little scrap of silk you were wearing in the circle in the desert," he added.

Lilly gave a husky laugh. "Don't get used to it," she said as she purposely rocked against him. "It's a sight you'll likely never see again. Skirts are more my style. I'd prefer not to be in britches at all."

Colt's dark pupils swallowed up the blue. The scent of leather and wild places that clung to him sucked her in and made her heartbeat thump hard and her stomach dip. "I can arrange that," he said, his voice deep and low as he reached for her buttons.

She grabbed the fabric of his shirt in both hands, pulling him even closer so they were nose to nose, hip to hip, and looked deeply into his eyes so he couldn't mistake her intentions. "So what's stopping you?" she breathed.

There was nowhere for them to go, not until the room stopped its rotation and revealed the next exit to them. The vibrating movement of the floor only agitated his state to a higher level.

His voice sounded rough and ragged, a man on the brittle edge of control. "It's wrong. Darkin and Hunters don't do this. There's rules." He slipped his hand slowly up her spine and into her hair, stroking his fingers through her curls, cupping the back of her head. The light throbbing in her blood grew more insistent in response.

"So?" Lilly went up on her tiptoes and grazed his lips lightly with hers in a teasing, seductive touch that twisted the need building inside her into an even tighter knot.

"I know you're a succubus, but that doesn't stop me from wanting you." His eyes intently searched her face, looking for answers and lingering on her mouth, making it tingle, his shoulders rock hard with tension. "It just plain don't make sense. I know what I'm supposed to do, but I don't give a damn."

He pressed his mouth hard to hers in a kiss that speared right to her very core, making her temperature soar and her bones liquefy. They melded together in the searing heat between them. There was no more him or her—only them. His touch ignited a breathtaking fire that threatened to consume them both from the inside out. She arched into him, wanting, needing, greedy for more.

He broke their fevered kiss and pulled back, his shallow and fast breathing matching hers as he rested his forehead against hers. "I can't think straight when I'm around you," he said, fine lines of pain appearing around his eyes as he closed them. "How do I know you aren't just using your succubus powers on me?"

Lilly only wished she had, and far earlier. She gave him a slow, wicked smile. "If I were, there's no way we'd have lasted this long."

"I think—"

She kissed him hard, nipping his lip. "Maybe you shouldn't be thinking at all, just feeling." Lilly rucked the ends of his shirt up out of his pants, then ran her hands underneath the cloth. Her hands glided along the ridged planes of muscle along his abdomen and sides, then up and across the broad expanse of his back. His skin was hot, gloriously hard and smooth beneath her fingers.

Colt sucked in a hissing breath. "Still don't make it right."

Lilly placed a finger over his lips to silence him, then replaced it with a lingering kiss that was part nibble, part flick as she slowly undid the buttons of his shirt and peeled it down his muscular shoulders. "Maybe this doesn't fall into wrong and right."

Colt groaned. His hands spread and tightened on her sides, his thumbs rasping back and forth over the soft sides of her breasts. "Everything falls into right and wrong."

"Not everything." She snapped her fingers, replacing her boots, buckskin britches, short blue jacket, and broadcloth shirt with the black silk sheath he'd summoned her in, placing only the most insubstantial barrier between his touch and her skin. "Like this. Is it wrong or right?" she teased.

His eyes widened a fraction and then he shut them tight and blew out a harsh breath as he cupped the globes of her breasts in his heated palms. "Very right," he growled.

She leaned in close, pressing herself to his chest, with only the hot silk between them as she wrapped her arms around his neck and whispered in his ear. "That's my Hunter."

Colt cried out, kissing her hard, his arms tightening around her as he lifted her up off her feet hard against him. His tongue was slick and soft, brushing, feasting on her mouth. Lilly thought she might just explode. Slowly he lowered her to her feet, her whole body brushing the full length of him as they both panted. But as she reached for the buttons in the rough fabric of his pants, the rotation of the room stopped abruptly and another grinding of gears filled the chamber.

He tensed. "Something's wrong. It's a trap!"

There was nowhere to go. No exit.

"But you said the lion's head was the Hunter's signal of what to do next!"

"It was, is, but maybe that one was intentionally placed there to mislead."

The floor in the circular room shifted beneath their feet, lifting to one side, creating a smooth, angled surface with nothing to hold on to. Colt slid, trying to climb up the floor as it tilted higher and higher, opening into a dark chasm beneath them. He grabbed the upper edge of the floor as she went sliding past him with a scream. He reached out to grab her, the yank and pull of contact making her whole arm burn, but he held fast to her wrist. He groaned, clenching his teeth, his jaw flexing and muscles in his arm bulging as he held them both by his one hand clamped on the edge of the upended floor. Their contact was smooth and slick and his fingers slipped against her skin, making the bones in her wrist twist with the pressure.

"Don't let go!" she begged, eyes wide and terrified.

Her skin was too slick, too smooth. The muscles in his arm burned and the metal edge cut into the palm of his gun hand as he held both her weight and his by one hand as they dangled precariously above the abyss.

"I can't hold us much longer," he muttered through tightly clenched teeth. "But we're going to go together. On the count of three, ready?"

"What? No! I'm not ready!" she said as she twisted frantically beneath him, grabbing hold of his arm with her other hand, her fingers digging into him hard enough to bruise.

Colt caught her panicked gaze and held it. "It'll be all right. Trust me." He had no idea if that was true or not, but her movement was shortening what little time they had left to hold on. It made no sense. Why had the lion head led them to a trap? The blood oozed out of the cut, making the metal slick beneath his fingers. Maybe it hadn't. Maybe this was the only way through this metal rabbit warren. His grip on the edge of the metal began to slip.

"One."

"Colt! You don't know what's down there."

"Two."

"Don't do it!"

"Three."

At the same time he let go, he pulled her up with every ounce of his remaining strength to hold her against him and cushion their fall into the darkness.

The drop was fast, a skidding free fall that sent them spinning off in the darkness on a slide that looped back on itself over and over in a spiral like a giant corkscrew. His hat came flying off, and with a thud they came to a stop on a pile of filthy rags.

The bronze walls were less tarnished here, and parts of their original golden luster showed in spots of the verdigris. The space they'd been unceremoniously dumped in was not much bigger than a sleeping compartment on a train, with four walls and only one, regular-sized, bronze door with a crystal doorknob and a keyhole beneath it.

Colt glanced upward at the smooth rounded tube they'd just fallen through and pulled his shirt back up around his shoulders. "There's no way we can get back up that way."

A stunned expression made Lilly's green eyes even wider. The hem of her black silk chemise had ridden up high, nearly to the juncture of her thighs. Colt's pulse pounded hard and he cleared his throat. "Allow me." He offered her his uninjured hand.

Lilly glanced at the black grease smeared on her legs from the pile of rags and grumbled in disgust. "This will never do."

She snapped her fingers and the boots, buckskin britches, white shirt, and short blue jacket reappeared as if they'd never been gone. "Much better."

Colt suddenly felt exposed. He buttoned up his shirt and quickly located his hat, tugging it firmly back into place. He picked up his pack, which had slid down with them, and put it into place on his back.

"Well, shall we?" Lilly asked, looking at the door.

"From the looks of things, sweetheart, it's try it or plan on staying here for an extended visit."

Lilly eyed the thin red line of light coming from beneath the door. "Do you hear that?"

The vibrating thrum of moving gears and shushing steam was louder in the room than it had been their entire trek through the death machine.

Colt touched the door with his fingers. "It's warm. Maybe we've reached the heart of the machine."

He turned the crystal knob in his hand. The door didn't budge. "Locked, and we don't got a key."

"We may just have to improvise," Lilly said, pulling the

copper wire and a nail from her pocket. She knelt before
the door, sliding the tip of the nail into the rounded part of
the keyhole and sliding the end of the wire in alongside it.

"Lock picking?"

"Another skill my father insisted I learn."

She wriggled the wire and listened carefully for the lock
to give way. She straightened up and gave Colt a grin as she
twisted the knob and opened the door.

A blast of wet, stagnant air hit them. Lilly covered her
mouth, gagging at the stench of death and decay and sulfur
that permeated the air. It reminded her so much of Rathe
that her skin tightened in revulsion.

Skeletons lay scattered about in different poses of their
last moments in what seemed to be an engine room. One
sat propped up against a wall, dressed in dusty gentlemen's
clothes, grasping an empty bottle whose peeling label read
absinthe. Another dressed like a roughed-up miner had a
bony hand clutched at the dagger handle stuck firmly
through his plaid shirt in one of his ribs. A third dressed in
a lab coat and goggles lay facedown at the table, his bony
fingers uptilted in a last fruitless effort to beg for help.

"Whatever happened here wasn't pretty," Colt muttered,
taking her hand firmly in his as they walked into the room
and he looked from one body to the next.

Behind them the door slammed shut, making a fine
powder of rock dust drift down from the exposed ceiling.
There was no knob or lock on this side of the door. "We
better start looking for an exit, if there is one," Colt muttered.

Lilly surveyed the room cut into the bedrock. The only
metal wall was the one behind them. Along the rough rock
wall ahead of them were the men in different stages of
decay, wooden crates full of gears and equipment, and a
small rickety table with two chairs, one occupied by the
skeleton with the goggles. On their right the rock wall
curved away. A small pool of water bubbled and boiled,

sulfur-laced steam rising in wisps and curls from its surface. Huge black pipes of cast iron with pressure gauges and wheel-controlled valves twisted from the pool and disappeared into the rock. And to the left there was a large bronze door similar to the one behind them.

Colt touched the pipe. "Damn." He shook his singed fingers. "Hot spring. Must be what provides the steam to power the machine."

"Do you think they"—she indicated the bones of the men behind them—"were in charge of the machine?" Lilly skimmed her finger along the curve of one of the cracked pressure gauges above the pipes.

"Judging by what they're wearing, they were treasure hunters who ended up trapped down, just like us." Colt pulled the goggles off the skeleton's shriveled face, and they tangled in the long, stringy hair still clinging to the skull of the corpse. "Whoever they were, they've been here a long time."

The fact that Colt believed them to be treasure hunters, and that the bones had been there a long, long time, wasn't exactly encouraging to Lilly. She could imagine herself and Colt only too well as one more pair of fools to be caught in this maniacal death trap machine. "Do you think they were looking for the Book?"

Colt kicked a mining headlamp on the floor aside. "Nope. I think they were looking for the Lost Dutchman's gold and stumbled into more than they bargained for and went mad."

Lovely. One more thing she'd considered, but didn't need to hear. "They had to be pretty good to make it this far."

"Either that, or this is where everyone ends up sooner or later to die."

"Do you think you could try a little harder to be optimistic?" Lilly rubbed her arms, suddenly cold in the room.

"Let's try to figure out how to get out of here, rather than pulling up a chair and waiting to die of old age."

Colt pulled off his hat and plowed his fingers through his hair. "How do I know?"

"You're the Hunter!"

"Yeah, well, Pa's notes on hunting down supernaturals didn't exactly cover disabling a dynamic killing machine," he said, settling his hat back in its customary place.

He glanced to their left at the silver door set into the rock, embossed with the head of a roaring lion. His mane flowed away from his head in silver streamers and his glittering eyes were cut golden topaz. There were no handles, no hinges on the beautiful door. But beside it was a silver plate set into the wall, with three small round openings as large as a quarter and a series of dials and a hand crank.

Lilly had never seen anything like it. She followed Colt as he walked over and began his examination. "It's beautiful, but how is it going to get us out of here?" she asked.

Colt cracked his knuckles and gave her a grin. "It's good luck."

"What?"

"I recognize it. It's a frequency transponder mechanism. Marley gave me a set of crystals with strict instructions to only use one type of crystal at a time. Each crystal resonates at a different frequency, giving it different levels of power, which technically should do different things. At least I think that's most of the theory he was blathering on about." He swung his pack off his back and dug into it.

Colt swore under his breath, then dug deeper. "Where are those damn crystals?"

A chill threaded through Lilly's veins as her hand slipped into her pocket and closed around the small velvet pouch. "What do they look like?"

"Three sparkly rocks, velvet drawstring bag," he said,

digging farther into his pack. "Marley said only to use them in an emergency."

"Well, I'd say this qualifies," Lilly muttered as she gave the small velvet pouch in her front pocket a squeeze.

His eyes narrowed as he glanced at her hand. "You took them." It wasn't a question, but an accusation. "Why?" Hurt mingled with suspicion in his eyes. Lilly didn't like either one.

Lilly's heart shrank a size smaller at his accusation, and the fury on his face. "Just when I begin to trust you," he muttered. "Serves me right."

"I—I didn't think it'd matter to you," she stuttered as she pulled the pouch from her pocket and proffered it to him. "I've always had the habit of picking up things like the wire and nails, especially when I'm nervous. It makes me feel more secure."

Colt took the bag from her. "That doesn't mean you had any right to take them." He gently pulled the puckered edge of the velvet, opening the pouch, and withdrew a small bit of clear quartz about the width of his thumb.

Heat suffused Lilly's cheeks. She balled up her hands on her hips. "If that's the worst thing I've done, I hardly think that's reason for you not to trust me."

"Oh, really?" He grasped the bag tighter, crushing the velvet.

"You're just mad that you liked kissing me. That you wanted more, even though you knew you shouldn't," she challenged.

Colt cursed under his breath. "You've been using your succubus powers on me all along, haven't you?" His knuckles tightened white as his grip on the crystal increased.

All the starch left Lilly's spine. All they'd been through and he still didn't see what was happening to them. She leaned against the rough wood of the stacked crates beside her. "No. I haven't. If I did, the moment you were satisfied, you'd go numb to everything else around you except the sound of my voice. Has that happened?"

Colt didn't answer. He didn't need to. While she sure as hell had set off sparks in him and given him heart palpitations fit to kill a man, she knew he'd never once lost his ability to feel around her. Hell, if anything, all his feelings became so intense they were difficult to bear.

"So what I'm feeling—"

"Is coming straight from you," she finished for him. "What's happening between us is as real and honest as it gets."

"Then I owe you an apology."

He couldn't have stunned her more if he'd shot her with his inventor friend's gadget. Hunters, especially the Chosen, were supposed to be ruthless. Not—apologizing.

"All I want is for us to find the Book so you can get it back together and I can escape Rathe."

Colt twisted the crystal between his fingers, the light bouncing off it and sending refracted sparkles over the walls of the machine room.

He looked at it, then handed it to Lilly. "How about you do the honors."

Chapter 21

"Go on, give it a try," Colt urged.

Lilly gazed at the imposing roaring lion emblazoned on the silver door before her and then gingerly plucked the clear quartz crystal from his thick fingers and shoved it into the first round hole in the silver panel of the transponder. "Now what?"

Colt turned the hand crank several times, then twisted the dial beside the crystal. A high keening noise began. The crystal lit with white light from below and the silver door beside the transponder shuddered, the topaz crystal eyes of the lion's face on the door beginning to glow.

"Try another one," Lilly urged, grabbing hold of his arm.

"But Marley said—"

"He doesn't know everything!" she retorted.

Colt pulled an amber-colored citrine from the bag and plugged it into the transponder above the quartz. Again he cranked, then turned the dial farther. The keening sound grew into a wail. The crystal glowed yellow. Slowly the door lifted and stopped halfway. Enough room to get through if they crawled on their bellies.

"Put in the last one."

This time Colt didn't even bother to argue. He took the piece of amethyst from the pouch and plugged it in the last hole on the transponder's receiver board, gave the hand crank several vigorous spins, and turned the dial. The keening sound turned into a high whine, purplish light shot up through the crystal, and the door lifted completely, revealing a huge two-story chamber unlike anything Colt had ever seen.

Large bronze lions, taller than Colt, sat as silent sentinels on either side of a metallic floor checkerboarded with different colors of metal tiles—silver, greenish copper, gleaming golden brass, and black wrought iron. All along the base of the walls behind them, greenish light pulsated and arced in long cylindrical glass tubes. But his gaze was drawn to a stream of bright pale moonlight streaming in a blue white shaft from high above at the far end of the chamber.

The eerie light illuminated a black marble pedestal atop a raised dais, and atop the pedestal sat a large rectangular box.

"This is it." Lilly tugged Colt's hand, prodding him forward when he just stood there staring. "Come on." She stopped because he wasn't budging. "What's the matter?"

"What if—Dammit, Lilly. What if we've gone through all this, endured death-defying experience, only to find that we did all that and this isn't what I'm looking for?"

She tugged harder. She understood wanting something so badly she could taste it. She understood bitter disappointment. "We won't know unless we go over there and look, will we?"

Colt's feet unglued from the floor, and he moved forward. Far too slowly for Lilly's taste. "Get moving, Mr. Jackson."

"You don't think that the light beam will act like that other one we encountered, do you?"

Colt wrapped an arm around her and held her tightly to his side. "You mean as a trigger to send out a bolt of electricity that's designed to kill rather than stun? Yes, that's exactly what I think."

"But we've gotten through their traps. Surely even that is enough of a test for the best of Hunters."

"Unless whoever put it here intended for it to never be moved."

Colt peered at the floor and bent down, examining the array of metal tiles in the floor. Some were greenish copper, others paler brass, some looked silver, and others were nearly black. The silver tiles looked like they were slightly elevated from the others. He stood and grabbed Lilly's shoulders. "Listen to me carefully. The colored tiles in this floor are pressure plates. You step on one and it will act as a trigger."

"To what?"

"I don't know, and I don't want to find out. Just follow close behind me, and step where I step. Stay on the silver tiles."

Lilly sighed. She'd had just about enough of Hunters and their traps.

They started across the floor, Colt going first. He stepped carefully from one pale silver tile to another, then turned back to assist Lilly. The tiles weren't large enough for two, so their reach had to stretch from one spot to the next. The problem was, his legs were longer than hers. At one point she had to hop to reach the spot where he'd last been. While one foot landed solidly in the middle of the silver tile, the other landed half on the proper tile and half on the dark iron one beside it.

The dark tile dipped down, making her ankle twist. She shrieked, windmilling her arms backward as she lost her balance. Colt grabbed the waistband of her pants and pulled her forward, flush up against him. *Shush. Thwang!* A rush of air stirred over the back of her neck. Lilly glanced at the wall where the shaft of a small crossbow arrow quivered. Both of them had narrowly missed getting shot where their heads would have been. Looking at where it must have come from, she noticed that each large lion had an opening in its mouth. Clearly the statues were not just pompous decorations.

"Now we know what happens when we step on the iron tiles," Colt huffed. Lilly's frantic heartbeat pounded against his chest like a frightened rabbit's. "How's your ankle?"

Lilly stepped down on it and winced. "Hurts, but I can walk on it." She swiveled and gazed at the pedestal still halfway across the room. "There's no way we're going to make it. I'll stay here and you keep going."

"We can make it together, we just need to go slow and be careful."

She tried hard to keep up with him. At one point she misjudged his movements and bumped into him, sending him off balance. His toe caught on a copper tile in front of him. He quickly withdrew it. A drop of something liquid hit where his foot had been a second before, and the small spot sizzled and fizzed, turning bright orange. Colt glanced upward. "Acid. Avoid the copper tiles."

Lilly bit her lip and nodded. The problem was, the closer they got to the pedestal and the elusive box, the farther and farther apart the silver tiles seemed to be spaced. She wasn't certain she could make the jump from one tile to the next, and Colt was already two moves ahead of her.

Exhaustion was beginning to take its toll. She leapt for a silver tile and missed, her foot landing on the brass one next to it. The hard bite of an electric shock clamped down on her foot, shooting up her leg, burning and causing her leg muscles to twitch involuntarily. Colt yanked her to the silver tile and she collapsed into his arms.

"I can't go on anymore. You go and get it," she pleaded.

"Nonsense. A Hunter never leaves his partner behind. We're in this together, you and I. We started this together and we're going to finish this together." He scooped her up into his arms and deftly crossed the last three silver tiles leading to the base of the dais.

Up close, the case on the pedestal looked far larger and more imposing. Colt took the steps two at a time, Lilly still clutched tight to his chest, and set her down only when they reached the top of the raised dais. He kept a firm arm around her waist and kept her tucked in close to his side.

A thick coating of dust made it difficult to see precisely what was inside the box, but upon closer inspection she saw the ledger-sized box was actually a glass case with seams made of metal. Lilly blew on it, coughing a little at the cloud it created.

Inside the glass case on black velvet was what looked like an ancient illuminated manuscript, the pages created from yellow matte vellum, the gilt lettering and hand-colored images glittering in the light of the torch. Lilly gasped. "It's beautiful."

"And in the right hands it's deadly to all Darkin."

She locked gazes with him. "And in the hands of the Chosen, a key to saving this world." Excitement tingled in her fingers and toes, sparkling and fizzing up inside her until she felt light-headed, like she'd drunk champagne. They'd done it! They'd actually done it!

Colt pointed at the ragged edge of the dark leather binding on the spine of the Book. "Part of the key anyway." His voice had a catch to it as if the sight choked him up. It took a moment but Lilly realized how much this stack of vellum pages really meant to Colt. This was more than a tool. This was his family legacy, the legacy of all Hunters.

"This is Cadel's piece of the Book," he said quietly. "See there? That's the back cover. And those loose pages at the back, those are my pa's notes."

"So that's the last third of the Book of Legend."

He nodded, never taking his eyes off the Book in the case.

"Well, get on with it."

He turned and gave her a questioning look. "What?"

"We didn't come through all this to just stand here and look at this relic, did we? Pick it up so we can take it with us."

"Right." Colt put his hands on the case. Blue sparks shot out, the current arcing up his arms and making the hair on his arms rise. He let out a yelp and jerked back, shaking his hands. "Damn thing is electrically charged!"

"It must be the gold on the edges acting as a conductor."

Colt stared hard at her for a moment. "So no case, no conductor."

"It seems logical to me."

Colt stripped off his shirt and wrapped it around his right hand several times. The moonlight highlighted with silvery fingers the ridges and ripples of his bare torso. Lilly's heart sped up in response. She tightened her hands into knots to prevent herself from reaching out and touching him while he was concentrating.

"What are you doing?"

"Getting rid of the case." He pulled back his hand and hit the glass hard, shattering it.

Lilly squeaked at the impact.

The fabric had done its job, protecting his hand. He unwrapped his hand and gingerly reached between the shards, careful to avoid the gold and the razor-sharp edges of the glass. As his fingers wrapped around the edges of the Book, a warm heat flowed through his hand and up his arm. Whatever else could be said, the Book was a powerful thing. It was also far heavier than it looked.

Colt pulled the manuscript from the ruins of its housing and shook off the glass shards glittering on the surface.

"We've got it! We've actually got it!" Lilly squealed with sheer delight.

"Finding it is only half the battle. Getting it out of here and to the Gate is the other half," Colt murmured. He was too awestruck by what he held in his hand. This was legend in physical form. An ancient depository of secrets from the ages meant to enlighten Hunters and protect humanity.

Lilly peered at it, a gleam in her eye. "What shall we do with it?"

Colt pulled an oilcloth out of his pack and gingerly wrapped the Book in the cloth, then tied it shut with a length of twine. "We're taking it out of here," he said as he tucked it into his pack and swung the pack over his bare shoulders.

Their plans were short-lived. The walls began to tremble and Colt heard what sounded like thunder.

"Must have been a pressure safety switch," he muttered. He glanced at the pedestal where the Book had lain and only now noticed the small section of raised velvet. He tried pushing it downward, but the thunder only grew louder. "Damn."

A deep rumble started in the recesses of the darkness above them. All the hairs on Colt's body lifted as he glanced upward. "That sounds like water, coming fast." He glanced back at the maze of colored tiles behind them, knowing now what each colored tile held in store for them. There wasn't time to walk from silver tile to silver tile. The safe route wasn't going to save them from whatever was coming.

Beneath their feet the floor trembled. A section of the wall slid open slowly far above them.

He grabbed hold of Lilly's hand and ran. Crossbow bolts

zinged behind them and the drips from the ceiling created an acid rain in their wake as they sped across the booby-trapped floor.

A rush of water came cascading down through the opening, an artificial waterfall that turned the room into a giant lake. The torrent had been designed to drown intruders, then flush away what was worthless, leaving the precious metal room intact.

Colt sputtered and gasped as the water caught them mid-run, extinguishing the torch and plunging them into a cold, wet rush and darkness. He held Lilly with an iron grip, determined not to lose her in the flash flood. His lungs and eyes burned, but in the tumult and dark there was no way to tell which end was up.

He broke through the surface and gasped, pulling Lilly up to join him. She wrapped her arms around him, her breath coming in short, desperate pants. The water twisted and swirled through the labyrinth of smooth metal tunnels, rather like pipes beneath a drain. There was no way to keep his bearings or even see.

Colt tried to keep his boots pointed downstream in case they came too close to smashing into anything, so he could kick away from it as they rocketed through the smooth rock tube inside the mountain, but the water carried them along so fast, he couldn't find purchase to hold on to anything to slow down their rapid momentum.

They shot out of the rock face of the mountain into open space and the night sky. Lilly shrieked, arms and legs flailing.

"Hold on to me!" he yelled above the roaring of the water. She latched on to him tight, and together they sucked in a great gulp of air as they plunged down toward the torrent.

Chapter 22

"Whatever you do, don't let go!" Colt knew it was a useless warning. Nothing could be heard over the roar of the tumultuous rush of water. The power and force of the deluge drove them over the edge in a chaotic waterfall of thousands of gallons of frothing, twisting, turning water. All he could do was hold tightly to Lilly and pray they survived. The night stars were streaks of light overhead as they were inextricably swept in a tidal wave with no up and no down.

Nothing to grab hold of, nothing to brace their bodies. They hit rock, were flipped end over end, feet first, then head down. He dragged in a gasp of air when he could, and felt his lungs burn when he couldn't.

They plummeted down hundreds of feet until they hit the roaring torrent below. It was more like slamming into solid rock than water, rasping his bare skin, jarring every bone in his body, tearing off his hat and threatening to rip the pack from his back. Colt wanted to cry out, but he had enough sense to know he'd just suck in more water.

The raging water carried them down the narrow rock crevasse, the narrow opening causing their trajectory to increase as the water deepened and moved even faster between the narrow rock walls. There was no stopping the flood. No way to control it.

The water was a merciless fury of nature with a mind of its own. If they hadn't landed in Hell, it was damn close.

Branches cracked and snapped in the onslaught, echoing like gunfire off the canyon walls. Dirty water cascaded into his mouth and ears. He choked and sputtered, desperate for a sip of air. But as long as he felt the tight grip of Lilly on his skin and the strap in his hand, he had something else to focus on instead of the exploding panic in his gut.

Lilly and the Book. That was all that mattered, he firmly told himself. He was a Hunter. Expendable for the greater good. But to have it end like this, dying in a flash flood, was embarrassing.

He was saved from his own morose thoughts when they slammed into a snag of mesquite trees caught up in the flood. The impact jolted him so hard he lost all his breath and nearly lost his hold on Lilly.

He struggled against the beating force of the water trying to drag him under. "Hold tight to the tree," he ordered. In the moonlight her wet hair had a silver sheen, and he saw her nod. Teeth chattering, Colt placed his face against the rough, wet bark, dug his fingers into the wood, and held on for all he was worth.

Slowly the force of the water lessened, and the level of the water lowered. The earthy scent of wet rock and wood permeated the air. Colt opened his eyes, blinking back the moisture on his lids, and glanced around. His limbs were numb with cold and exhaustion, but as he moved every muscle screamed.

"Lilly?" It came out a barely audible rasp. "You all right?"

* * *

Lilly knew she wasn't dead. She just hurt enough to wish she was. But thanks to being Darkin, the bruises and lashes in her skin were already beginning to heal. She stirred beside Colt, wet hair plastered to her head and across her shoulders in heavy, wet ropes.

"I'm alive, if that counts," she murmured, then coughed hard, her chest burning.

Colt set his head back down beside hers and gave a small laugh. "Yeah. It counts."

"Remind me never to follow you into a Hunter-devised death trap again," she said slowly. "Or ride on that mechanical monstrosity of yours."

He laughed off her asperity. "I'm just glad that we're still alive." He reached over and brushed the wet hair from her cheek with a tender touch and looked into her eyes. "We did it, sweetheart. We got the Book."

She managed a tremulous smile. "We did."

The cool wash of desert air, scented with the heavy sweetness of night-blooming cactus flowers, caressed her cheek. Lilly should have felt elated. She should have been able to fly. They had done the near impossible, and if they were capable of that, she might actually stand a chance of escaping Rathe. But deep down, everything within her just hurt.

In the moonlight the water had turned into a silver ribbon on black wet rock. It still burbled and flowed beneath the snag, but it was slowly going back to being the small stream they'd first encountered in the gulch.

"Our pact is complete," she said softly.

He closed his eyes. "Not yet," he croaked. "I promised to free you from Rathe, and I will."

A small shimmer of hope welled up inside her. Colt had never said he loved her, but perhaps he really, truly did.

He cracked open one eye. "The first thing we need to do

is get down this mountain. Then we can figure out how to get the Book of Legend reunited."

"That's mighty ambitious. Perhaps we ought to consider taking this at a more manageable pace."

"Such as?"

"Such as being able to walk first," she suggested, her voice tinged with sarcasm as she groaned.

He chuckled. "You've got a point, sweetheart."

He grunted as he peeled himself off the snag and struggled down the tangle of wet wood. "Are you coming or not?"

Lilly took a deep breath and started moving. The wet buckskin britches were growing clammy and tightening as she climbed down to the canyon floor. Colt offered her a hand at the last bit, and she took it and stepped down on firm soil once more. Then he swung his pack off his back and checked on the oilcloth package containing the Book.

"Looks like the Book made it through all right." He cast a glance at her, and swallowed hard. "You'd best get out of those britches before we have to cut them off you," Colt said, as if he'd had the experience to back up his claim. "They'll only get tighter as the leather dries and shrinks."

"Purely suggested with my comfort in mind, I'm sure." She cast him a flirtatious glance as she wrung out her hair.

He had the audacity after all they'd just been through to wink. "Of course."

That was fine by Lilly. She felt far more comfortable in skirts anyway. She snapped her fingers and materialized a fresh set of clothing for herself, including a cream-colored linen calf-length skirt and fitted jacket, thin cotton shirt-waist, a hardy pith helmet wrapped near the brim with a swath of sheer cream silk, and a sturdy walking stick.

Colt quirked a brow at her change in clothing. "Planning on another grand adventure so soon?"

"I have the distinct impression that this kind of thing is

your normal *modus operandi*, and therefore I'm dressing appropriately."

"To go where? Deepest darkest Africa?" He smiled as he slung his pack off his shoulder to rest at his feet. "My pa only taught me enough Latin to be able to passably read the incantations he taught me, so would you mind translating that Modus opera-endy?"

"How you do things."

He gave her a boyish grin, which seemed at odds, and yet perfectly suitable, to the shadows on his roguish face. "That about sums it up. Being a Hunter isn't fancy dress and tea parties, if that's what you're sayin'."

She couldn't help but notice how his wet clothing clung to the hard ridges of muscle, and the gleam of moonlit water on his torso. There wasn't an ounce of fat on Colt. Every hardened, scarred inch of him was earned through hard work. For a moment she considered how he might look with no clothing at all, and her heart responded by going from a trot to a full-out gallop. She shook her head to realign her thoughts more appropriately.

"Would you like a change of clothing as well?"

His eyes held a shimmer of suspicion as he paused, his hand flexing around the edge of his gun belt, and considered her offer. And really, was there so much to consider? He was wet as a drowned kangaroo rat. Finally he replied, "As long as you don't gussy me up and you get me back my hat. Sure, I could go in for some fresh clothes. Just make sure you don't mess with my weapons or my pack."

She snapped her fingers and his wet, heavy denim pants were replaced by dark pants, a fresh white cotton shirt accented with a black ribbon tie at the neck, and his favorite blue and black brocade vest, along with a long brown duster jacket and of course his hat, which she made sure was dried out and free of mud. If possible, he looked even more devastating and dangerous with a bit of polish.

"I look like Remy or Wyatt Earp." His sculpted mouth pressed into a line with distaste. "I said nothing fancy."

Lilly crossed her arms "That hardly constitutes formal dress. And besides, it looks good on you."

"Well, it's dry." Colt grumbled out his thanks, but it wasn't exactly convincing.

The water had all but disappeared, running in a rush out of the gulch and into some distant arroyo. Only the wetness on the rock walls of the gulch and the thin stream of water running in between the rocks indicated that there'd been any gully-washer at all.

They picked their way through the flotsam and jetsam of the flood and climbed out of the darkness of the gulch into pale moonlight. Before them spread the wide expanse of the desert floor. The rocks of the mountain behind them, rust-colored in the daylight, rose up like stacks of silver bars. The crescent moon was sinking in the western sky, still bright white against a sky that was growing blue with pre-dawn light.

Tempus waited for them, just where they'd left him, brass hooves glinting in the waning moonlight. Colt peered out over the immense darkness of the desert. He took the winding key from his pack, unstrung a section of the leather hide covering, and wound the beast. He then secured the hatch and cover back in place and strapped his pack to his horse. When he saddled up without so much as a hand to help her, Lilly gave him a sour look. "You could have helped me mount."

He tipped back the brim of his hat to reveal a twinkle in his blue eyes that made her distinctly aware he'd seen her in far less than she was wearing now. "Thought you weren't comfortable riding my monstrous machine," he said smoothly.

"I'm not. But neither am I a fool. We'll get to where we need to get the Book faster if we both ride."

He gave her a wicked smile. "I'd be happy to give you a ride."

Heat crept hot and fast into her cheeks. She was certainly succubus enough to know precisely what his tone implied. Worse, she'd been thinking about it too.

He pulled her up to sit atop his lap in the saddle. "You'll be more comfortable up here than riding behind," he said by way of an explanation.

Lilly would have debated that point as she rearranged her skirts, since there was a very firm ridge at her posterior, but she didn't think it would make matters any better to mention it.

"And you'll need to take off that hat, otherwise I'll be hitting my chin on it," he said, giving her pith helmet a tap.

With reluctance she removed her headgear and settled it on the pommel. "Better?"

"We'll see." Colt flipped the GGD switch on Tempus, and the clockwork inside the mechanical horse began to click and whirr. He lifted his head, stomped once, then started moving forward.

Letting her ride up front on his lap had to be just about the stupidest thing he'd ever done. With every step forward Tempus took, the soft curve of Lilly's bottom shifted against his shaft, making it both exquisite torture and a pleasurable pain.

They rode on through the desert in companionable silence as the sun rose, an orange fireball riding the ridge of the mountains. The desert spread out in a wash of tans and reds before them, punctuated only by the cactus, short bushy scrub, and spindly junco that looked more like thorny tall sticks than anything else.

Her sweet voice broke the stillness. "How long do you think it'll take us to get to Bodie?"

"About four days."

She twisted, her hair a cloud of ruby-colored flame in the morning's rays, and gazed at him. "Isn't that cutting things a little close?"

"As long as Remy and Winn show up with the other portions of the Book of Legend, it should all work out just fine."

"Hypothetically," she said, turning back to face front.

"Now who's being the pessimist?" he jibed.

"And then what?"

Colt shrugged. "Well, if we manage to close the Gates, then Rathe won't have a hold over you any longer. You'll be free and can go find your sister, just like I said."

An awkward silence stretched between them, filled up with all the things that he wanted to say but found himself too tongue-tied and distracted to express without mucking it up.

Lilly sighed, the movement brushing her small shoulder blades over his chest, making Colt wince. "But I'll still be a demon and you'll still be a Hunter," she said softly as she deflated against him. Colt shifted his hold on the reins to one hand and wrapped the other tightly around her middle, splaying his hand over the soft curve of her hip.

"Do you really think that matters to me at this point?" he said near her ear, his voice rough. He caressed the soft shell of her ear with his mouth and inhaled the unique feminine scent that was all Lilly. Damn, even there she was softer than silk and sweet-smelling.

"It has."

"Hmm," he said as he moved his lips lower, tasting the tender hollow just beneath her ear. "Things change."

Her head tilted slightly, giving him better access. The pulsing rush under his skin increased. "Colt?"

"Mmm," he responded between slow, soft kisses against her nape.

"If I were just a human girl, would you still find me alluring?" She wriggled in his lap and he kept himself as still as he could, which on a moving mechanical horse was nearly impossible. He blew out a slow, steady breath.

"Definitely."

He left it at that. There was no point telling her that somewhere between entering the dynamic machine inside the cave and trekking soaking wet out of the gulch, Colt had discovered one critical thing his pa had never mentioned.

Sometimes the rules just didn't apply.

There were times black faded and white became spoiled. Times when you had to listen to your gut, your heart, and not your head. Times when science and reason didn't hold the answers and intuition did. And right now his gut was a huge throbbing ache, and the only thing that seemed to make it any better was the same thing that made it worse: the woman he held in his arms.

Demon or not, she'd wormed her way into his heart in a way no other female had ever done before. And it wasn't just the chemistry between them burning like a lucifer to kerosene. It was her keen mind, the sweet curve of her cheek, the way she looked at him that made him feel like he was more than just a man. He was somebody.

He'd spent so long hiding in the shadows, blending, he'd become as dismissible as imagination and as fleeting as time. His brothers, his horse, and Marley were about as normal and stable as his life got, and that wasn't saying much.

Hell, to put it simply, he craved more. More of whatever it was that Lilly offered him.

The day wore on. Hot stretches of desert floor dotted with cactus, scrub, and jonco scented with the smells of hot rock and creosote turned into hills. Hills gave way to steep, rocky trails ending in cooler brown flat-topped mesas bristling with little junipers and pines. The sky stayed a vivid cloudless blue. No matter how many times the words were on the tip of his tongue, Colt couldn't seem to master them enough to verbalize. What could he possibly say? He had nothing to offer her. No future. She couldn't even live among normal folks for long without her demon powers beginning to infect the relationships around her. Sooner or later the men wouldn't be able to resist her and the women-folk would be hateful. He wanted to protect her from that. He wanted to give her the normal peaceful life that had been snatched away from her as a little girl.

They leaned forward as Tempus took a zigzag dirt road up the mountains and Colt gripped the reins tighter.

"What do you want from life, Lilly?"

She shook her head, her curls rippling across his cheek, teasing him in the slight breeze. "I want to matter to someone."

Her words were simple, but they hit him like a punch in the gut. She was just as lost, just as battered as he was. She mattered, dammit. She mattered to him.

"You *do*."

Her laugh was hollow, brittle and fragile, revealing the depth of her emptiness inside and making his heart contract. "I want to matter not just for what I can offer or do for another person, but just because . . . well, just because I'm me."

"You matter to me."

"For the moment. But there's no future in it, for either of us. You know that."

He stiffened, rejecting the idea. "What I know is that there's no predicting the future, prophecy or no prophecy. We're going to go into this together, side by side, and by the end of it you'll be free. Trust me."

She turned, gazing up at him, her green eyes bright with yearning, and placed a dainty hand against his cheek and said two words that stripped him down to his bones. "I do."

Colt kissed her hard and fast, letting all the things he couldn't say flow into that one kiss that slanted his mouth across her soft willing one. He slipped his arm beneath her legs, lifting her from her position on his lap and settling her across it instead. She was warm and soft beneath his hands.

"You're tired and so am I. We deserve a rest."

"But what about getting the Book to Bodie?"

"There's only so many miles we can travel in a day, sweetheart. One night's rest isn't going to end the world."

"You're certain?" she hedged, gazing at the sickle of moon already visible in the growing twilight that changed the high desert mountains from shades of red and brown to hues of purple.

"New moon ain't until a few days from now." He splayed his hand over the curve of her hip, and her stomach quivered. "Besides, we deserve a chance to celebrate finding our part of the Book."

Lilly looked up into his rugged face. Colt wasn't just handsome, he was devilishly so. His dark hair was clean and slicked back, making his strong cheekbones and the hard line of his nose more pronounced. The blue of his eyes sparkled with wicked intentions. Her heart bucked.

"What exactly did you have in mind?"

His gaze shifted to the cluster of buildings on the ridge above them. They were getting closer to Prescott. "A special little dinner for two."

As Lilly gazed at the enormous crystal and gas jet chandelier sparkling overhead in the coffered silver lobby ceiling of the Silver Swan Hotel, she briefly wondered exactly what the desk clerk at the long walnut counter had thought when Colt had checked them in without any luggage. She'd never worried about seeming inappropriate before. What was it about being around Colt that made her conscious of her every movement and emotion?

She kept trying to reason out her strange reactions to him as they climbed the wide, sweeping staircase to the second floor.

Situated at the end of the hallway, the little engraved brass plaque on the door of the room they'd been given read HONEYMOON SUITE. Lilly put her hand on his bicep, which flexed beneath her fingers.

"Are you going to carry me over the threshold?" she teased.

Colt pushed the door open, gave her a devastating smile, then swung her up into his arms like she weighed the same as a feather pillow. Lilly gave a little squeak of protest. She hadn't thought he'd seriously take her up on her jest.

But somehow, having his arms around her felt absolutely right. For the first time Lilly felt cherished. And that was an altogether different sensation than being protected. Someone could protect you and still not touch your heart. This reached down into the deepest parts of her and stirred the remnants of her soul. She'd never felt more human than she did right now. Or more loved.

Colt had spared no expense. Gleaming brass gas lamps topped by elegantly frosted glass shades and dripping with long cut crystals at the base lent a soft yellow glow to pale green watered silk and gilt crown moldings along the walls. A small settee with deep-buttoned cushions of forest green brocade and an elaborately carved edge, and two matching wingback chairs accented with black tassels sat around an elegant little tea table of cherrywood topped with white marble before the large white marble fireplace. A polished silver tea set and a cut crystal vase of fresh flowers both flickered with reflected firelight. The small sitting room had one door leading to the bedroom. Clearly the suite was the nicest the hotel had to offer.

He set her down gently on the thick carpet and closed the door behind them with a soft click. Lilly rubbed her arms at the unexpected chill that invaded her body once she was no longer in his arms.

"How did you get them to give you this suite?" Lilly asked.

"I told them we were newly wed. They couldn't very well refuse the honeymoon suite then, now could they?" His heart-stopping smile warmed her all the way to her toes. His appreciative gaze lingered, creating a trail of heat almost like a physical caress. Her skin suddenly felt a size smaller. She turned away, for the first time as a succubus not certain how to respond. A honeymoon was something she had no right to. Something she'd never anticipated she'd have.

Lilly chided herself for her foolishness. After all, she was a succubus, not some milk-water miss fresh out of the nursery with not a clue to what a man wanted from a woman.

Lilly ran her fingers over the pale green moiré silk on the walls as she slowly walked around the sitting room. The problem was, she'd never had her soul at stake, and certainly not her heart. With Colt she feared it would be both.

If she let herself truly indulge all the desire he stirred in her, he might be able to get her soul back from Rathe, but Colt would never return her heart. 'Course if she hadn't been trying to con herself, she'd have admitted the truth; he'd had her heart in his back pocket all along. From the moment she'd laid eyes on him within the circle he'd conjured in the dark desert night, she'd been helpless to resist the yearning that smoldered inside her.

Lilly glanced through the open door into the adjoining bedroom. The elegant curves of the brass headboard and footboard made the wide mattress, covered in dark green velvet and heaped with colorful pillows sporting an impressive array of tassels and lace, look even bigger. She jumped a little as his hand came to rest, warm and heavy, on her shoulder.

"You hungry?" His voice rumbled all the way through her, making the coiling sensation curl into an even tighter spring.

"Absolutely famished." She didn't tell him her hunger had nothing to do with food.

"I thought you might be."

"We could go downstairs and eat," she offered half-heartedly.

There was a knock at the door. Colt winked at her. "I hope you don't mind, but I already ordered dinner for us." He opened the door and ushered in a man in spotless dark green bellhop uniform who pushed in a cart covered with shiny domed silver trays.

Lilly considered for a moment that it might be quite possible that Colt could read minds. The scent of roast chicken, mashed potatoes, and steamed vegetables drifted up from the cart, making her stomach grumble. Beside the trays was a bottle of champagne tucked into a bucket of ice and a small silver bowl of ripe red strawberries. The height of extravagance, yet she couldn't help but smile. If she'd learned anything about Colt, it was he never did anything in half measure.

"Would sir like me to serve?" the bellhop asked. Colt shook his head, slipped the young man a quarter dollar, and efficiently herded him to the door. He shut it and put his back to the door, his gaze heavy and intense.

"It seems you've thought of everything," Lilly murmured.

"Thought, perhaps," he said with a slight sly smile, "but rarely indulged in."

A small laugh welled up in her throat. "I find that very difficult to believe, you being a Hunter."

"So what do you want to try first?"

Colt's blue eyes glittered, revealing that it wasn't the repast on the table he was interested in sampling. He popped the cork of the champagne and poured a glass for each of them, handing her one. "To unlikely allies."

"To the Chosen," she replied. They both took a sip, his gaze never leaving hers. The tart liquid bubbled and fizzed on her tongue, but not nearly as much as the fizzing, bubbling sensation that was building in her blood.

He plucked a strawberry out of the bowl, dipped it in champagne, and traced a slow, cool path across her full bottom lip.

Lilly closed her lips around the berry and took a bite. Colt's pulse thrummed harder, a roar in his ears. Damn. There was only so much a man, any man, even a Hunter could endure. Hell, he was only human.

Her lashes dipped down halfway, a sultry smile curving her mouth. "Colt, you're looking at me like you want to eat me," she said, her tone low and seductive.

He swallowed hard. It wasn't too far from the truth. Try as he might, he couldn't resist the allure of her. He tossed the berry down on the table and pulled her toward him, bringing her soft body up tight against his. "I told myself I'd free you and walk away. But I'm not sure I can."

"Free me?"

"Walk away." He took her lips like a starving man. They were warm and lush, and tasted of strawberry and dry champagne, but also of something more. She tasted of trust, of freedom, of a thousand cravings he'd had since he'd become a Hunter that he denied himself.

Her hot hands slowly and deliberately peeled the jacket

from his shoulders, kneading them, as she kissed him deep and slow, letting her tongue glide along his. Everything inside him tightened and ached. Colt let go of his hold, letting her pull the jacket from him and fling it to the floor. It knocked the tea service sideways, causing a loud crash. He broke their kiss. "We should—"

"Ignore that." She finished for him and gently pushed away. Colt watched in agony as she lifted her arms and snapped her fingers, materializing herself into an exotic harem girl ensemble he'd only seen drawn on a postcard his Hunter friend Marcus had sent him from a hunt in Egypt for wayward mummies.

The gauzy azure fabric that swirled about in long strips from the short skirt at the juncture of her hip to her well-turned ankles was so sheer it revealed far more than it hid, turning nearly transparent in the firelight. Her long legs were glorious. Her breasts, plump and pale white, nestled in a miniature black corset outlined in tiny blue jewels that only extended to the upper edge of her ribs, leaving her the smooth expanse of her stomach and her graceful shoulders scandalously bare. Colt nearly swallowed his tongue. He'd never seen anything like it.

"So, how do you like it? They say it's the latest fashion in the harems of Marrakech."

He had no prayer of answering her.

Her lips curved in a seductive smile as she sauntered forward, the heat of her body threatening to send him up in flames. She reached toward him, sliding her hands down his chest, then suddenly yanked on the fabric of his vest so hard that buttons went flying to ping off the wall. His shirt fared no better.

"Much better," she murmured.

The moment Colt's system woke from the shock of encountering a succubus in all her glory, his libido kicked in with a vengeance. He grasped her about the waist, marveling at the softness of her skin and letting his hands encircle her waist and follow the indention of her spine down to the smooth sweep of her derrière.

"I think I have a far greater appreciation for the power of a succubus," he breathed.

She slowly blinked, her lashes whispering against his cheek. "Then you're still thinking too much. Let me show you," she purred.

Colt's whole chest contracted, then exploded with fire the moment her heated fingers found his bare skin and began to explore. He closed his eyes as her hands trailed across his ribs and followed the line of hair down his abdomen.

Her kisses were warm, sensual, and sexy as hell as she trailed them back up his chest. She pressed a hot kiss right over his heart. It sped up in response.

Lilly locked her half-lidded gaze on his, then captured his mouth with a slow swirl of her tongue. Her bare leg slid up along his, curling over his thigh. He couldn't resist; his hand found nothing but the hot silk of her skin, smooth and warm as he touched her from her delicate ankle up around the curve of her calf to the soft delicate spot behind her knee. So tender, so fragile, so very feminine beneath his hands.

Maybe it had nothing to do with being a succubus, he thought as he slid one hand up over her dainty ribs to the small corset she wore. He cupped the soft, warm globe of her breast in his other palm, enjoying the firm, silky weight of it. Maybe it was just because it was Lilly and she'd somehow become as necessary to him as air. Her soft whimper in response to his touch made the frenzy inside him worse. Overhead the gas jets in the lamps flared even brighter and the fire crackled and popped, sending up a shower of sparks.

He kissed her neck and along her collarbone, her skin even softer there than he had imagined. She smelled like heaven and promises, a spicy rose garden on a lazy warm summer's day. He wanted to taste and touch every inch of her skin, see if the dips and hollows were just as sweet. He wanted to feel her welcoming warmth and sink home. He wanted her.

She sank her fingers into his hair, bringing his face back to hers. "You're thinking again." Her full lips pouted slightly and he couldn't resist kissing the soft, supple mouth. His hands slid up to her thigh. Lilly gave a small hop, deftly wrapping her other leg around him like an acrobat so that she was locked about his middle, her damp heat exactly where he wanted it most.

"And you're not playing fair," he growled as he cupped her bottom to support her and found not only was she not wearing a stitch of clothing beneath the sheer silk skirt, she was slick with feminine need. He cursed and let out a rattling breath, trying to control the way his body shook and his shaft throbbed. Desire sparked into a full-out inferno of need. He knocked over one of the wingback chairs in his haste as he turned and pressed her back against the wall, bracing his feet to steady them both. Wanting to feel every exquisite inch of her inside and out.

"Who said I'm playing," she answered, her eyes twin points of emerald flame that seared his senses, burning away all thought, all reason, leaving only the throbbing rush in his blood that told him to take her fast and hard. The jets of the gas lamps grew dangerously high, making their frosted glass shades crack.

"If you are, it's a dangerous game. I won't give you my soul."

"I don't want your soul. What I want is far more carnal." Lilly's sultry gaze never left his as she slowly and deliberately slid one hand down between them, deftly undoing the buttons on his black pants. She captured the hot, hard length of him in her hand and stroked it up and down, cupping it in her wicked fingers and pressing it against her slick wet heat. He pulsed and ached, using every shred of sanity he had not to sink in to the hilt.

"Last chance," he whispered harshly, trying to maintain his control and failing miserably. A sheen of fine perspiration glowed on her skin, turning her into a gilt goddess.

"You're safe with me. I promise you, your soul is your own," she replied.

Colt couldn't take any more. He sank into her, letting her heat sear away all rational thought. Sparks popped before his vision as her warm smoothness tightened and convulsed around him. Lilly cried out, her head tilting back, her eyes closed. Deep within him something snapped, unleashing a flood of emotion. His chest tightened, constricting around his heart, making the ache and throb extend to every inch of him. For the first time there was peace—not the lull of it, but the absolute certainty that this one moment was perfect and complete. And God help him, he never wanted it to end.

She met him measure for measure, her breath in frantic little pants, their bodies in unison in a run to the finish. She pitched against him, her hips rocking, her fingers digging into his shoulders, all of her tightening around him as she cried out. The fire roared out of the hearth in a blast of heat and light as though tethered to their response, sending the settee, wingback chairs, and tea table up in a blaze. For Colt, it was like being snockered on Kentucky Red Eye, only with a mule kick to the head to boot. He couldn't think or feel beyond where they connected together, skin to slick skin. Her heart was still pounding so hard he could feel it in his own chest. She clung to him, and he wasn't positive he could let her go.

Chapter 23

Lilly waited until late that night when his warm chest beneath her cheek rose and fell with a slow, steady rhythm. They lay skin to skin beneath the blankets and velvet coverlet, which were warm and heavy. A sense of false security, to be sure, but oh so comfortable.

Outside, the room still smelled of smoke. Remnants of the sitting room continued to smolder from the fire, which had responded to her emotions. Soot streaked the ceiling. She hadn't realized making love to a Hunter could be dangerous, not just to your soul, of course, but the room around you. Her response to him had gone to the very marrow of her bones, calling forth powers she didn't even realize she had, let alone could control.

Certain he wouldn't wake, she carefully slipped out from the covers, her skin dimpling with the chill of the air. On silent bare feet she padded toward the discarded pile of Colt's belongings and opened his pack. She pulled out the oilcloth package containing his portion of the Book, her hands tingling. The Book wasn't just a historical remnant or long-kept journal of knowledge. It held power. It radiated a warm, throbbing power that shimmied up her arms, up her torso to the top of her head, raising all the hairs along the way. She held the key to everything she'd ever wanted right here in her hands. The key to her bargain with Rathe to become human. The start of Colt and the Chosen reuniting the Book of Legend and holding the Gates of Nyx closed.

A twinge of insecurity grew larger in the bottom of her throat, just above her heart, making it difficult to breathe. Ever since they'd begun to look for the Book, it had become very clear to Lilly that both the Darkin and the Hunters would do anything to possess it. Having it with them only increased their risk, and Colt rode a fine enough line as it was. Alone, the two of them were hardly enough to fight off a group of trail bandits or Darkin determined to get it.

She held the Book, cold and hard, to her chest, letting herself fill up with the vibration of it traveling straight through her. Then she held it out. "No more thinking, Lillith Marie Arliss," she whispered, voice thick with emotion. "You know what must be done. *Do* it!"

The Book vanished in a shift of smoky particles.

Sending it to Winn's office at the jail might not be the best idea, but it was certainly safer than risking it on the journey to Bodie. The Book would be there, waiting for them. And for once she might be able to do something to help keep Colt safe. Well, as safe as she could manage, at any rate. She knew Colt well enough to know if she had told him of her plan, he would've never agreed. He was all about doing things himself and wouldn't want the Book out of his sight, even to protect it.

She clasped her hands together, waiting until they grew warm, then started to separate them, letting the glowing green ball in her hands expand until it was the shape and size of the Book she'd just sent away. She tucked the replica in Colt's pack, then carefully slipped back into the bed beside his big warm body. Now, should anyone think to relieve Colt of his prize, they'd have nothing in their hands but a faux book. The real section of the manuscript was safe. She planned to keep it that way for as long as it took.

They left the hotel before first light, Colt dressed in his usual garb of denim, a button-down shirt, and his hat. The only thing he still wore that she'd given him yesterday was the long brown duster. Lilly had donned her adventurer's clothing once more. It was light-colored and would be more comfortable in the heat than denim, and far more practical than a bustled gown while riding.

"I still don't understand why we're leaving so early," she muttered, readjusting her position on his lap.

"Did you see what happened to that hotel room?"

She blushed furiously. "Yes, but—"

"But nothing. They're going to have to completely tear it apart and rebuild. And one night's tariff isn't going to pay for that, and we don't have extra time to stick around while they sort it all out."

They moved slowly down out of the mountain trails toward the desert floor. The breaking light of dawn cast them into a long, solitary shadow moving among those of the saguaro cacti, their thick prickly arms raised to greet the sun.

At least they weren't riding into it. She wasn't looking forward to another few long days in the saddle because of how sore it would make her, but then those days were precious to her as well. After the Chosen brought the Book of Legend together, there was no telling what would happen. This could be the last time she had a chance to be with Colt.

"Once I meet up with my brothers and we join the Book together, then we can set about freeing you from Rathe." Colt sounded bold and confident. Too bad she didn't share his certainty that such a thing was possible.

She hated to voice her growing doubts, but the closer they got to restoring the Book, the more doubtful she was becoming of her own happy ending. "Do you really think Rathe is going to do you or me any favors once you close the Gates?"

Colt tightened his arms around her and leaned down, putting his lips close to her ear, eliciting an all-over body shiver from her. "Once we have the Book, we can do whatever we wish. Rathe won't have a choice."

She sighed and twisted to gaze into his shadowed face. "You know this isn't just about the Book of Legend anymore, don't you?" She pressed a small fist to her aching sternum. "It's bigger than that. The prophecy about the Chosen is true. Without the three of you, we lose. The world ends. It's not enough to put the Book together, it will take all three of you to close the Gates. The *three* of you to stand against Rathe."

He grunted. "I'm flattered you think I'm that important," he eyed her critically, "but right now it's not about either of those things. We have only one thing to focus on, and that's bringing the pieces of the Book together so we can close the Gates of Nyx."

She couldn't deny that it was an excellent place to start, but it wasn't going to be enough. She needed to do whatever she could to ensure Colt made it back to his brothers intact. He might not believe in the prophecy, but gut deep Lilly had always known he was part of the Chosen. And as such, he was more important than even the Book itself. If the prophecy was true, it would take the powers of all three of the Chosen to seal the Gates and defeat the rise of the Darkin.

A flash of copper light blazed at the horizon just over Colt's shoulder. Lilly gasped. "That can't be good."

Colt turned to see what had made her stiffen. For a moment he frowned, thinking the sun was rising from the wrong direction. Then he instantly saw that it was not the sun rising.

The hard-packed ground trembled beneath them. At first he thought it might be an earthquake, but there were no sounds of grinding earth or rolling motion to the land . . . and the tremors were getting stronger, rather than weaker. Whatever it was, it was moving quickly toward them.

Colt had a bad feeling about this. A really bad feeling. "Whatever it is, it's big and metal and headed our way," he muttered as the earth continued to tremble beneath them.

Colt pressed hard against the accelerator panel in his horse's sides. Tempus took a few steps and lurched into a trot that quickly became a gallop. Puffs of dust trailed along in a growing stream behind them as the horse picked up the pace, moving at a steady clip across the stretch of desert.

But Tempus was no match for the mechanical beast closing in. Across the sand and rock came the metallic clank and thunder of an enormous machine, growing louder. Colt glanced behind them. What was once a glint became a blinding glare as a gigantic mechanical brass scorpion rumbled closer, a column of white steam following it, glowing with orange light as the sun rose higher.

"Sister Mary Margaret Margarita. What in the blazes is it?"

Lilly twisted to get a look and squeaked at the sight. "Can't this bucket of bolts move any faster?"

Colt glanced at the timer set into the saddle. At this pace, Tempus would need a rewind in less than half an hour. There was only so far the machine could go at this speed. But even that meant nothing. The scorpion was still gaining on them.

"What does it want?"

"Breakfast?" Lilly suggested unhelpfully.

"Not if I can help it," Colt muttered, clutching Lilly

tighter about the middle. He gave the reins a pull and headed for the smudge of purple mountains in the distance.

The ground grew so unstable as the scorpion closed in that Tempus faltered, stumbling to his knees. Colt and Lilly were jettisoned from the saddle. They sailed over the horse's head to the ground, a tumble of limbs, the pack and Colt's hat flying in different directions.

Colt couldn't breathe. Pain throbbed in every bone. He heard Lilly groan and felt her shift against him. Good, she wasn't dead. Neither of them were. *Yet.* He struggled to scramble to his knees, knowing that they needed to make it to the safety of the rocks.

Suddenly everything went cold as a shadow blotted out the sun. Colt twisted, glancing up, then scuffled through the dirt, trying to put himself between the enormous, hinged, metallic claw and Lilly.

With a hiss of steam and the ratcheting click of moving gears, the massive brass claw extended to snap around Colt's waist and lift him from the ground. Lilly scrabbled for Colt's pack, then screamed as the second claw picked her up from the ground, leaving them both suspended twenty feet above the desert floor, level with one another.

She struggled, pushing and prodding against the claw that held her in its grasp. They rose together until they were level with the enormous bulbous glass eyes of the scorpion and the platform in between them. At the helm of the enormous machine was a man in a red brocade jacket with a black broad-brimmed hat and black satin cravat, which matched his black goatee and thin elegantly waxed mustache.

"Dr. Adder Morpheus, at your service," the man introduced himself to Colt in a smooth Southern drawl. He touched the edge of his hat with a gray-gloved hand and gave a slight bow as he winked at Lilly.

Lilly grimaced. "Hardly. What do you want, Morpheus?"

"You know this man?" Colt demanded between his clenched teeth.

Dr. Morpheus didn't even give her a chance to answer. "Oh, Miss Lilly and I go way back, don't we, darlin'? Her father and I were old friends."

Colt's eyes narrowed with distrust.

Still struggling to break free from the metal claw, Lilly glared at the man. "He's a snake-oil salesman," she said with disdain.

"Inventor and doctor of extraordinary curatives," Dr. Morpheus corrected her mildly.

"Either way, you're Rathe's," she countered. "*Doctor* Morpheus gave up his soul in exchange for immortality. Now he exists by stealing the life and souls of his customers." The sarcasm in her tone came through loud and clear. He certainly wasn't a doctor, and their health was not at the top of his agenda.

"So he's a demon like you?" Colt's fingers itched to get at the sting shooter, but his arms were pinned so tightly to his sides in the scorpion's grasp that he couldn't move a muscle.

"Of a fashion," Lilly answered as she glared at Dr. Morpheus. "Are you going to tell us what you want or not?"

"Tsk, tsk, darlin'. Your manners have truly become appalling since your dear daddy's demise." He twisted the waxed end of his mustache around his finger, making it curl like a sly smile.

Lilly clenched her fists tightly. "If you don't want to risk the same fate, I suggest you let him go."

Dr. Morpheus chuckled. "I'm only holding on to your young man because I do believe you're holding something of interest to me. I suggest we make an exchange."

"Stand in line, Morpheus," Lilly said with asperity. "You're not the only one interested in the Book."

"Yes, but I *am* the one with the scorpion at my disposal."

"True."

"So be a good girl, won't you, and just hand over the pages to your uncle Morpheus."

"Won't do you any good."

"Oh, I highly doubt that. You see, that Book is my ticket out of Hell, or should I say more like my pardon."

Colt let out a bark of laughter. "I should have known a con artist like you would make a deal with the devil."

Dr. Morpheus grinned and glanced over at Lilly, a knowing look passing over his face that Colt didn't like one bit. "Oh, we're used to making deals with all sorts of folks, aren't we, darlin'? What'd you promise this young man of yours in exchange for his help?"

"That doesn't concern you." Lilly's mouth flattened into a grim line.

Dr. Morpheus turned back to Colt. "Well, son, let me just say that whatever this delightful young lady promised you, it'll hardly compare to what *I* can offer you if you'll just have her hand over those pages."

"Oh, and what's that?" Colt replied.

"Your life." To illustrate his point, Dr. Morpheus pulled a lever on the panel in front of him, and the mechanical claw of the scorpion squeezed tighter, making stars pop in Colt's vision. A large glass-tipped scorpion tail arced into view, a vile yellow-green liquid sloshing around inside the enormous glass stinger. "That stinger is filled with oil of vitrol. Just one prick, and you'll have about an hour left to live, if you're lucky. Sometimes the acid works faster."

"I'd rather have her burn the Book than give it to you."

"I can arrange that." Dr. Morpheus pulled another lever on the panel before him, and the stinger started to lower in Colt's direction.

* * *

"Stop!" Lilly shouted.

"Did you object?" Dr. Morpheus said with obvious delight.

"Of course!"

"Then what are we to do about it, my little daylily?"

"Let him go. Take the Book. Take me, but let him go." It was really no risk. The pages in the pack she held were a mere forgery, a copy, and a hastily created one at that.

"NO!" roared Colt.

Lilly looked at him, tried beseeching him with her eyes, unable to tell him the Book she held was a fake. "If I go with him, you'll at least be alive."

"But he'll only take you back to Rathe!"

Lilly forced herself not to tremble at the thought. "We always knew that was a possibility."

Colt squirmed against the grasp of the mechanical scorpion. "No. Hell no. Don't do this!"

"I'm sorry," Morpheus interjected, "this is so entertaining. But I do have other pressing engagements. Miss Lilly, am I taking you and the Book, or am I killin' this young man, then taking you and the Book?" To emphasize his point, he lowered the glass stinger a few more feet until it was poised, glistening a few inches above Colt's chest.

"Let him go," Lilly said simply. Colt stared at her hard. Didn't she know she was goddamn ripping his heart out of his chest?

Dr. Morpheus's smile turned pointed up at the edges in a grotesque semblance of delight. "There now. See, I knew you could be a reasonable girl." He fingered the lever that controlled the claw holding Colt. Colt grunted as it tightened up another notch, making stars pop again in his vision. "Just remember, son," Morpheus drew the *s* out so it hissed, "you come after me and I'll kill her first, slowly, so you can watch. *Then* you. Do we have an understanding?"

Colt couldn't draw in enough air to speak, so he nodded.

"Good." The scorpion rider pushed the brass lever down with his elegantly gloved hand.

With a hiss of steam, the pistons on the claw opened the metal pincers, letting Colt fall twenty feet to the ground in a heap. He groaned.

His vision was blurred and began to darken, but he turned to his side and watched the big metallic scorpion clank off toward the horizon and the open desert, Lilly still clutched in one enormous claw and the pack still clutched in her arms.

Lilly wriggled and struggled against the metal pincer holding her securely about the middle. "You got what you wanted, Morpheus. Let me out of this infernal contraption!"

"Tsk, tsk. Manners, Miss Lilly. We must mind our manners."

"*Please*, will you let me out of this thing?"

Adder Morpheus twirled the long end of his mustache as he considered her request. Lord, how she loathed him, especially when he did that like some sanctimonious judge. He'd done that for as long as she could remember. He flicked a lever with his finger and the claw came up still farther until she was poised over the metal plate deck where he stood. He extended a gloved finger, paused for a moment, watching her wriggle, then pushed a button on the panel. Lilly was unceremoniously dropped onto her feet beside him. She stood, holding the pack in one hand, trying to brush the dirt and wrinkles from her skirts.

Adder yanked the pack from her, then grabbed hold of her wrist in a hard unyielding grip as he snapped a pair of brass-colored handcuffs on her and then himself, linking them together. "There, now. Just in case you got the notion to shimmer off somewhere else, you'll know I'll be right there with you."

Lilly yanked against the cuff in annoyance, but knew he was right. She wasn't going anywhere without him until he took off the special cuffs. "Are we planning on riding this thing all the way to Rathe?"

Adder chuckled. "That would be somethin', wouldn' it? But we're goin' to meet him in neutral territory. That way when I hand you and the Book over, I'll be on my way a free man that much sooner."

"You trust him to let you walk away?" Lilly asked, sliding him a sideways glance. She sighed with a slight bit of dramatic flair. "You must be losing your touch."

"Don't think you can out-con a con man, my dear. I've already got my arrangements with Rathe, same as you. He'll abide by them, you'll see."

Lilly maintained a nonchalant expression, but inside she was fuming mad.

After several hours, the swaying motion mixed with the smell of hot metal and machine oil from the scorpion and the noxious sweet odor of pipe tobacco that clung to Morpheus made Lilly nauseous. She gripped the railing looking out at the dry stretch of desert before them. "How much farther?"

"Just over that ridge into Death Valley."

Lilly sighed. Rathe was sadistic, cruel, and power-hungry, but not overly creative.

The wide salt flats spread in an endless, mind-numbing stretch of crisp white crust from one brown mountain range to the other. Not a plant, not a single living thing, drew breath out here. The mechanical scorpion never slowed, and took them up with crunching steps through the valley floor to where it narrowed, then spread out into miles of pale sand dunes. The undulating mounds of sand were sculpted by the wind into thousands of ripples without a single tree, bush, or blade of dried grass to hold the shifting sands back.

Dr. Morpheus pulled a large lever and pushed a pedal in the floor downward. With a hiss of steam the scorpion slowly descended, the portions of its articulated legs sliding one over the other as they collapsed into shorter stubs. With a rattling shake, the monster came to rest.

Dr. Morpheus pulled at the edge of his broad-brimmed black hat, making sure it was securely in place, then looked over his shoulder at her. "Are you ready, my dear?" He walked over to the edge of the scorpion's massive head, and flipped a switch. Lilly watched in horrified fascination as a set of stairs made from open-worked lattice began to sprout and unfold from the machine's cranium.

"You do like your toys, don't you, Morpheus."

He smiled, offering her a hand. "After you, Miss Lilly."

Lilly would have preferred to slap him rather than take his hand, but they were still high above the ground and she didn't want to fall. Instead of touching him, she grasped her skirts in one hand and the brass rail in the other, and slowly made her way unaided to the ground.

"I'm assuming you didn't bring me all this way for nothing."

"Patience, my daylily. I'd hardly be eager to see Rathe if I were you."

"You do realize he'll be furious you forced me to let Colt Jackson go."

Dr. Morpheus eyed her speculatively. "But I have the Book." He shook the pages in his hand, making them flutter in the light wind blowing over the dunes, whipping the sand into a stinging spray that scoured her cheeks.

"Yes, but you don't have the Hunter."

"He's hardly of any use. Hunters are a penny a pound."

"Even when they're part of the Chosen?"

His eyes narrowed. "You purposely neglected to share that little tidbit with me, didn't you, darlin'."

She gave him a supercilious smile. "Always hold back something for yourself. Wasn't that the first lesson you and Father taught me?"

A rumble, like a stampede of buffalo across the plains, grew louder, the earth beneath their feet beginning to tremble. Sand shifted beneath their feet as the largest dune before them shivered. "Oh, look, and just in time for you to explain it all to Rathe," she said blithely.

A great chasm in the ground opened up before them, red and violent, spitting out steam, the sand spilling into the gap like an hourglass. And through it came Rathe in elegant topcoat and tails, great black overcoat and top hat, looking fit for a night at the opera, followed by several of his thralls. Two of them, flanking Rathe, were stone Scoria soldiers, great rock men with glowing coal-like eyes and dark open maws, spewing dust in little puffs from their joints as they moved with thunderous steps. Behind them were a chimera, who shook his great lion mane and his scaly snake of a tail, with eyes like Rathe's, flicking its tongue and tasting the air, and a hellhound, big as a buffalo and dark as sin, its glowing red eyes and enormous white canines dripping shiny strings of deadly saliva made more visible by its dark coat.

Dr. Morpheus gave an elegant old-fashioned bow, one leg bent, bringing his head to the level of his knee. "My lord." His voice was unctuous and tinged with fear.

"Good day, Dr. Morpheus. I see you have brought me my wayward demon, but have you the Book?"

Dr. Morpheus took the pages from beneath his arm and held it out to Rathe, his head bent in sycophantic supplication.

Rathe slipped it from Morpheus's hands and flipped through the pages. His pale, waxy skin glowed faintly in the brilliant daylight. The vertical slits in the demon lord's yellow eyes widened a fraction, his slash of a mouth creasing wider in his deathly pale face. Lilly waited one heartbeat, then two, and knew the exact instant when Rathe realized what he held was a fake.

The earth shook and the faux Book burst into orange-yellow flames in his hand. Dr. Morpheus jerked his head upward. "My lord! The Book!"

With demon speed Rathe kicked him in the jaw, sending him sprawling back into the dirt. Dr. Morpheus moaned, his eyes glazed with shock. Lilly froze, watching in horrified fascination as the tips of Rathe's fingers extended into long black talons that glinted in the sunlight. The demon lord's elegant black cloak swirled about him in a spin of darkness as he leaned down, putting his long, razor-sharp talon against Morpheus's throat. The skin dimpled in and oozed a drop of scarlet blood where the doctor's pulse beat hard and fast.

"The next time you displease me, Doctor, I shall slice you from ear to ear and drink your blood and eat your entrails like sausages while you watch, then make you grow them back so I can feast again the next day and the next. Are we clear?"

Rathe moved his hand from one side of Morpheus's throat to the other in a slow slicing motion.

Dr. Morpheus stared, eyes wide with fear. It was the last thing he ever did. His head rolled off his shoulders and into the dirt.

Lilly stood rabbit still as Rathe's gaze swiveled in her direction. "Lillith Marie Arliss. I want the real Book. Now."

For a moment she considered materializing another forgery, then she took a look at the doctor's sightless eyes staring at her and thought better of it. If Rathe had been able to detect her first forgery, he certainly could tell another.

But she wasn't going to give in without a fight.

"You promised to give me my freedom if I brought you the Book."

"Yes."

"Will you still?"

"I grow weary of your childish games." Within one heartbeat he was beside her, his talons digging into the flesh of her neck as he lifted her off the ground, his hand squeezing hard on her windpipe and cutting off her air. "Give. Me. The. Book."

She hesitated as stars and streaks began to cloud her vision.

"Time's up, Lillith Marie Arliss."

Using what little strength she had left, Lilly brought her hands together. The warmth expanded as she brought the Book back from Winn's office and into her hands.

Rathe dropped her like a used rag in a heap on the sand dune. She coughed and wheezed, getting both sand and air in her lungs. She rolled over gingerly, massaging the painful dark bruises on her throat and struggling to her knees in the soft sand.

"Take her down below and pick up his head. I have plans for it," Rathe ordered with a flick of his hand. Lilly tried to crawl away as a Scoria soldier and the hellhound bracketed her. The Scoria soldier snatched her up from the ground as if she were a child's doll, crushing her to the granite wall of his chest, making it impossible to move while the shifter bound her wrists and feet with silver chain.

"But you promised to give me my freedom!"

Rathe glanced at her. "And you promised to get me Colt Jackson. I've grown bored with your games. It's time for some entertainment."

Pure unadulterated dread clamped down hard on her gut. Rathe's idea of entertainment never turned out well for the participants. Lilly struggled against the strong ties binding her. As a succubus, there wasn't much she could do to seduce a Scoria soldier, and her other demon powers were neutralized in Rathe's presence.

"Let's call it not so much a change of heart as an insurance that your Hunter will come for you."

"But I've given you Colt's portion of the Book."

"Yes, and at one time you suggested I might be able to get the rest of it with Colt as bait. Very ingenious, really. I can see why your father valued you. You're quite an accomplished con artist, penny-girl."

Lilly winced. She had never regretted anything more than telling Rathe about the Chosen's ability to get all the portions of the Book together. He'd use them, all of them, to further his own agenda.

Rathe stared at her hard—as if peeling back her skin to see what lay beneath, laying bare bone and muscle, heart and soul. "He won't save you. You know that, don't you?"

Lilly was stunned. He'd dug into her mind discovering her greatest fear. "H-h-h-ow?" she stammered.

The slash of his mouth twisted with a kind of malevolent pleasure. "I was counting on it when I chose you. Oh, he'll come, but I'll never let him leave. And once I've stripped him of what I need to open the Gates, I'll use him as bait for his brothers and string all their heads together on my chain."

Lilly shuddered, her skin drenched in the icy realization of what she'd done. Without even knowing it, she'd unwittingly helped Rathe with his plan. An image of Colt flitted through her mind. His blue eyes imprinted in her vision like a sunspot—present no matter where her gaze moved. He'd never forgive her for this betrayal. Never.

Her legs began to shake and she collapsed to the ground when her knees gave way. Only now did the con come full circle. She'd never seen it coming and now dreaded knowing that Rathe had won and she'd forsaken the only man she'd ever come to care for.

There would be no chance of escaping now or ever. He'd win. The Gates would be opened and the world would fall to the Darkin with Rathe at the helm. It wouldn't matter that Colt and his brothers were the Chosen. In an effort to grab at her own freedom, she'd doomed them all.

"So what happens now?" she asked, her voice sounding small and fragile to her own ears.

"We wait."

Chapter 24

Colt wasn't about to be beaten by an overgrown tin can, a snake-oil salesman, and a demon lord.

He hightailed it to Marley's as fast as he could get Tempus to go. It wasn't train speed, but it was a damn sight more direct, which made up for the difference.

Just seeing Marley's strange house made his insides twist about with urgency. Who knew what Rathe was doing to her? He was a sadistic sonofabitch. Colt was already crazed with worry and fear. He honestly didn't want to dwell on it until he had some form of game plan in place to free Lilly.

He hopped off Tempus, flicked the GGD switch, and turned to find Marley's door ajar. A fizzle of wariness started at the back of his neck, making all the hairs on his head come to attention, but his gun hand didn't itch.

He peered into the dark interior of Marley's abode. "Marley? Marley, you there?" Colt called out. The door creaked open as he pushed it a bit with his shoulder and stepped inside. It took a moment for his eyes to adjust to the gloom. Marley wasn't much of a housekeeper, but he at least organized his things in piles and teetering stacks in some semblance of order, if only to his own eyes. But what Colt saw was chaos.

Twisted metal, fallen bookcases, smashed equipment, and broken glass littered the floor. Panic seized him by the throat and squeezed hard. He pulled his revolver out and cocked it in one lightning-fast motion. "Marley, dammit, answer me!"

Zzzot. An arc of electricity shot past him, setting the wall ablaze. Colt dove behind an upended table for cover.

"You shan't fool me twice!" Marley called out. "Step one toe out in the open and I'll have you torched to a crisp."

Colt took off his Stetson and waved it above the level of the table. "Marley, it's me, Colt."

"That's what you said last time," Marley replied.

Zzzot. Colt pulled down his hat to find a smoking hole through the middle of it. "Dammit to blue blazes, Marley, I'm Colt Ambrose Jackson and you're buying me a new goddamn hat!"

There was a rustling sound as Marley moved closer amid the fallen papers and debris, but Colt didn't stick his head out to look.

"Who bought you the last one?" Marley asked, his voice tinged with suspicion.

"My pa."

Marley's cotton-tufted head and enormous goggled brown eyes, round with surprise, peered over the edge of the table and down at Colt. "Bloody hell. It is you!"

"That's what I've been sayin'. What the hell happened?"

Marley slipped the goggles to his forehead, making the liquid in the lenses slosh around. The goggles left the part of his face that had been covered white against the rest of his soot-blackened skin, so he looked like a demented raccoon. "I was attacked by a shape-shifter."

"That's no reason to shoot my hat."

"The shifter was disguised as you. I let that fiend in my

home and the detection sensor in my utility belt went berserk. Then it attacked me."

Colt glanced around at the destruction in Marley's home, then back at his friend. "You all right?"

Marley stiffened his upper lip and nodded.

"And Balmora?"

"She's intact."

"Good." Colt rubbed the back of his neck. "Marley, I know this isn't a good time for you and all, but I need a favor."

Marley shook his head. "I couldn't possibly—" He gestured to his home, falling silent, then fiddled with his lip between his fingers, curiosity making his brown eyes bright. "Oh, bother. What is it?"

"I need you to send me to Hell."

Marley spluttered. "Are you bloody well mad? Why on earth would I do that? Don't I work myself to the bone creating inventions to ensure that you *don't* end up there?"

"Pa's part of the Book is there. And so is Lilly."

Marley's dark brows bent together forming a bushy V beneath the edge of his goggles. "That does present a conundrum. I'm not at all certain how to get you there."

"I bet that book you let me borrow could tell us."

"The one you used to summon that succubus?"

For a second he pictured Lilly the first time he'd seen her—her hair licking like red flames against her alabaster skin, her womanly curves accented by the black silk sheath she'd worn. But what made him twinge was the memory of her subtle smile, her light lilting laughter, and the twinkle in her eye. "Yep."

"Well, I suppose. I mean, I hadn't consider—" Marley was starting to ramble. Which meant he was thinking hard, but Colt needed more concrete results, and fast.

"Dang it, Marley, I don't got time to shilly-shally around

with this. You gonna send me to Hell or do I got to summon another demon to get me there?"

"No, no. I'll do it." He climbed around the remains of a bookcase and over to the desk littered with broken glassware and the marble bust of President Lincoln, now cracked in half down the forehead like an egg.

Marley reached into a drawer and pulled out the familiar heavy, musty book. He pulled his goggles down, which magnified his eyes like a wise old owl, and flipped through the pages, muttering to himself. "Hell, Hell, Hell, how to send oneself to Hell. Ah!" He pointed at the page and grinned up at Colt. "Here it is, although it says it's performed on a lingering soul of bad repute."

"You mean a bad ghost."

"Precisely."

Colt holstered his gun. "Is this like an exorcism?"

"No. That's for demons inhabiting a body."

"So, what do you need?"

"Well a body, for one thing—"

"Marley . . ."

"Oh, ah, let's see."

Colt grabbed a piece of paper and scrounged up a pencil and began writing things down as Marley rattled off a half-dozen herbs, candles, a silver knife, and some salt. Colt shrugged out of his duster, stripped off his jacket, and rolled up the sleeves of his shirt. Together they made their way around the dismantled portion of Marley's home and into the kitchen, where Marley fiddled with his assortment of brown and green bottles.

Colt couldn't read Marley's indecipherable handwriting on the labels, so he didn't even try to help. Instead he searched through the drawers and found a salt cellar and a silver bowie knife. He let out a long, low whistle as he rubbed his thumb up along the lethal, flattened edge of the foot-long blade. "That's some knife, Marley."

"A gift."

"From a friend or an enemy?"

Marley gave him a crooked smile. "Neither. An old flame, I'm afraid."

Colt gave the blade a wary gaze. "She didn't use it to try to cut out your heart, did she?"

"No, nothing so dramatic, old chap. Left it wedged in my door with a note."

"A woman Hunter?" Colt guessed.

"Precisely." Marley dusted the salt off his hands. "There now, we have a proper circle. Just place the candles as you did before, light them, and we can begin."

"Before you send me back, I got to ask you for one more favor."

Marley simply stared at him.

"I need you to find out what happened to Lilly's sister Amelia Arliss and tell her. Can you do that for me?"

"Anything else, or shall I fetch Her Majesty for tea as well?"

Colt chuckled. "Nah, I wouldn't advise it. She'd take a fancy to Balmora, seein' as what a fine job you did with her."

Marley actually blushed. "Are you ready, then?"

"As I'll ever be." Colt did as instructed and stood back at the edge of the circle. In the center of the circle surrounding the five-pointed star, Marley placed a bowl containing absinthe, balsam wood, juniper berry, thistle, skullcap, and cloves. He lit the mixture on fire and beckoned Colt closer. "Your hand, please," he said as he picked up the bowie knife.

Colt cautiously held out his hand, palm up. "What are you planning on?"

"Just a bit of your blood."

Colt snatched his hand back. "Now hold on a second."

Irritation flashed in Marley's eyes. "Do stop being such an infant. I'm not going to cut off your fingers or anything drastic."

Colt eyed the long, deadly sharp blade, not nearly as sure as Marley about that assertion.

True to his word, Marley left his hand intact and only sliced a thin line across the fleshy pad beneath Colt's thumb. He held Colt's hand above the smoking mixture in the bowl as he continued to read from the book. A thin rivulet of scarlet dripped down the length of Colt's thumb. He watched it well up into tear-shaped drops before they fell. One. Two. Three.

The smoking mixture in the bowl flared into a small greenish fire. Marley pulled a vial of something black and viscous out of his belt and shook it hard, then put a drop in the fire, where it sizzled and smoked even more. The plume of noxious smoke smelled strongly of sulfur.

"What's that?"

"Vampire blood. Gives the blighter something to hold fast to instead of you."

Then Marley pulled a large gun-like apparatus with enormous glass bulbs enmeshed in a fine net of copper wire.

"And that?"

Marley's smile widened, almost reaching his ears. "This is my Aether Particulate Enhancer. Should give the whole process a little boost. It uses revolving magnets at a high velocity to amplify—"

"Later, Marley."

"Oh, yes, of course." He picked up the bowl and poured the entire flaming mixture into the glass bulb at the back end of the gun. Snapped it shut and flipped a switch. The entire apparatus began to hum loudly.

Colt eyed the gun nervously. "Ever tested it?"

"Not yet. But there's nothing a little applied science can't improve." He leveled the barrel of the device at Colt, squeezed his eyes shut, and pulled the trigger. Out shot a bolt of green electricity.

Colt's skin began to dissolve into dark particles, ripping apart tiny bit by tiny bit until he looked like smoke and felt as insubstantial. Marley muttered a final line of Latin, and with it Colt disappeared completely.

The sensation was worse than drowning. Not only could Colt not draw a breath, he had that peculiar sensation of being buoyant, like he was floating suspended in water. Particle by particle his form knit itself back together. And it was excruciating. Every bit of him burned, and he prayed that as his body reassembled everything would go back in its proper place.

The minute he could, he sucked in a gulp of air, coughed and wheezed. His lungs burned. The floor beneath his hands was highly polished cold black marble that gleamed with the reddish glow that seemed to emanate from the edges of the room. Colt lifted his head to see he was in an enormous audience chamber hewn from the rock. At the far end on an upraised marble dais was a throne of glittering black obsidian, occupied by a well-dressed, gruesome gentleman.

Even from where he knelt on the floor, Colt could see the menacing yellow of the demon's eyes and the way the vertical pupil flexed with interest at his arrival.

"Welcome to Hell," Rathe said by way of a greeting. The pale, waxy skin of his face stretched tight over high cheekbones and a blade of a nose and was a shade more gray than the pristine white of his cravat, shirt, and vest, and accentuated by his black formal dress. His hair was slicked back, and red rubies glittered in the cuffs at his wrists and in the snowy folds of his cravat.

Great. The Demon of the Opera. Just what he didn't need. Colt swallowed hard against the dust-dry sensation in his mouth and staggered to his feet. "Where is she?" he rasped, quickly feeling for his gun holster only to find it, and his special Colt revolver, were missing. They hadn't made it along with him in the transport. *Damn. Double damn.* A defenseless Hunter in Hell.

The demon leaned forward, balancing an arm on his knee. "Come, come, Mr. Jackson, you'll have to be more specific than that. There are literally millions of souls under my control."

Colt ached, but he was also angrier and more determined than a wet cat. "Lilly."

The vertical pupils grew thicker. A predator scenting its prey. Rathe gave an absent tug to one of his cuffs. "Oh, you mean my servant, Lillith Marie Arliss? She's been waiting for you right over there."

Colt swiveled and saw Lilly clothed in nothing but a bloodstained corset and thin cotton bloomers, suspended from huge rusted hooks impaled in the flesh of her chest. The hooks linked to great thick lengths of chain that disappeared into the darkness of the cavern above them. She hung like a side of beef in a butcher shop window, her dead weight swaying slightly, her skin a spiderweb of newly healed pink scars where she'd been sliced repeatedly. Bile rose up hot and thick in the back of his throat. Colt thought he was gonna puke right there on the demon's highly polished floor.

He locked his narrowed gaze on Rathe. "Is she alive?"

Rathe sighed, toying with the red ruby stickpin in his immaculate white cravat. "You Hunters are so tiresome," he muttered. He slowly withdrew six inches of long gleaming silver, topped with a glittering teardrop-cut ruby, from the cloth and flung it in Lilly's direction. Rathe's aim was true—

Suddenly unable to move anything but his head, Colt followed the trajectory with his gaze, his feet stuck to the floor, as the silver picked up glints of red light in its path toward Lilly. His heart almost stopped. What cruel trick was the sonofabitch—

Ah, hell.

The long pin, sharp as a needle, pierced her soft breast over her heart like a hot knife through butter, causing a trickle of blood. It stuck in her chest, and her eyes opened wide and she let out a bloodcurdling scream.

"Stop!" Colt yelled. He'd never felt more helpless in his life as he did at that moment.

"Her predicament is your fault, Hunter. She never would have been dragged into this if she hadn't been sent out to follow you."

She bucked and thrashed against the pain, the stickpin jiggling violently with her movements. Colt couldn't stand it. He would rather have been flayed alive than watch her torment. Colt struggled and pulled at the invisible bonds encasing his limbs, leaving him frozen to the floor. "Enough!"

Finally her body went rigid, her eyes wide, her mouth open in a silent scream. And suddenly she went pliant and heavy, like a wet burlap sack.

Rathe curled his fingers in a come-hither fashion, and the pin pulled slowly from her chest and reappeared in his cravat. "You could easily stop her pain. Just give me what I want."

"Let her down and we'll talk."

Rathe snapped his fingers and the hooks and chains disappeared into smoke, dumping Lilly into a broken heap on the cold black marble floor. A cool breeze brushed past him, releasing him from his frozen state. Colt ran to her. He knelt and lifted her, holding her against his chest, supporting her body with his thighs, anything he could do to offer her comfort and ease her suffering.

She moaned quietly. Relief washed over Colt. At least she was still alive. The gaping holes the hooks had left in the skin around each collarbone and the pinhole in her breast from the stickpin began to heal before Colt's eyes. It had to be her demon powers. Whatever it was, he was profoundly grateful.

She shivered and he gathered her closer, stroking her hair, murmuring words of comfort that had no meaning, whispering words of hope that he couldn't back up. Dark circles marred the fine porcelain skin beneath her eyes, and beneath his fingers her red hair was dull and brittle. Seeing her like this affected him worse than the day Winn had nearly died. His brother had been a man. He'd been older. Colt loved him, but Winn hadn't been his to protect, his to care for. Lilly was. The dark fan of her lashes fluttered as her eyes opened slightly. Her lips were cracked and bleeding, and she swiped them with the tip of her pink tongue, trying to speak.

"Save your breath," he said to her softly. "I'm here now, and I'm not going anywhere."

She grew stronger by the moment, absorbing the strength he offered her willingly. "Y-you know the only thing h-harder than breaking into Hell is—is breaking out."

She was killing him. He stroked her matted hair off her face. "I kind of figured that."

"Then why did you do it? You shouldn't have come. Rathe is never going to let you or the Book leave."

Colt gazed at her. "I had to. I promised. And I always keep my promises."

"What do you have to prove? Just get the Book and get

out of here!" Colt could feel Rathe's malicious gaze, cold and piercing, on his back as he entertained himself by watching their struggles. He glanced at the demon lord, ensconced on his obsidian throne. On his lap was Pa's part of the Book. Rathe's fingers flipped the edges of the pages with a *thrip, thrip, thrip* sound that was driving Colt insane with the thought that the demon was touching it at all. He wanted to go punch Rathe straight in the face and take the damn thing. But Lilly was nearly broken and in his arms.

"No. I let a demon beat me once and nearly lost my brother because of it. I'll be damned if I'm going to let it happen again."

Colt fixed his gaze on Rathe's yellow eyes. "What do you want?"

"It's really more a question of what *you* want," Rathe replied, stroking his long, pale fingers over the front of the open vellum page of the Book. "You've caught me on a good millennium. I'm willing to negotiate with you, Hunter. You can leave. But Lillith and your portion of the Book of Legend stays with me."

Colt gazed at the fine network of angry red scars on her skin and realized how much she'd been tortured in his short absence. "No deal."

"You wish to counter my offer?"

"Yes."

Rathe leaned forward. "I'm listening."

"I'll stay. You turn Lilly human again and let her go with the Book. You get me, and a shot at the other two pieces of the Book when my brothers come looking for me."

"Tempting . . ." He paused as if truly considering it. "But no. I'd consider letting Lillith or the Book return to your realm if you stay, but not both."

Colt pondered that. There had to be another way around this.

"Think it over, Colt. Lillith or the Book? Which will you choose?"

Colt's gaze connected with Lilly's. She could see the thoughts flitting across his mind as if they were said aloud. He'd made a promise. He was going to get her out. She had no doubt Remington and Winchester would come for him and the Book. He probably thought he could endure anything Rathe could throw at him until his brothers got him out. But Lilly knew better.

She'd seen the particular enjoyment Rathe got from torturing souls—the barbed blades, the slicing razors, the hooks, axes, and acid he used. There was not a shred of doubt within her being that Colt would be tortured long and hard before he died and became yet another lost soul under Rathe's control.

Colt's brow bent in determination. He'd made his decision. And she could already tell it was the wrong one. He turned to Rathe and set his shoulders. The muscles along his jaw flexed as he gritted his teeth. "I choose Lilly's freedom."

No. Lilly gasped. He'd gone mad. What difference did it make if she was left to Rathe's torture? At least the world would be safe. "What are you doing?"

He caught her gaze and held it. She was stunned; his eyes were so cool, so hard and focused, they looked like deep river ice. "I'm doing what I have to. I made you a promise, and I've never broken my word."

Rathe clapped in a slow, measured beat as if applauding a theatrical performance. "How very touching. Now, if you don't mind, I should very much like to conclude our business."

He pointed a long finger at her, the fingernail extending and becoming a long, dark talon. "Lillith Marie Arliss," his voice boomed and echoed like thunder off the rock walls, "you are henceforth freed of your debt to me. I take back what I have given you."

A bolt of invisible fire speared her through the chest, knocking her off her feet as it spread like acid through her veins, eating away at her from the inside out. She let out a bloodcurdling scream and collapsed to the floor writhing, arching, unable to stop it.

"You said you'd free her!" Colt shouted, tensing against her.

"And so I have," Rathe replied, his tone dripping with sadistic pleasure. "No one said becoming human again would be painless."

Colt wrapped his strong arms beneath her and tried to lift her, but the burning only increased. She bucked and thrashed, trying to escape the pain. She tried to scream and a billowing cloud of blackness poured from her mouth instead, shooting up and out, spiraling through the air and into Rathe's open maw. In a last blinding flash, whatever warred inside her consumed her, leaving her feeling charred and fragile. She collapsed on Colt's lap as he sat beside her. His strength, his warm, loving touch were all that kept her tethered to her consciousness.

If only I could help him, she thought. But she could tell by how badly she hurt in every muscle and tendon of her body that she was nothing but a mere mortal now. Not a demon with powers. Not even a strong woman with a weapon.

Colt had given up everything for her to become human once more, and she could do nothing to save him.

Hot, fat tears streaked down her cheeks, and she whimpered. Colt gathered her up tightly in his arms and held her, kissing her hair, which only made her regret more acute.

"I'll find a way back to you. I promise," Colt whispered fiercely as they locked hands.

But she knew even if he believed that was possible, it

could never, *would* never happen. Once Rathe took, he rarely, if ever, gave back.

"Go," Rathe waved a clawed hand dismissively.

And with that her hand dissolved into a dark mist that dissipated between Colt's fingers. There was nothing left to grasp and hold on to. He was gone, and she'd never told him she loved him.

Chapter 25

For a moment Lilly couldn't breathe. She squeezed her eyes tightly closed at the blinding glare spearing red through her eyelids. Lord. Was she dead?

Would she *know* if she were dead?

She lay very still. Death was cold, wasn't it? But the light was warm, gentle. Tentatively she let her eyes flutter open, squinting as her eyes adjusted. Sunlight. Brilliant blue sky. The enormous brown eyes of Colt's inventor friend.

She gasped, scooting back crablike on the ground to get away from him. "Wh-what do you want?" she stuttered. The last thing she needed was to fight off a demon Hunter when she no longer was one.

"Are you hurt?" He held a red and white Navaho-style wool blanket out to her. Lilly waited for a moment, then grabbed it close, covering the tattered, stained remains of her undergarments, suddenly aware of how exposed and truly awful she must look.

His question took her by surprise. She frowned as she took mental stock of herself. There were aches and pains, but nothing abnormal, nothing she couldn't breathe through if she tried hard enough.

She looked around. The rugged brown rocks near her swept down into a valley with a little town at the bottom. She appeared to have landed at the top of a zigzagging path that led up the hill. The air smelled desert sweet, and the sagebrush near her head rustled and crackled with the breeze. "Where am I?"

Colt's inventor friend, his white tuft of hair askew, studied her through his elaborate multi-lensed brass and leather goggles. Lilly pressed a hand to her temple. Her head hurt so badly all her thoughts were fuzzy. What was his name? Merlin, Martin, Marlcy? Yes, Marley, that was it. Marley Turlock.

"Where am I, Mr. Turlock?"

"You've somehow landed, quite unexpectedly, in my front yard, Miss Arliss."

"Your yard?" She glanced around at the rocky patch of cactus and the strange squat wooden house with the multiple articulated arms with pincers and telescopes, magnifying glasses and cannon-like barrels, which extended from the roof like the appendages of an enormous insect.

"Where's Colt?" She sat bolt upright and groaned at the bruising pain in her solar plexus. It felt as though she'd been kicked in the chest by a horse. She tried to take a deep breath, but it knifed into her lungs, leaving her gasping and panting.

Mr. Turlock crouched beside her and put a hand on her back to steady her as she swayed. "Colt didn't arrive with you."

Her heart stopped for a moment, then picked up the beat to twice as fast. "Then he's still with Rathe!" She grabbed hold of the lapels of Marley's pale brown laboratory coat and shook him so hard his brass buttons rattled. "Mr. Turlock, we have to help him. You don't know what Rathe's capable of. I've got to go back to Hell. Now. Right this very minute!"

He covered her trembling hands with his own and gently removed them from his coat, pulling the slipping blanket more securely about her shoulders. "There, there, Miss Arliss. You haven't known the Jackson brothers as long as I have. If there's any way for Colt to return, he'll manage it."

Lilly shook her head violently. "You know the *Jackson brothers*, Mr. Turlock, but you have surely never come face-to-face with the archdemon Rathe. There is no way Colt will be set free. He's up against more than you can possibly imagine." A sob strangled in her throat, she hiccupped, but the hot pricking sensation behind her eyes wouldn't be stopped. "And there's nothing I can do now to help him."

The inventor glanced down at his utility belt and quirked a thick, dark brow, which barely arched above the edge of his brass goggles. "My word," he breathed, so it came out a fascinated whisper. "I thought it was a fluke, but it appears to be true." He peered intently at her, and Lilly had the ridiculous sudden urge to reach up and touch her face to make sure none of her features had been rearranged in transit.

From his leather utility belt he pulled out a long cylindrical copper tube with a crystal attached in a hollowed-out cavity in the middle of it. For a second Lilly held her breath as he passed it back and forth over her. It did nothing. No flare of red light. No shot of electricity, and she was immensely relieved.

"Miss Arliss, are you aware that you aren't a demon any longer?"

Lilly gave a short brittle laugh as she pressed a fist to the very real ache of regret lodged deep in her chest. "Very."

He shoved his goggles to the top of his forehead. Without them, his soft brown eyes looked normal-sized and full of wonder. "You actually managed to become human again? But how?"

"It was none of my doing. The demon lord I made a bargain with in the first place revoked my powers."

"But you haven't aged a bit. It's quite remarkable."

Lilly pulled the rough wool blanket closer around her shoulders. There was a cold, hollow feeling invading her bones that she couldn't stop. "And it couldn't have come at a worse time. There's nothing I can do now to help Colt escape Rathe."

Marley tucked his demon detector away in his belt. "I think you'll find our Colt is far better equipped to deal with a demon lord than you think."

Lilly didn't miss the part about Colt being ours, as if Marley was now including her in their close-knit Hunter group. Too bad it was too little, too late. "So you've said. Tell me, Mr. Turlock," she cocked her head to one side and looked at him, "now that I'm human again, am I more acceptable to you?"

The inventor had the decency to splutter "Well, I, you see, I say, really "

She closed her eyes for a moment and shoved her snarled hair away from her face, then took a deep breath and locked gazes with him. "Can you help me get Colt back?"

"I must say, she played her role even better than I imagined possible," Rathe drawled as he leaned back in his black throne, a picture of a wealthy gentleman at ease after a night at the opera.

Colt knew the demon was baiting him. He'd seen the truth in Lilly's eyes, felt it in the way her body shuddered when he'd held her close. The last thing she'd wanted was for him to exchange himself for her.

For him there wasn't even a choice. He'd promised. And he still had one more promise to keep. He would return to her.

"I don't believe you." Lilly would have never betrayed him.

Rathe chuckled, the sound grating and mirthless. "I suppose you wouldn't. The two of you have gotten fairly close while she's been with you, haven't you?" He paused, the vertical slit of his pupils widening slightly like a cat sighting its prey. "She's human now," Rathe said. "In exchange for bringing me the Book, and serving up one of the Chosen, I gave her her heart's desire. She got what *she* wanted. And I got what *I* wanted. You—" Rathe's mouth split in a parody of a smile. The black talons retreated into his fingertips once more and he brushed his hand over the folds of his snowy cravat, fingering the stickpin with the blood-drop ruby within the white folds. "What do you get, Hunter? You could go to her. Give up hunting, settle down, have the perfectly *human*," he shuddered in revulsion, "life you were born to lead."

Colt snorted. "I fail to see how that could possibly happen at this juncture. I'm stuck here." He gestured to the rock walls of Rathe's lair.

"Ah, but you don't have to be." The yellow in Rathe's eyes turned more poisonous as the pale skin around them tightened. "There is a way to have *your* heart's desire, Colt Ambrose Jackson."

Curiosity curled in Colt's belly, urging him to ask, while reason and every ounce of his Hunter instinct shouted at him to ignore the archdemon. Curiosity and his desire to see Lilly won out. "How?"

"Leave the Book."

Colt gave a bitter laugh. "That's amusing. Just the Book? I'm not that green. What else?"

Rathe's mouth split his face in a dark red line, a ghoulish grin that crinkled his waxy skin and exposed his sharp, angular teeth nestled in black gums. "Well, there is the matter of you taking my youngest daughter from me."

Colt tensed. Shit. He knew that was going to come back

to bite him like a stepped-on rattler. Didn't matter if it was an accident or not. "I killed her in self-defense."

Rathe's golden eyes bored into him. He didn't give a damn what Colt's puny human reasoning had been. The end result was Colt had killed his youngest daughter. The demon wanted more than the Book, he wanted retributi—

There was no warning.

The red-hot sting of a flaming Darkin whip stripped an inch-wide length of shirt and skin from across Colt's back with the force of a lash, knocking him to his knees and setting his shirt on fire. Colt rolled onto his back to put out the flames, but it did nothing for the wound already puckering and seething at the unnatural fire seeping into his skin. "That is for turning my demon against me."

Colt barely had time to suck in a breath before the whip struck again, this time across his chest like a hash mark, crossing over and reopening the nearly healed wounds the shifter had raked across his chest. Colt cried out in agony, slapping out the flames on his chest, his hands slick with his own blood, his shirt falling in singed tatters to the floor. "That is for my youngling."

Colt gasped against the pain. Out of the corner of his eye Colt saw the fiery length of the supernatural whip arcing toward him once more and tried to scrabble away. It wrapped around his neck, burning and growing tighter as it dragged him back toward Rathe, slicing through his skin like a wire through clay. Colt pulled at it with his hands, only to have his fingers blister. He couldn't breathe. The pressure behind his eyes increased, making them feel as if they were about to explode. Darkness crept in on all sides, crowding out Colt's field of vision.

"Oh, don't go anywhere until you've heard my offer."

And as fast as the whip had appeared, it vanished. Colt gasped, sucking in a great lungful of air tinged with the scent of his own blood and burning flesh. The moaning of a soul in agony filled his ears, and he realized it was his own voice.

"That's only a taste of what I have in store for you if you stay with me."

Colt panted against the pain, the burning as if all of him were still on fire, his knees and hands and cheek pressed against the cold marble floor. "What the hell do you want from me?"

"Your soul. Give it to me."

He raised his head and gazed at Rathe. "And become your demon? No. Way. In. Hell."

Rathe's eyes pulsed with yellow maliciousness. "You amuse me, Colt Ambrose Jackson. Tell me, would it make any difference if I told you that you can take my generous offer, or Lilly can take your place? I do so enjoy working on her." Rathe cocked his head like an inquisitive bird of prey inspecting the mouse caught in its talons before ripping off its head. "Your soul and the girl, or you refuse and I torture her while you watch. You must admit it is a tempting offer, though, isn't it?"

"Give up the Book and be your slave is what you mean," Colt panted.

Rathe held up his hands and gave a little shrug. "Oh, you've already lost your family's third of the Book of Legend." He leaned forward. "The question is not keeping the Book, but rather how you wish to spend your remaining years; here as my personal entertainment, or with her." He slowly pointed up.

"Speak plainly. What do you want?" Colt was afraid, deathly afraid, that he knew what this monster wanted. And everything in him fought off the bone-deep terror that was threatening to make him into a jibbering, mindless fool.

"I want your soul."

Pain speared Colt through the heart like a red-hot bullet.

As much as he didn't want to admit it, Rathe had a point. He'd lost. Now it was just a matter of bargaining to determine his future. And Lilly's.

He counted himself as hard to break, but everyone had a breaking point if you found just the right place to apply pressure. Colt hung his head and sighed, then struggled to his feet, swaying slightly, and locked his gaze on Rathe. "I'll give you one-tenth of my soul."

Rathe picked up the Book and tucked it under one arm, his gaze fixed on Colt's face as he stepped down from the dais and walked slowly toward him. "Three-quarters."

"One-quarter," Colt countered in desperation to preserve as much of himself as he could.

Rathe stood less than an arm's length away, close enough that the sulfur stench of him burned Colt's throat. "Half. And that's my final offer," the demon lord said quickly, his voice holding an edge of anticipation and excitement.

Everything within Colt balanced on a razor's edge. His heart seemed to slow, pounding harder, louder in his ears. This was it. There was only one thing he could do. "Agreed."

Rathe held out his long, thin hand. "I want your promise, Hunter."

Colt hesitated, then took it. Rathe's cold, dry, dead flesh made everything inside him shrivel. A suffocating blackness, like oily smoke but denser and far more vile, slithered out of Rathe's mouth and hung suspended in the air between them. They were the two hardest words he'd ever said, and it took everything within him to say them. "I promise."

The sulfuric blackness slammed into him, filling his nose and mouth, making it impossible to breathe, to even think, as it filled and burned in his chest. But even as his hand was still clamped in the cold hard one of the demon, that same strange sensation of being pulled apart infinitesimal bit by infinitesimal bit sparked again in his system.

Someone was trying to summon him out of Hell.

Rathe felt it too. His pupils instantly dilated into thin slits, and his grip tightened until the bones in Colt's hand cracked. Just before his skin began to fade into dark smoke-like particles, Colt grabbed the Book from Rathe's grasp.

Everything was a blur of pain.

"How long is this supposed to take?" Lilly's voice, sweet and impatient, filled his ears.

She squeaked as he transformed from a curl of dark particles into solid form. He'd never seen anything so beautiful as her surprised face lighting up with joy at the sight of him.

Her red hair was caught up in a twist, little spirals of flame silk curling about her sweet face. A long-sleeved red calico gown, fastened with little pearl-like buttons from chin to belly button, clung to her curves, and Colt staggered forward with the need to hold her.

The supernatural detection device on Marley's utility belt began to glow a furious red. Marley narrowed his eyes, pointing a crossbow at Colt's chest.

A spear of agony hit him in the heart when she moved toward him, but Marley stepped in front of her, confirming his worst fears. Now that he was half Darkin, she'd want nothing to do with him. "Careful, Miss Arliss. That shape-shifter is back."

Standing before them in nothing but his boots and black pants, Colt felt absurdly exposed. He rubbed his thumb over the smooth vellum of the pages in his hand and raised it to show them. "I got the Book." He swallowed hard. The raw marks upon his skin from the Darkin lash had some-how already healed but were still caked with dried blood.

Marley's gaze darted from the pages to Colt's face and back again. The tip of the crossbow dipped slightly but was still cocked and ready. "How do I know the demon lord—" Marley glanced at Lilly.

"Rathe," Lilly supplied.

"The demon lord, Rathe, hasn't sent you to fetch Miss Arliss back?"

Colt sighed. "You don't."

Marley glanced down at the still glowing indicator on his detection device. "You're Darkin. Admit it."

Colt didn't miss that Lilly's eyes widened with shock and fear. Her eyes, which had been impossibly green before when she was a demon, were now a softer sage color. The irony struck him to the heart. Wasn't that just the way of things? He knew their positions were now reversed. He was the evil thing and she the human. He the hunted and she on the side of the Hunters. All the faith she'd placed in her precious prophecy had gone up in smoke the moment he'd sold part of his soul to Rathe in exchange for his freedom. There was no way he could be part of the Chosen now. Hell, he wasn't even sure he'd be accepted by his brothers any longer.

But he'd done it because Rathe had found his one weakness: Lilly.

Colt blew out a harsh, frustrated breath. "It's not what you think, Marley."

"Then perhaps you should enlighten me," Marley retorted, raising the end of the crossbow level with Colt's heart once more.

"Oh, no. No, no," Lilly murmured, a sad softness to her voice. "I know that look. You've made a deal with him, haven't you?"

It hurt to gaze into her sad, accusatory eyes. They began to well, her lashes turning dark with tears before they spilled in a shining track over her cheek.

"Guess it means we're still not fit to be with one another."

Lilly surprised him by shoving past Marley and coming

at him in a rush. She threw her arms around him in a fierce hug that placed her smooth cheek against his bare chest. "Why? Oh, Colt, you shouldn't have. You should have chosen the Book."

Tenderly, gently, Colt stroked her hair beneath his fingers. The texture was silk under his touch, and the spicy-sweet fragrance that was all Lilly swirled around her in a seductive mixture he couldn't resist. She was even more alluring than she'd been as a succubus. "You were worth more than the Book," he whispered, his voice rough and ragged. She was worth a thousand Books of Legend.

She tipped her head up and stared at him, serious and not the least afraid of his new Darkin status. "How much of your soul did you exchange for your freedom?"

Colt tried to shrug it off as inconsequential, when the reality was his choice weighed like a lead yoke on his shoulders. "I bargained him down to half for a chance at a lifetime with you. It was worth it."

Lilly nodded, her fingers absently stroking the skin over his heart, making it tighten in response. "That's enough."

"For what?"

She peered at him, her eyes narrowing. "For you to have demon powers. That's why Marley's detector can sense you." She wiped away the blood on his chest with her sleeve. He flinched as she followed one of the dark pink lines that had been the open lash mark on his chest with her finger, her touch trailing fire in its path. "That's why you've healed so quickly."

Colt stiffened and tried to pull away from her, but she held on to him tightly. "Look, I know I'm not completely human anymore. I expect this changes everything."

Her generous lips tipped up at the edges in a soft smile. "You still don't understand, do you?"

Colt paused for a moment, thoroughly confused by her demeanor. Shouldn't she be shrinking back in fear or disgust? Truthfully, she'd been trying for so long to get out of being a demon that he didn't understand how she could stand to be around him with half a demon inside him. "I suppose I don't," he finally admitted.

"He may have taken half of your soul, but in return he's given you abilities he can't hope to defeat. He's given you powers of the Darkin."

He still wasn't seeing the positive in this particular situation. "And that's a good thing because—"

"Because when your new powers are combined with your brothers', the Chosen will be unstoppable."

Colt rubbed the uncomfortable itch on the back of his neck. "Yeah, well, about that. I'm not so sure my brothers are going to be as accepting of me having half a soul as you are. They're more apt to act like Marley here." He jerked his thumb in the direction of the crossbow still held at his chest.

"Perhaps you need to give them . . . and me a chance. People who love you don't worry about how you've changed. You're still you, aren't you?"

Colt puffed up a little bit. "Hell, yeah, of course I am. Just a little more scarred," he said, glancing at his new marks.

Lilly put her hand to his cheek and waited until his gaze connected with hers. "Then you're still the man I love, and that's really all that matters."

Colt pulled her in tight to his chest, afraid for a moment that this was all just a hallucination and would disappear at any moment. That the light feeling growing inside him would end and the weight that had lifted off his shoulders would somehow return.

"You love me?"

She nodded.

"Half-demon and all?"

"I loved you when you were all Hunter too, so what's the difference?"

He shrugged. "I don't know, I guess I just thought that it would make a difference somehow."

Lilly turned on Marley. "Oh, for pity's sake, put that thing away. This is Colt. I'd stake my mortality on it."

Marley hesitantly lowered the weapon, a strange gleam coming into his eye. "You say he should have demon powers now?"

Lilly nodded.

Marley looked Colt up and down, moving in a semicircle around him and Lilly. "Interesting, very interesting." A maniacal gleam lit his eyes. "This could be very useful. Would you mind if I ran some tests on you?"

"Not now," Lilly and Colt answered in unison. Marley looked a bit deflated.

Colt didn't want to let go of her, not for an instant. After what little he'd seen, there was no way he was taking a chance Rathe might find and take her away from him.

She looked up into his face. He'd never get tired of looking at her. "I've just one question I want you to answer for me, Colt."

"Anything."

"You could have taken the Book and left me behind. Why didn't you? Why'd you give up part of your soul when you didn't have to? And how did you get out?"

"That's not one question, that's more like two or three."

She slapped her hand on his shoulder. "Answer the questions."

"First, I got you out because I promised. Second, I gave up part of my soul to be with you. Last, he offered me a way out of Hell and a way to protect you, so I took it."

Lilly threaded her fingers through his hair, brushing her thumb against his cheek in a soft caress that sank down deep like a healing balm to his torn soul. "You were afraid he would torture me some more, weren't you." It wasn't a question, it was a statement.

"Yes."

"Colt Ambrose Jackson," she said softly as she brushed her lips against his, "you're in love."

Colt smiled. "Yes, ma'am. I do believe I am."

Joining the Book together and closing the Gates was the only way he was going to protect her, hell, all of them, from Rathe taking over the world. "We've still got three days until the new moon," Colt said.

"Time enough to unite the Book of Legend, if your brothers have recovered the other pieces," she replied, determination written all over her face.

"What about our pact? Are you still willing to come along?" Colt teased as he looked into the face of the woman he'd given his very soul for, and brushed a curl away from her cheek.

She blushed, glancing away from him for a moment, then gave him a sly smile. "Are you saying you want my help in exchange for a kiss?"

Colt cupped his hand around her hip and pulled her close. "I'll take it any way I can get it."

She laughed, rose up on her tiptoes, and kissed him soundly on the mouth. "Spoken like a true Hunter."

He shifted his hold, locking his arms around her waist. "Half Hunter or not, getting this Book together isn't going to be easy."

"Who gave you the mistaken impression that anything worthwhile ever is?" she said.

"You think you can trust a half-demon Hunter?"

She nestled closer her eyes full of admiration and desire. "With all my heart."

"Then let's beat them to Bodie. We've got a world to save."

Keep reading for a special sneak preview of *The Slayer*,
Winchester's search for the second part of
the Book of Legend, available April 2012!

And look for Remington's story, the exciting
conclusion to the Legend Chronicles—
The Chosen—in December 2012.

"Put down the gun, Hoss, afore I blow that oversized melon of yours to kingdom come." Winchester Jackson's cold, steady voice cracked through the canyon sure as a shot. Although the other hefty man, seated on his horse, had his rifle stuck under the leather flap of the stagecoach window, Winn knew Hoss Dalton never robbed alone. Somewhere, hidden by the rock walls, sagebrush, and dead grasses of the canyon, his ragged band of fellow thieves lay in wait.

Inside the stage, halted precariously on the shaley edge of the dirt road leading from Carson City to Winn's town of Bodie, a woman whimpered, and a small dog yipped.

"Hoss? You hear me?"

The female whimper was cut off instantly, and even the hot desert air scented with creosote and sagebrush in the rocky chute of the canyon stood still.

Hoss, two bricks shy of a load and perpetually half-drunk, turned slowly. His rifle, which was pointed at the occupants hidden within the dark interior of the steam stage, wavered just a bit at the sound of the sheriff's voice.

Attached to the front of the stage, the mechanical horses, big copper beasts the size of Clydesdales, pinged, hissing steam through their venting nostrils as the metal and gears cooled.

Winn kept Hoss in his sights. The old man's eyes, rheumy from too much rotgut whiskey, flicked to the star-shaped silver badge on Winn's chest, but his rifle didn't waver. Sonofabitch, was the old fool going to shoot a stage full of people right here, ten minutes from town, for a lousy payroll?

The brilliant sun stood white hot overhead in a cloudless field of pale blue.

"Countdown is at three, Hoss. Drop that, or swear to God, I'll shoot you where you stand! Tommy Sutton? You stay right where you are!" he yelled. He didn't know if Sutton was there or not. Didn't have eyes in the back of his head either, but the rustle in the grasses off to his right stopped.

"Damn, Winn. You ain't nothin' like your old man." The man's tone conveyed his deep disappointment born of familiarity.

Winchester Jackson peered down the length of his rifle barrel aimed at his quarry's heart. "Thank you for the compliment." The fact was, anything that distinguished him from his notorious outlaw father and supernatural Hunter, Cyrus "Black Jack" Jackson, pleased him enormously. He didn't want any part of that life. Not now. Not ever again.

"Cain't you jest let me go, for old time's sake?" Hoss and his group of bandits had once been Hunters along-side his father. But tough times had turned them from pro-tecting humanity to protecting their own self-serving interests. They'd robbed this stage four times in the last month, taking the Black Gulch Mine's payroll.

Winn was damned if he was going to let it be five. He'd tried hard to ignore their activities because it'd just been stealing and he had a murder a day to contend with in the

rowdy mining town, sometimes more. But enough was
enough.

"Then I wouldn't be doing my job, now would I? Get your
hands where I can see them." Winn cocked the hammer back.

Click. Click. Click. Click. Four other guns cocked and
pointed at Winchester's head as the rest of Hoss's group
emerged from the jagged tan rocks of the canyon where
they'd stopped the steam stage.

Damn.

"Not this time, Winn." Hoss stepped forward, his wide
smile a mess of gaps and yellowed teeth, and pulled the
rifle from Winchester's hands. "No one would have figured
you for the rotten apple in the barrel. A lawman. That
would jest make your pa spit nails."

Winchester resisted the urge to tug on the hardened tips
of his heavily waxed black mustache, a habit he'd developed when agitated during his last five years as sheriff of
Bodie. "My pa would have spit anything he could chew."

A metallic clink alerted Winn to the steps of the coach
being lowered. "Stay inside," he shouted to the fool preparing to alight on a mountain pass with five armed men holding up the stage.

A rustle of taffeta accompanied a dainty half boot and a
length of silky calf onto the first step.

From the dim recesses of the stage stepped an elegant
woman, her dark, glossy curls capped with a jaunty little
top hat heavily accented with a cloud of black feathers. Her
expensive bustled gown, the blue-black iridescent color of
raven wings, hugged her slim waist and suggested a silhouette that was amply curved by nature rather than artifice.
But more stunning than her figure was her face. Lips, a
shade too full to be fashionable, and high cheekbones accented a pair of piercing whiskey-colored eyes that stole
his breath away.

The woman's dusky beauty was both dark and alluring,

but the undercurrent of danger surrounded her like a storm cloud charged with lightning. Upon the black kidskin leather of her gloved hand was a large ruby ring, which matched the blood-like droplets of rubies at her ears. Her every mannerism screamed wealth and privilege.

"Is there a problem, gentlemen?" Her voice was soothing and rich like warm honey, and her heavy Eastern European accent made "gentlemen" sound more like "zhentlemen."

Hoss gave an impatient jerk of his head toward the stage, even though his gaze lingered on the woman. "Wait your turn, missus. Get back in that coach. We'll have us a fine time when I'm done with my business." His suggestive tone made Winchester want to punch him—hard, and preferably more than once.

"I think not," she replied smoothly.

The hair pricked up porcupine fashion on the back of Winchester's neck as the scent of sulfur tainted the air. Something about this situation wasn't right. He turned away from the woman, focusing instead on taking down Hoss. Sure, he'd probably get shot, but if he did it right, it wouldn't be more than a flesh wound and Hoss would take the brunt of his gang's shots. He bent his knees slightly, preparing to lunge at Hoss's middle, but before he could even move, all hell broke loose.

The woman's face warped, her brows protruded, her eyes turned crimson, and her full lips bracketed a pair of perfect pearly fangs. She hissed and every head turned.

"Vampire!" Hoss yelled to the others.

Taken off guard, they fumbled with their weapons, trying to exchange regular bullets for silver, but they weren't fast enough. In a blink she had stripped the men from their horses, and savagely ripped out their throats with her delicate gloved hands and her fangs.

Winchester grabbed his rifle out of Hoss's loose grip

and trained the weapon on the monster in taffeta. She turned back, facing them, her lips slicked with bright red blood. The tip of her soft pink tongue stroked one fang, making Winchester's gut tighten involuntarily.

"A bit rustic, and a little too well marinated in whiskey, but substantial," she said, as if discussing the vintage of wine. She pulled a black silk handkerchief from the sleeve of her gown and dabbed at the blood remaining around her lips and chin, removing the last traces of her unladylike activity.

"Well, don't just stand there, shoot her!" Hoss yelled, as he shuffled behind Winchester. Winn stood his ground, the rifle pointed straight at the vampiress's heart. Not that it would do much good. What he really needed was a ma-chete or a broadsword to lop that lovely dark-haired head from her slim shoulders.

"Don't come any closer," he warned.

She tilted her head slightly like an inquisitive bird of prey, her eyes returning to their tawny color and her face returning to its regal profile. Only the fangs still remained. "You have nothing to fear from me. Look around you, Hunter. Have I harmed the innocents in the coach? Have I harmed you? No. I took only the lives of those who were contributing nothing to your society in the first place. Hardly a crime." She peeled the soiled black gloves from her fingers one at a time, then tossed them into the air where they disappeared in a swirl of dark smoke.

Winn's finger rested heavy on the trigger, just needing a finite amount of pressure to fire the rifle at the vampiress. Only one thing held him back.

Everything she'd said was true.

He glanced at the steam stage. The occupants huddled inside the wooden stagecoach, whispering and peering with wide frightened eyes from behind the dusty leather window coverings, afraid to come out, but they were unharmed.

Hoss's men lay in crumpled bloody heaps and Hoss himself was still huddling behind him, but she hadn't attacked him.

"What d'you want, vampire?"

"I am Lady Alexandra Porter, Contessa Drossenburg, embassary of his vampiric majesty, Emperor Vladamir the Fifth. I've come to seek out the eldest of the Chosen, Winchester Jackson. I was told he resides in Bodie." Her gaze flicked to the cluster of sun-bleached wooden buildings down in the valley below, then drifted to the star on his chest. "Do you know him?"

"Lady, I *am* him."

Her eyes widened slightly. "Then we have business to discuss."

Winn slowly lowered his gun, but not his guard. Apparently Hoss was stupider than he looked; he tried to wrestle the repeating rifle away from him. But Winn had lost his patience. He clocked Hoss on the side of the head with the butt of his rifle, and the other man slid unconscious facedown into the powder-fine dirt.

Winn glanced up at the vampire. "I don't work with supernaturals."

She gave a shrug of her petite shoulder, her fangs retreating completely, leaving behind an even, white smile. "I expected as much, but the Emperor does not share my view. He thinks it is time for vampires to join with the Chosen if we are to defeat a mutual enemy."

"The enemy of my enemy is my friend?"

"*Da.* But perhaps it is best if we discuss this elsewhere." She threw a meaningful glance over her shoulder at the stunned occupants of the steam stage. "May I have your leave to glamour them? It is not safe for them to know so much. Don't you agree, Mr. Jackson?"

Much as he didn't like it, she did have a point. The last thing he needed was a stage full of frightened travelers to come rolling into Bodie spouting off about a vampire killing the Dalton gang. People, as a general rule, were panicky, stupid, and rash. And chances were ten out of ten, if the travelers talked, the town would come beating down his door demanding him to fix it. No, it was far better if she glamoured the lot of them and made them forget this unpleasantness had ever happened. He nodded his approval.

The vampire Contessa dipped her head as she bent in a curtsey, then gingerly picked up her skirts and turned back to the stage. The low, husky quality of her voice rustled like the taffeta she wore, sultry and smooth, completely absorbing the total attention of the travelers.

"You have had a most pleasant trip, with only the slightest delay for a mechanical horse that needed an application of oil," she said slowly. Winn tried to block out her voice, but glanced over her shoulder to see the wide, glassy stares of the occupants of the stage. She certainly did know how to throw a glamour. Good thing he was practically immune.

That was the second thing Pa had taught him about hunting. The first had been never to trust a supernatural being. The Darkin were the scourge of the universe — children of the night—dedicated to eliminating humans so they could claim the earth for themselves.

No matter how elegant, sophisticated, or well-mannered the Contessa seemed, she was still just a damn vampire, and sooner or later he was going to have to slay her.

The knowledge bit down deep and hard into his bones, refusing to let go. Winn silently cursed in four different languages. As the oldest Jackson brother, he'd been exposed to the life of a Hunter the longest. Pa had started drilling it into him from the time he could toddle.

Which made all of this so much worse. Because ten years ago he'd given it up, walked away, and vowed to stay good and gone from Hunters and anything to do with the Darkin. He'd tried to lead a normal life—be an upstanding citizen with a clean reputation—something neither of his brothers would know about. For while the Jackson brothers looked similar on the outside with their pa's jet hair and broad shoulders and their ma's blue eyes and winning smile, they were as different as could be on the inside.

Winn turned away from her bidding the travelers a kind good-bye, shaking their hands and waving to them as the horses gained steam and began to huff and chuff, ready to resume their journey into Bodie.

It didn't help that his little brother Colt, the hothead of the three and a self-styled outlaw, had come waltzing in that afternoon, determined to locate their pa's long-lost piece of the Book of Legend.

He'd told him the truth. Only a Darkin could access the Book. Well, Colt was welcome to it. Nothin', but nothin', was going to change his mind about taking up arms as a Hunter again.

White puffs of steam and darker smoke from the steam carriage's boilers mixed with the dirt, creating a dark smudge in the otherwise cloudless clear blue sky as the stage clanked and rolled on toward Bodie.

The vampire eyed him with a mixture of curiosity and respect mingling in the whiskey depths of her eyes. "You are not exactly what I expected, Mr. Jackson." She clasped her bare hands together, the dark ruby ring winking on the ring finger of her right hand.

"What'd you expect?"

The corner of her mouth tipped up in a way that made his skin tighten, and he had to keep himself from leaning forward to sample those tempting lips.

"From the legends we've been told," her gaze raked him over, assessing him, "someone bigger."